an
vel for

AN UNOFFICIA FOR MINECRAFTERS

CHASING HEROBRINE

Sky Pony Press books may be purchased in bulk at special discounts for sales promotion, corporate gifts, fund-raising, or educational purposes. Special editions can also be created to specifications. For details, contact the Special Sales Department, Sky Pony Press, 307 West 36th Street, 11th Floor, New York, NY 10018 or info@skyhorsepublishing.com.

Sky Pony® is a registered trademark of Skyhorse Publishing, Inc.®, a Delaware corporation.

Visit our website at www.skyponypress.com.

10 9 8 7 6

Library of Congress Cataloging-in-Publication Data is available on file.

Special thanks to Cara J. Stevens, David Norgren, and Elias Norgren

Cover design by Brian Peterson
Cover illustration by David Norgren

Print ISBN: 978-1-5107-1818-0
Ebook ISBN: 978-1-5107-1827-2

Printed in China

Designer and Production Manager: Joshua Barnaby

INTRODUCTION

If you have played Minecraft, then you know all about Minecraft worlds. They're made of blocks you can mine: coal, dirt, and sand. In the game, you'll find many different creatures, lands, and villages inhabited by strange villagers with bald heads. The villagers who live there have their own special, magical worlds that are protected by a string of border worlds to stop outsiders from finding them.

When we last left off in the small border world of Xenos, Phoenix, T.H., and Xander had just conquered the Ender Dragon and reclaimed the legendary Dragon Scrolls, only to return and find Phoenix is no longer welcome within the gates of her own village.

She and her family have settled into their new home outside the village, along with a growing number of supporters. Their small town has expanded to include a farm, some stores, and even a small school.

Our story resumes on Halloween, as Phoenix and her friends are getting ready for a night of fun and a touch of mischief. But none of them are prepared for the real-life ghost story they are about to encounter that may make this Halloween celebration their last…

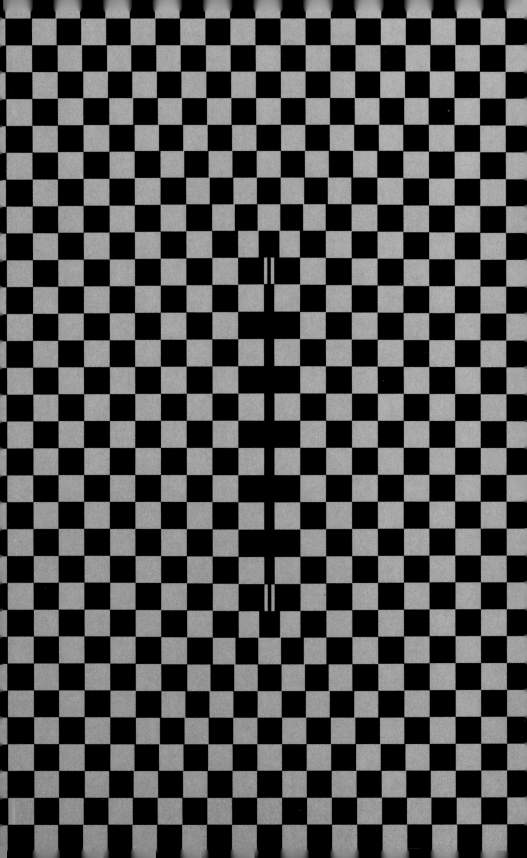

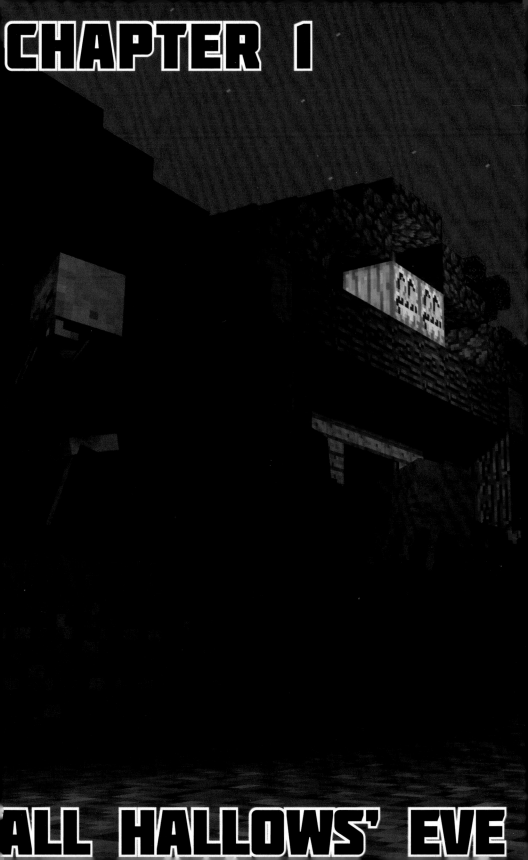

CHAPTER 1

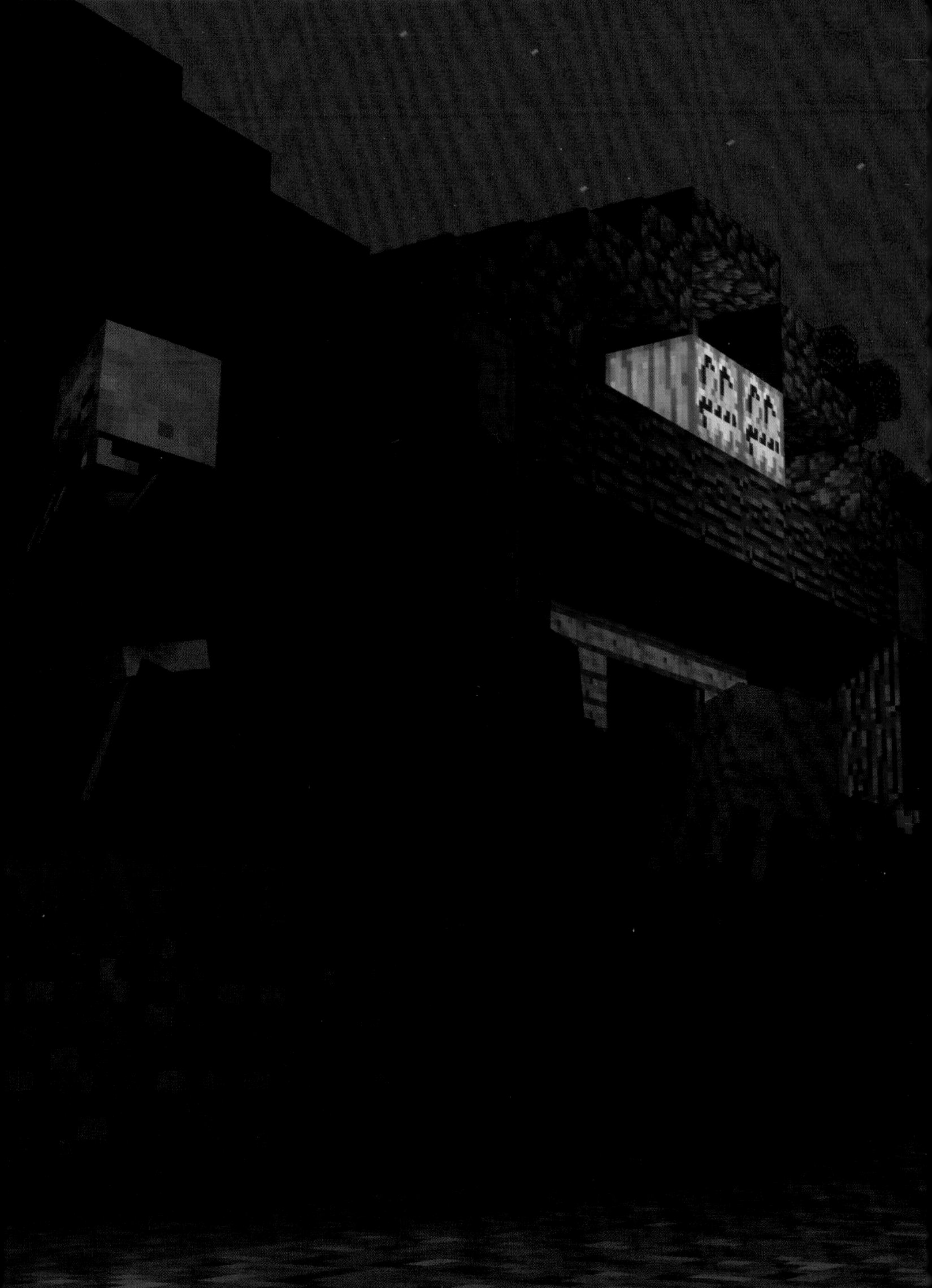

ALL HALLOWS' EVE

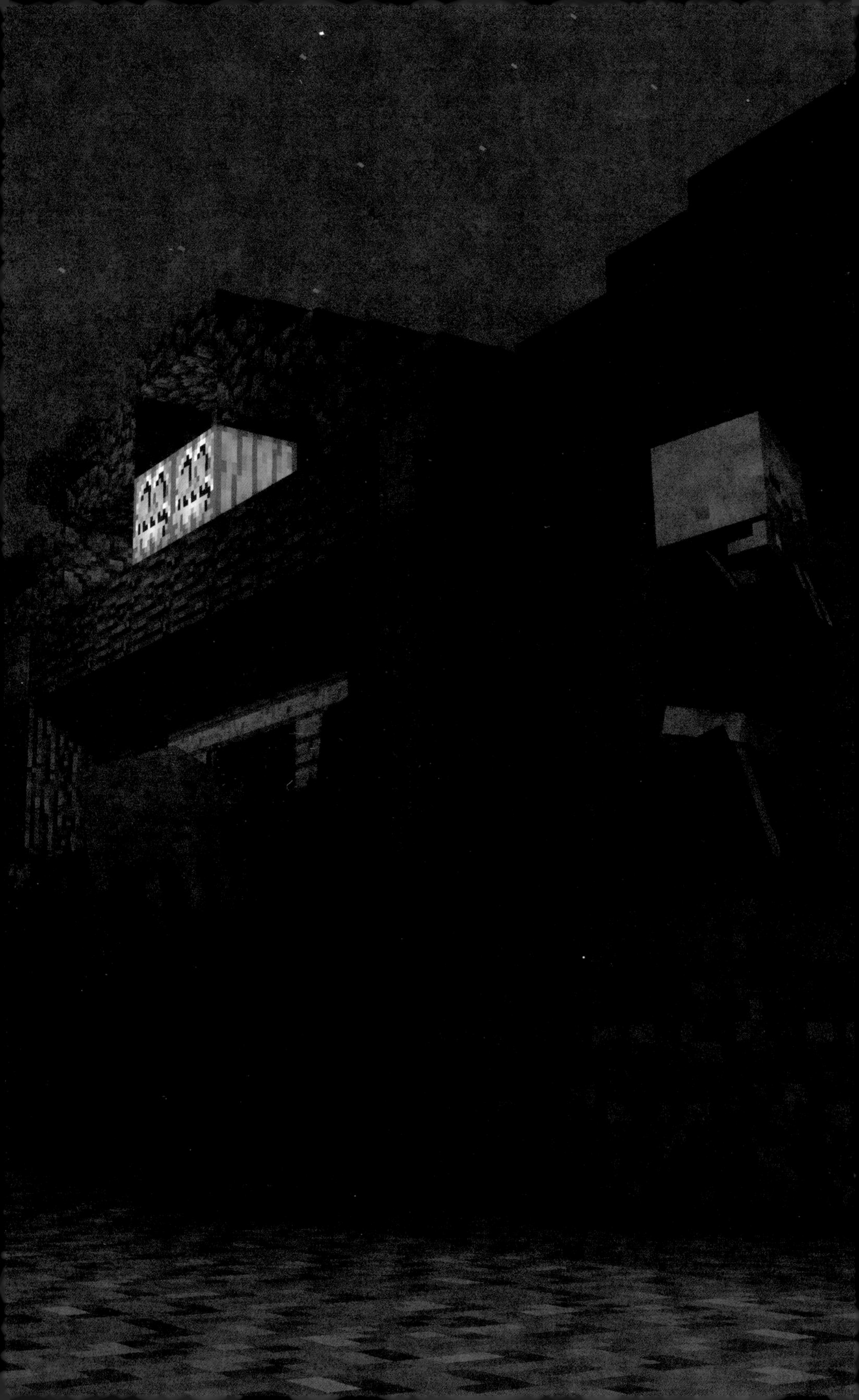

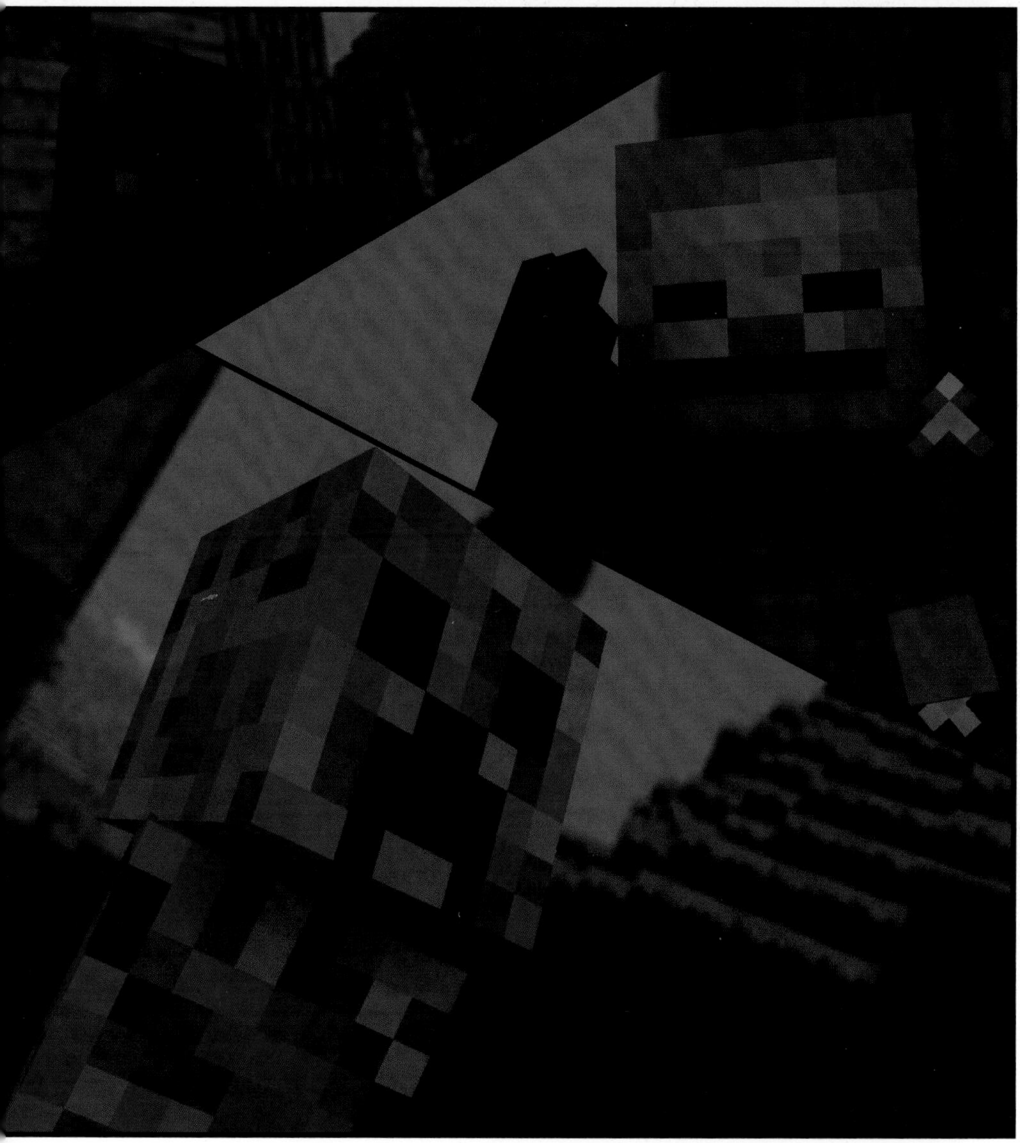

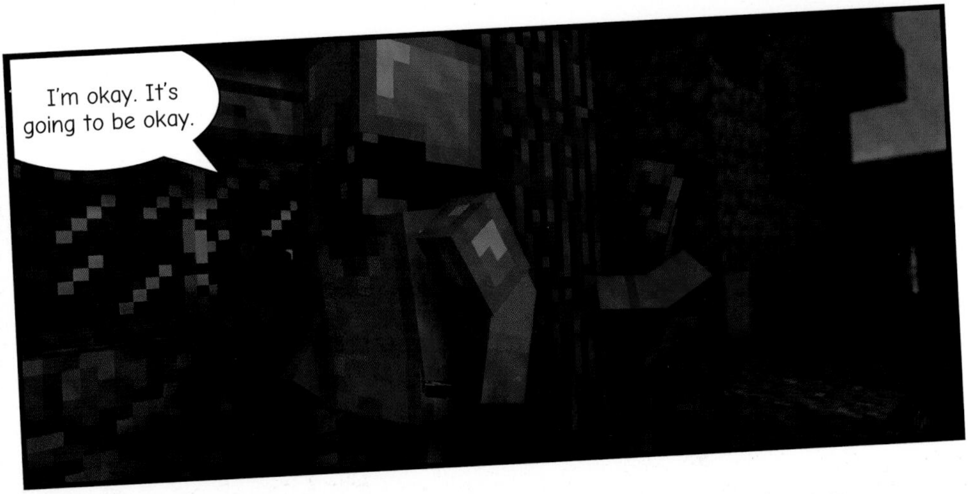
I'm okay. It's going to be okay.

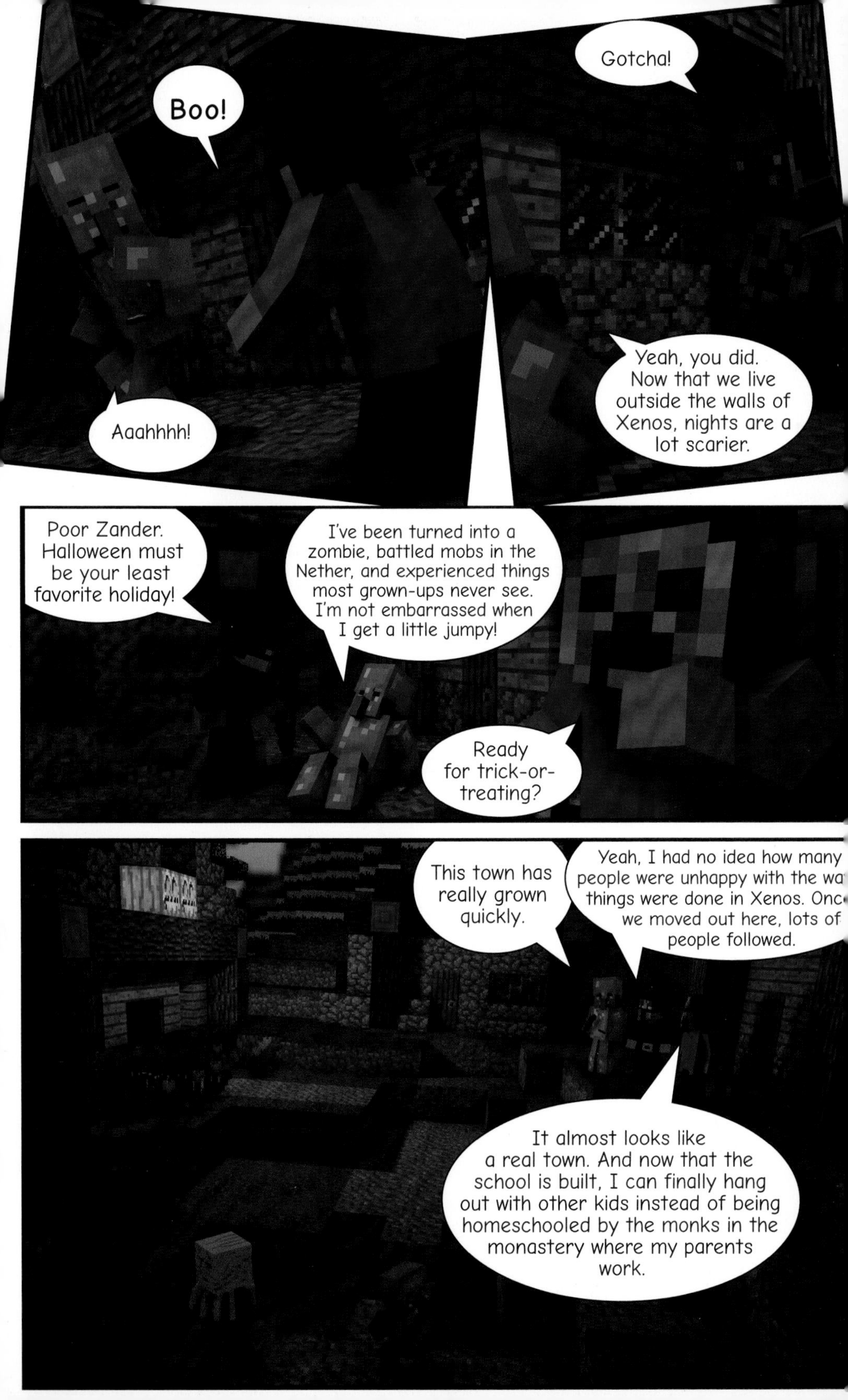

Boo!
Aaahhhh!
Gotcha!
Yeah, you did. Now that we live outside the walls of Xenos, nights are a lot scarier.
Poor Zander. Halloween must be your least favorite holiday!
I've been turned into a zombie, battled mobs in the Nether, and experienced things most grown-ups never see. I'm not embarrassed when I get a little jumpy!
Ready for trick-or-treating?
This town has really grown quickly.
Yeah, I had no idea how many people were unhappy with the wa things were done in Xenos. Onc we moved out here, lots of people followed.
It almost looks like a real town. And now that the school is built, I can finally hang out with other kids instead of being homeschooled by the monks in the monastery where my parents work.

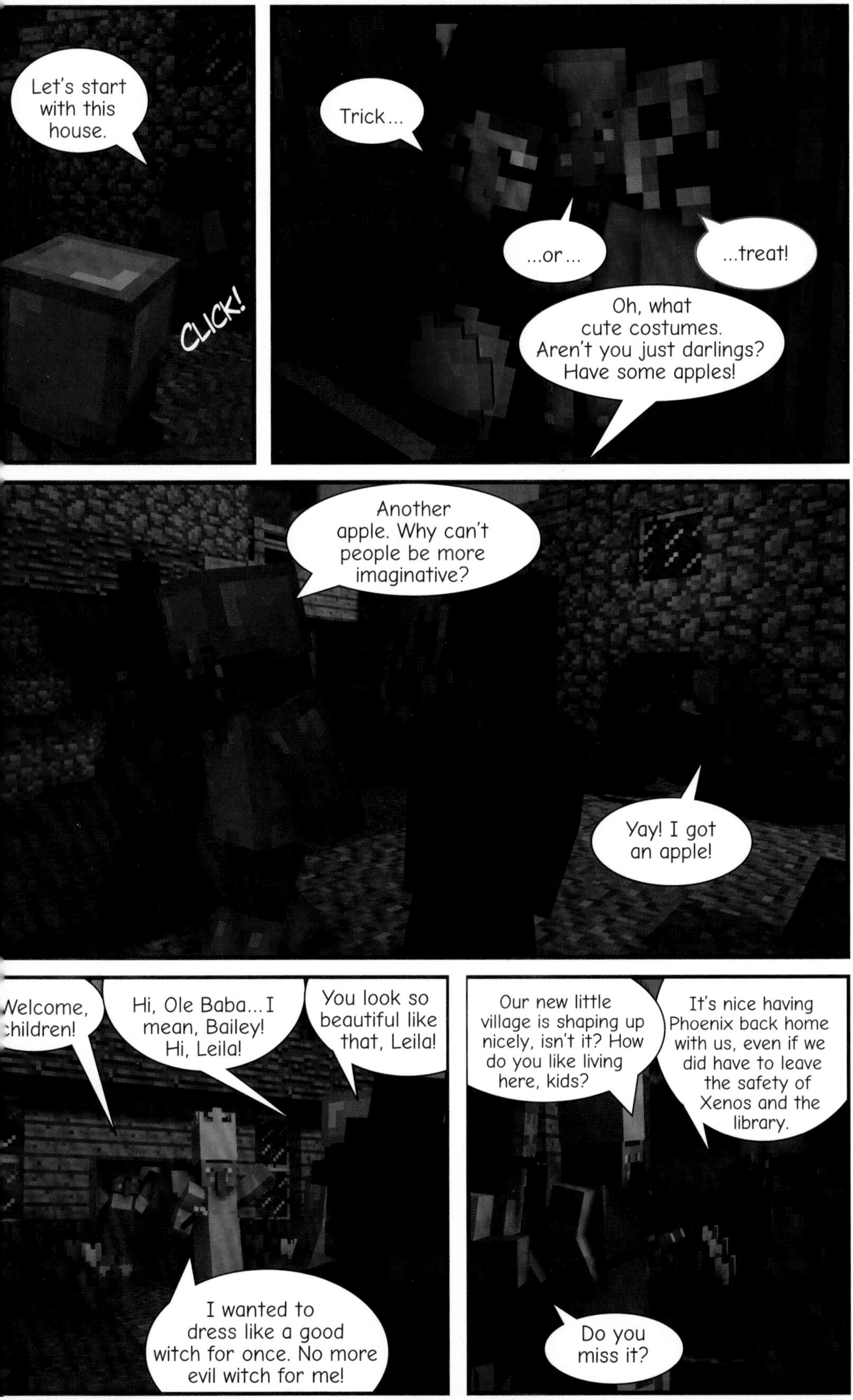
Let's start with this house.
CLICK!
Trick...
...or...
...treat!
Oh, what cute costumes. Aren't you just darlings? Have some apples!
Another apple. Why can't people be more imaginative?
Yay! I got an apple!
Welcome, children!
Hi, Ole Baba... I mean, Bailey! Hi, Leila!
You look so beautiful like that, Leila!
I wanted to dress like a good witch for once. No more evil witch for me!
Our new little village is shaping up nicely, isn't it? How do you like living here, kids?
It's nice having Phoenix back home with us, even if we did have to leave the safety of Xenos and the library.
Do you miss it?

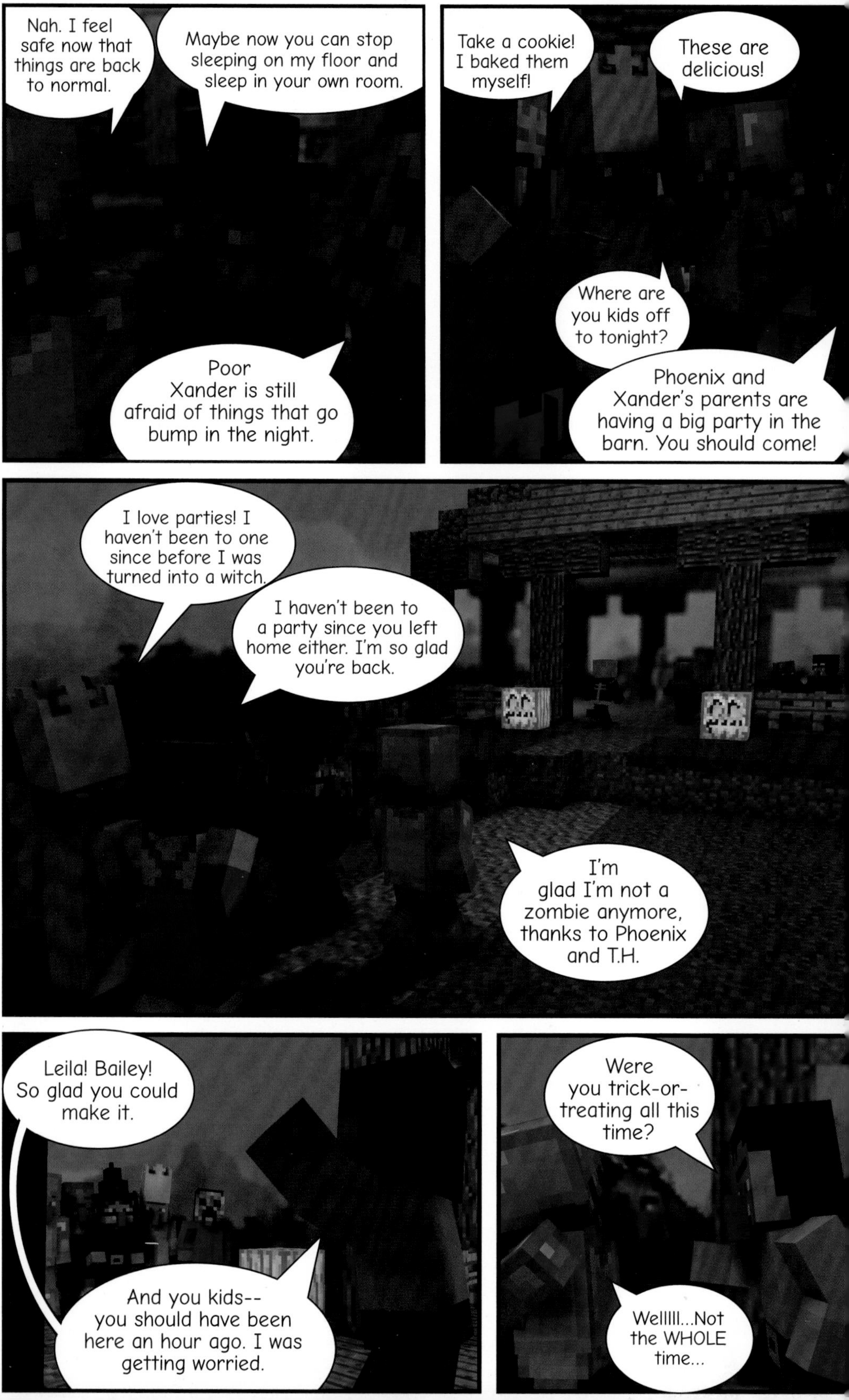
Nah. I feel safe now that things are back to normal.
Maybe now you can stop sleeping on my floor and sleep in your own room.
Poor Xander is still afraid of things that go bump in the night.
Take a cookie! I baked them myself!
These are delicious!
Where are you kids off to tonight?
Phoenix and Xander's parents are having a big party in the barn. You should come!
I love parties! I haven't been to one since before I was turned into a witch.
I haven't been to a party since you left home either. I'm so glad you're back.
I'm glad I'm not a zombie anymore, thanks to Phoenix and T.H.
Leila! Bailey! So glad you could make it.
And you kids--you should have been here an hour ago. I was getting worried.
Were you trick-or-treating all this time?
Welllll...Not the WHOLE time...

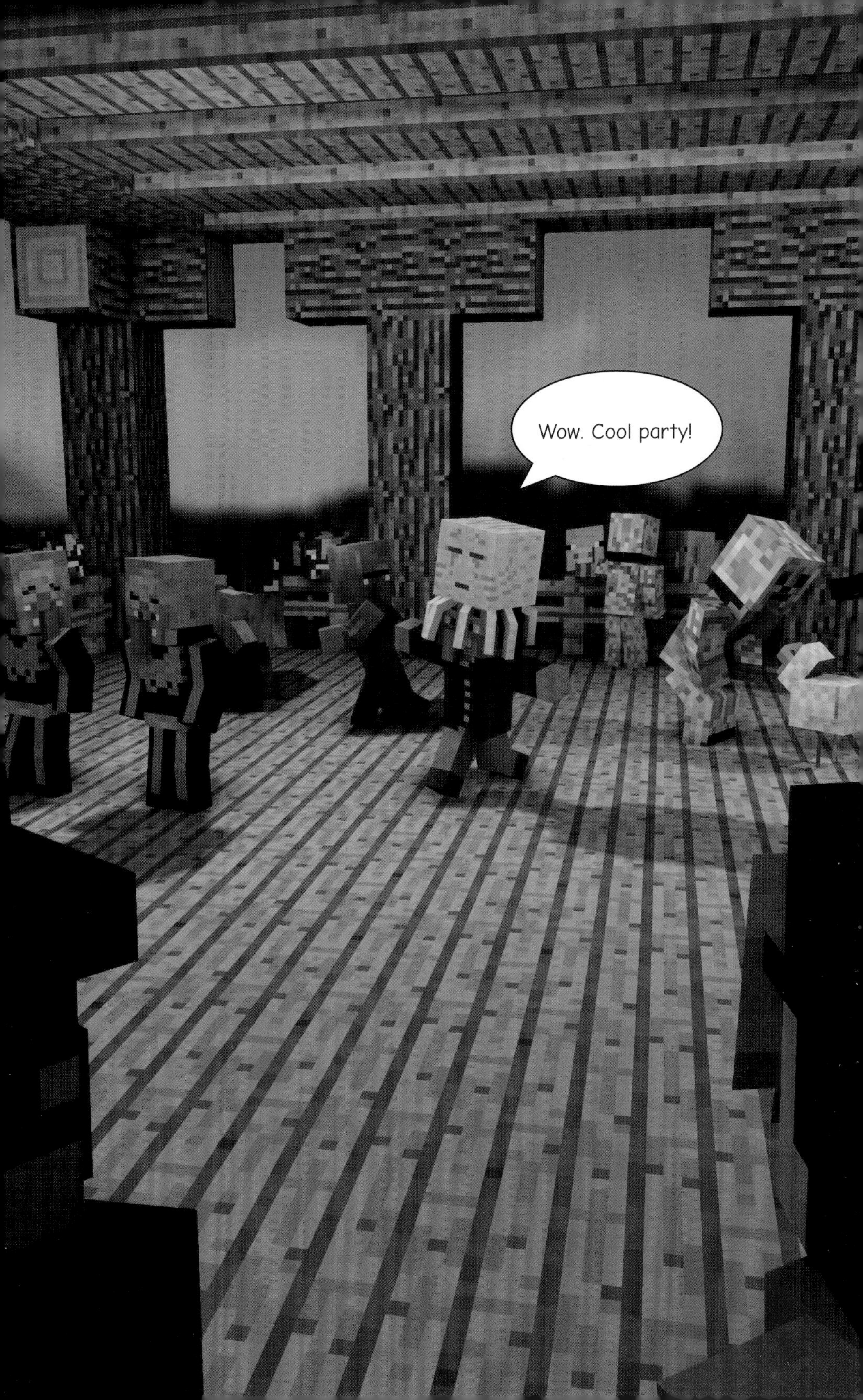
Wow. Cool party!

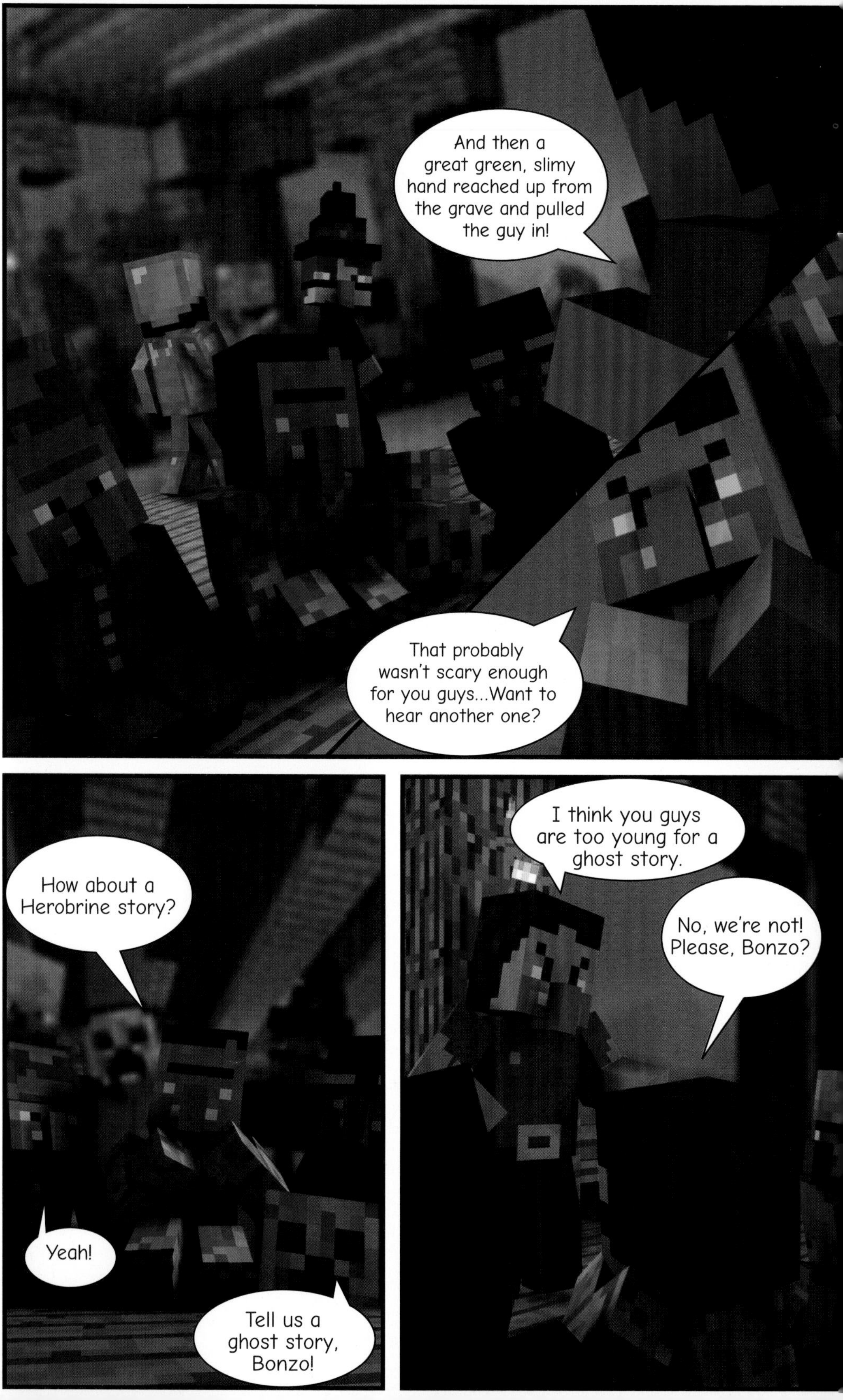
And then a great green, slimy hand reached up from the grave and pulled the guy in!
That probably wasn't scary enough for you guys...Want to hear another one?
Tell us a ghost story, Bonzo!
Yeah!
How about a Herobrine story?
I think you guys are too young for a ghost story.
No, we're not! Please, Bonzo?

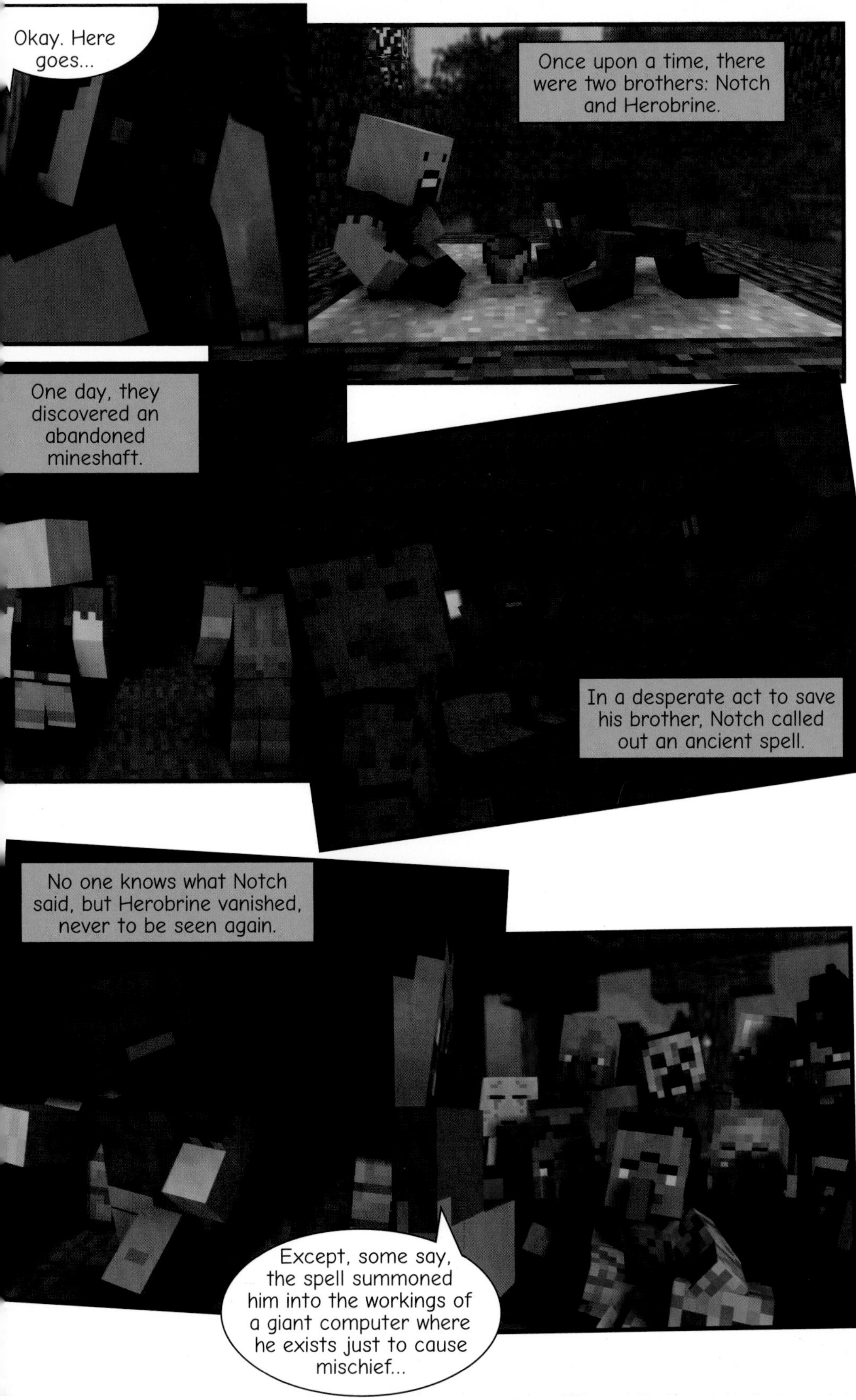

Okay. Here goes...
Once upon a time, there were two brothers: Notch and Herobrine.
One day, they discovered an abandoned mineshaft.
In a desperate act to save his brother, Notch called out an ancient spell.
No one knows what Notch said, but Herobrine vanished, never to be seen again.
Except, some say, the spell summoned him into the workings of a giant computer where he exists just to cause mischief...

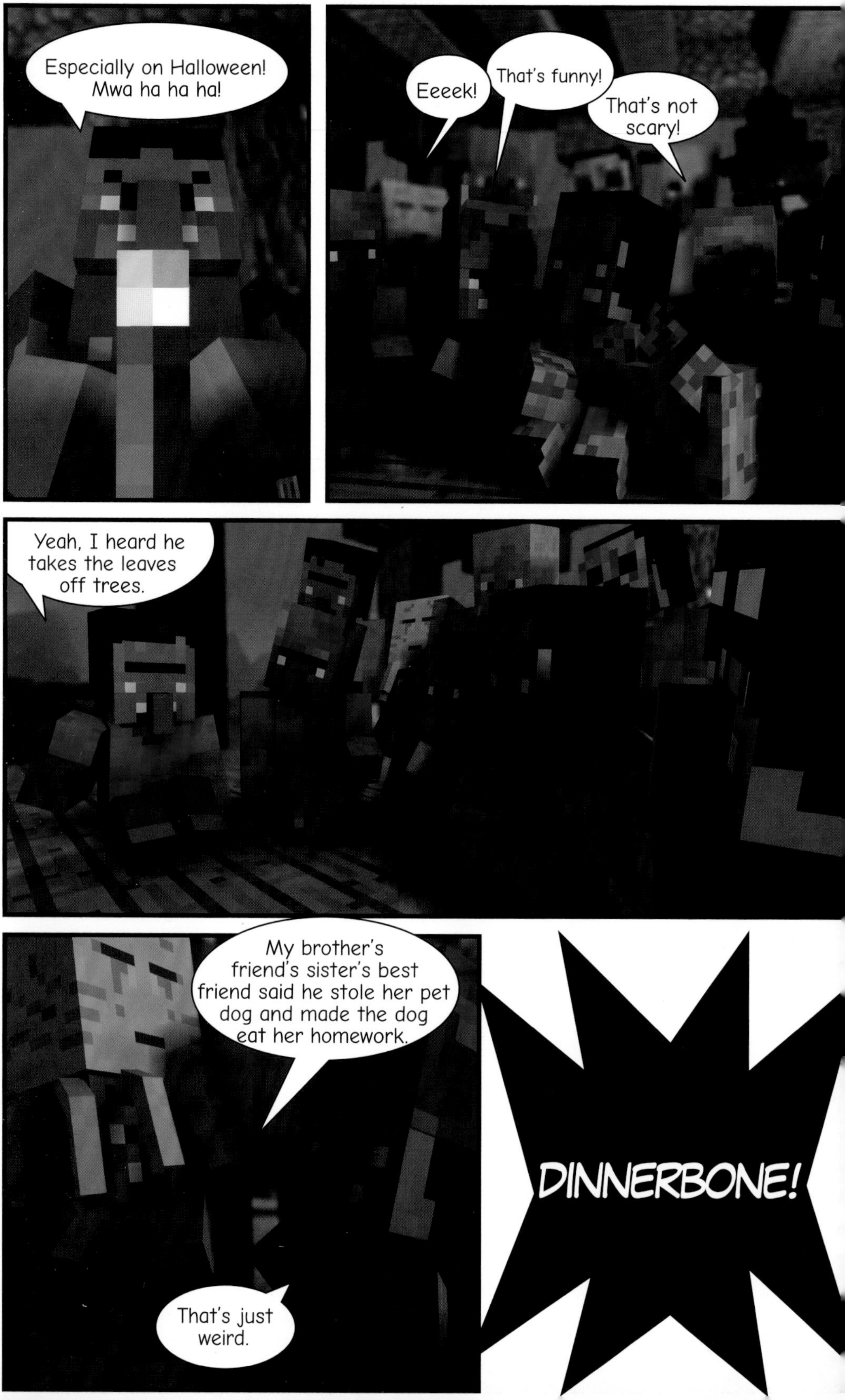
Especially on Halloween! Mwa ha ha ha!
Eeeek!
That's funny!
That's not scary!
Yeah, I heard he takes the leaves off trees.
My brother's friend's sister's best friend said he stole her pet dog and made the dog eat her homework.
That's just weird.
DINNERBONE!

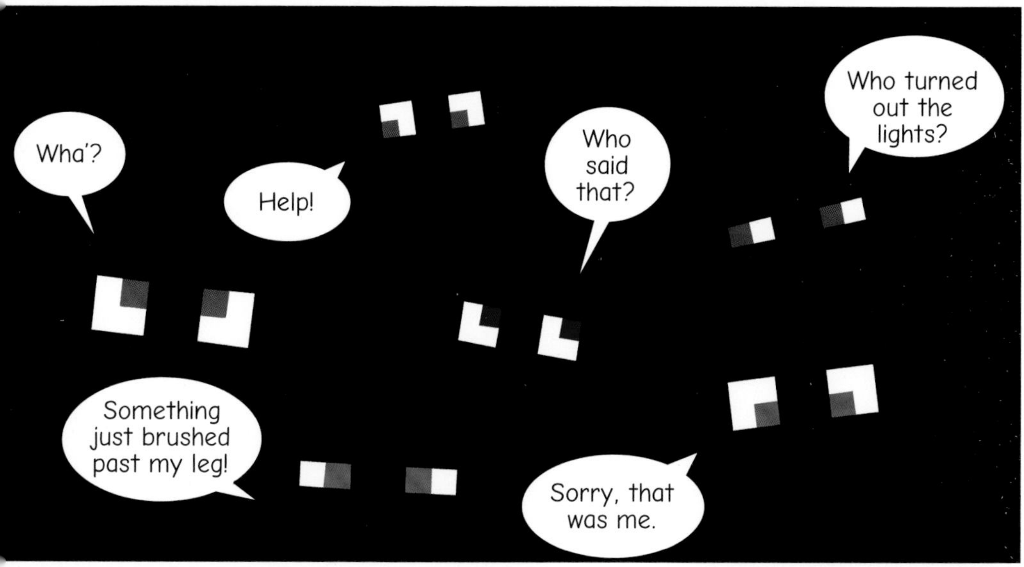
Wha'?
Help!
Who said that?
Who turned out the lights?
Something just brushed past my leg!
Sorry, that was me.

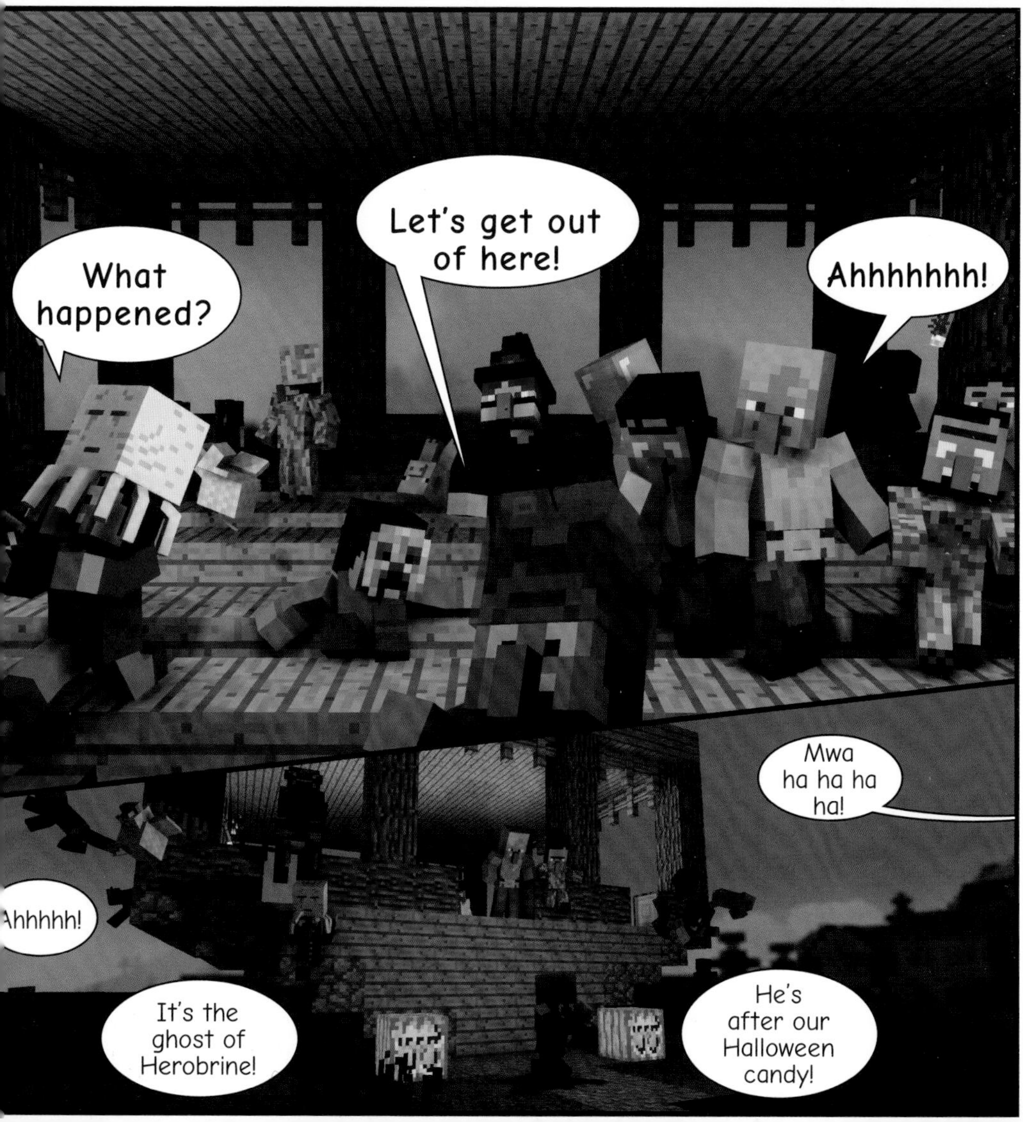
What happened?
Let's get out of here!
Ahhhhhhh!
Mwa ha ha ha ha!
Ahhhhh!
It's the ghost of Herobrine!
He's after our Halloween candy!

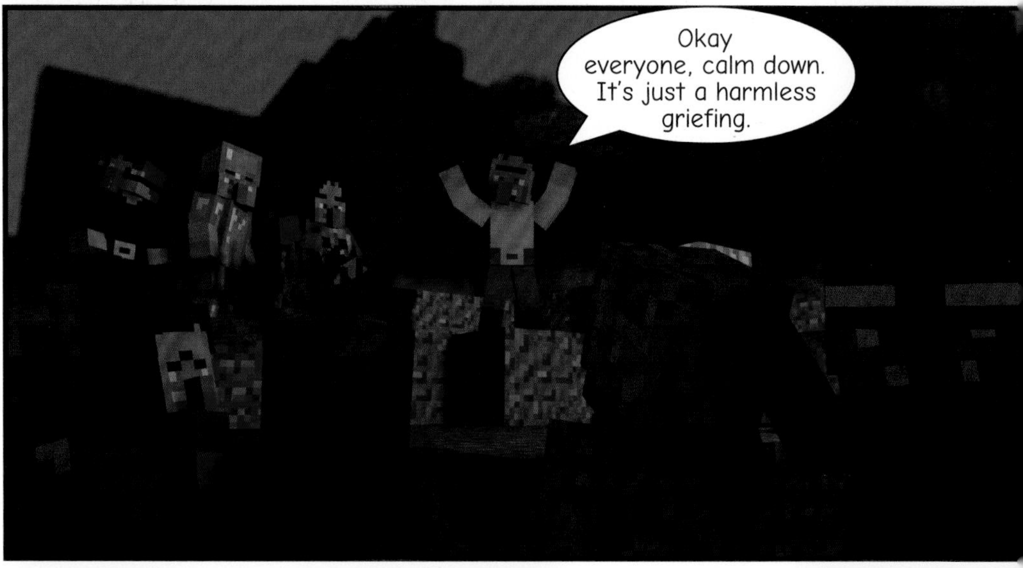
Okay everyone, calm down. It's just a harmless griefing.

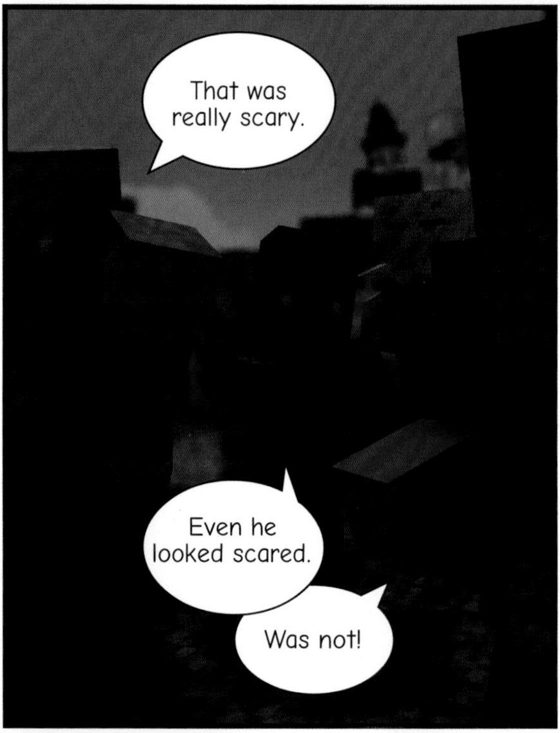
That was really scary.
Even he looked scared.
Was not!

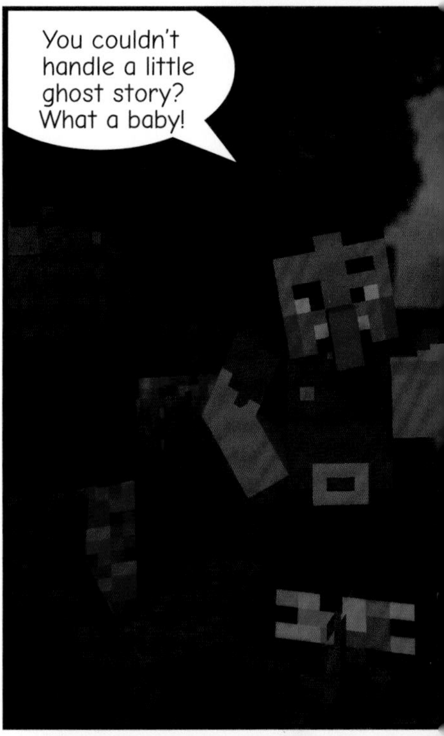
You couldn't handle a little ghost story? What a baby!

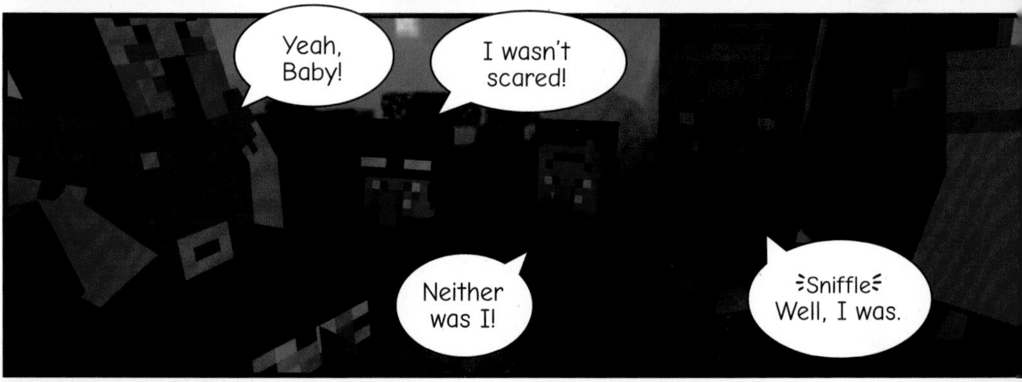
Yeah, Baby!
I wasn't scared!
Neither was I!
Sniffle
Well, I was.

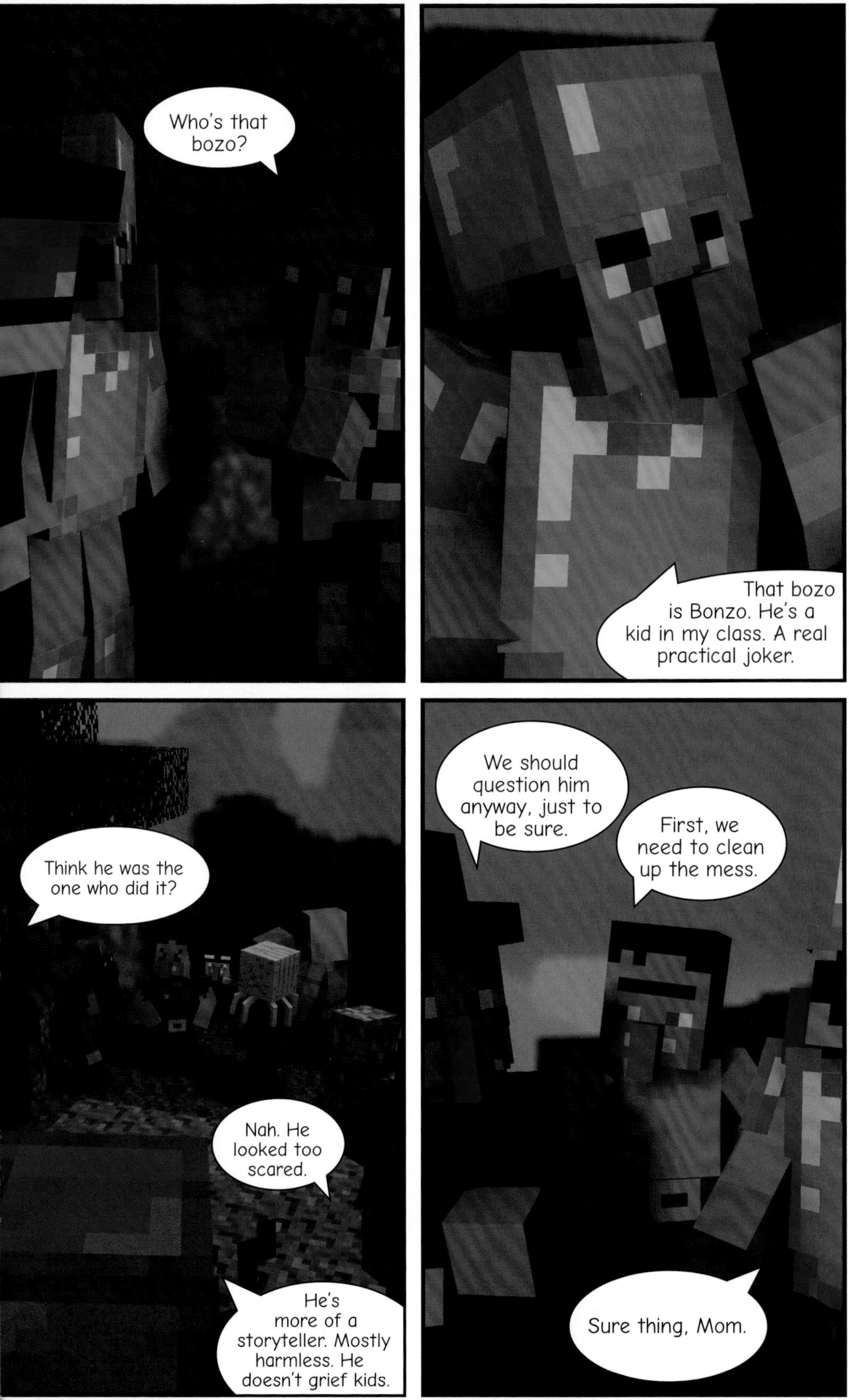
Who's that bozo?
That bozo is Bonzo. He's a kid in my class. A real practical joker.
Think he was the one who did it?
Nah. He looked too scared.
He's more of a storyteller. Mostly harmless. He doesn't grief kids.
We should question him anyway, just to be sure.
First, we need to clean up the mess.
Sure thing, Mom.

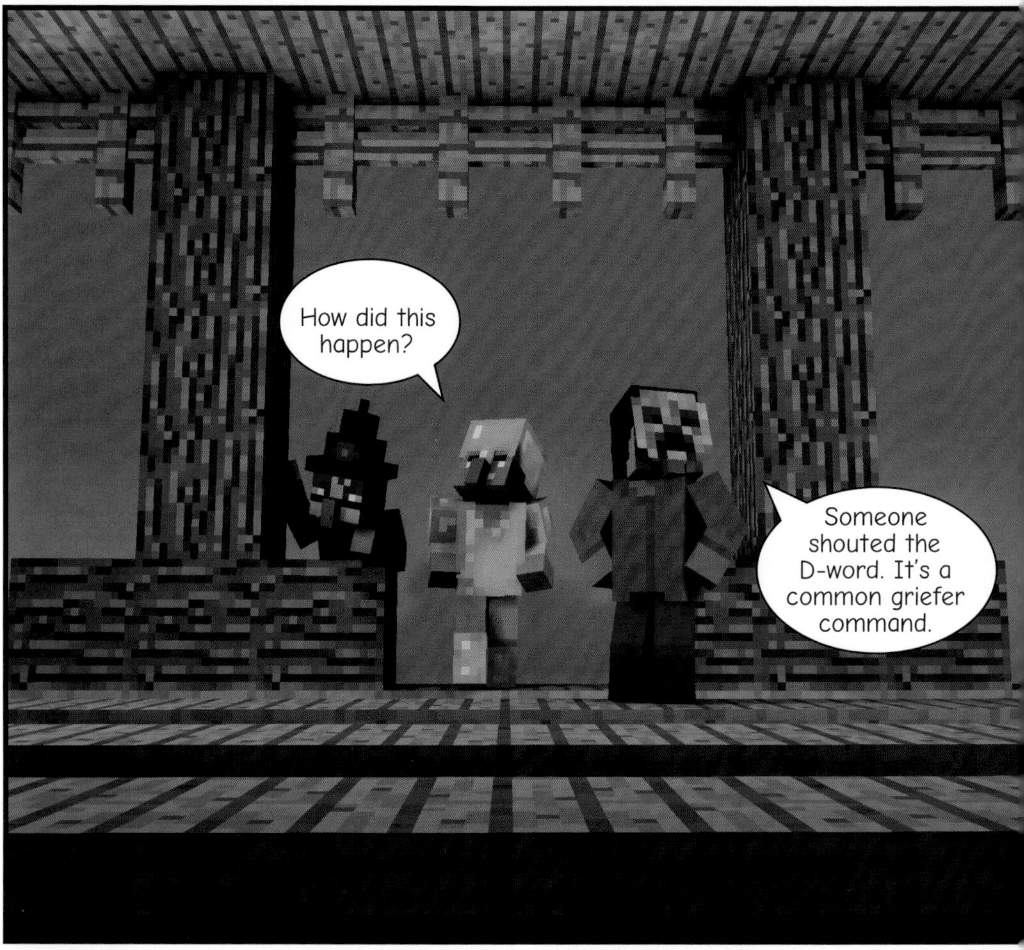
How did this happen?
Someone shouted the D-word. It's a common griefer command.

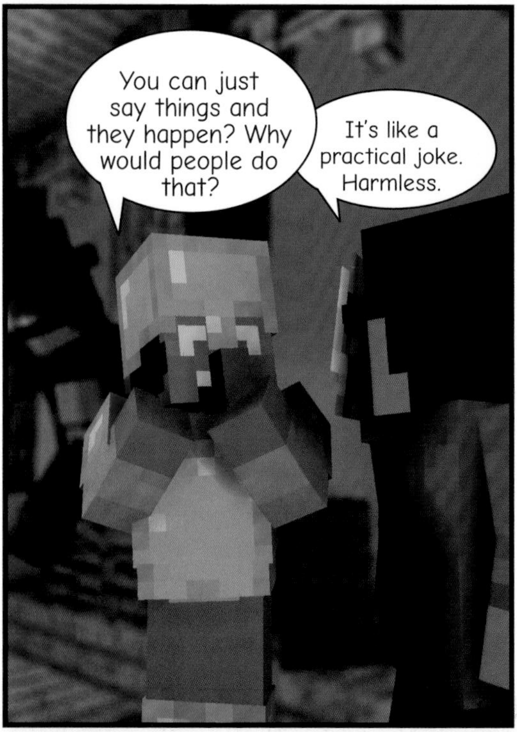
You can just say things and they happen? Why would people do that?
It's like a practical joke. Harmless.

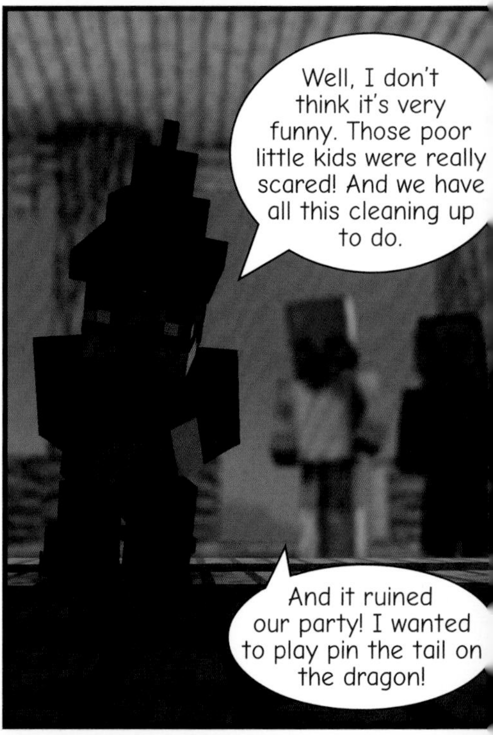
Well, I don't think it's very funny. Those poor little kids were really scared! And we have all this cleaning up to do.
And it ruined our party! I wanted to play pin the tail on the dragon!

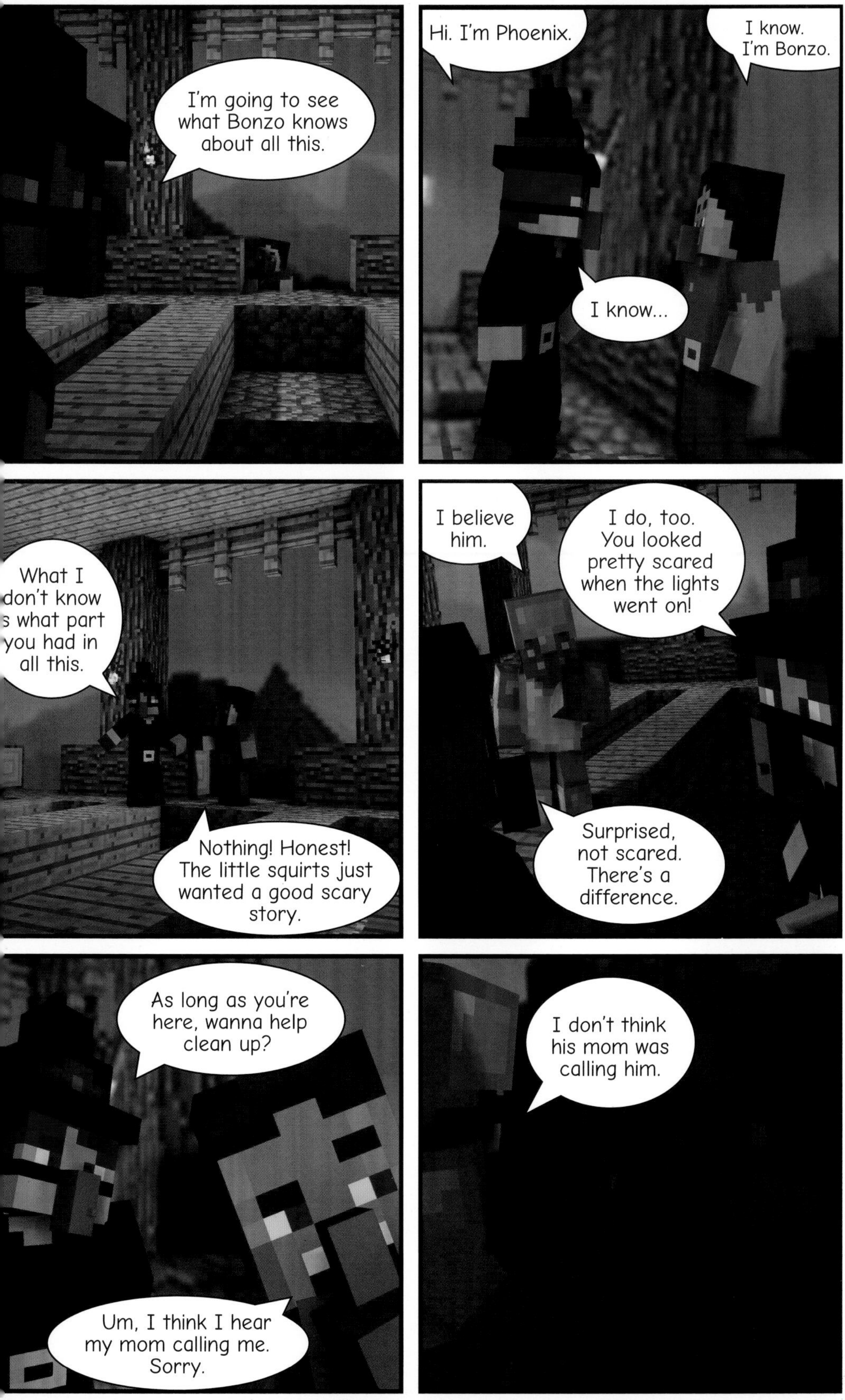
I'm going to see what Bonzo knows about all this.
Hi. I'm Phoenix.
I know. I'm Bonzo.
I know...
What I don't know s what part you had in all this.
Nothing! Honest! The little squirts just wanted a good scary story.
I believe him.
I do, too. You looked pretty scared when the lights went on!
Surprised, not scared. There's a difference.
As long as you're here, wanna help clean up?
Um, I think I hear my mom calling me. Sorry.
I don't think his mom was calling him.

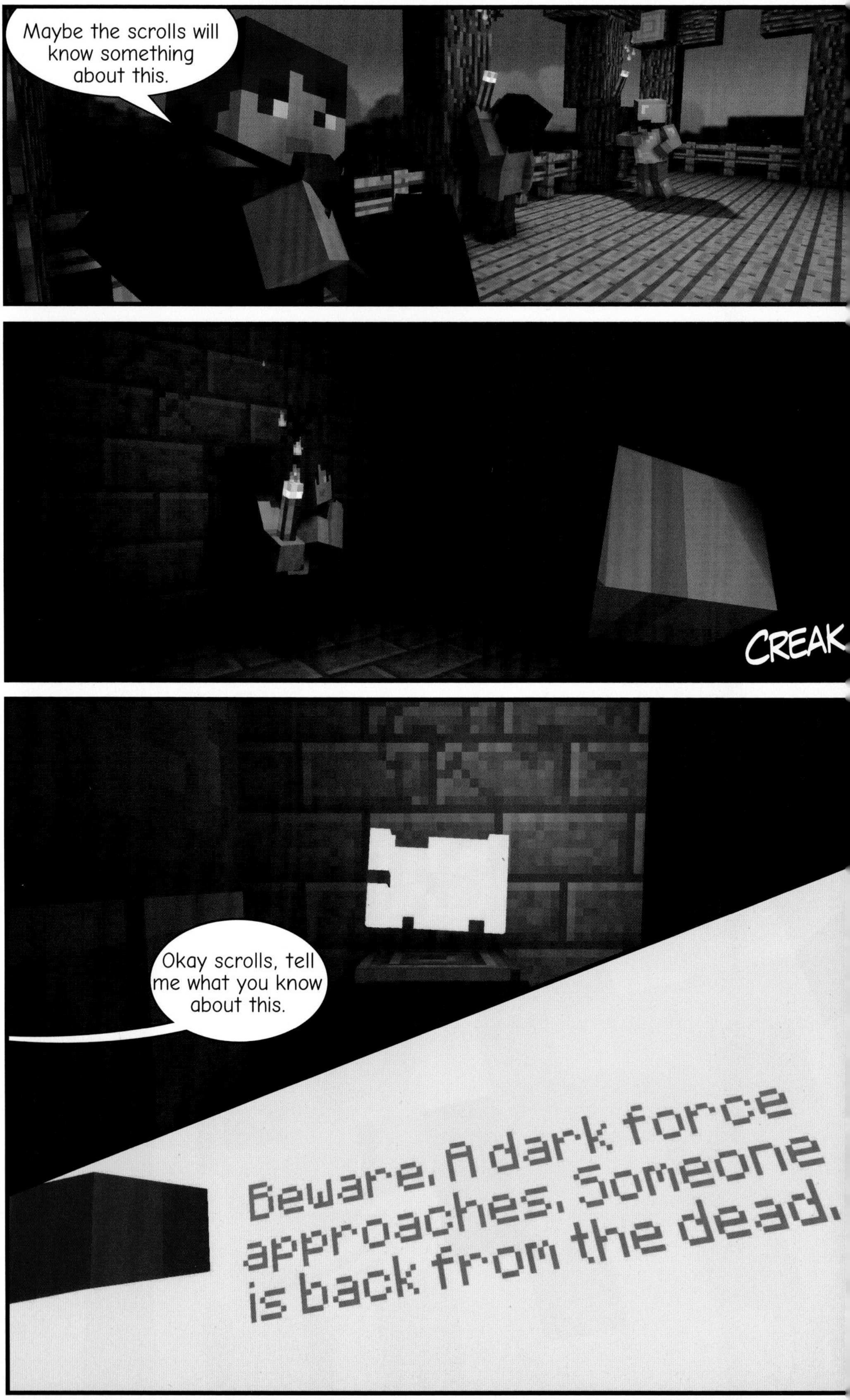
Maybe the scrolls will know something about this.
CREAK
Okay scrolls, tell me what you know about this.
Beware. A dark force approaches. Someone is back from the dead.

CHAPTER 2

THE MARK OF HEROBRINE

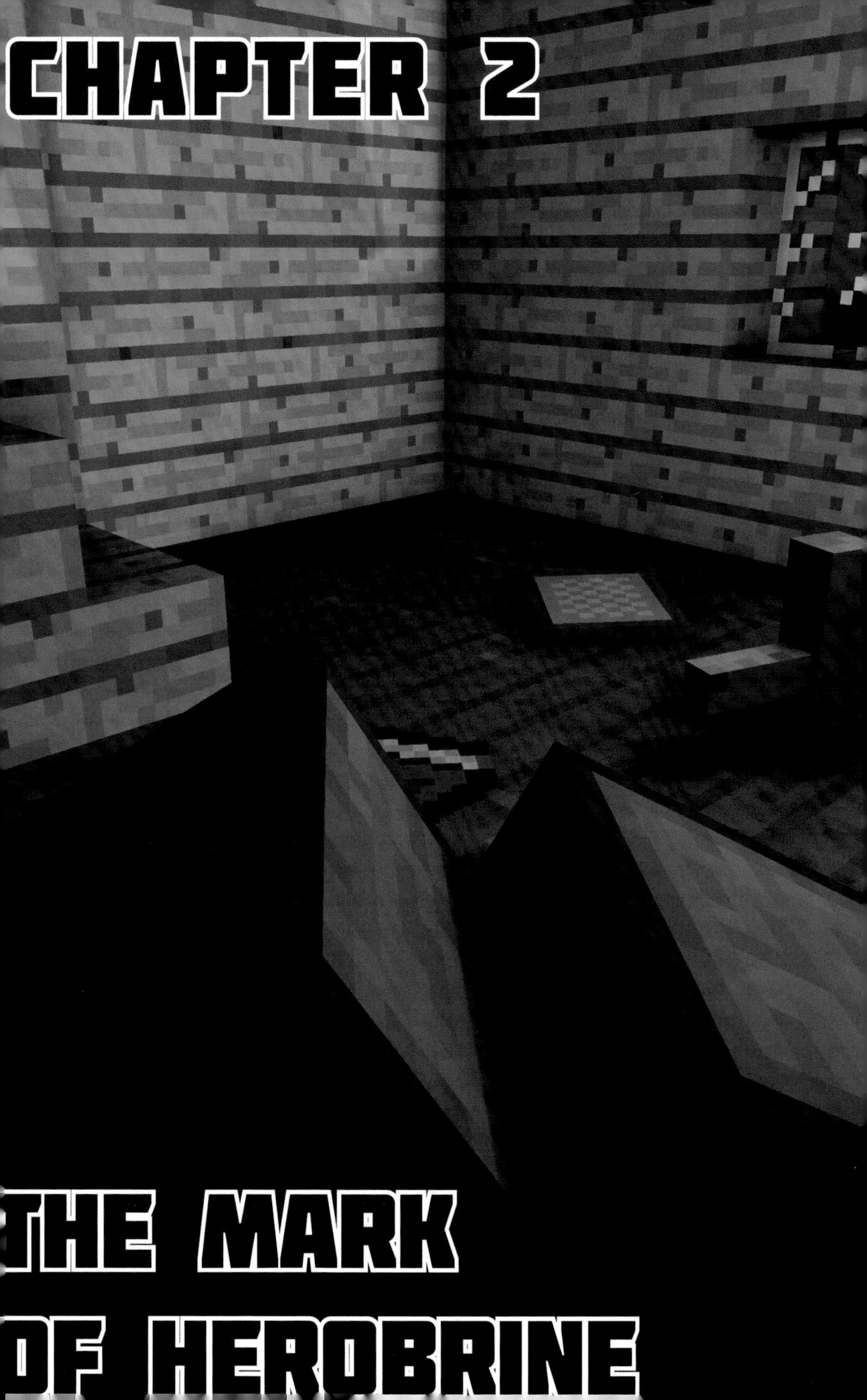

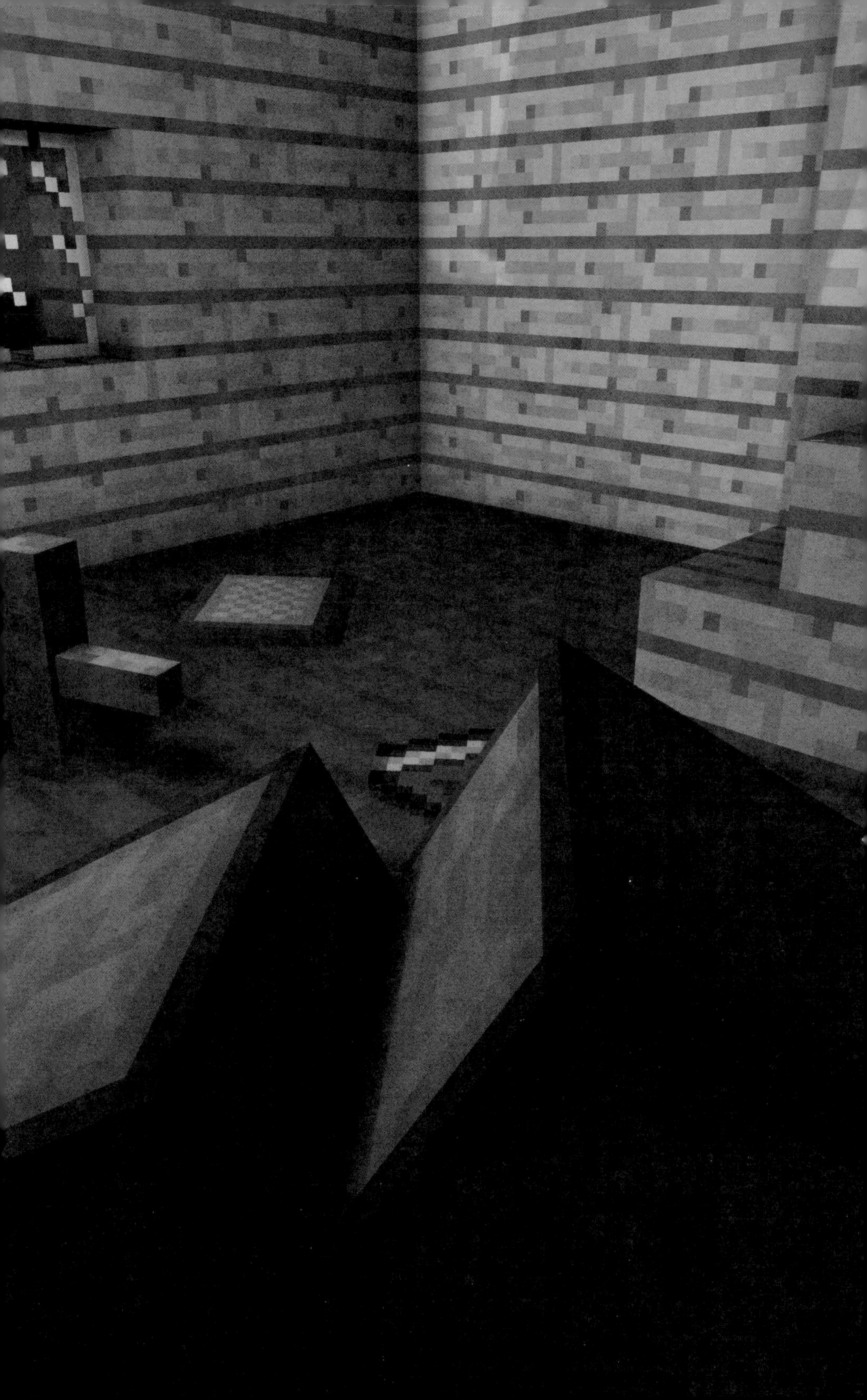

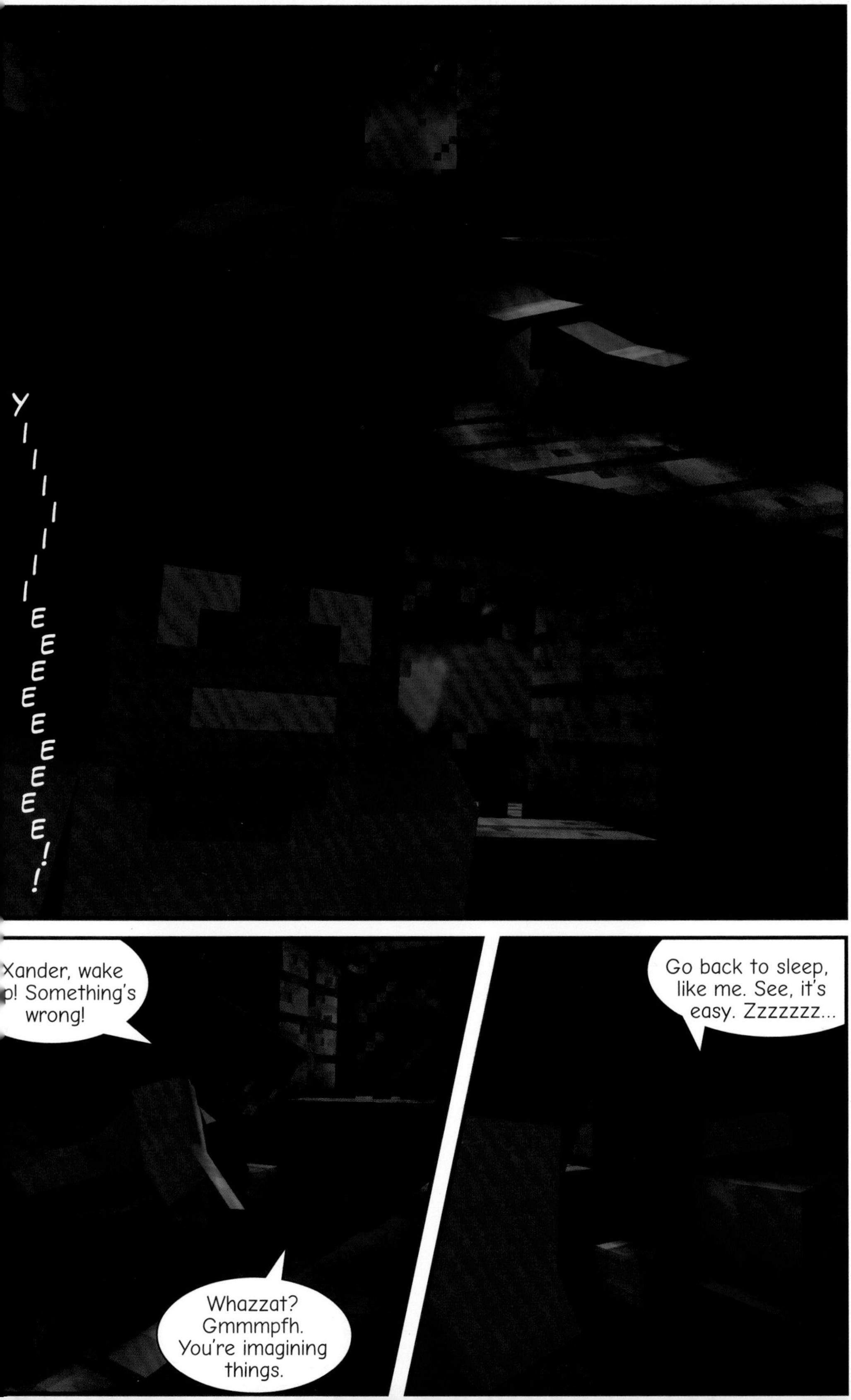
YIIIIIIIEEEEEEEEE!!
Xander, wake p! Something's wrong!
Whazzat? Gmmmpfh. You're imagining things.
Go back to sleep, like me. See, it's easy. Zzzzzzz...

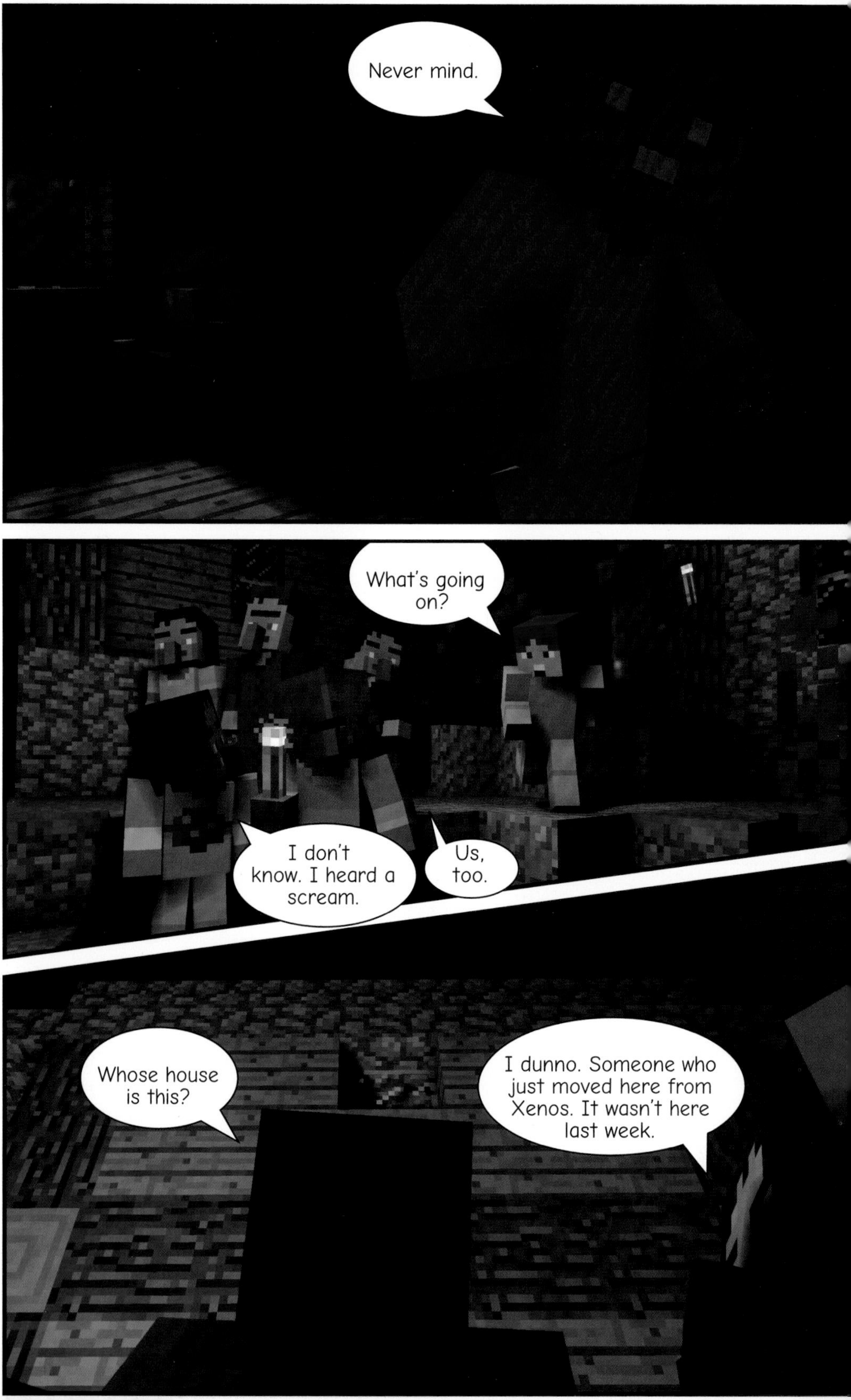
Never mind.
What's going on?
I don't know. I heard a scream.
Us, too.
Whose house is this?
I dunno. Someone who just moved here from Xenos. It wasn't here last week.

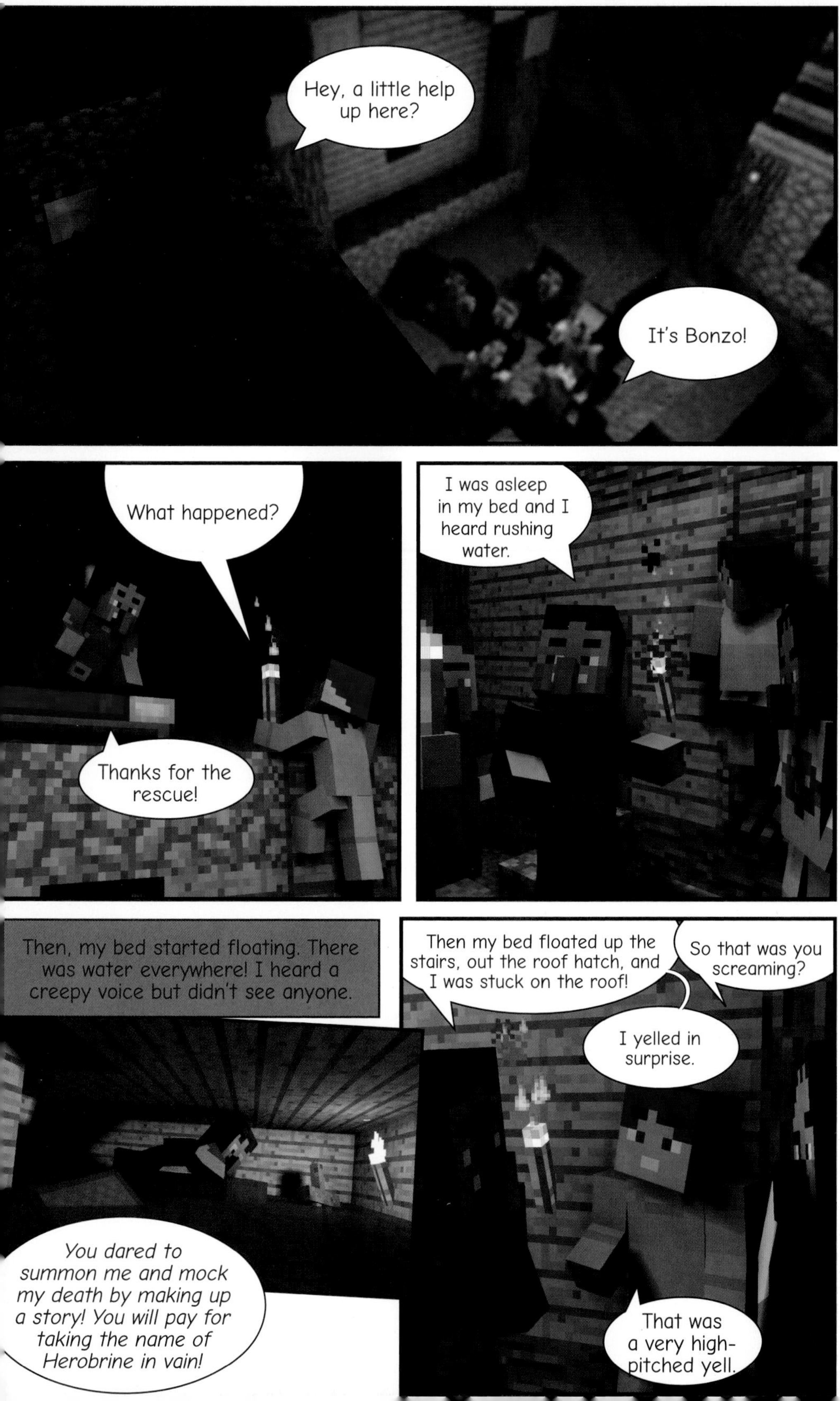

Hey, a little help up here?
It's Bonzo!
What happened?
Thanks for the rescue!
I was asleep in my bed and I heard rushing water.
Then, my bed started floating. There was water everywhere! I heard a creepy voice but didn't see anyone.
You dared to summon me and mock my death by making up a story! You will pay for taking the name of Herobrine in vain!
Then my bed floated up the stairs, out the roof hatch, and I was stuck on the roof!
So that was you screaming?
I yelled in surprise.
That was a very high-pitched yell.

Looks like you have a little water problem, Bonzo.

If only there were a way to dry this house out quickly...

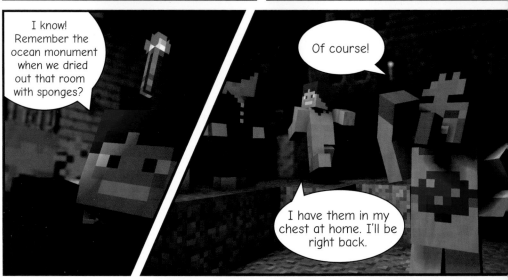

I know! Remember the ocean monument when we dried out that room with sponges?

Of course!

I have them in my chest at home. I'll be right back.

Bring Xander with you. We need all hands on deck for this one.

We're back! Who wants a sponge?

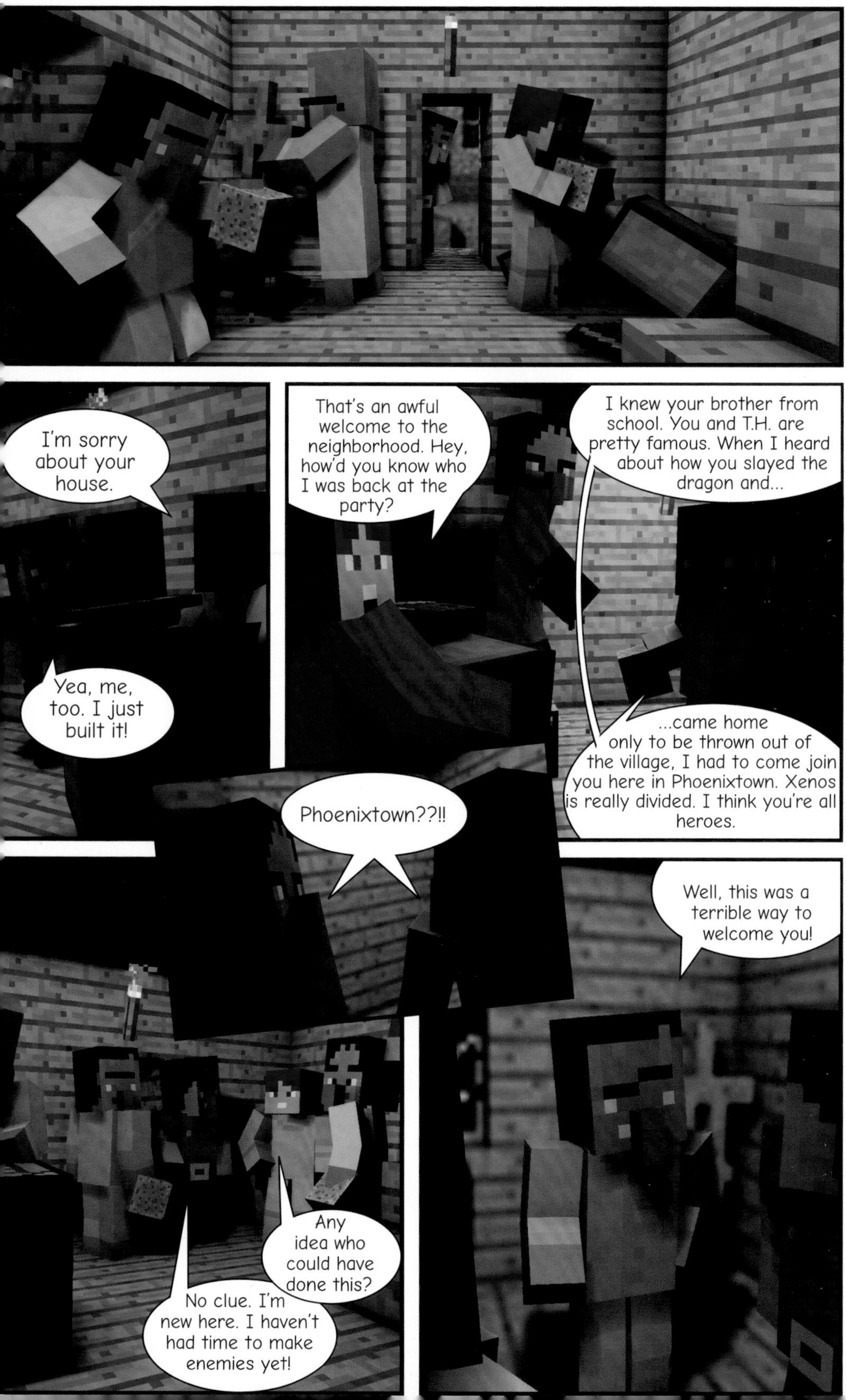
I'm sorry about your house.
Yea, me, too. I just built it!
That's an awful welcome to the neighborhood. Hey, how'd you know who I was back at the party?
I knew your brother from school. You and T.H. are pretty famous. When I heard about how you slayed the dragon and...
...came home only to be thrown out of the village, I had to come join you here in Phoenixtown. Xenos is really divided. I think you're all heroes.
Phoenixtown??!!
Any idea who could have done this?
No clue. I'm new here. I haven't had time to make enemies yet!
Well, this was a terrible way to welcome you!

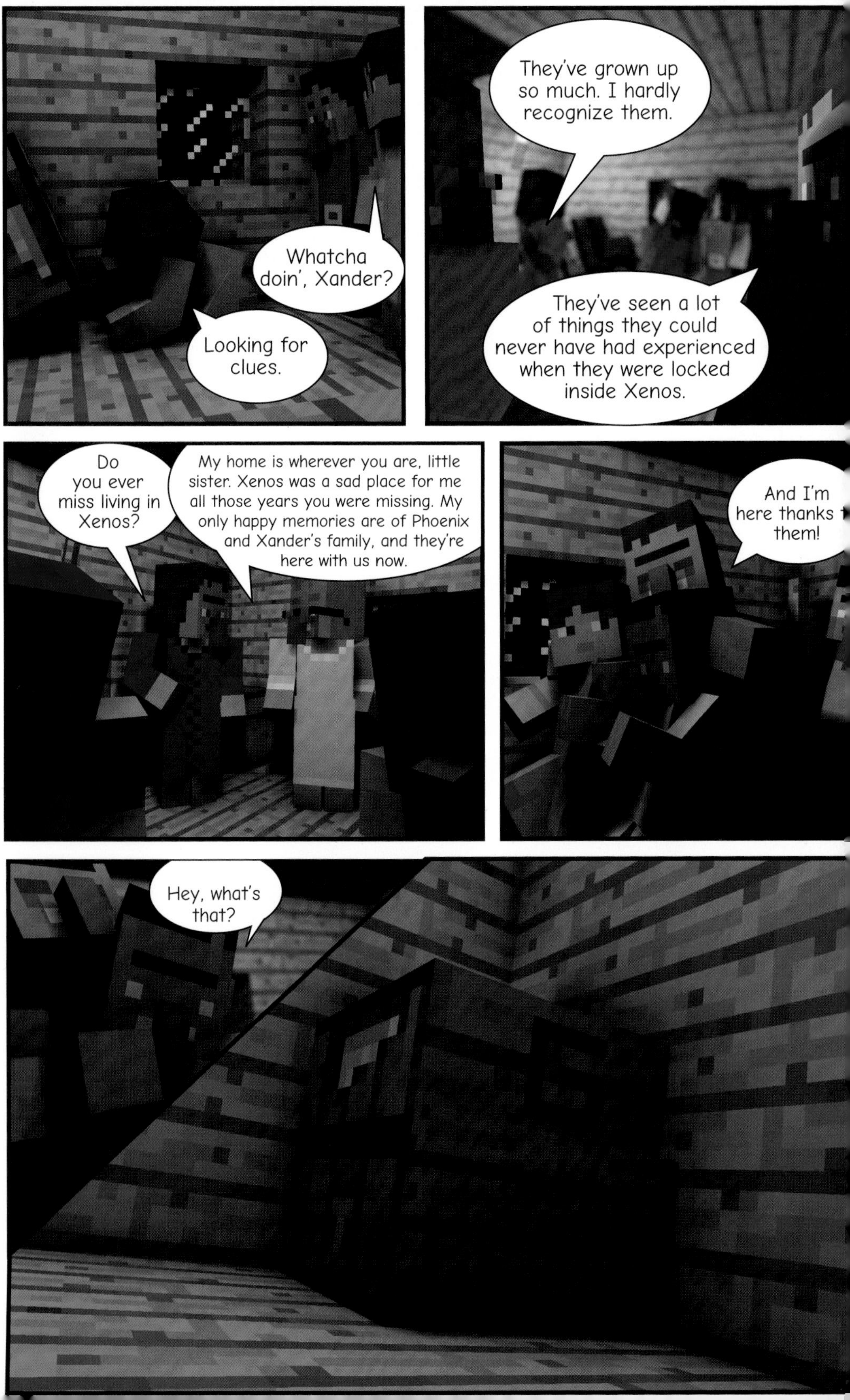
Whatcha doin', Xander?
Looking for clues.
They've grown up so much. I hardly recognize them.
They've seen a lot of things they could never have had experienced when they were locked inside Xenos.
Do you ever miss living in Xenos?
My home is wherever you are, little sister. Xenos was a sad place for me all those years you were missing. My only happy memories are of Phoenix and Xander's family, and they're here with us now.
And I'm here thanks to them!
Hey, what's that?

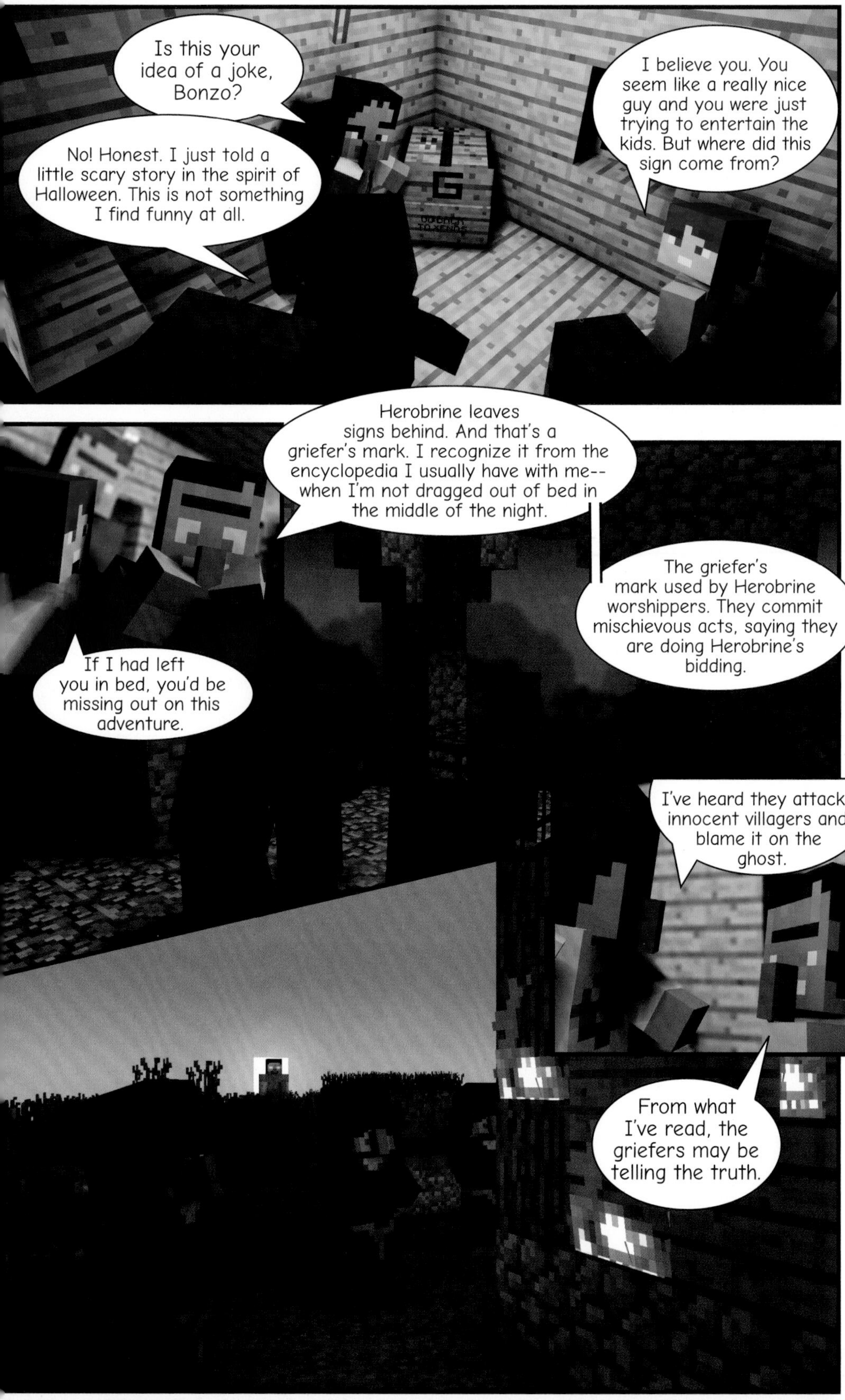
Is this your idea of a joke, Bonzo?
No! Honest. I just told a little scary story in the spirit of Halloween. This is not something I find funny at all.
I believe you. You seem like a really nice guy and you were just trying to entertain the kids. But where did this sign come from?
Herobrine leaves signs behind. And that's a griefer's mark. I recognize it from the encyclopedia I usually have with me--when I'm not dragged out of bed in the middle of the night.
If I had left you in bed, you'd be missing out on this adventure.
The griefer's mark used by Herobrine worshippers. They commit mischievous acts, saying they are doing Herobrine's bidding.
I've heard they attack innocent villagers and blame it on the ghost.
From what I've read, the griefers may be telling the truth.

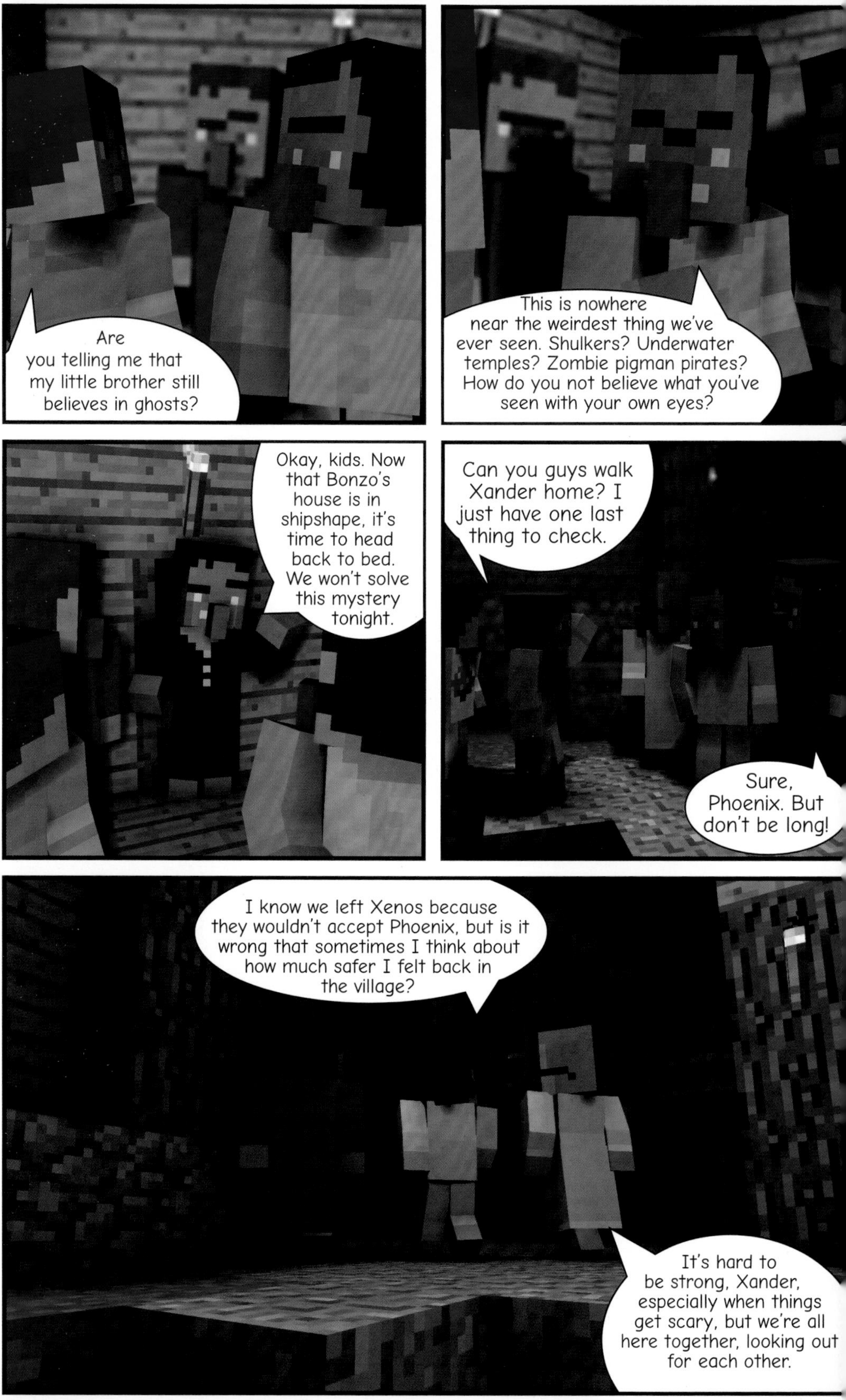
Are you telling me that my little brother still believes in ghosts?
This is nowhere near the weirdest thing we've ever seen. Shulkers? Underwater temples? Zombie pigman pirates? How do you not believe what you've seen with your own eyes?
Okay, kids. Now that Bonzo's house is in shipshape, it's time to head back to bed. We won't solve this mystery tonight.
Can you guys walk Xander home? I just have one last thing to check.
Sure, Phoenix. But don't be long!
I know we left Xenos because they wouldn't accept Phoenix, but is it wrong that sometimes I think about how much safer I felt back in the village?
It's hard to be strong, Xander, especially when things get scary, but we're all here together, looking out for each other.

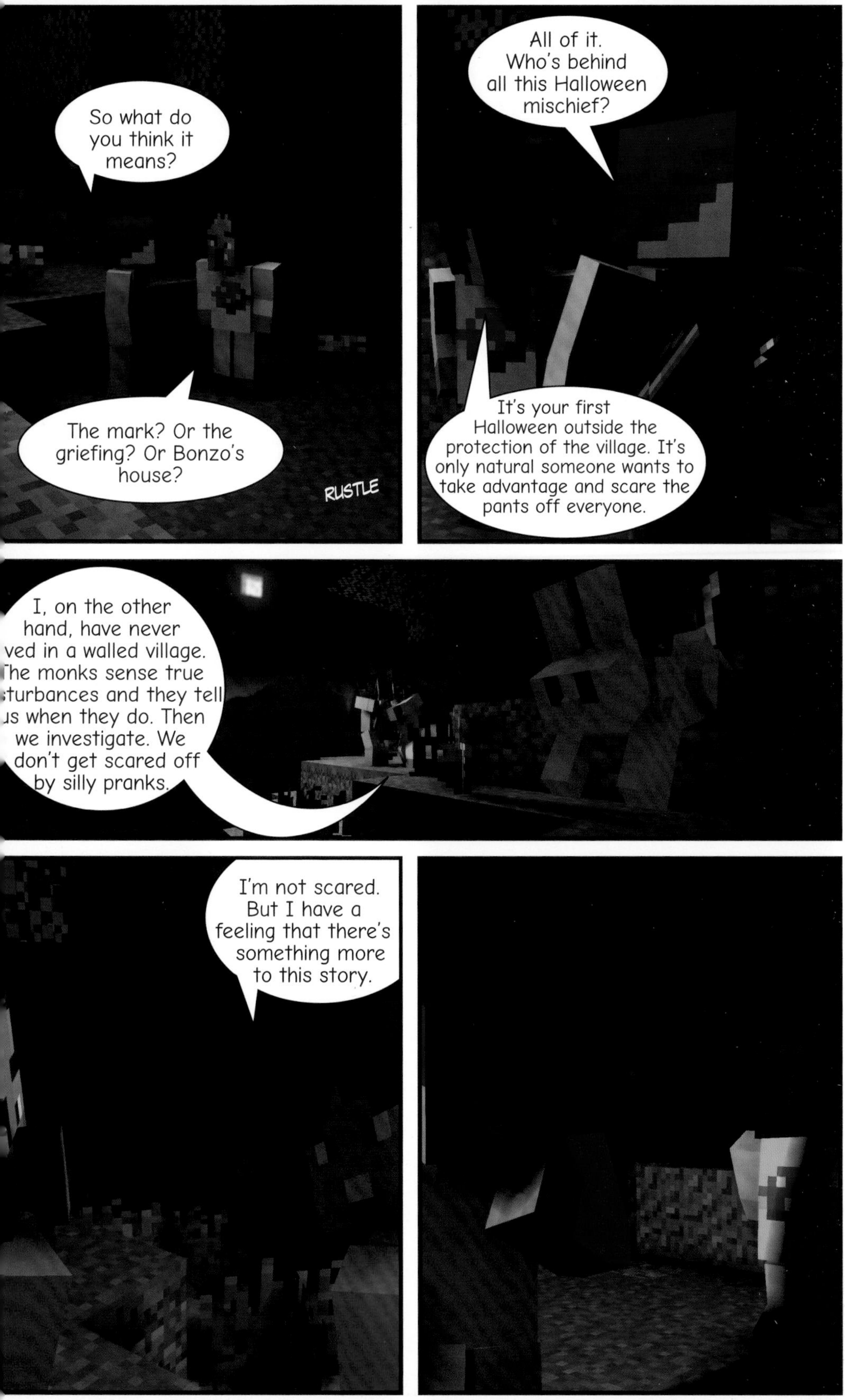
So what do you think it means?
All of it. Who's behind all this Halloween mischief?
The mark? Or the griefing? Or Bonzo's house?
RUSTLE
It's your first Halloween outside the protection of the village. It's only natural someone wants to take advantage and scare the pants off everyone.
I, on the other hand, have never ved in a walled village. The monks sense true sturbances and they tell us when they do. Then we investigate. We don't get scared off by silly pranks.
I'm not scared. But I have a feeling that there's something more to this story.

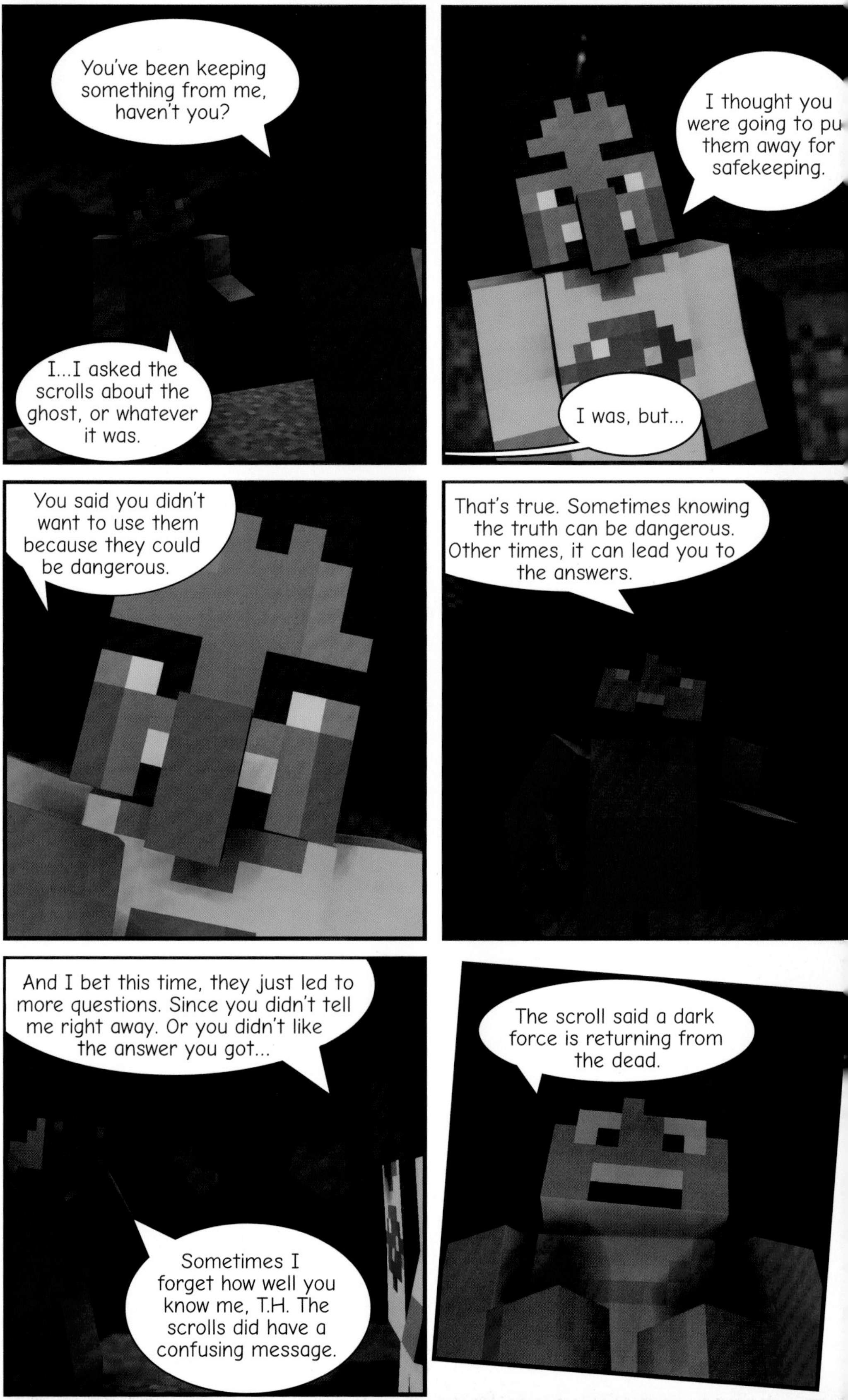
You've been keeping something from me, haven't you?
I...I asked the scrolls about the ghost, or whatever it was.
I thought you were going to pu them away for safekeeping.
I was, but...
You said you didn't want to use them because they could be dangerous.
That's true. Sometimes knowing the truth can be dangerous. Other times, it can lead you to the answers.
And I bet this time, they just led to more questions. Since you didn't tell me right away. Or you didn't like the answer you got...
Sometimes I forget how well you know me, T.H. The scrolls did have a confusing message.
The scroll said a dark force is returning from the dead.

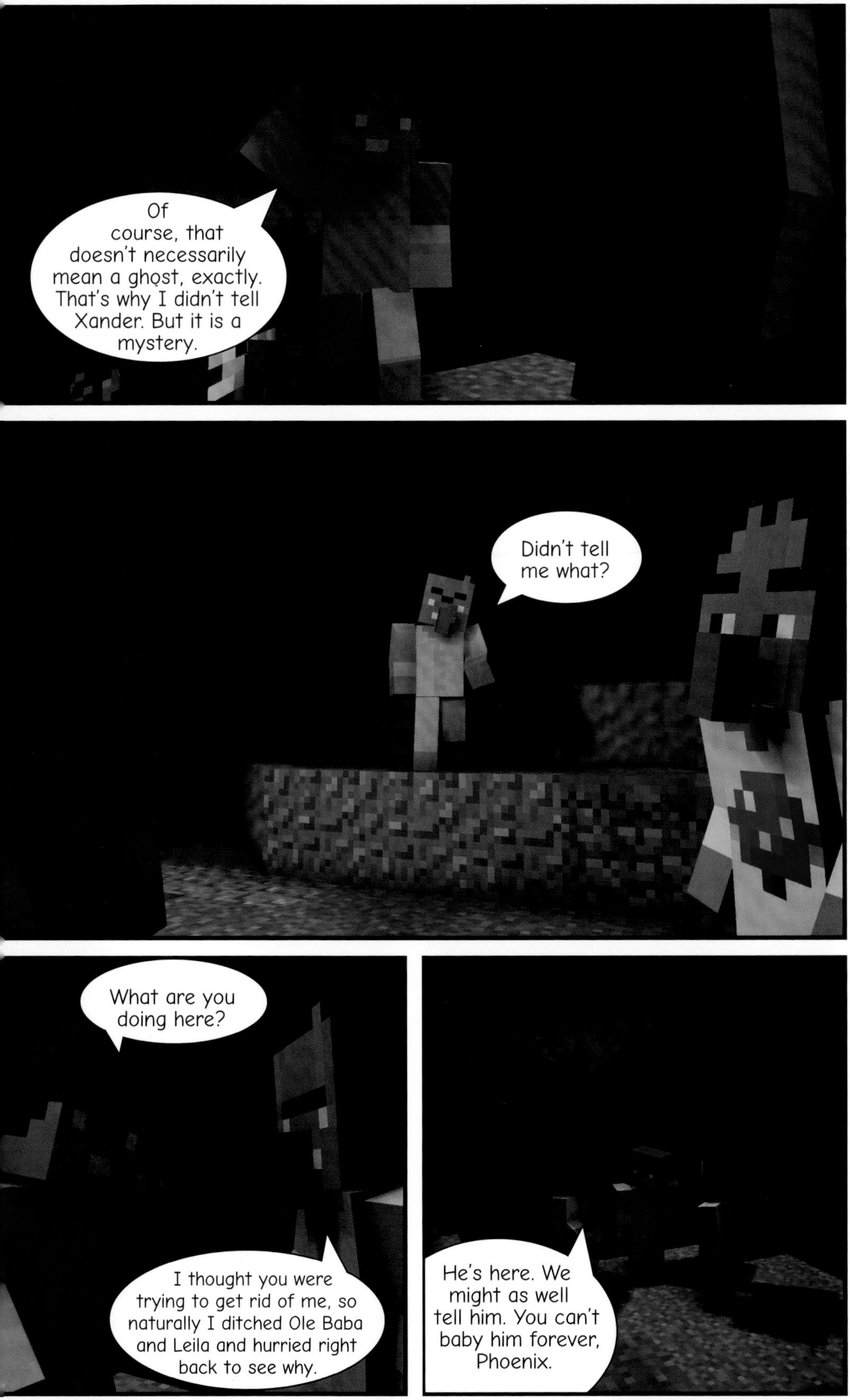
Of course, that doesn't necessarily mean a ghost, exactly. That's why I didn't tell Xander. But it is a mystery.
Didn't tell me what?
What are you doing here?
I thought you were trying to get rid of me, so naturally I ditched Ole Baba and Leila and hurried right back to see why.
He's here. We might as well tell him. You can't baby him forever, Phoenix.

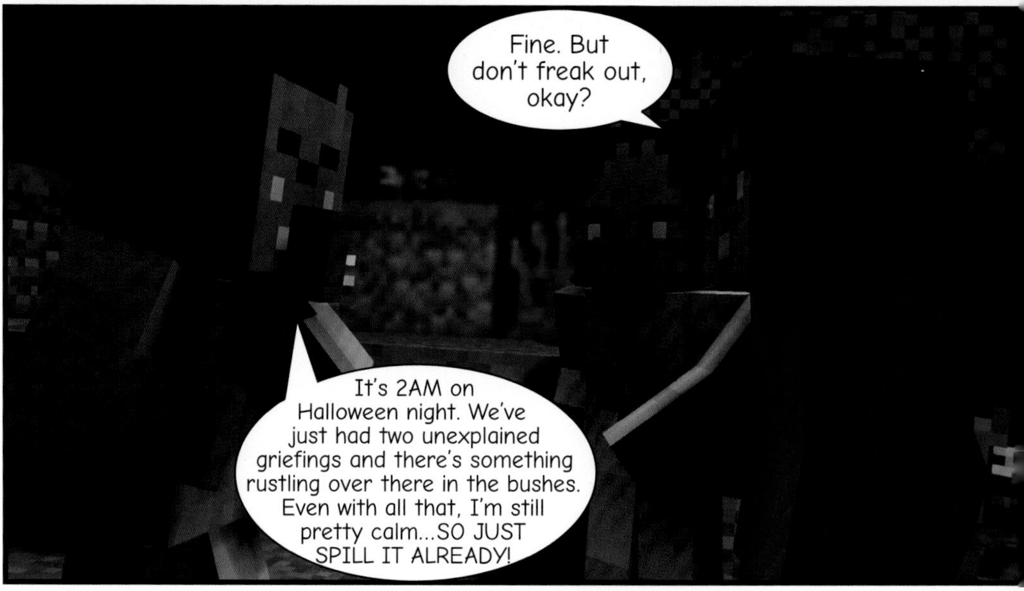
Fine. But don't freak out, okay?
It's 2AM on Halloween night. We've just had two unexplained griefings and there's something rustling over there in the bushes. Even with all that, I'm still pretty calm...SO JUST SPILL IT ALREADY!

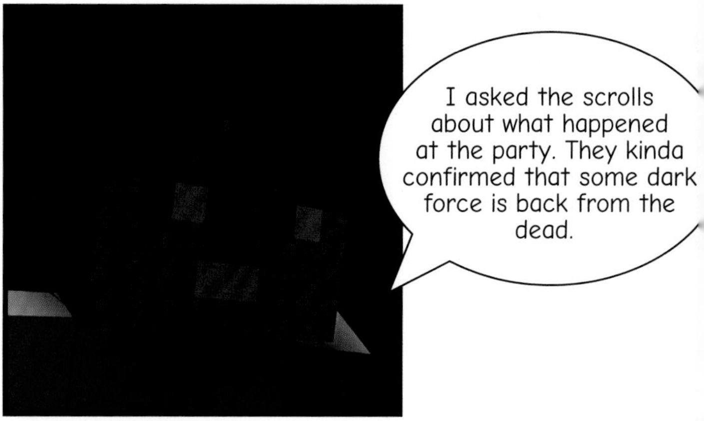
I asked the scrolls about what happened at the party. They kinda confirmed that some dark force is back from the dead.

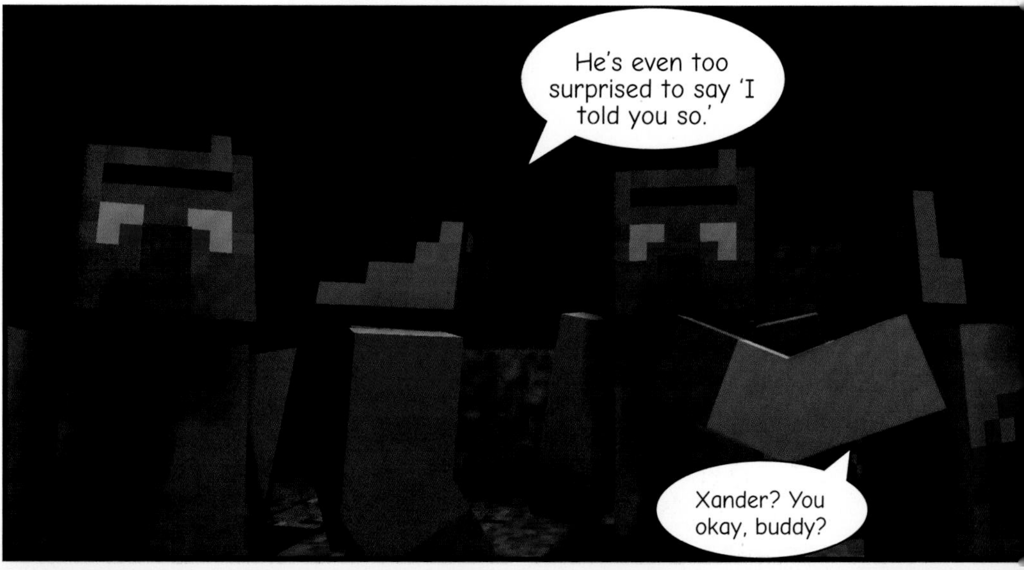
He's even too surprised to say 'I told you so.'
Xander? You okay, buddy?

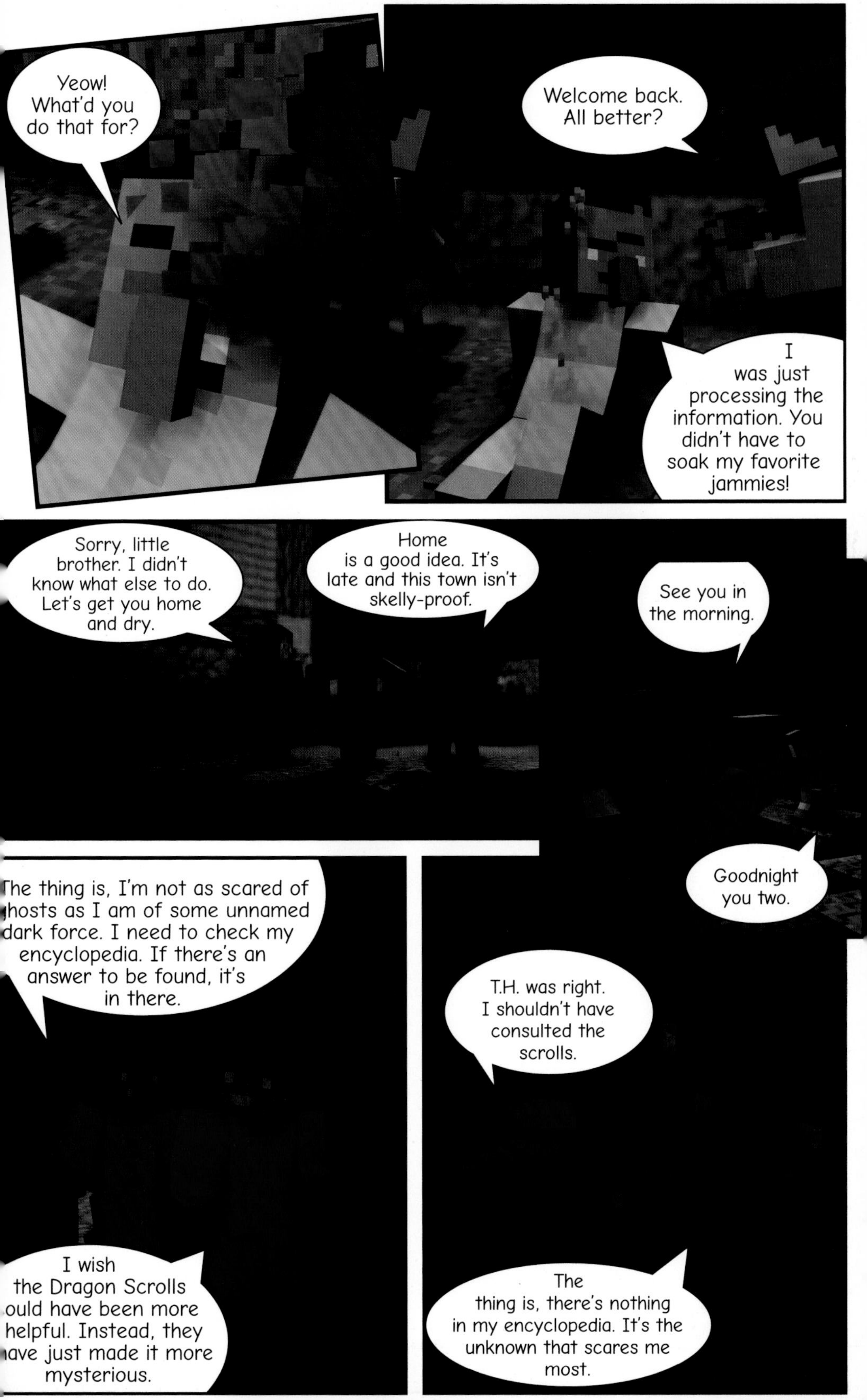
Yeow! What'd you do that for?
Welcome back. All better?
I was just processing the information. You didn't have to soak my favorite jammies!
Sorry, little brother. I didn't know what else to do. Let's get you home and dry.
Home is a good idea. It's late and this town isn't skelly-proof.
See you in the morning.
Goodnight you two.
The thing is, I'm not as scared of ghosts as I am of some unnamed dark force. I need to check my encyclopedia. If there's an answer to be found, it's in there.
T.H. was right. I shouldn't have consulted the scrolls.
I wish the Dragon Scrolls could have been more helpful. Instead, they have just made it more mysterious.
The thing is, there's nothing in my encyclopedia. It's the unknown that scares me most.

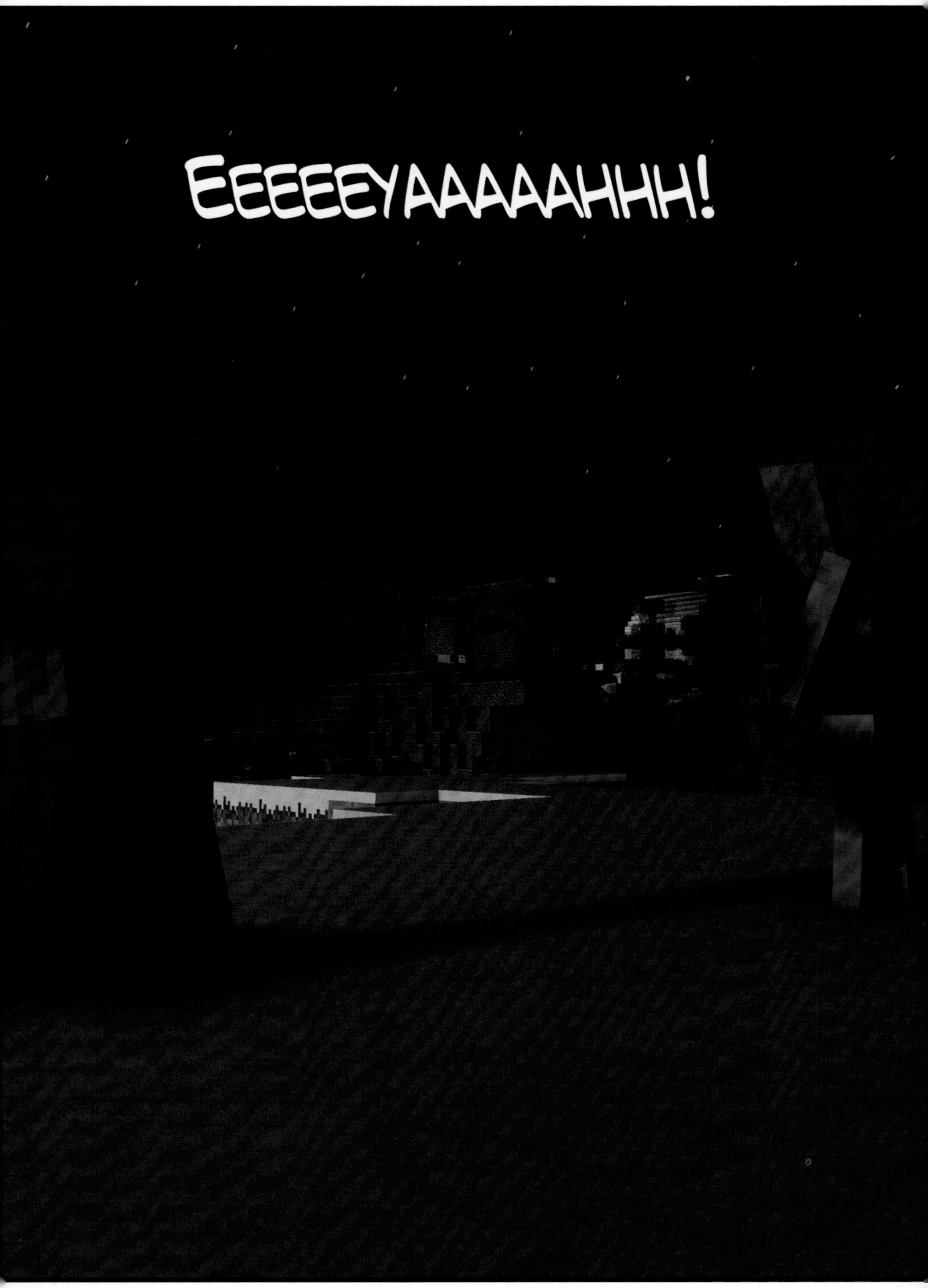
EEEEEEYAAAAAAHHH!

CHAPTER 3

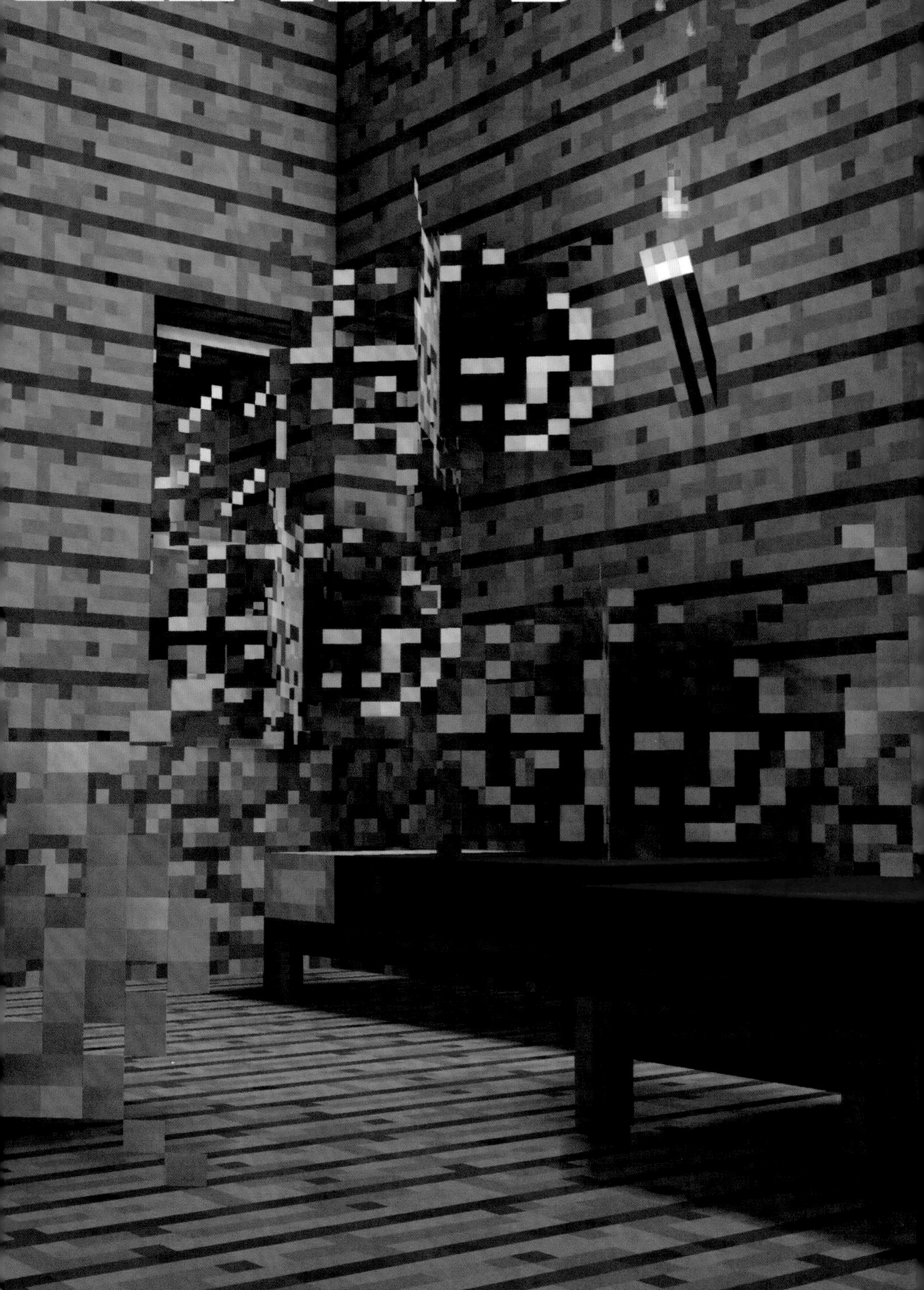

GOOD GRIEF

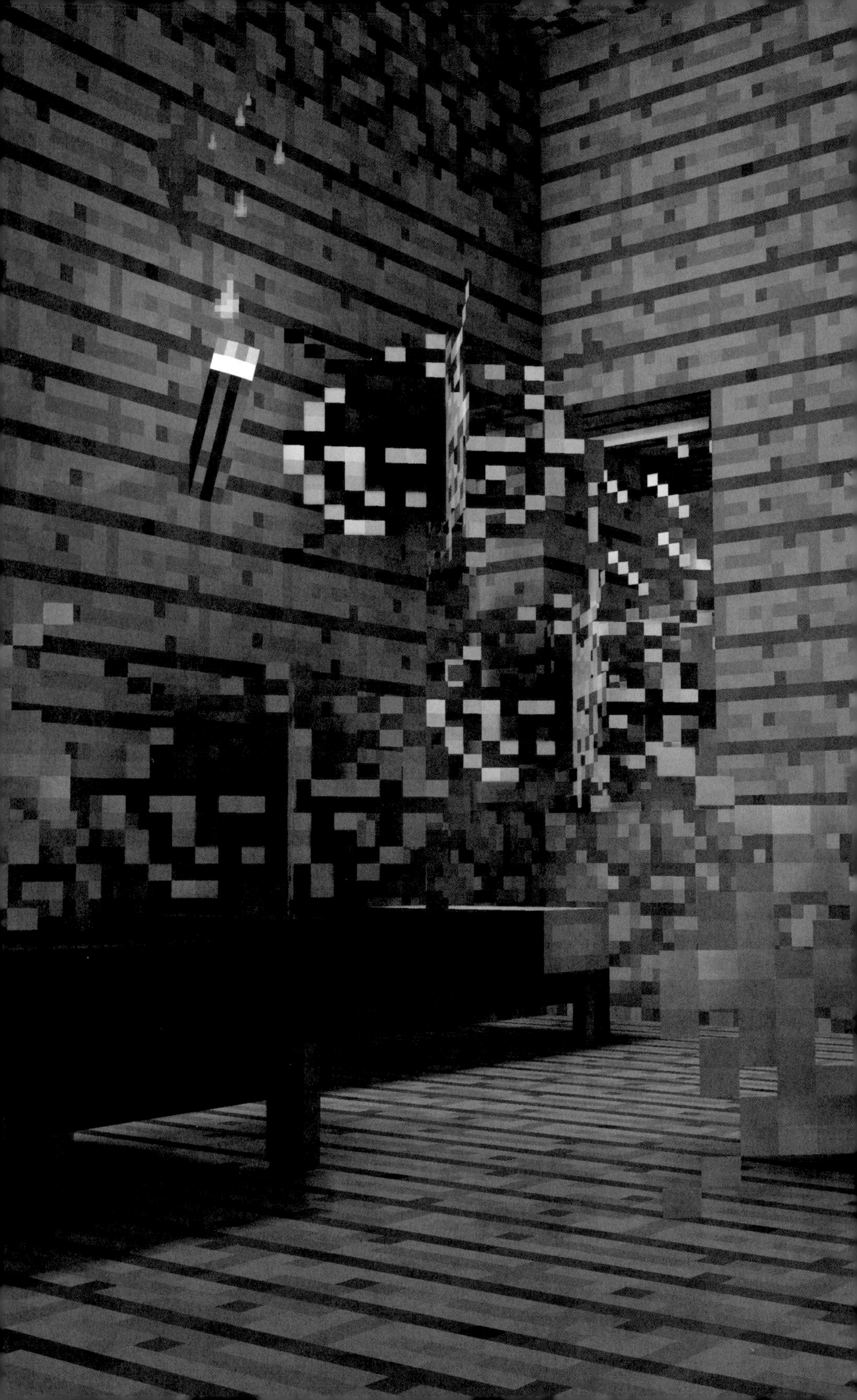

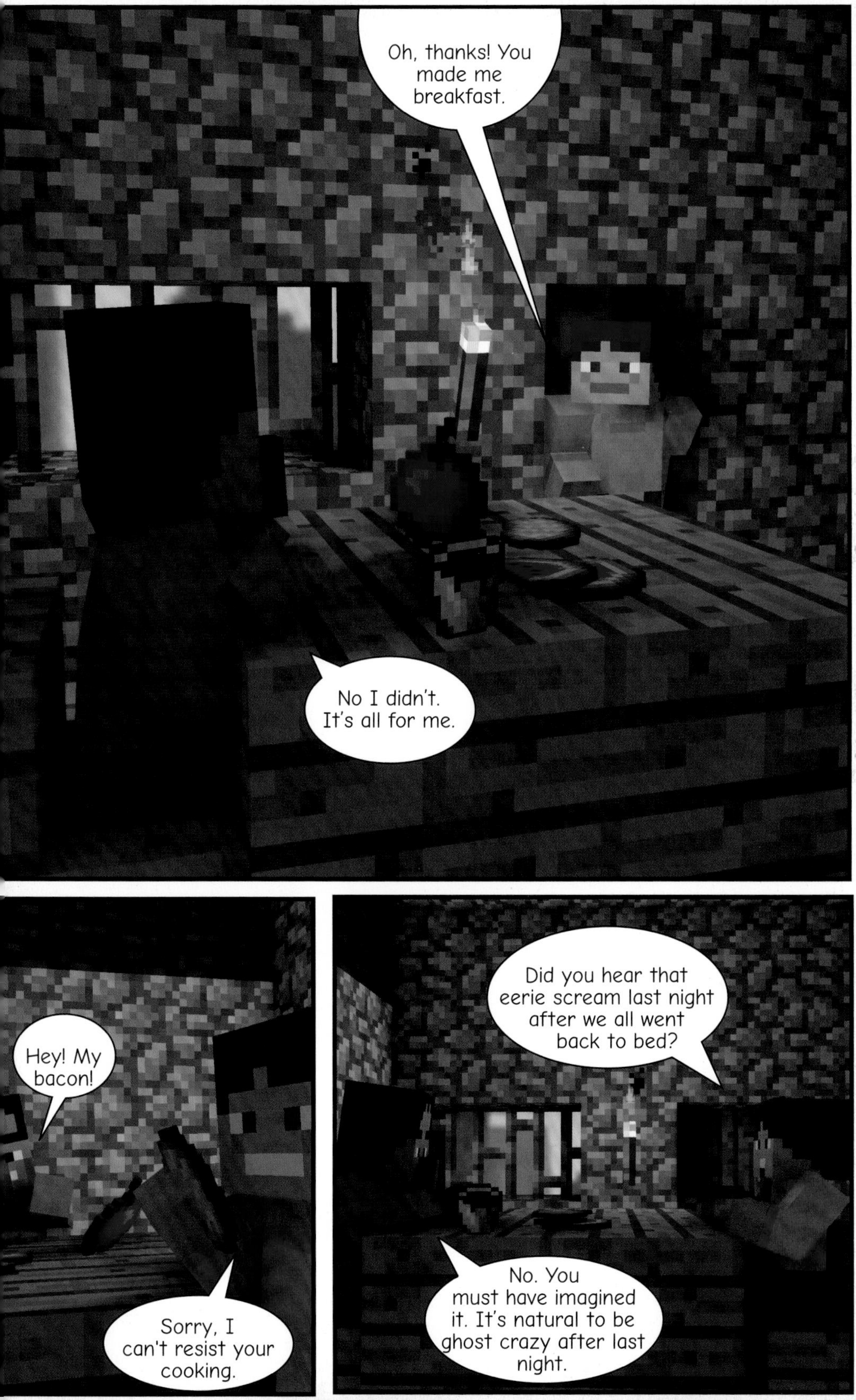
Oh, thanks! You made me breakfast.
No I didn't. It's all for me.
Hey! My bacon!
Sorry, I can't resist your cooking.
Did you hear that eerie scream last night after we all went back to bed?
No. You must have imagined it. It's natural to be ghost crazy after last night.

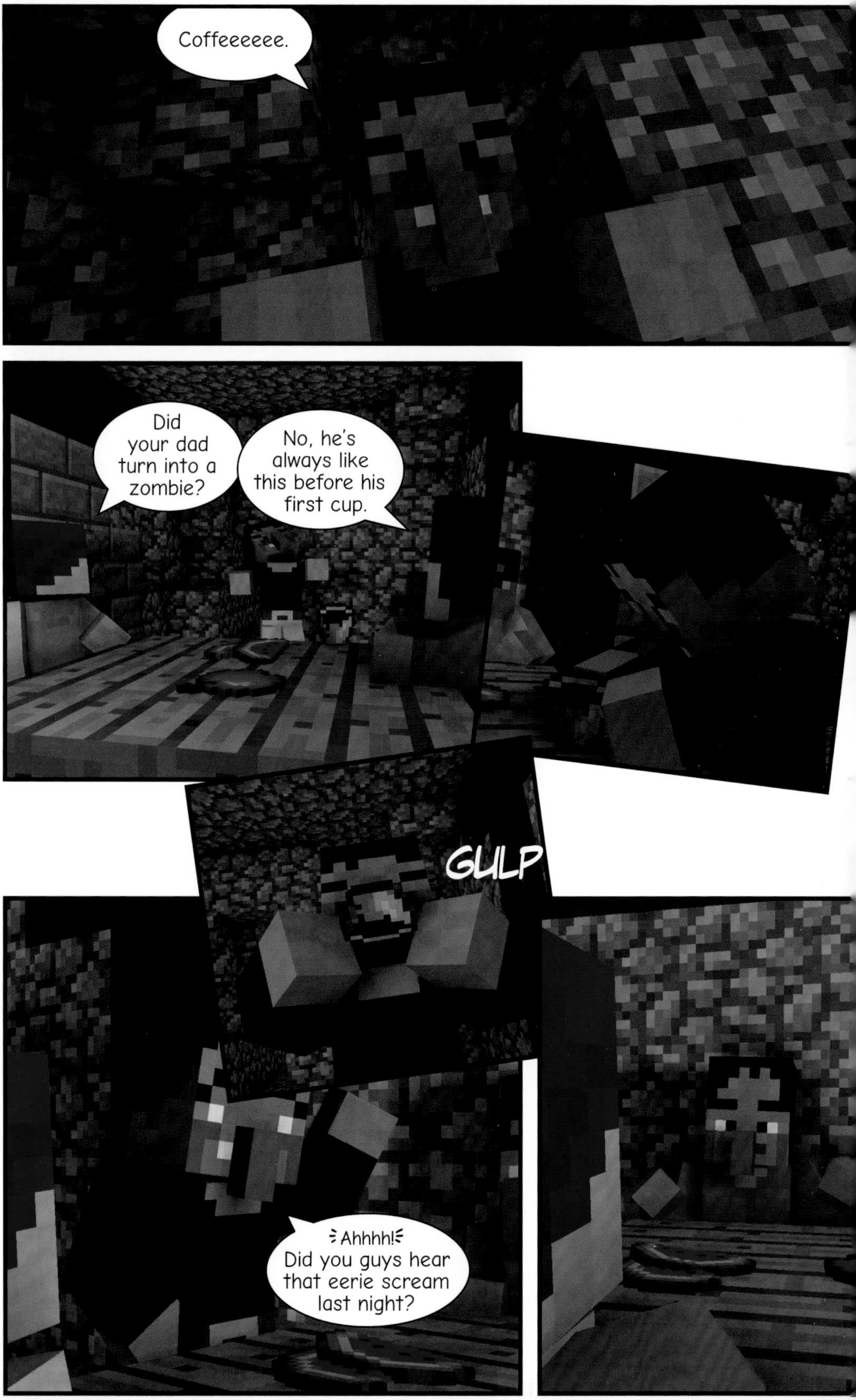
Coffeeeeee.
Did your dad turn into a zombie?
No, he's always like this before his first cup.
GULP
Ahhhh!
Did you guys hear that eerie scream last night?

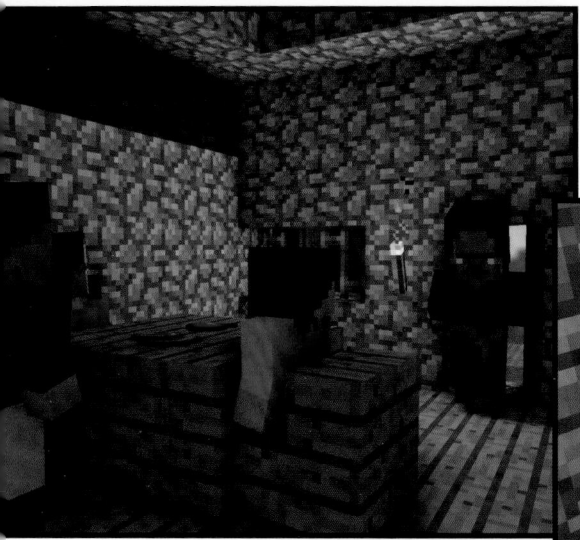
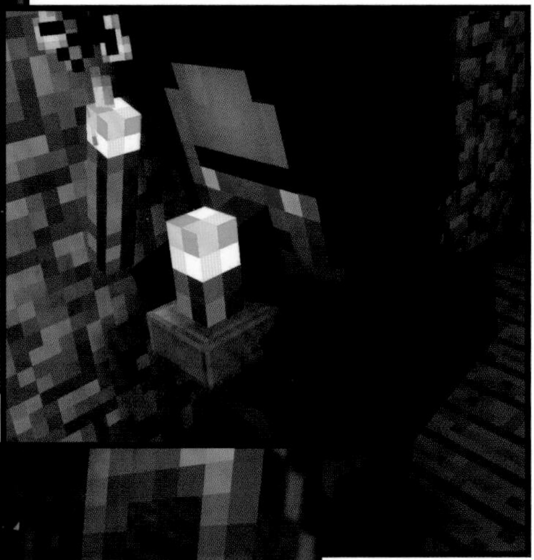
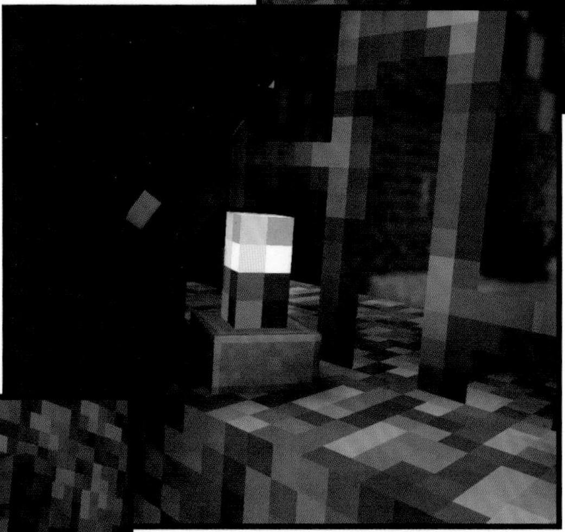
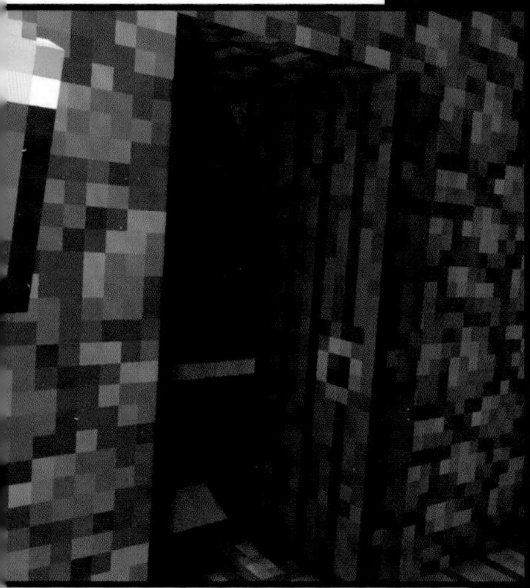
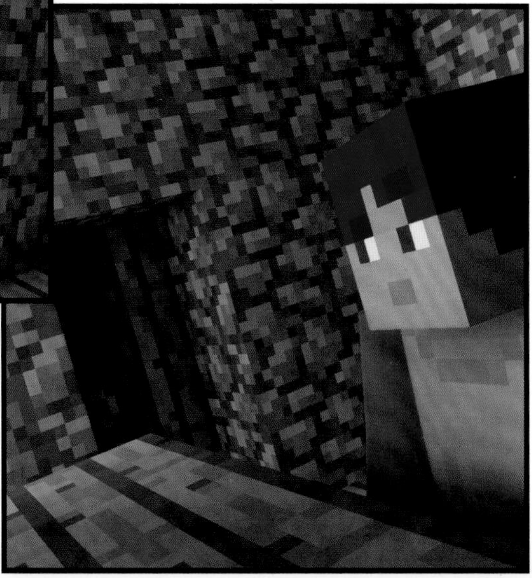

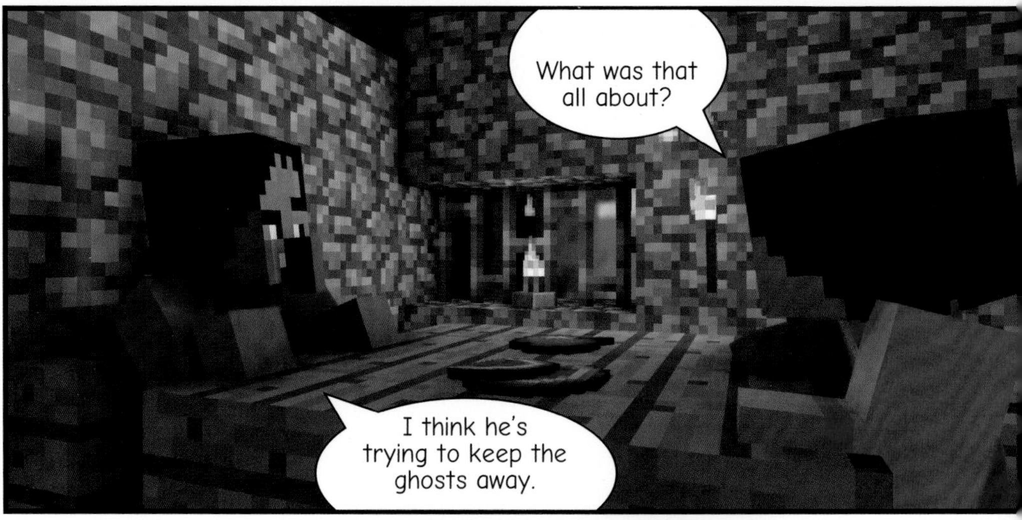
What was that all about?
I think he's trying to keep the ghosts away.

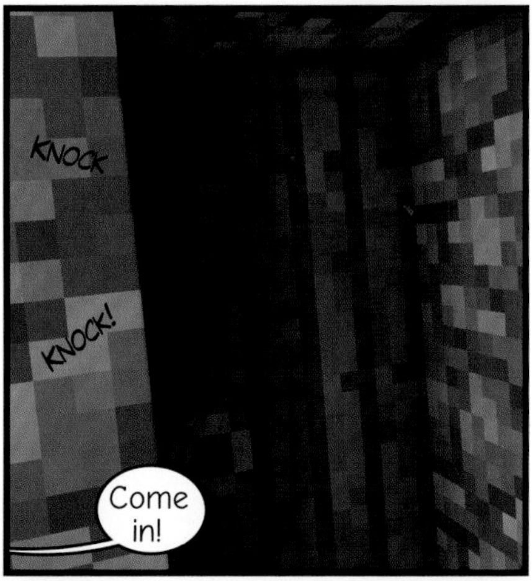
KNOCK
KNOCK!
Come in!

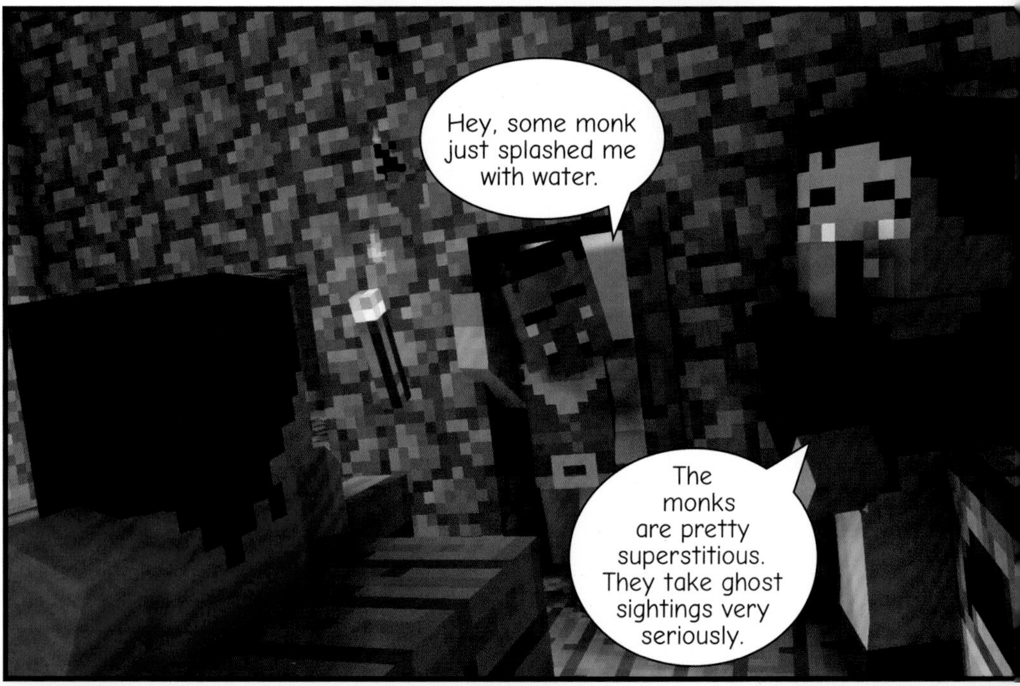
Hey, some monk just splashed me with water.
The monks are pretty superstitious. They take ghost sightings very seriously.

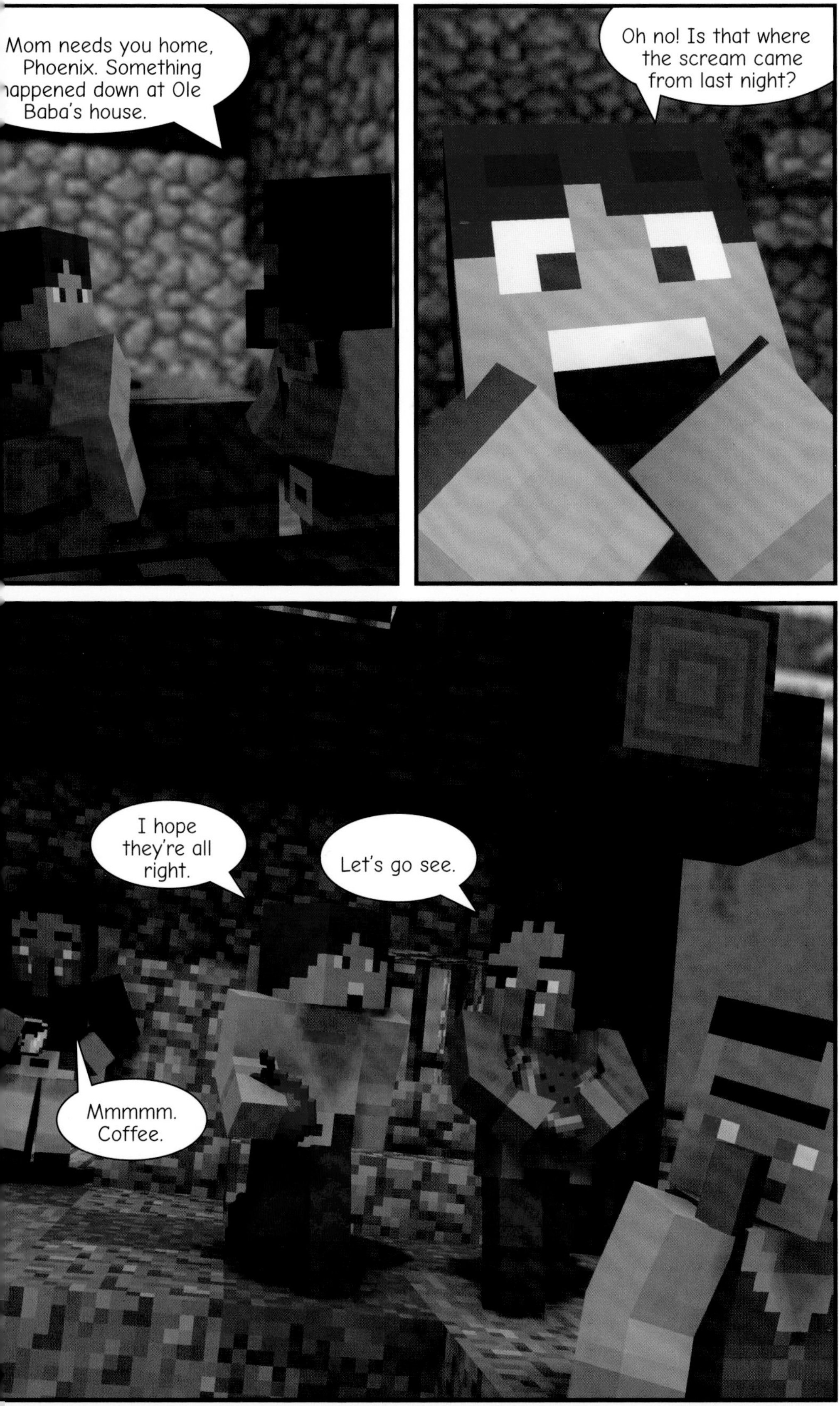
Mom needs you home, Phoenix. Something happened down at Ole Baba's house.
Oh no! Is that where the scream came from last night?
I hope they're all right.
Let's go see.
Mmmmm. Coffee.

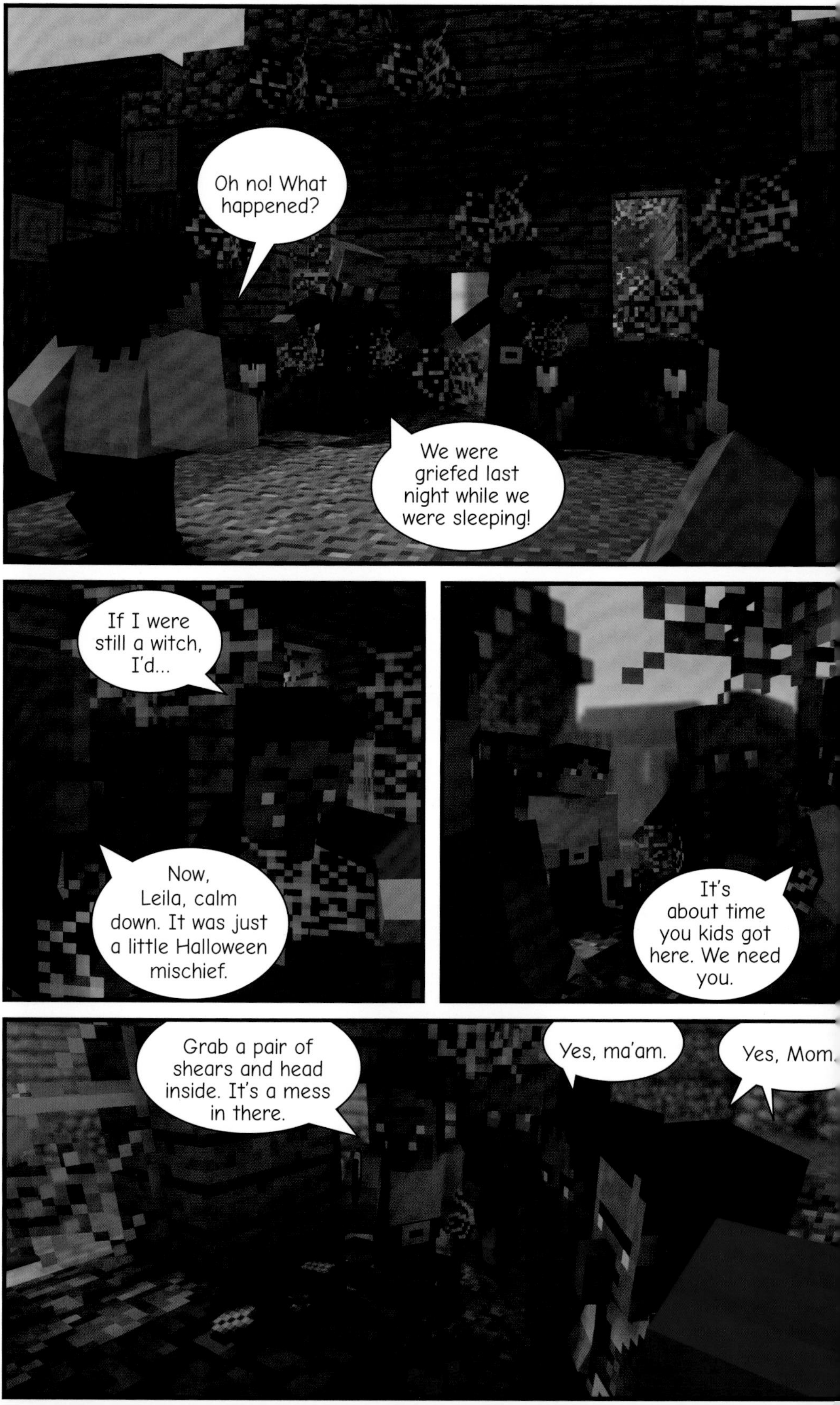
Oh no! What happened?
We were griefed last night while we were sleeping!
If I were still a witch, I'd...
Now, Leila, calm down. It was just a little Halloween mischief.
It's about time you kids got here. We need you.
Grab a pair of shears and head inside. It's a mess in there.
Yes, ma'am.
Yes, Mom.

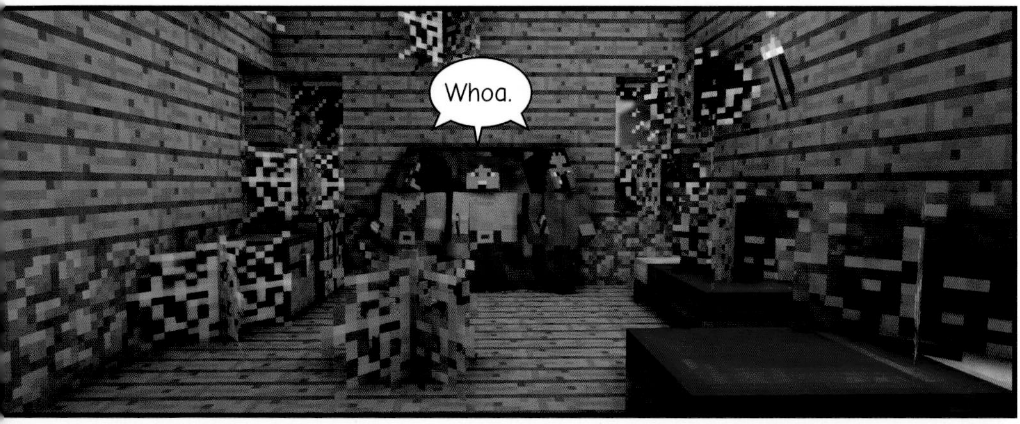
Whoa.

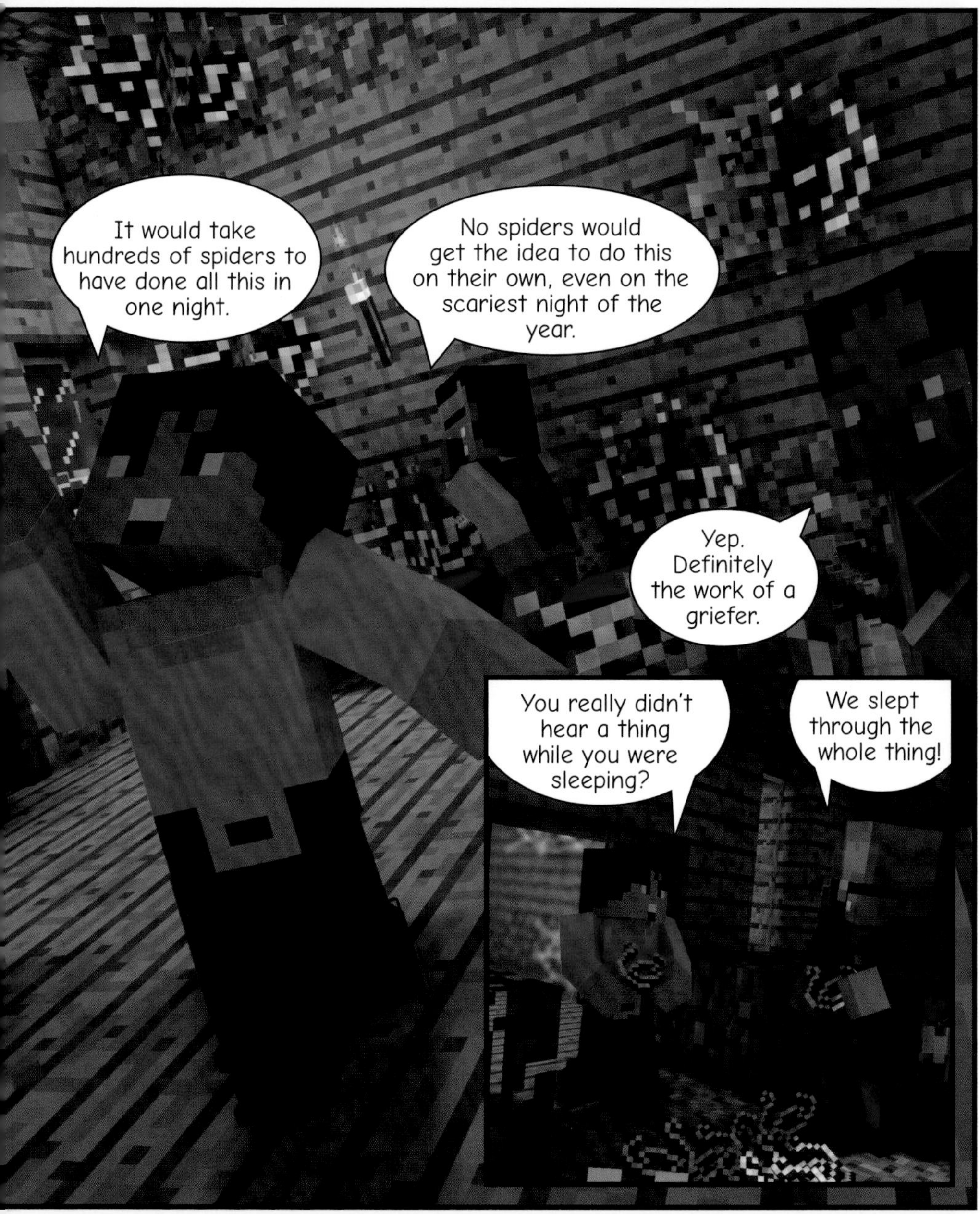
It would take hundreds of spiders to have done all this in one night.
No spiders would get the idea to do this on their own, even on the scariest night of the year.
Yep. Definitely the work of a griefer.
You really didn't hear a thing while you were sleeping?
We slept through the whole thing!

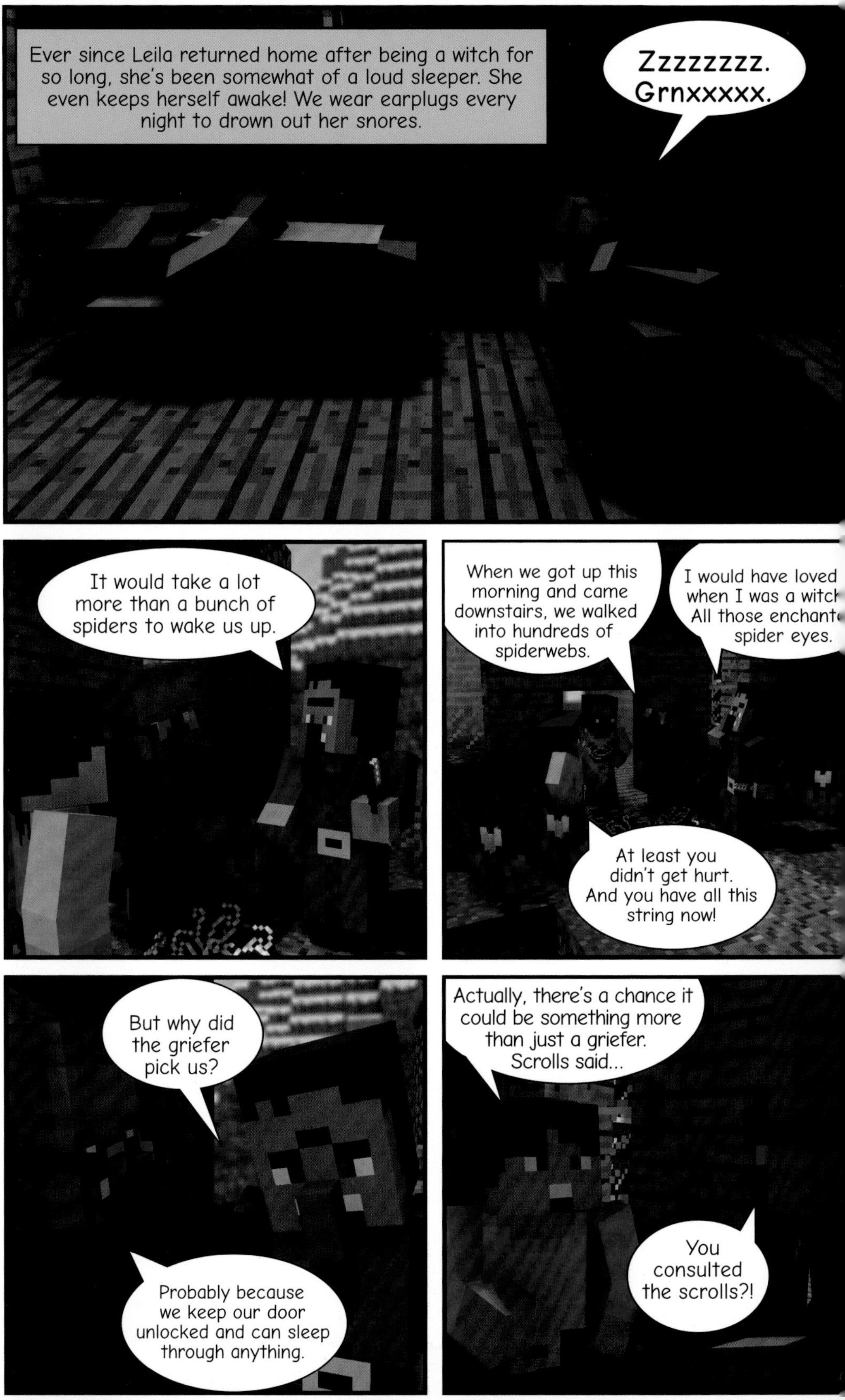
Ever since Leila returned home after being a witch for so long, she's been somewhat of a loud sleeper. She even keeps herself awake! We wear earplugs every night to drown out her snores.
Zzzzzzz. Grnxxxxx.
It would take a lot more than a bunch of spiders to wake us up.
When we got up this morning and came downstairs, we walked into hundreds of spiderwebs.
I would have loved when I was a witc All those enchant spider eyes.
At least you didn't get hurt. And you have all this string now!
But why did the griefer pick us?
Probably because we keep our door unlocked and can sleep through anything.
Actually, there's a chance it could be something more than just a griefer. Scrolls said...
You consulted the scrolls?!

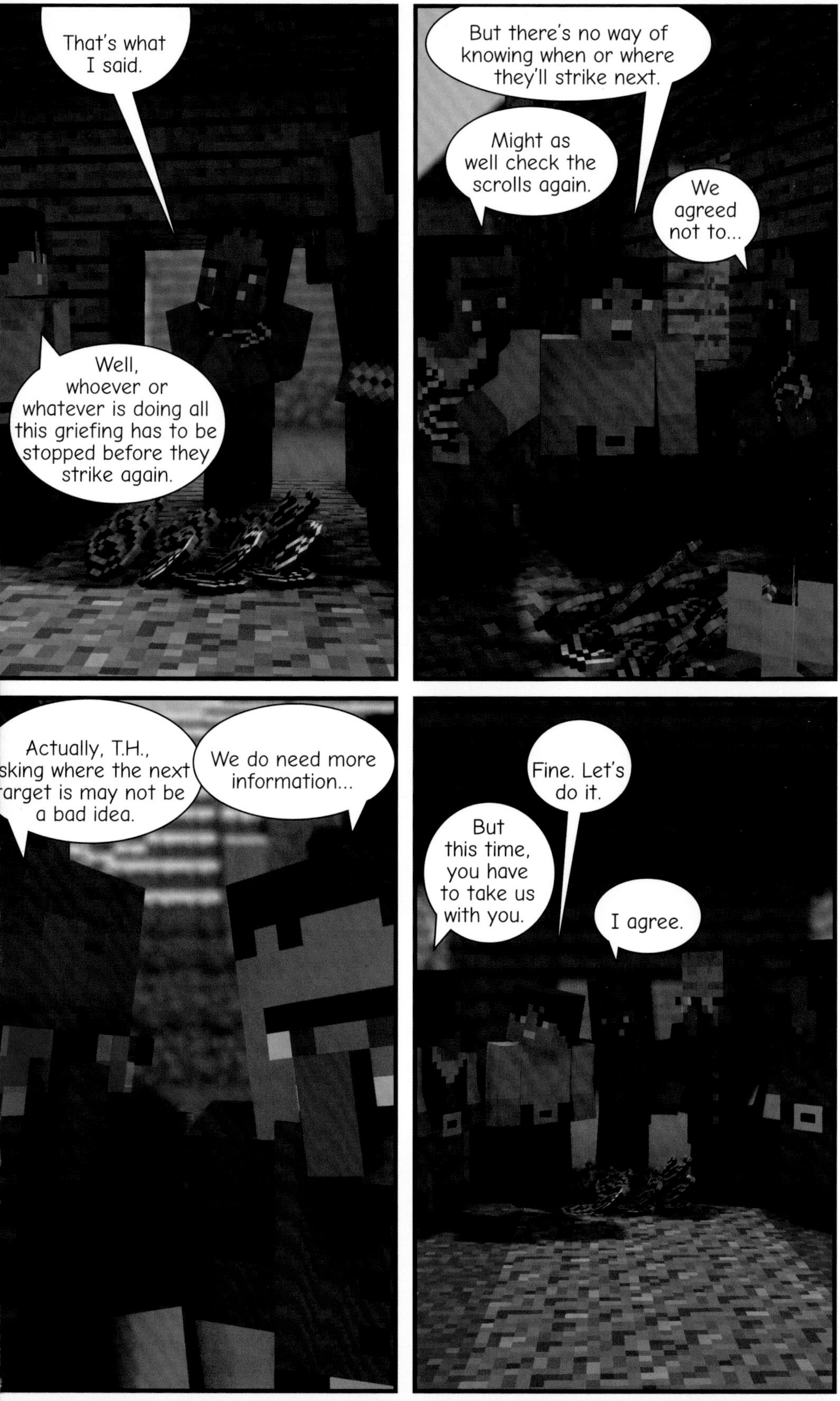
That's what I said.
Well, whoever or whatever is doing all this griefing has to be stopped before they strike again.
But there's no way of knowing when or where they'll strike next.
Might as well check the scrolls again.
We agreed not to...
Actually, T.H., sking where the next arget is may not be a bad idea.
We do need more information...
Fine. Let's do it.
But this time, you have to take us with you.
I agree.

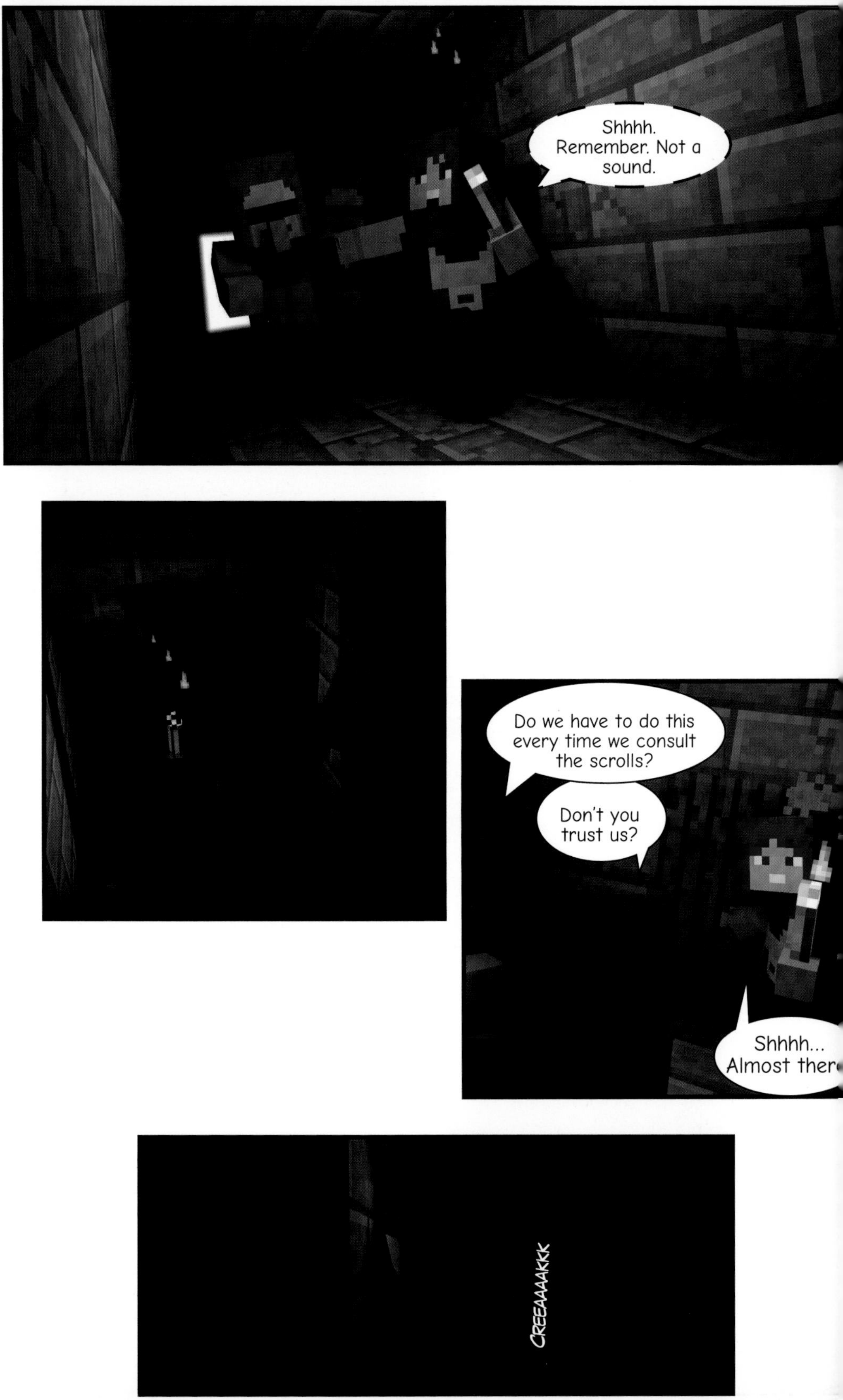
Shhhh. Remember. Not a sound.
Do we have to do this every time we consult the scrolls?
Don't you trust us?
Shhhh... Almost ther
CREEAAAAKKK

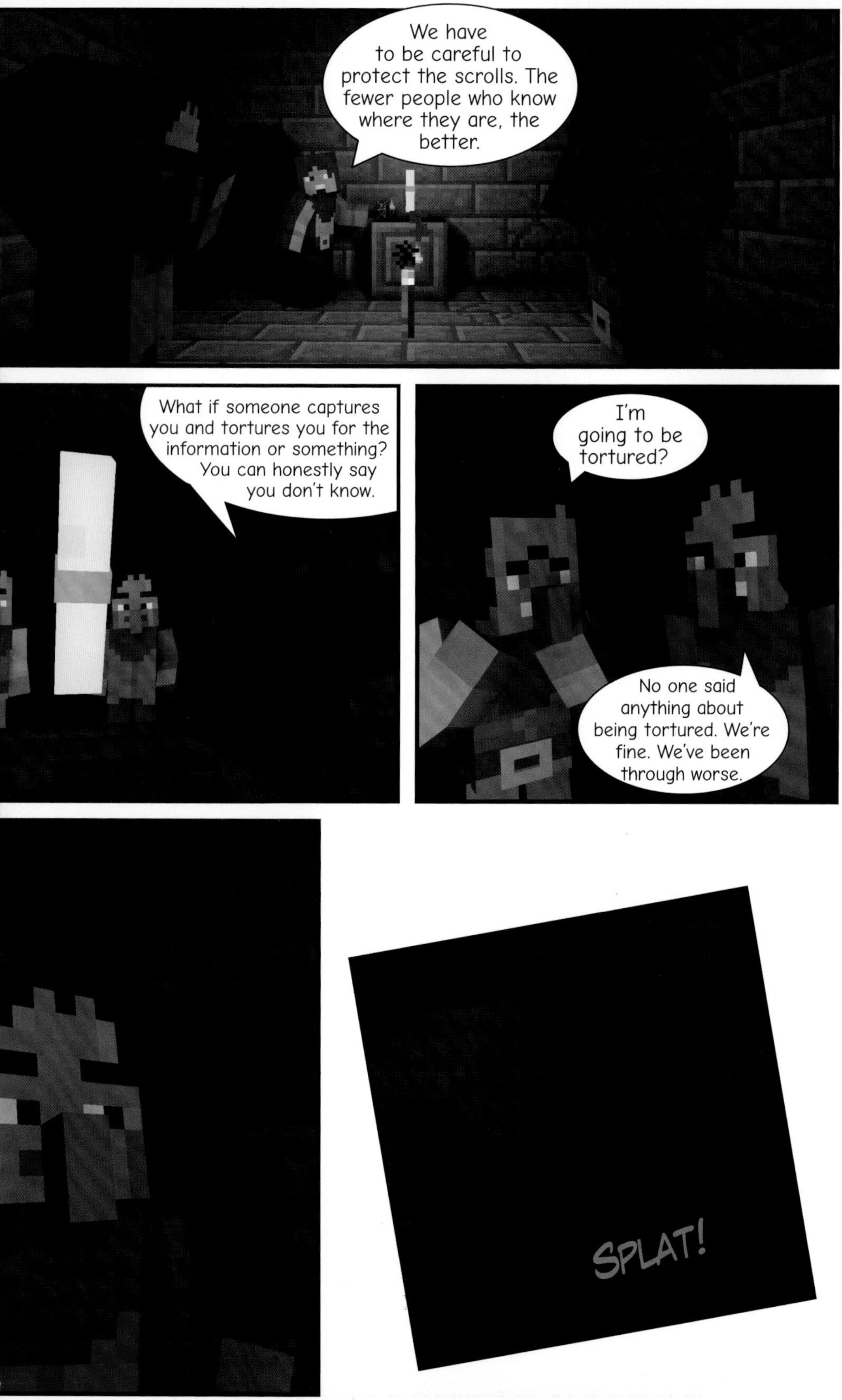

We have to be careful to protect the scrolls. The fewer people who know where they are, the better.
What if someone captures you and tortures you for the information or something? You can honestly say you don't know.
I'm going to be tortured?
No one said anything about being tortured. We're fine. We've been through worse.
SPLAT!

No matter how many times I see it, it's still really cool.

Me, too.

I have to keep the scrolls safe at all costs, you know that.

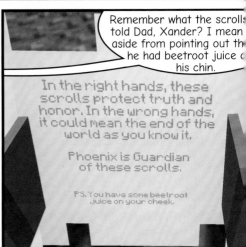

Remember what the scroll told Dad, Xander? I mean aside from pointing out th he had beetroot juice his chin.

In the right hands, these scrolls protect truth and honor. In the wrong hands, it could mean the end of the world as you know it.

Phoenix is Guardian of these scrolls.

P.S. You have some beetroot juice on your cheek.

What if something happens to you? They could be lost forever.

Then the scrolls will be even safer because they'll be protected.

That's a creepy thought.

Well, actually...

Who did you tell if you didn't tell us?

Ole Baba...I mean Bailey...knows.

You told her and not us?

Let's leave this argument for another time...Ready to ask the scroll?

Okay, Dragon Scrolls...Please tell us where the griefer will strike next.

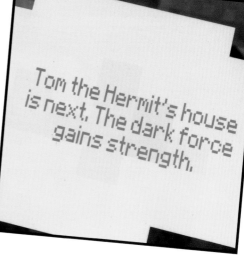

Tom the Hermit's house is next. The dark force gains strength.

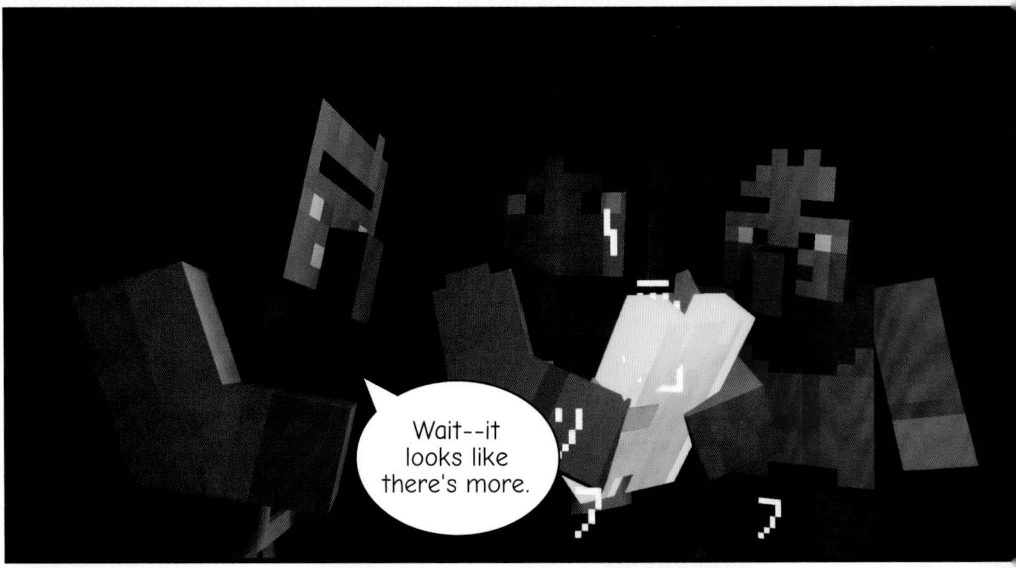
Wait--it looks like there's more.

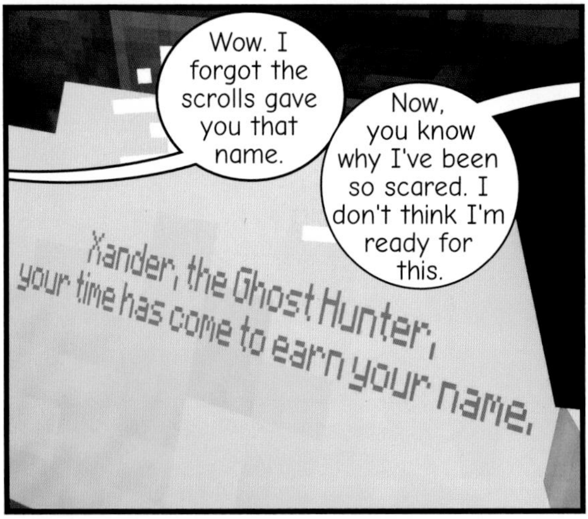
Wow. I forgot the scrolls gave you that name.
Now, you know why I've been so scared. I don't think I'm ready for this.
Xander, the Ghost Hunter, your time has come to earn your name.

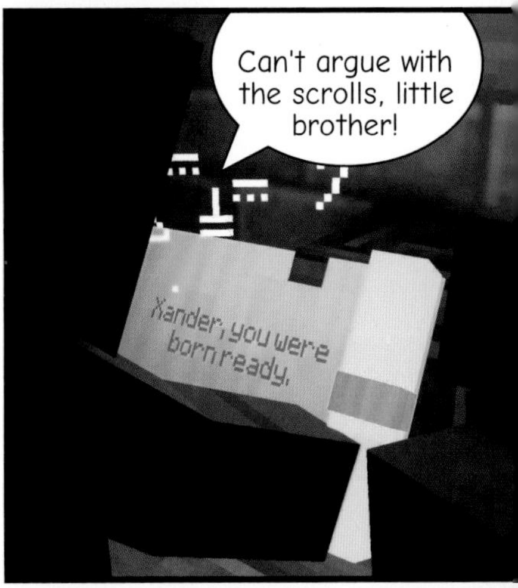
Can't argue with the scrolls, little brother!
Xander, you were born ready.

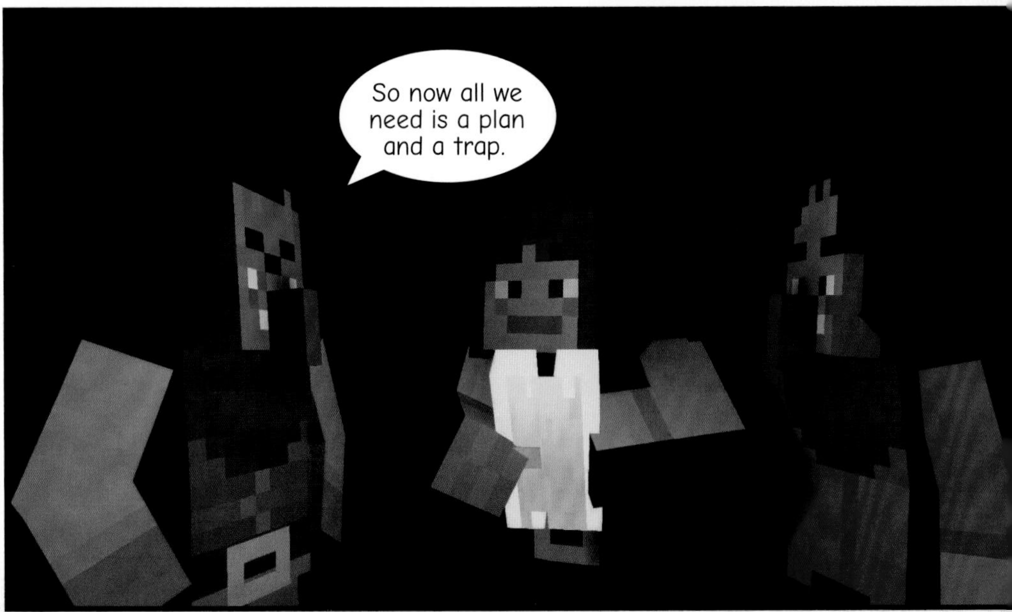
So now all we need is a plan and a trap.

CHAPTER 4

TRAPPED

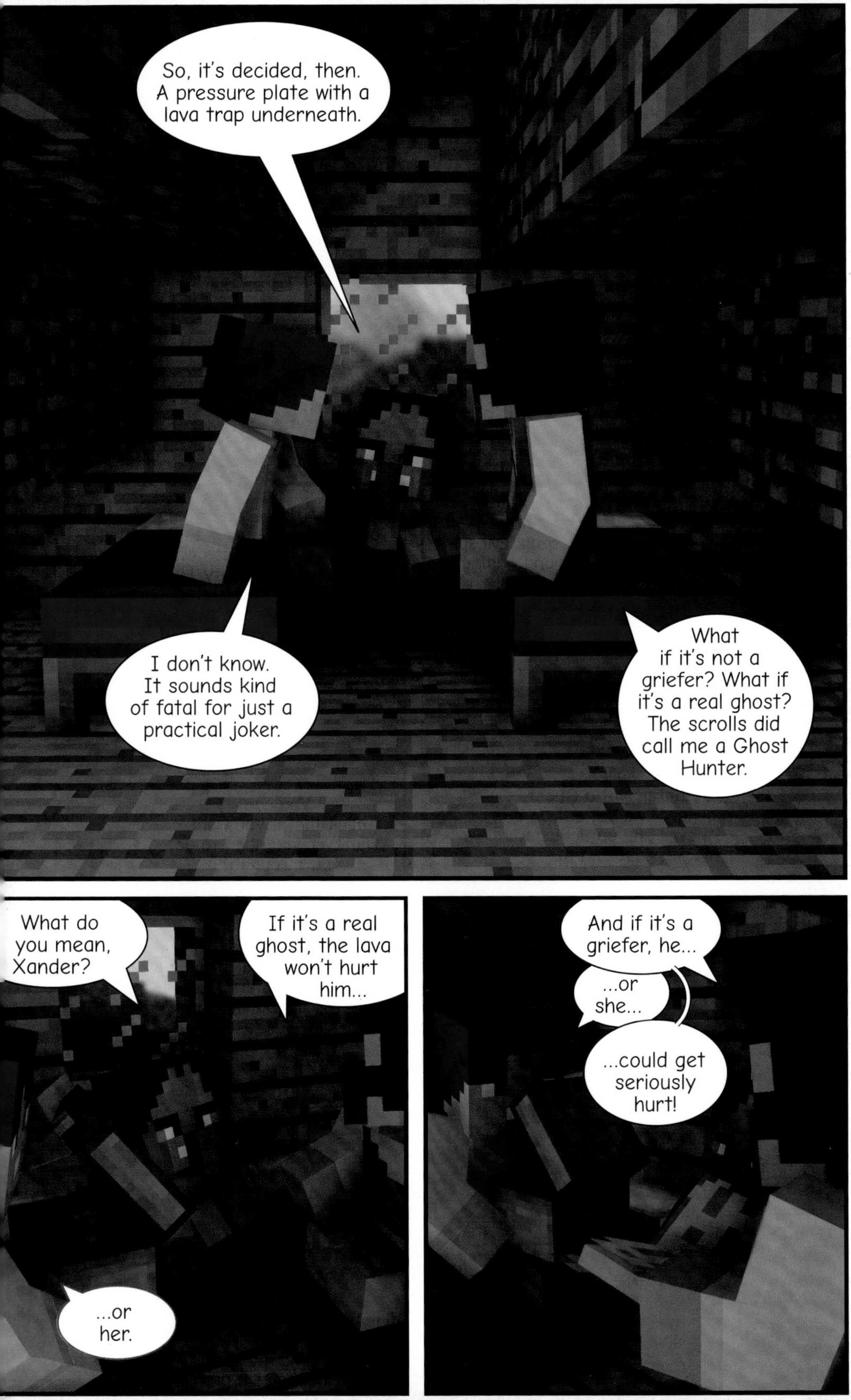
So, it's decided, then. A pressure plate with a lava trap underneath.
I don't know. It sounds kind of fatal for just a practical joker.
What if it's not a griefer? What if it's a real ghost? The scrolls did call me a Ghost Hunter.
What do you mean, Xander?
If it's a real ghost, the lava won't hurt him...
...or her.
And if it's a griefer, he...
...or she...
...could get seriously hurt!

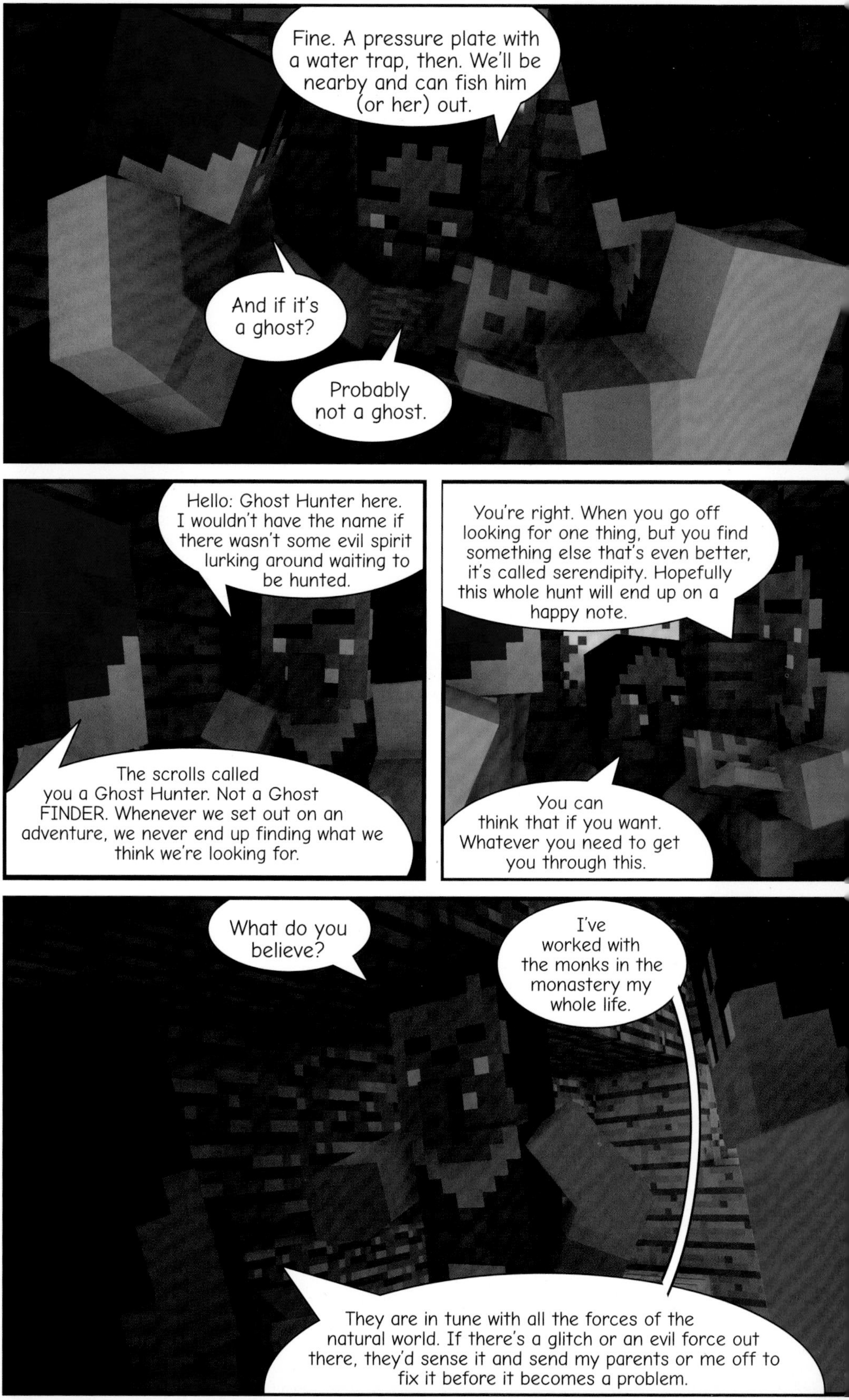
Fine. A pressure plate with a water trap, then. We'll be nearby and can fish him (or her) out.
And if it's a ghost?
Probably not a ghost.
Hello: Ghost Hunter here. I wouldn't have the name if there wasn't some evil spirit lurking around waiting to be hunted.
The scrolls called you a Ghost Hunter. Not a Ghost FINDER. Whenever we set out on an adventure, we never end up finding what we think we're looking for.
You're right. When you go off looking for one thing, but you find something else that's even better, it's called serendipity. Hopefully this whole hunt will end up on a happy note.
You can think that if you want. Whatever you need to get you through this.
What do you believe?
I've worked with the monks in the monastery my whole life.
They are in tune with all the forces of the natural world. If there's a glitch or an evil force out there, they'd sense it and send my parents or me off to fix it before it becomes a problem.

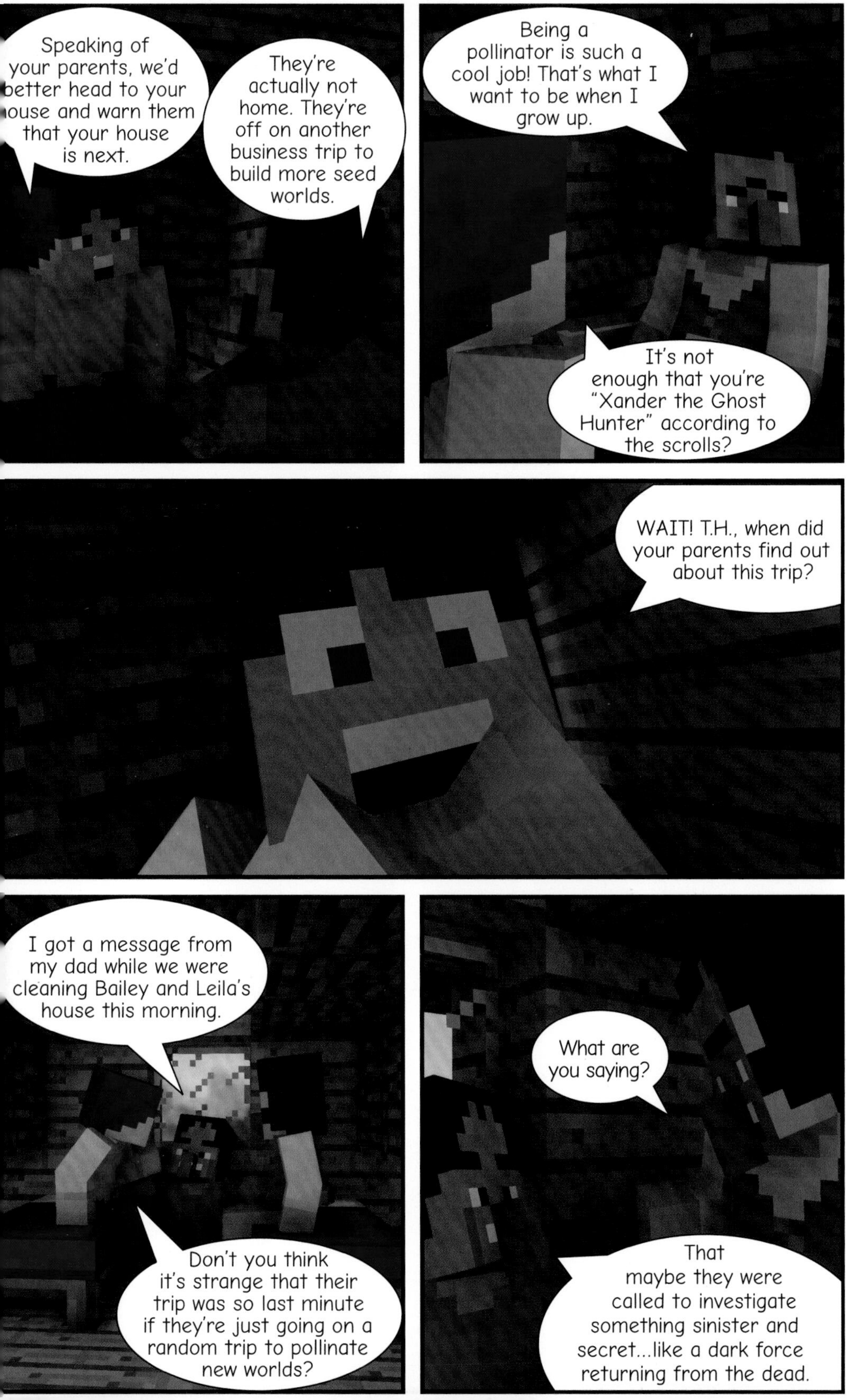
Speaking of your parents, we'd better head to your house and warn them that your house is next.
They're actually not home. They're off on another business trip to build more seed worlds.
Being a pollinator is such a cool job! That's what I want to be when I grow up.
It's not enough that you're "Xander the Ghost Hunter" according to the scrolls?
WAIT! T.H., when did your parents find out about this trip?
I got a message from my dad while we were cleaning Bailey and Leila's house this morning.
Don't you think it's strange that their trip was so last minute if they're just going on a random trip to pollinate new worlds?
What are you saying?
That maybe they were called to investigate something sinister and secret...like a dark force returning from the dead.

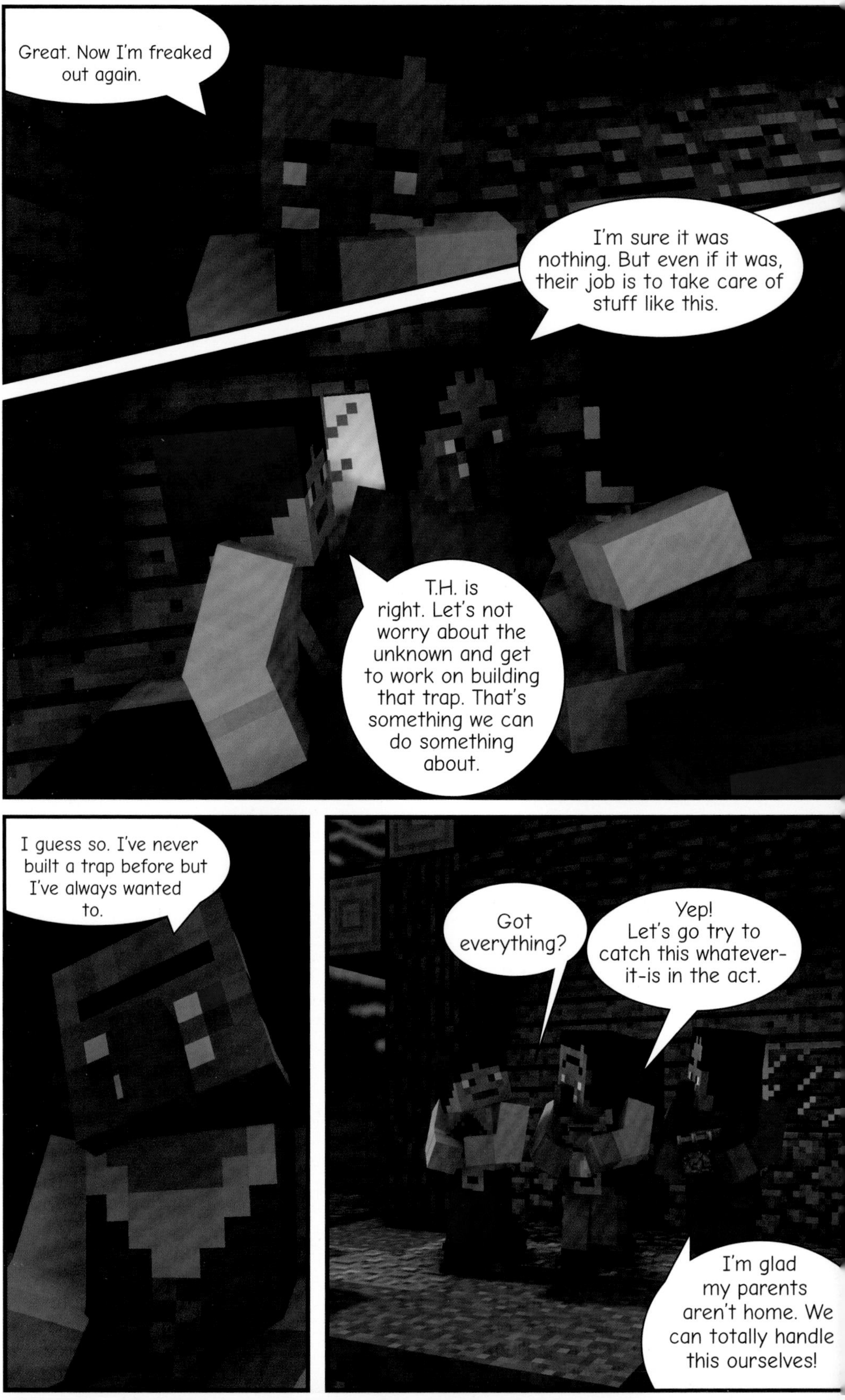
Great. Now I'm freaked out again.
I'm sure it was nothing. But even if it was, their job is to take care of stuff like this.
T.H. is right. Let's not worry about the unknown and get to work on building that trap. That's something we can do something about.
I guess so. I've never built a trap before but I've always wanted to.
Got everything?
Yep! Let's go try to catch this whatever-it-is in the act.
I'm glad my parents aren't home. We can totally handle this ourselves!

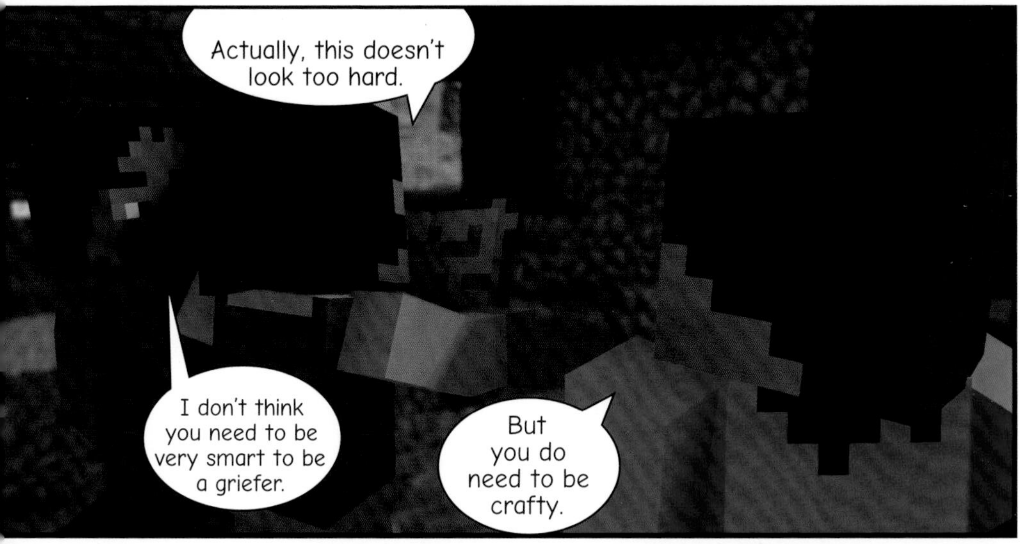
Actually, this doesn't look too hard.
I don't think you need to be very smart to be a griefer.
But you do need to be crafty.

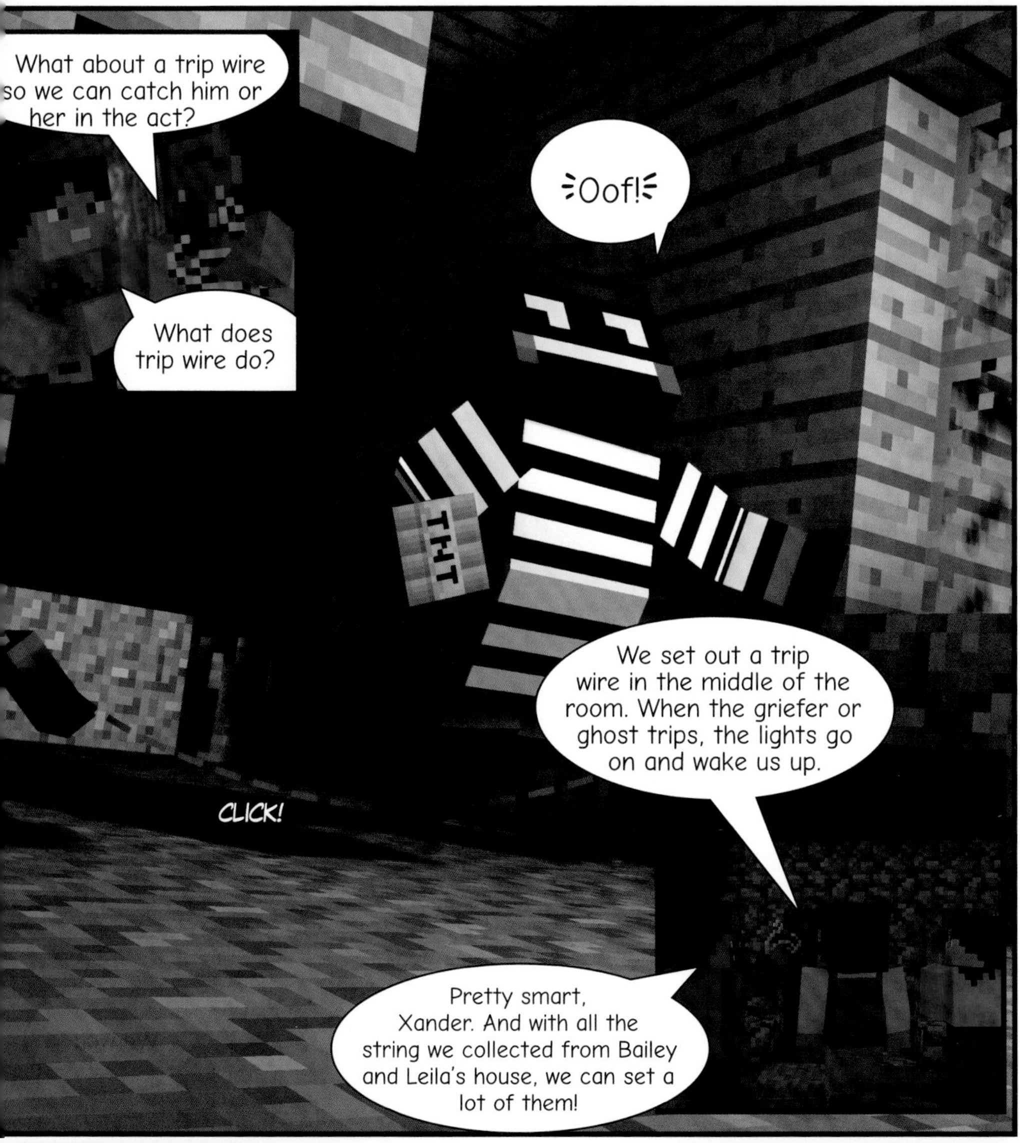
What about a trip wire so we can catch him or her in the act?
What does trip wire do?
Oof!
TNT
We set out a trip wire in the middle of the room. When the griefer or ghost trips, the lights go on and wake us up.
CLICK!
Pretty smart, Xander. And with all the string we collected from Bailey and Leila's house, we can set a lot of them!

STAKEOUT

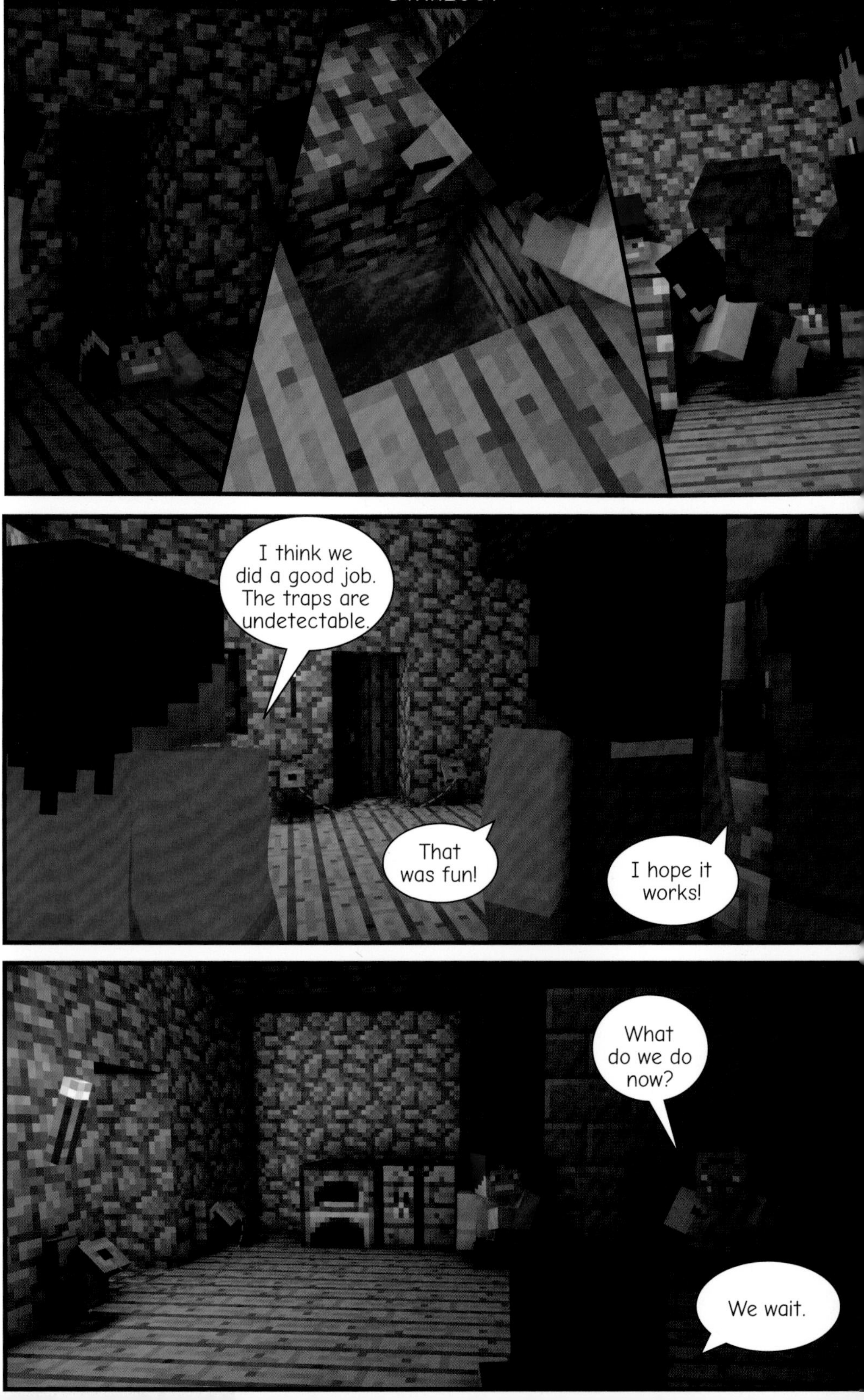
I think we did a good job. The traps are undetectable.
That was fun!
I hope it works!
What do we do now?
We wait.

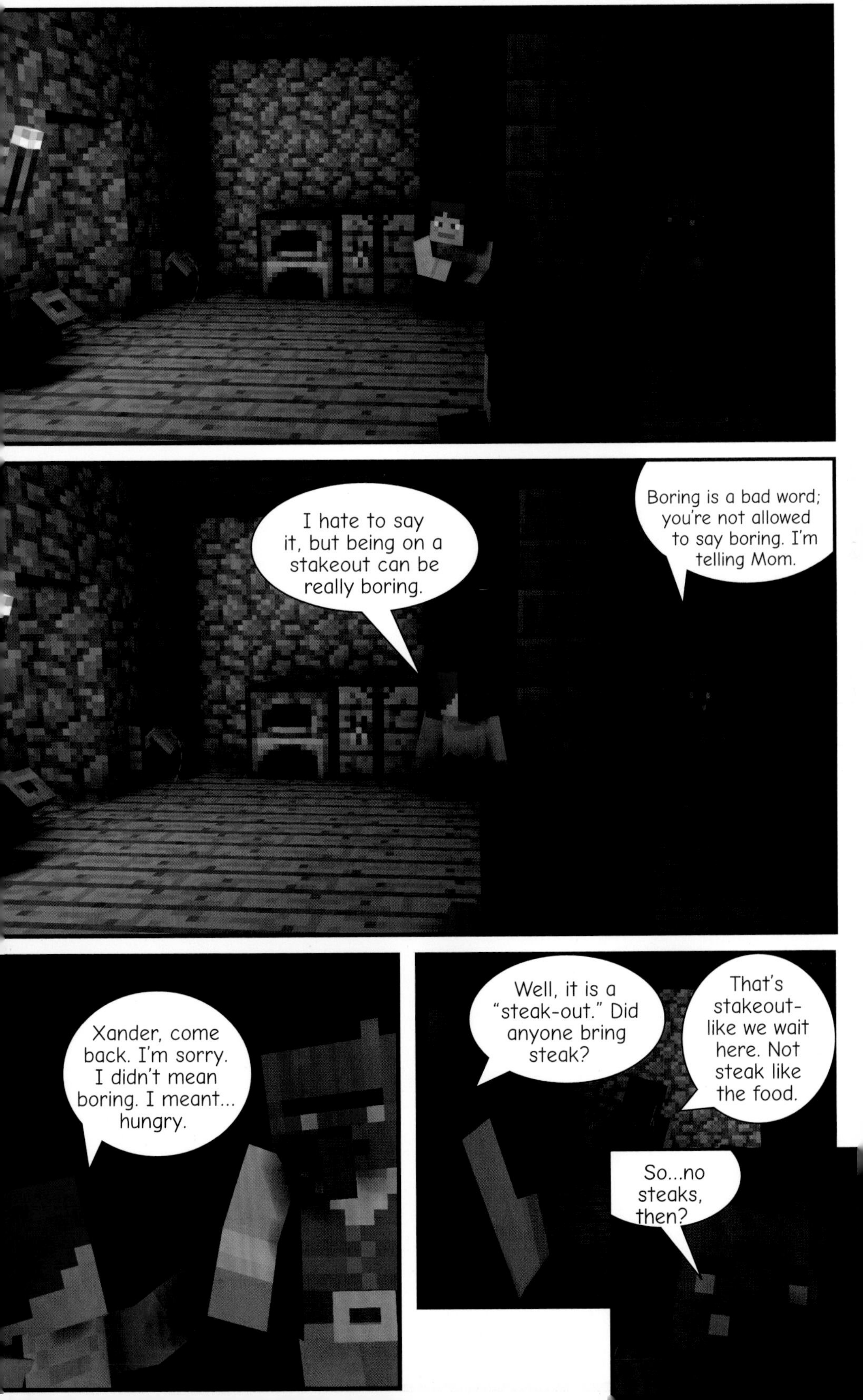
I hate to say it, but being on a stakeout can be really boring.
Boring is a bad word; you're not allowed to say boring. I'm telling Mom.
Xander, come back. I'm sorry. I didn't mean boring. I meant... hungry.
Well, it is a "steak-out." Did anyone bring steak?
That's stakeout-like we wait here. Not steak like the food.
So...no steaks, then?

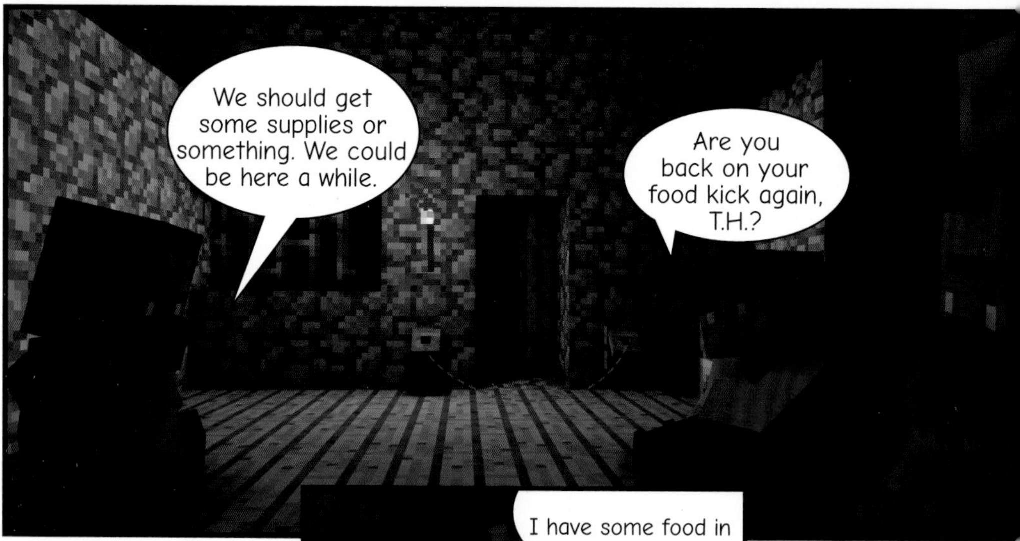
We should get some supplies or something. We could be here a while.
Are you back on your food kick again, T.H.?

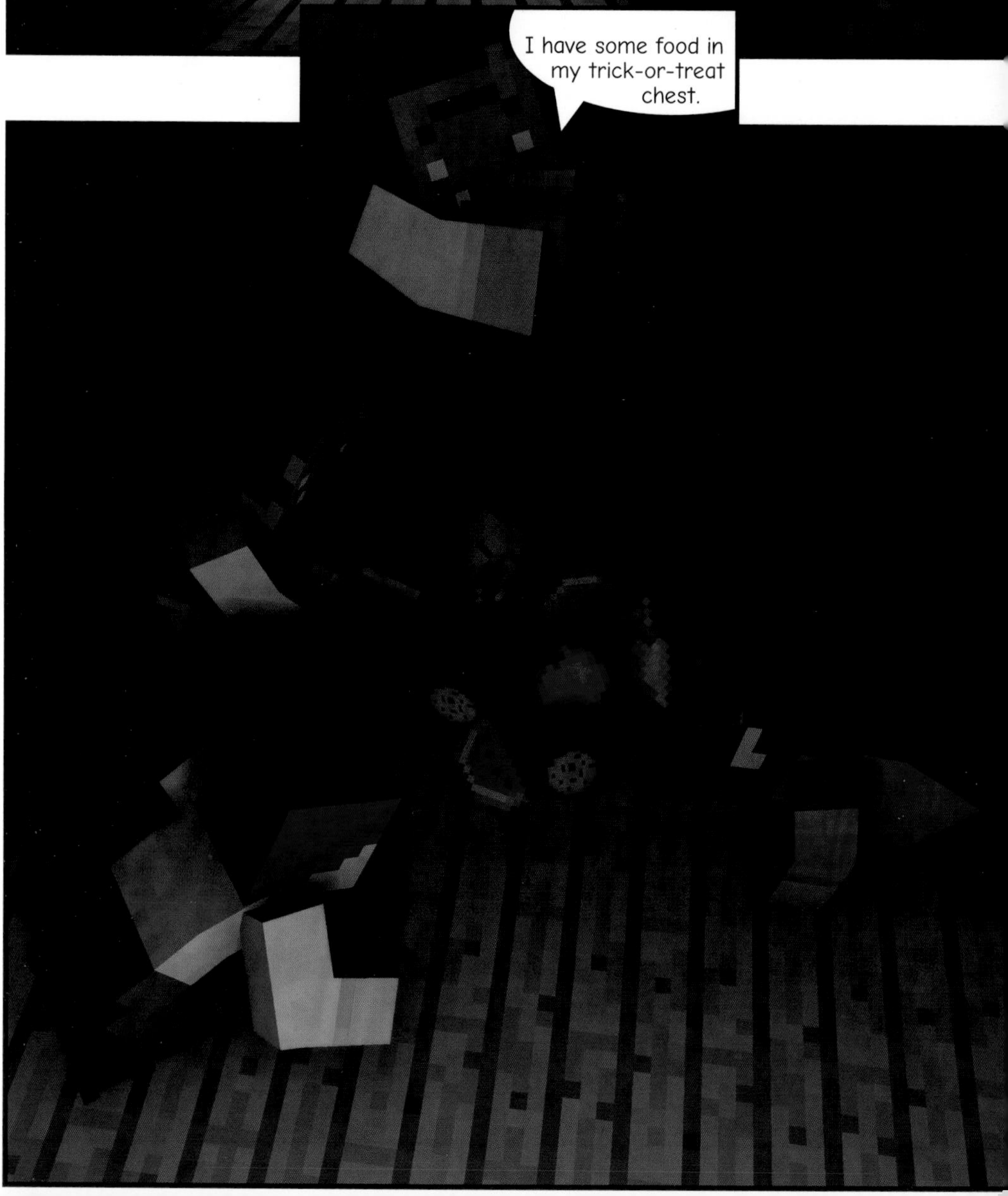
I have some food in my trick-or-treat chest.

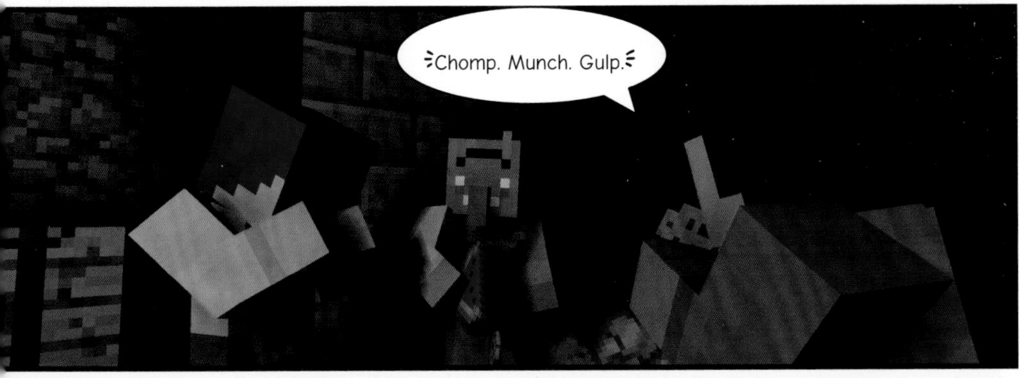
Chomp. Munch. Gulp.

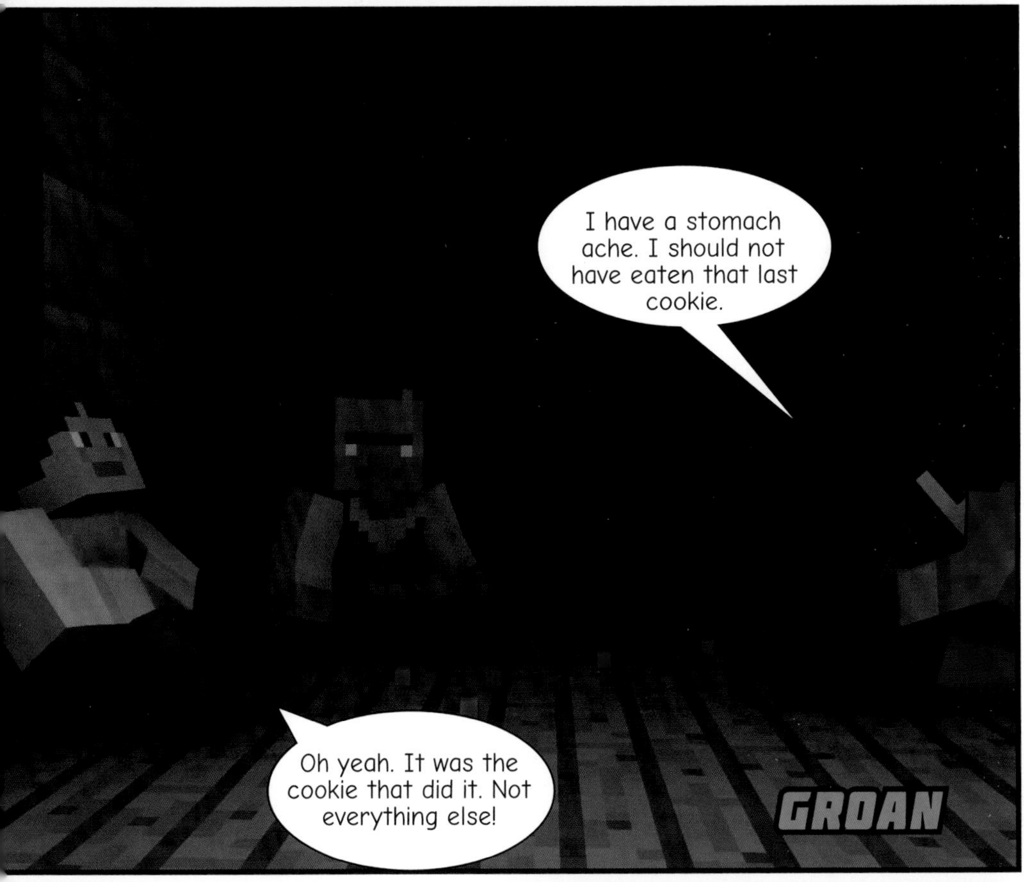
I have a stomach ache. I should not have eaten that last cookie.
Oh yeah. It was the cookie that did it. Not everything else!
GROAN

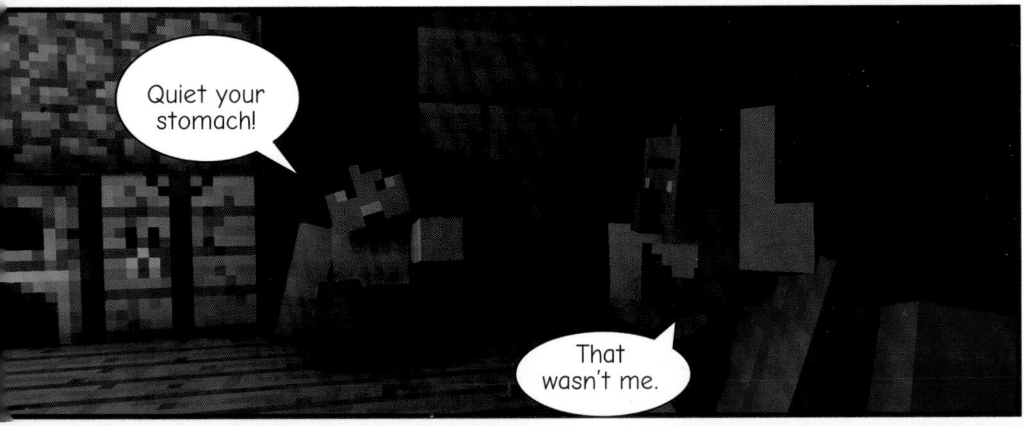
Quiet your stomach!
That wasn't me.

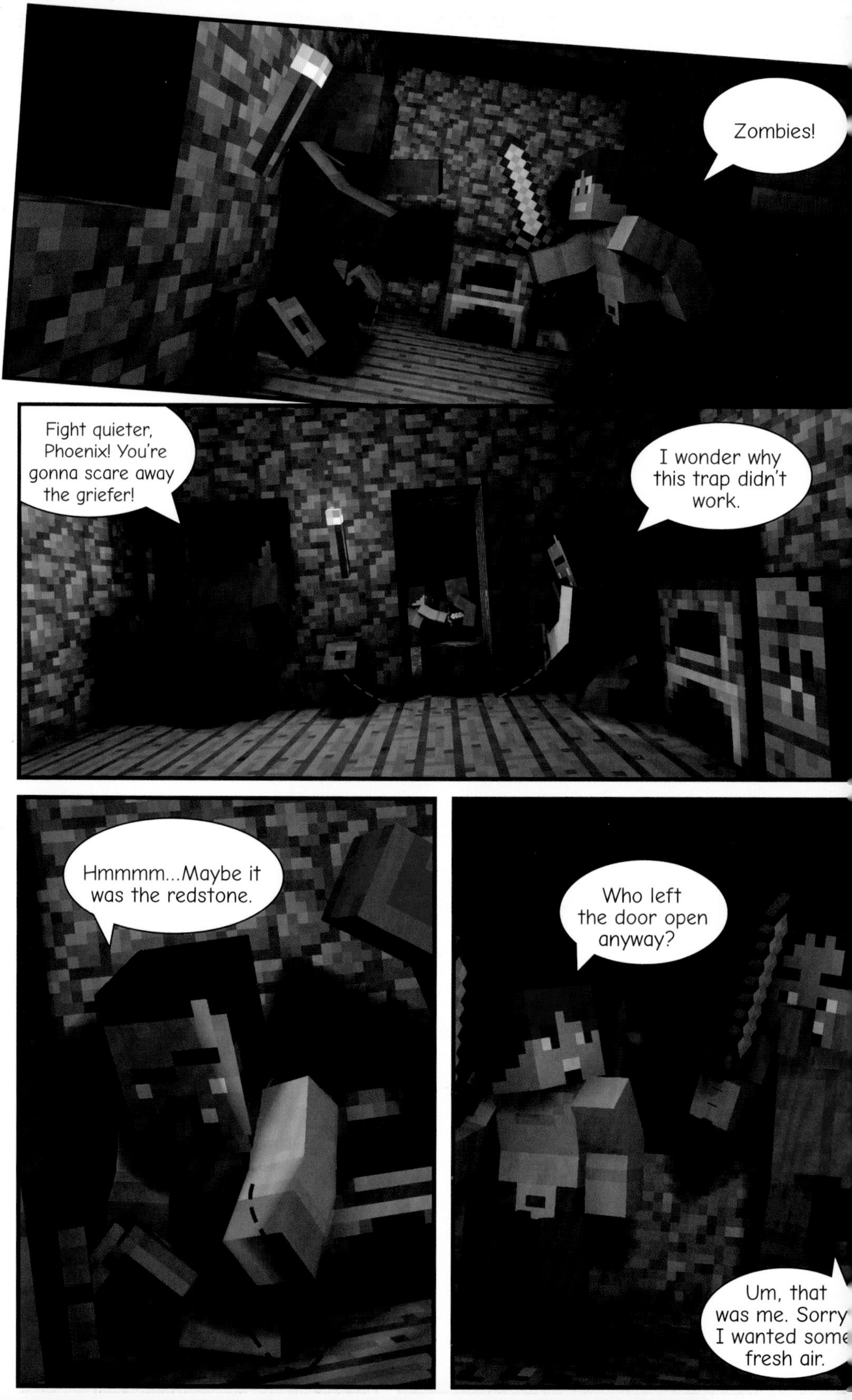
Zombies!
Fight quieter, Phoenix! You're gonna scare away the griefer!
I wonder why this trap didn't work.
Hmmmm...Maybe it was the redstone.
Who left the door open anyway?
Um, that was me. Sorry I wanted some fresh air.

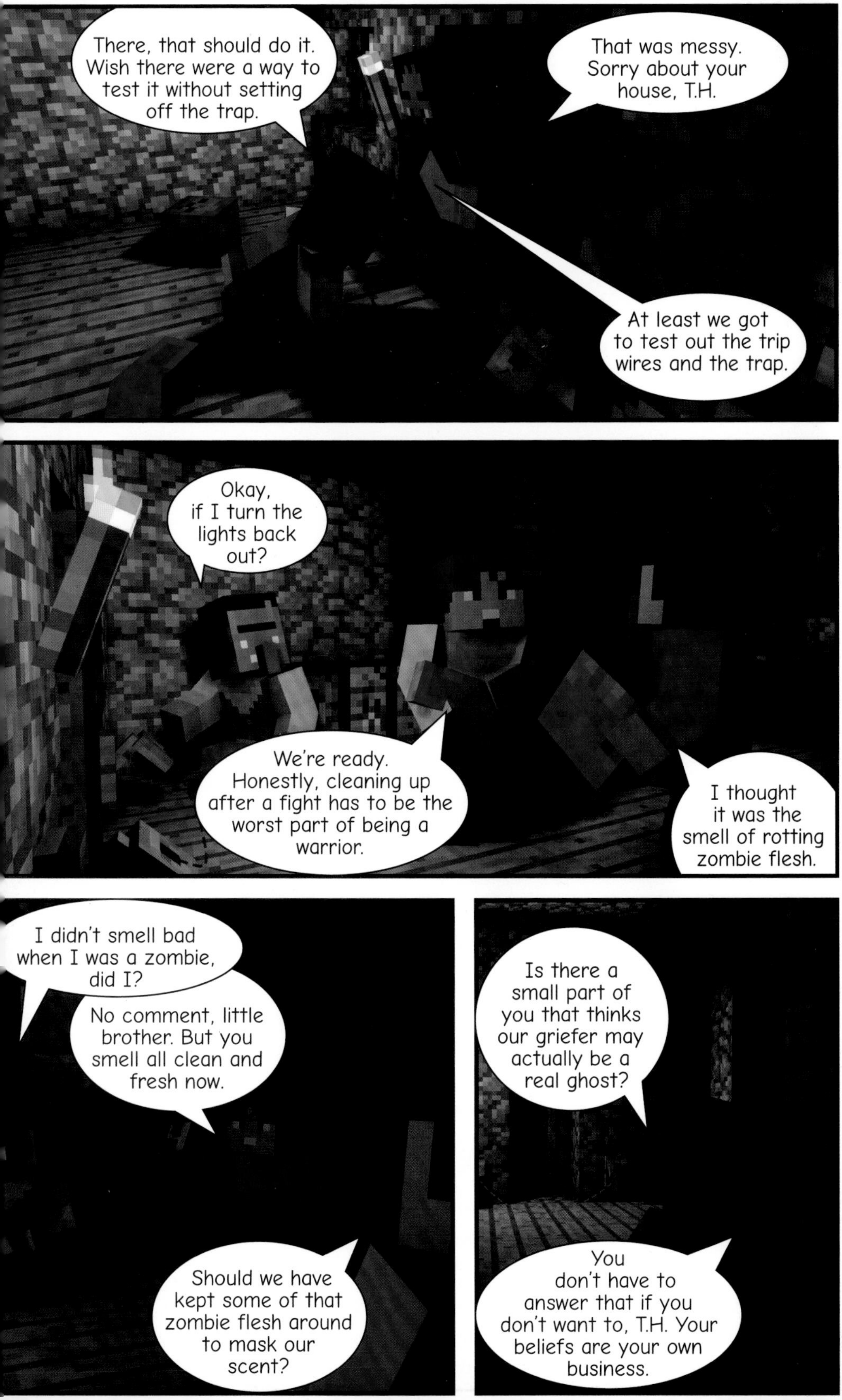
There, that should do it. Wish there were a way to test it without setting off the trap.
That was messy. Sorry about your house, T.H.
At least we got to test out the trip wires and the trap.
Okay, if I turn the lights back out?
We're ready. Honestly, cleaning up after a fight has to be the worst part of being a warrior.
I thought it was the smell of rotting zombie flesh.
I didn't smell bad when I was a zombie, did I?
No comment, little brother. But you smell all clean and fresh now.
Should we have kept some of that zombie flesh around to mask our scent?
Is there a small part of you that thinks our griefer may actually be a real ghost?
You don't have to answer that if you don't want to, T.H. Your beliefs are your own business.

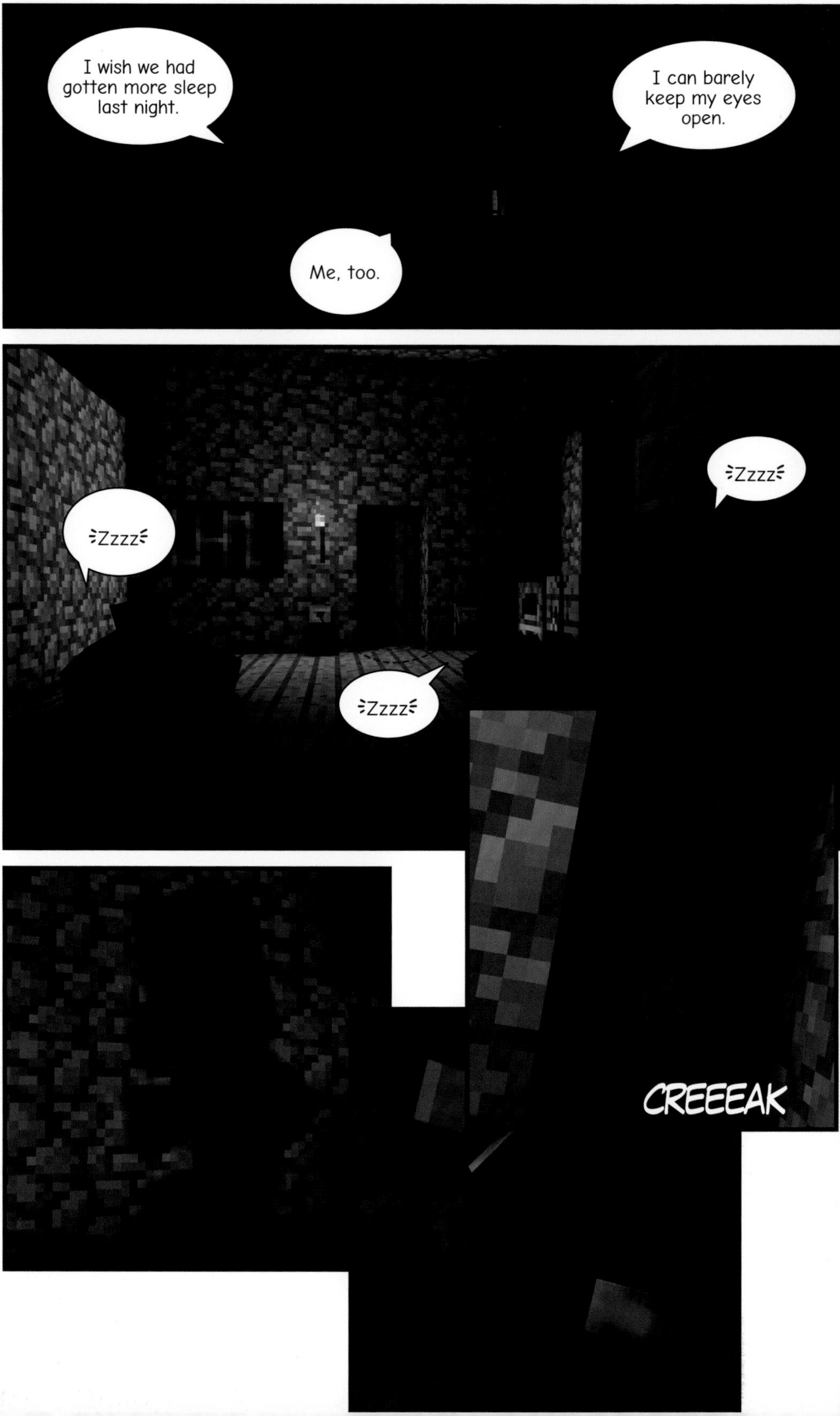
I wish we had gotten more sleep last night.
I can barely keep my eyes open.
Me, too.
Zzzz
Zzzz
Zzzz
CREEEAK

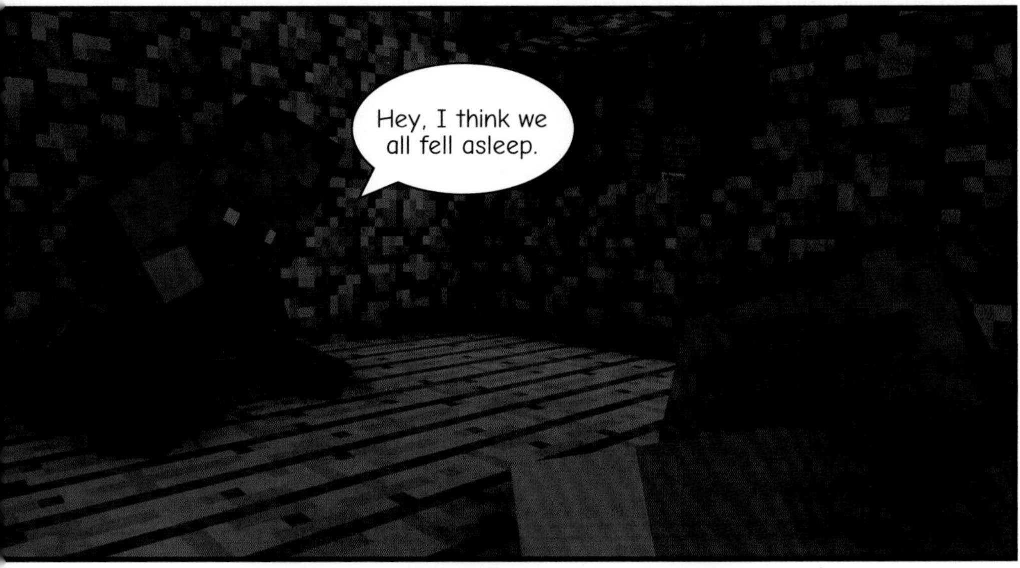
Hey, I think we all fell asleep.

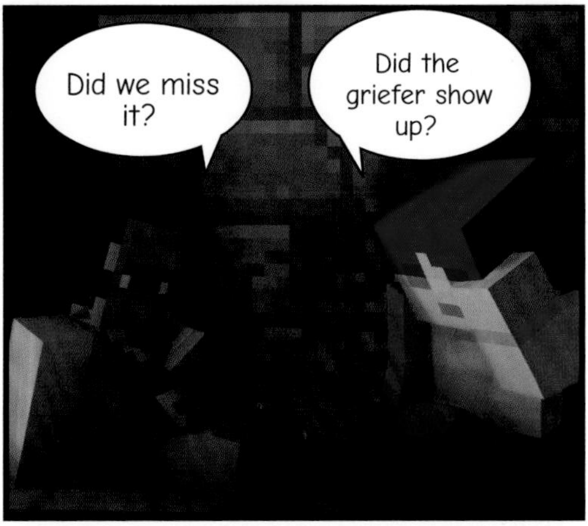
Did we miss it?
Did the griefer show up?

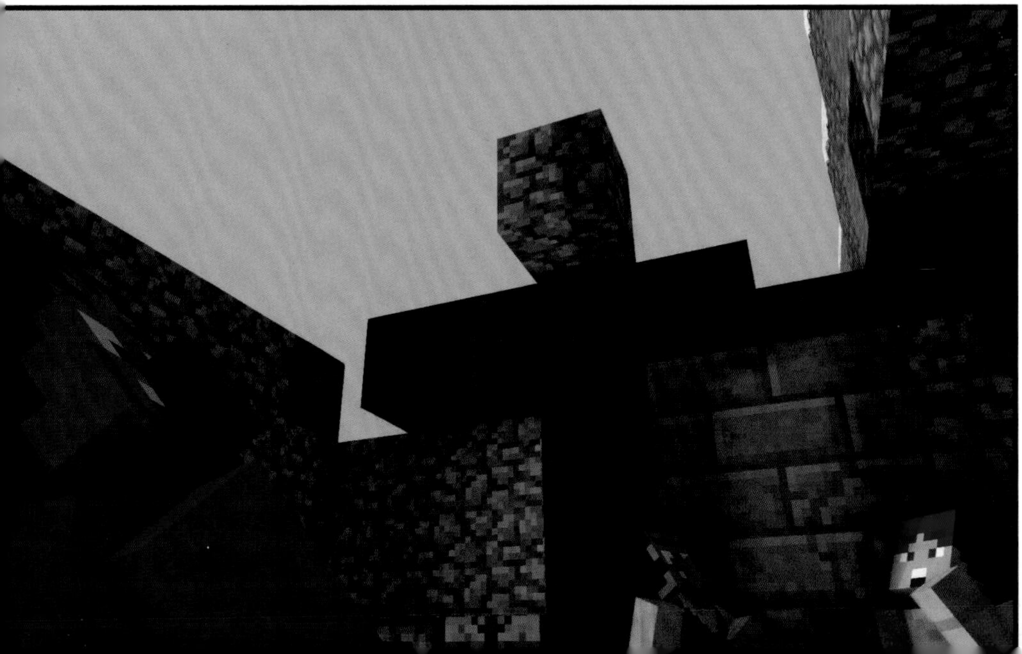

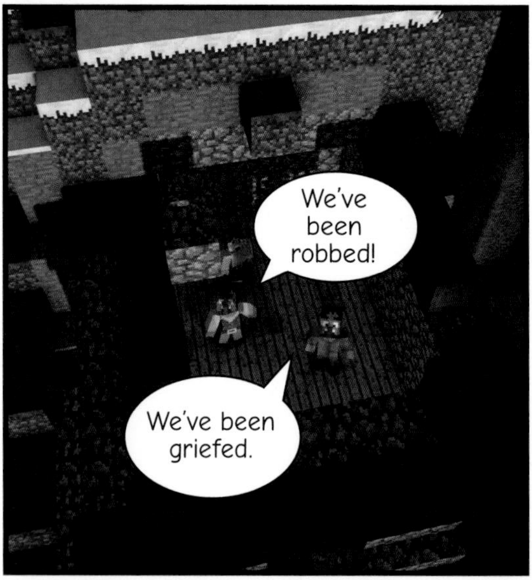
We've been robbed!
We've been griefed.

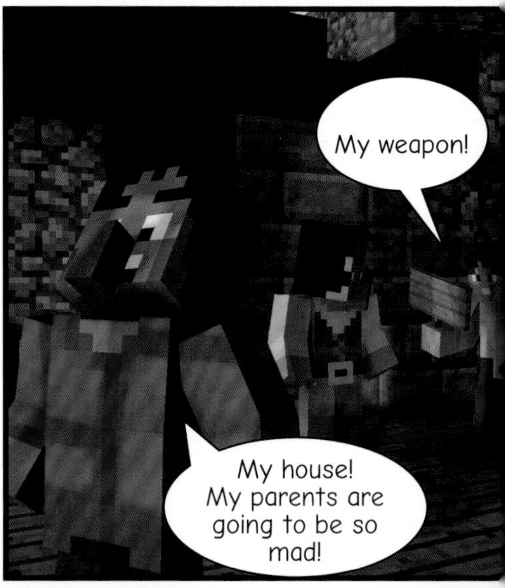
My weapon!
My house! My parents are going to be so mad!

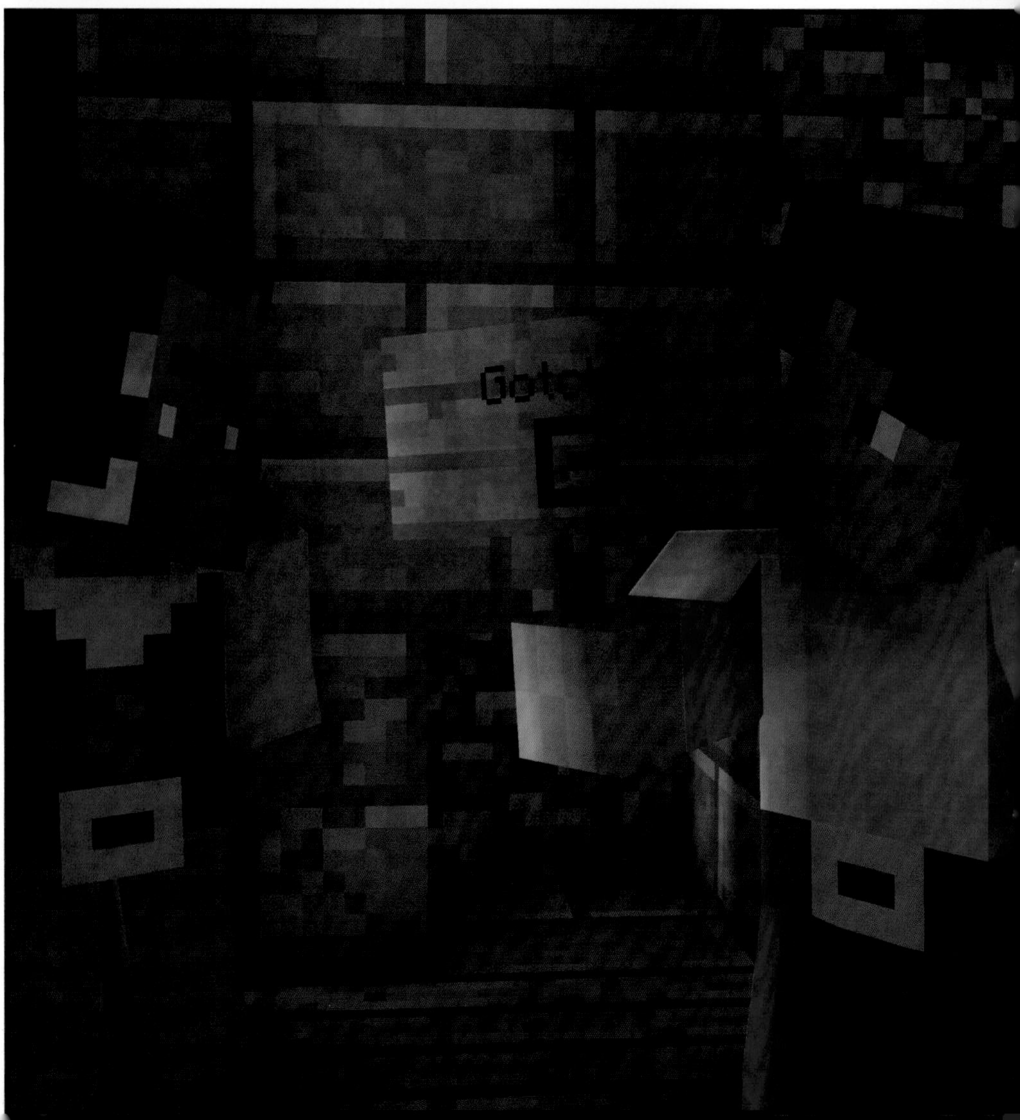

CHAPTER 5

BAIT

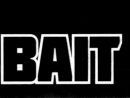

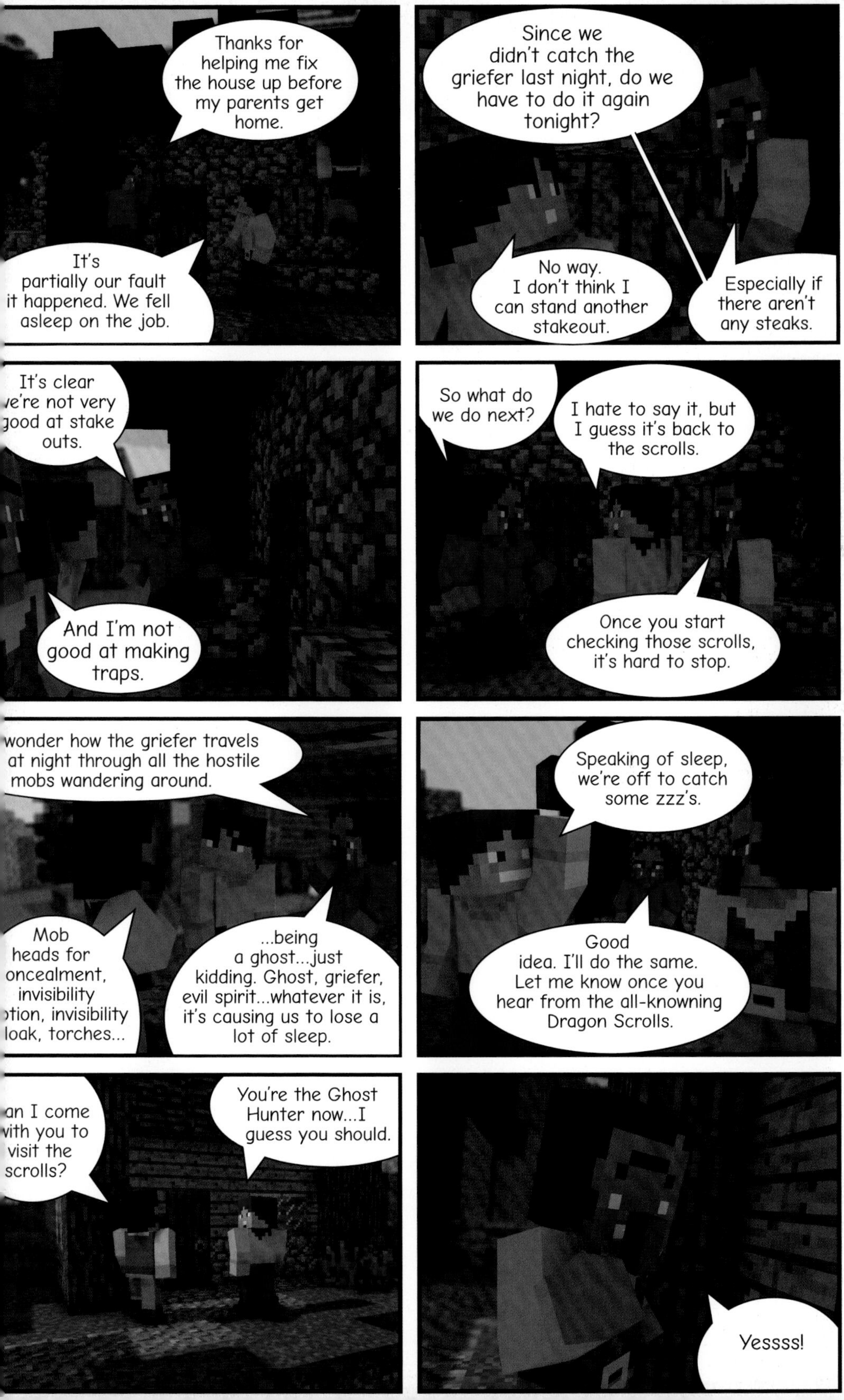
Thanks for helping me fix the house up before my parents get home.
It's partially our fault it happened. We fell asleep on the job.
Since we didn't catch the griefer last night, do we have to do it again tonight?
No way. I don't think I can stand another stakeout.
Especially if there aren't any steaks.
It's clear ve're not very jood at stake outs.
And I'm not good at making traps.
So what do we do next?
I hate to say it, but I guess it's back to the scrolls.
Once you start checking those scrolls, it's hard to stop.
wonder how the griefer travels at night through all the hostile mobs wandering around.
Mob heads for oncealment, invisibility otion, invisibility loak, torches...
...being a ghost...just kidding. Ghost, griefer, evil spirit...whatever it is, it's causing us to lose a lot of sleep.
Speaking of sleep, we're off to catch some zzz's.
Good idea. I'll do the same. Let me know once you hear from the all-knowning Dragon Scrolls.
an I come vith you to visit the scrolls?
You're the Ghost Hunter now...I guess you should.
Yessss!

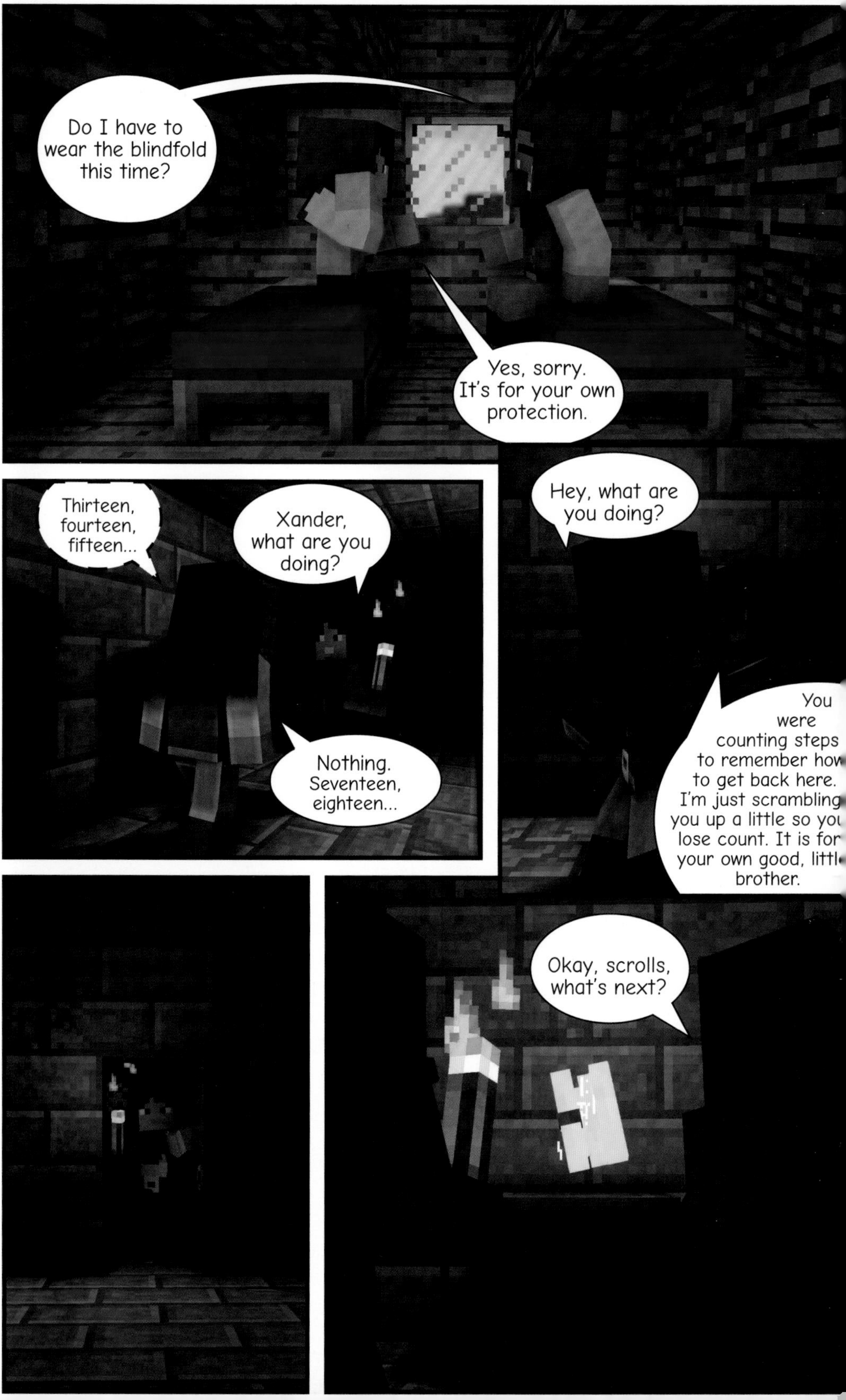

Do I have to wear the blindfold this time?
Yes, sorry. It's for your own protection.
Thirteen, fourteen, fifteen...
Xander, what are you doing?
Nothing. Seventeen, eighteen...
Hey, what are you doing?
You were counting steps to remember ho to get back here. I'm just scrambling you up a little so yo lose count. It is for your own good, littl brother.
Okay, scrolls, what's next?

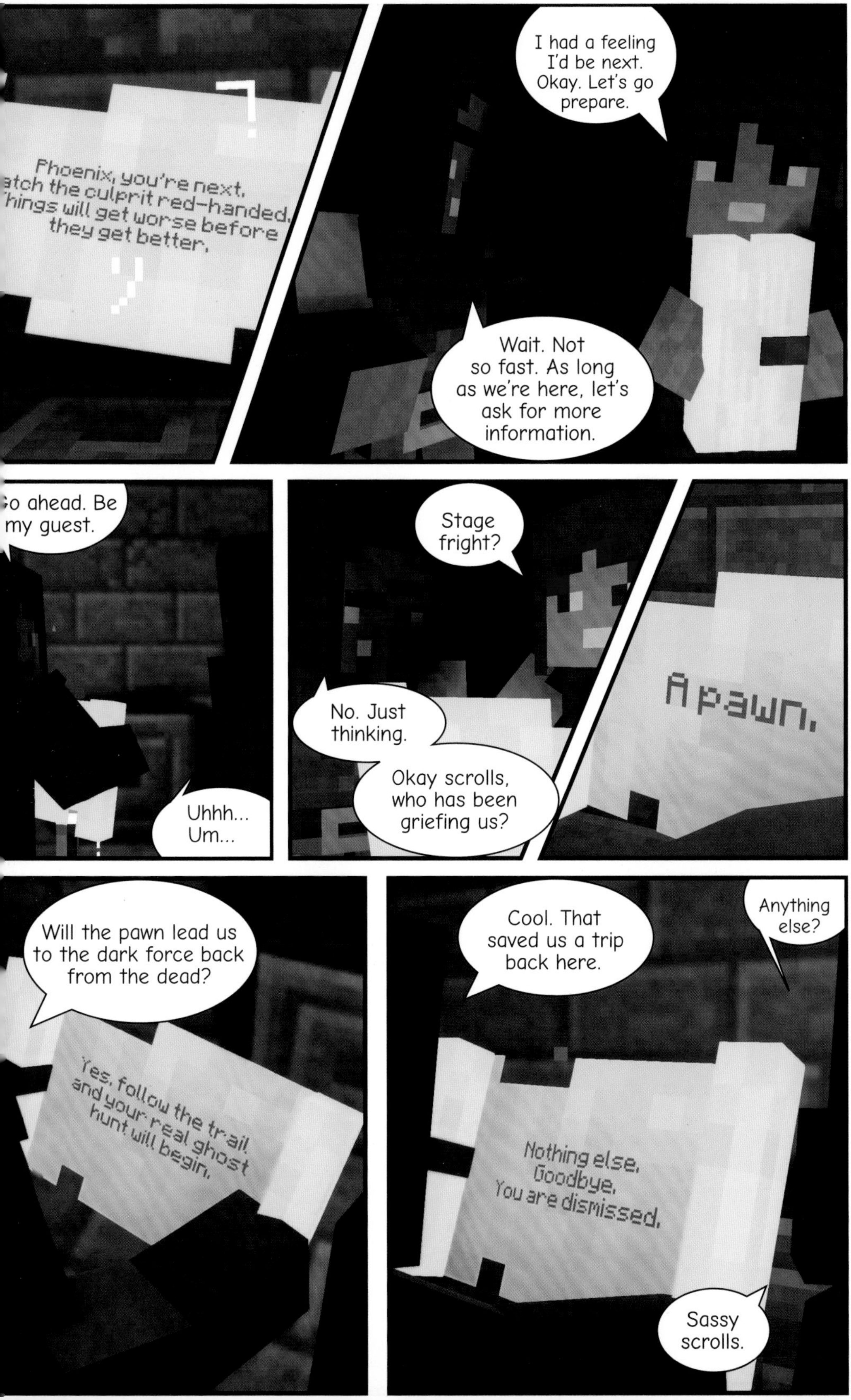
Phoenix, you're next.
atch the culprit red-handed.
hings will get worse before
they get better.
I had a feeling
I'd be next.
Okay. Let's go
prepare.
Wait. Not
so fast. As long
as we're here, let's
ask for more
information.
o ahead. Be
my guest.
Uhhh...
Um...
Stage
fright?
No. Just
thinking.
Okay scrolls,
who has been
griefing us?
A pawn.
Will the pawn lead us
to the dark force back
from the dead?
Yes, follow the trail
and your real ghost
hunt will begin.
Cool. That
saved us a trip
back here.
Anything
else?
Nothing else.
Goodbye.
You are dismissed.
Sassy
scrolls.

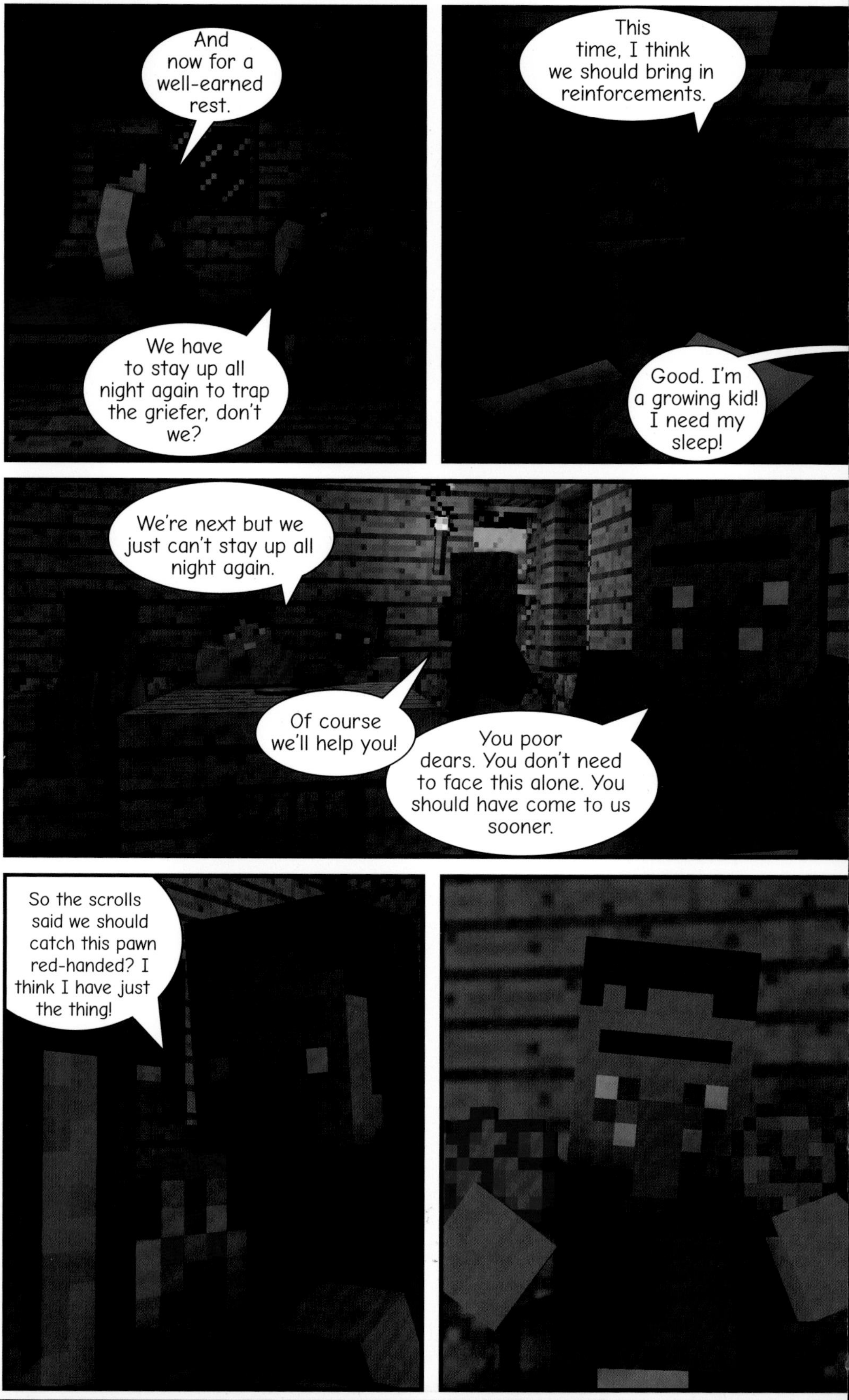

And now for a well-earned rest.
We have to stay up all night again to trap the griefer, don't we?
This time, I think we should bring in reinforcements.
Good. I'm a growing kid! I need my sleep!
We're next but we just can't stay up all night again.
Of course we'll help you!
You poor dears. You don't need to face this alone. You should have come to us sooner.
So the scrolls said we should catch this pawn red-handed? I think I have just the thing!

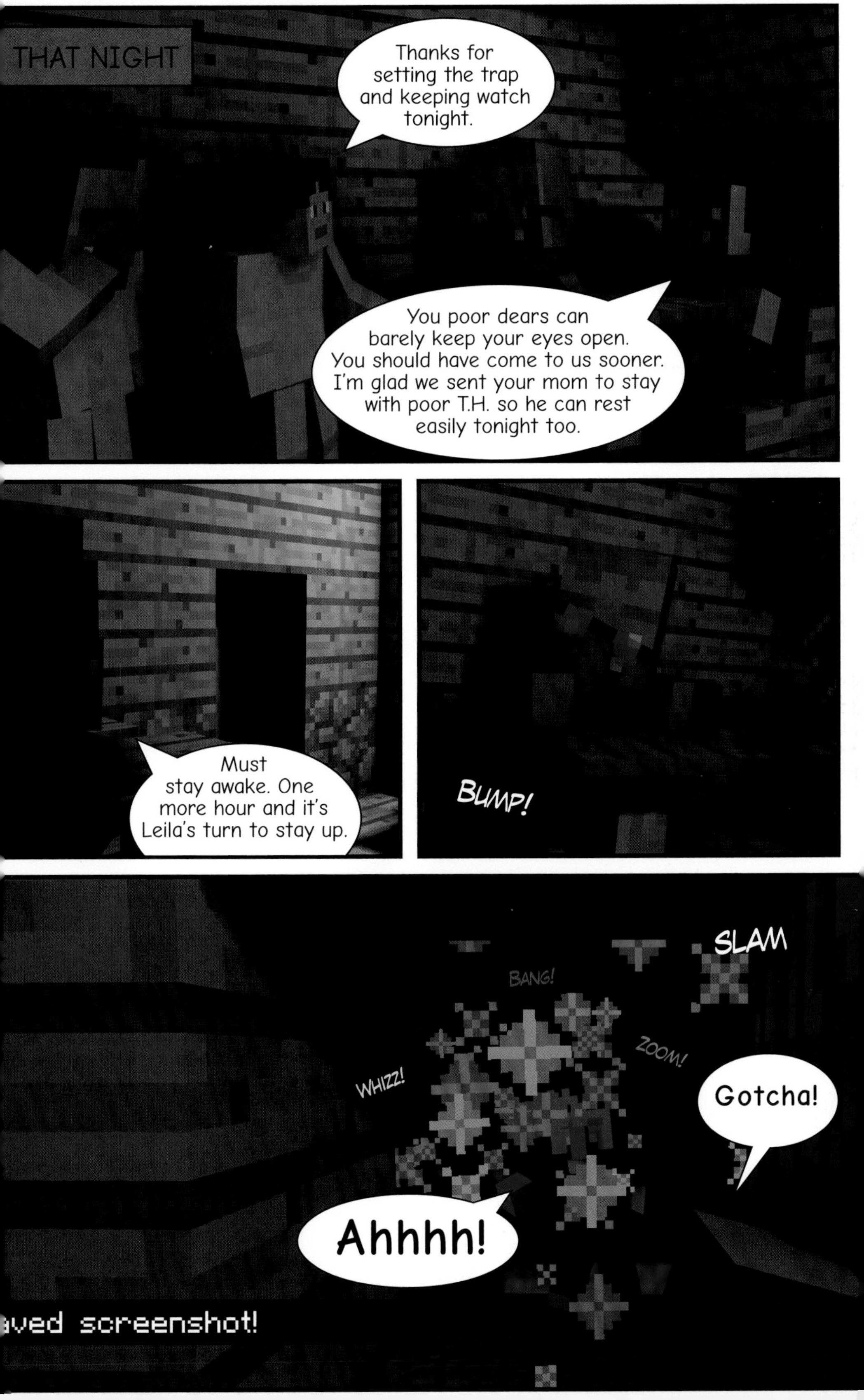
THAT NIGHT
Thanks for setting the trap and keeping watch tonight.
You poor dears can barely keep your eyes open. You should have come to us sooner. I'm glad we sent your mom to stay with poor T.H. so he can rest easily tonight too.
Must stay awake. One more hour and it's Leila's turn to stay up.
BUMP!
SLAM
BANG!
ZOOM!
WHIZZ!
Gotcha!
Ahhhh!
aved screenshot!

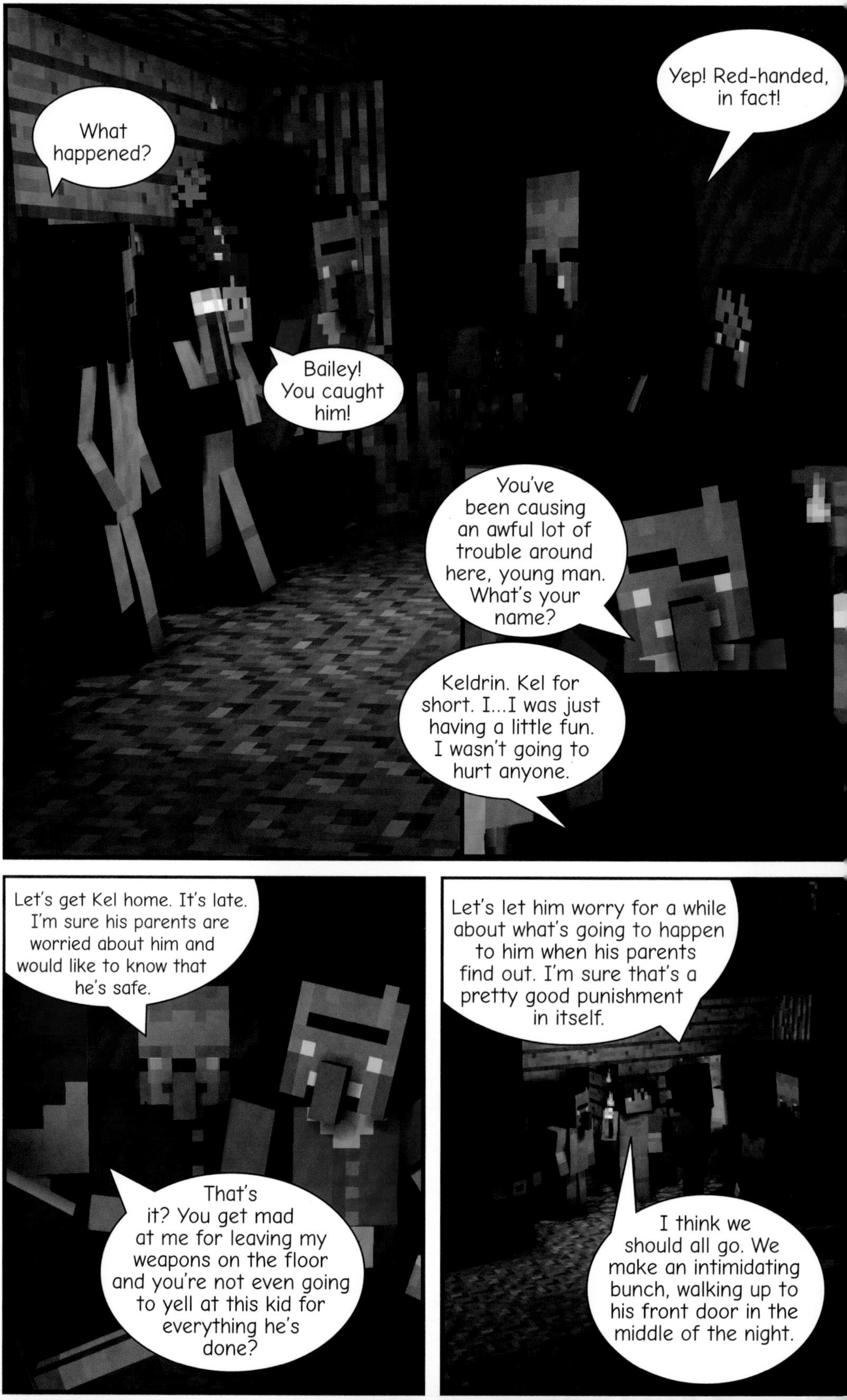
What happened?
Yep! Red-handed, in fact!
Bailey! You caught him!
You've been causing an awful lot of trouble around here, young man. What's your name?
Keldrin. Kel for short. I...I was just having a little fun. I wasn't going to hurt anyone.
Let's get Kel home. It's late. I'm sure his parents are worried about him and would like to know that he's safe.
That's it? You get mad at me for leaving my weapons on the floor and you're not even going to yell at this kid for everything he's done?
Let's let him worry for a while about what's going to happen to him when his parents find out. I'm sure that's a pretty good punishment in itself.
I think we should all go. We make an intimidating bunch, walking up to his front door in the middle of the night.

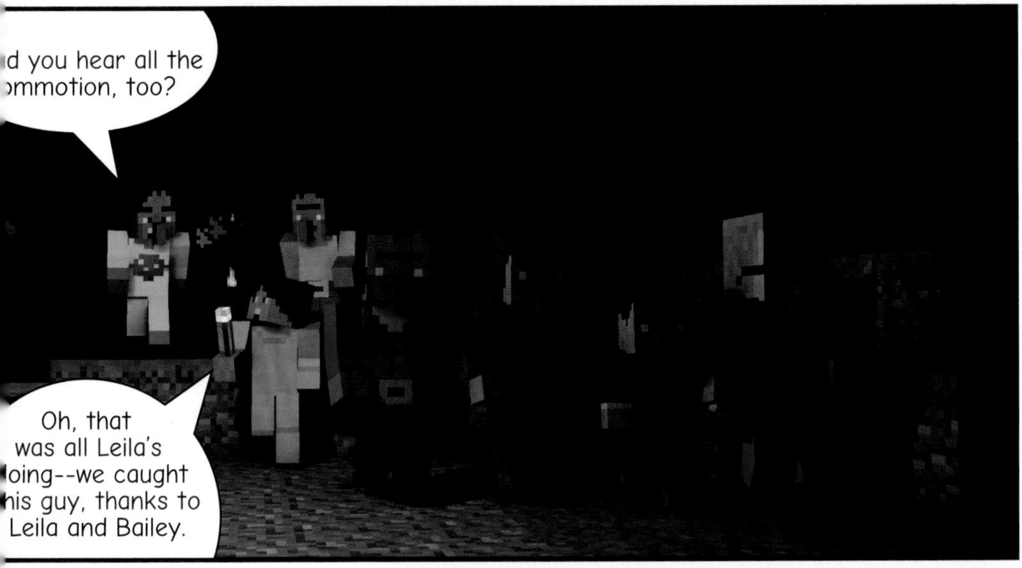
d you hear all the ommotion, too?
Oh, that was all Leila's oing--we caught is guy, thanks to Leila and Bailey.

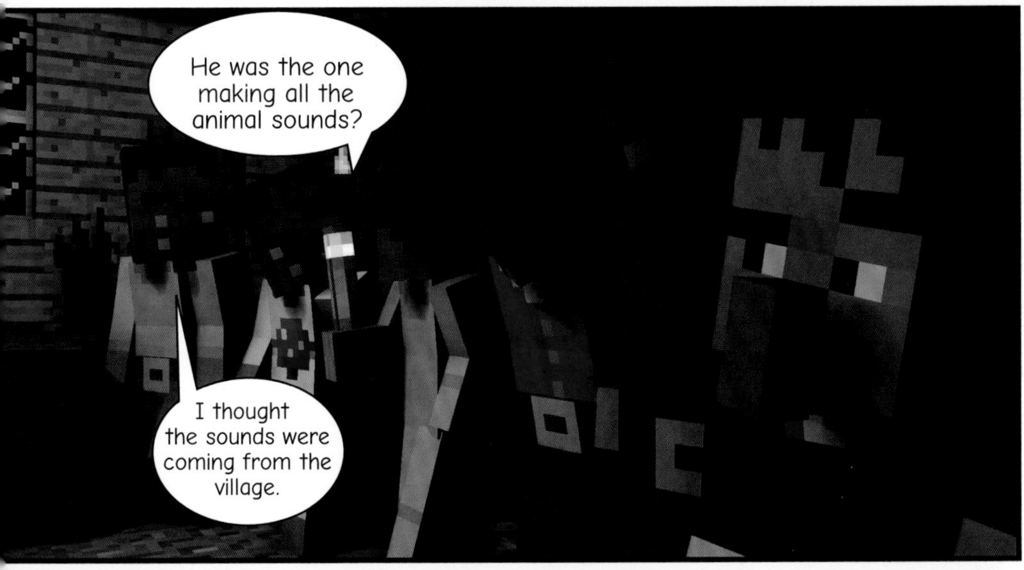
He was the one making all the animal sounds?
I thought the sounds were coming from the village.

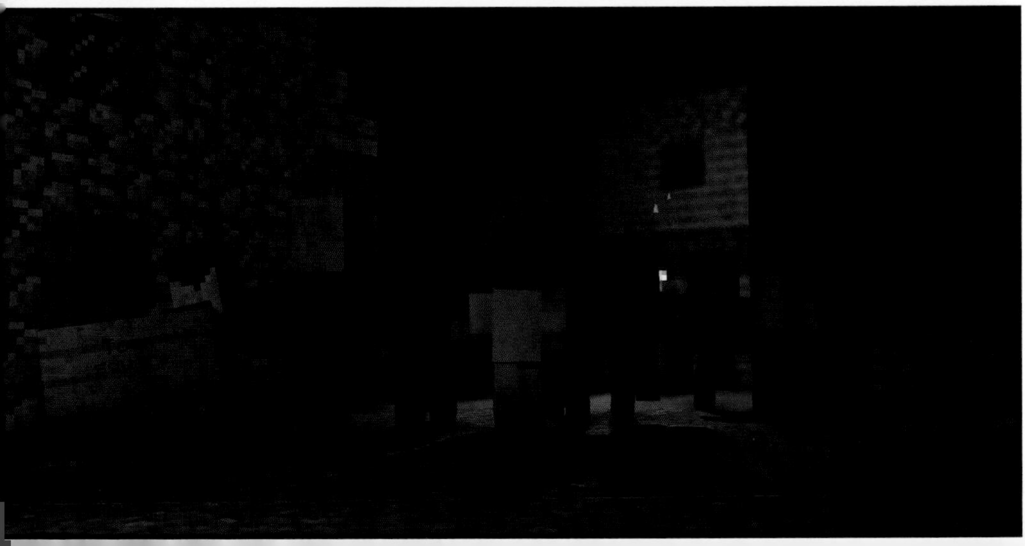

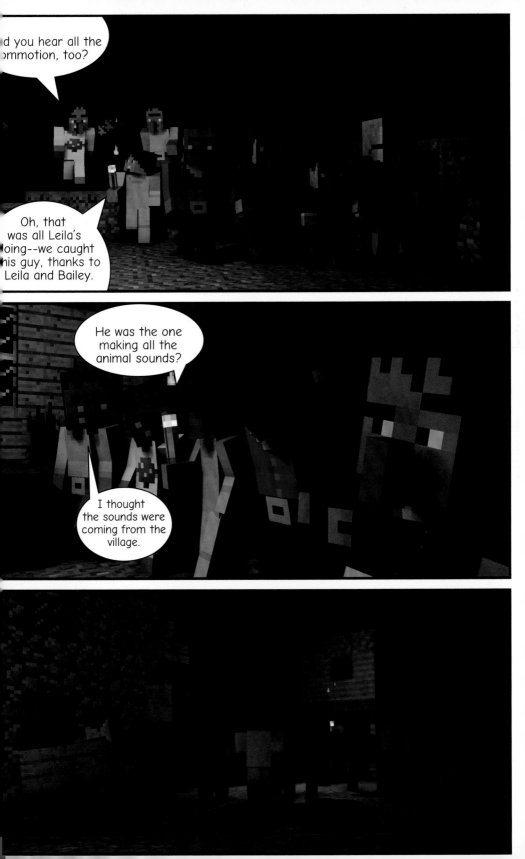

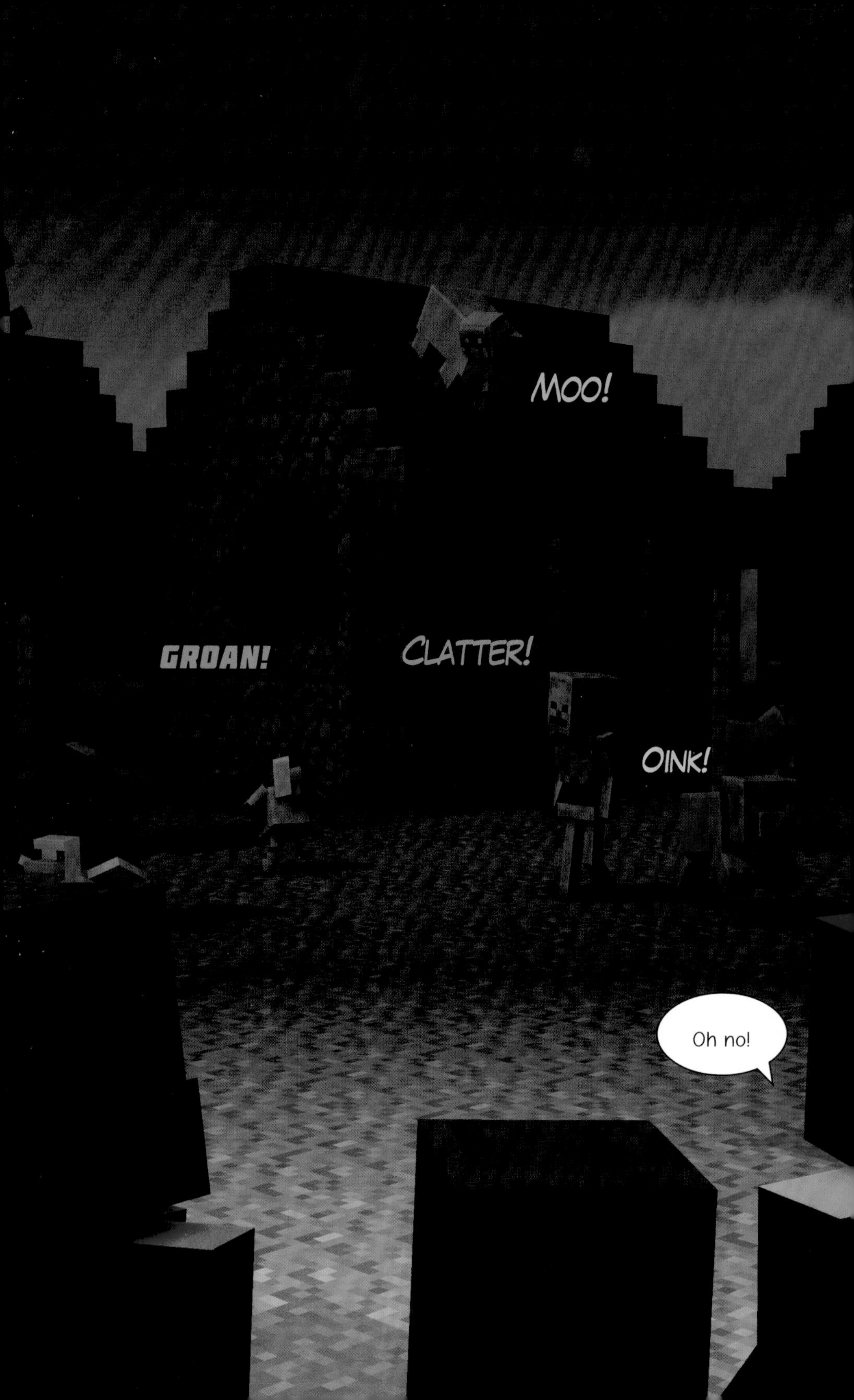
MOO!
GROAN!
CLATTER!
OINK!
Oh no!

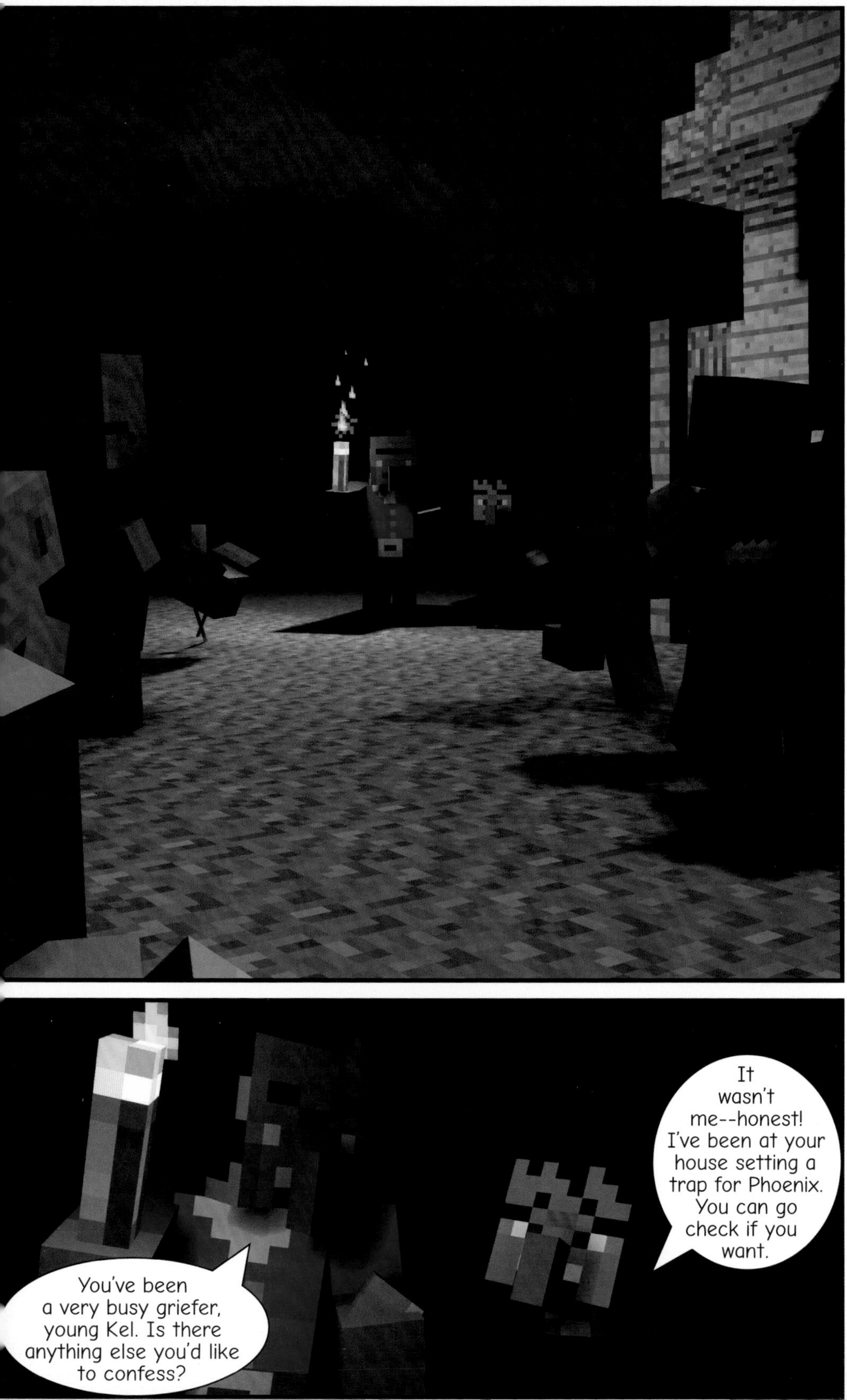
You've been a very busy griefer, young Kel. Is there anything else you'd like to confess?
It wasn't me--honest! I've been at your house setting a trap for Phoenix. You can go check if you want.

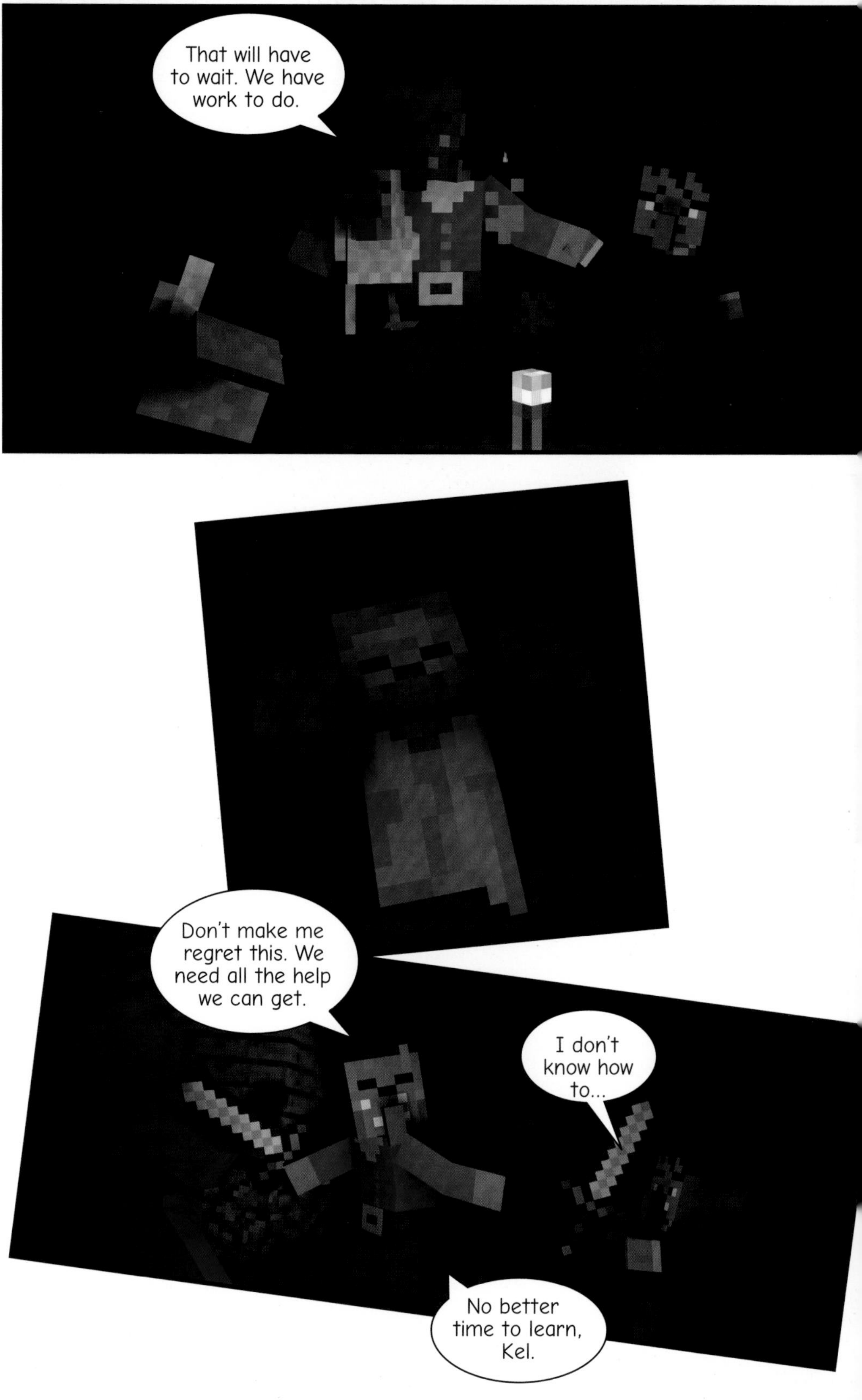
That will have to wait. We have work to do.
Don't make me regret this. We need all the help we can get.
I don't know how to...
No better time to learn, Kel.

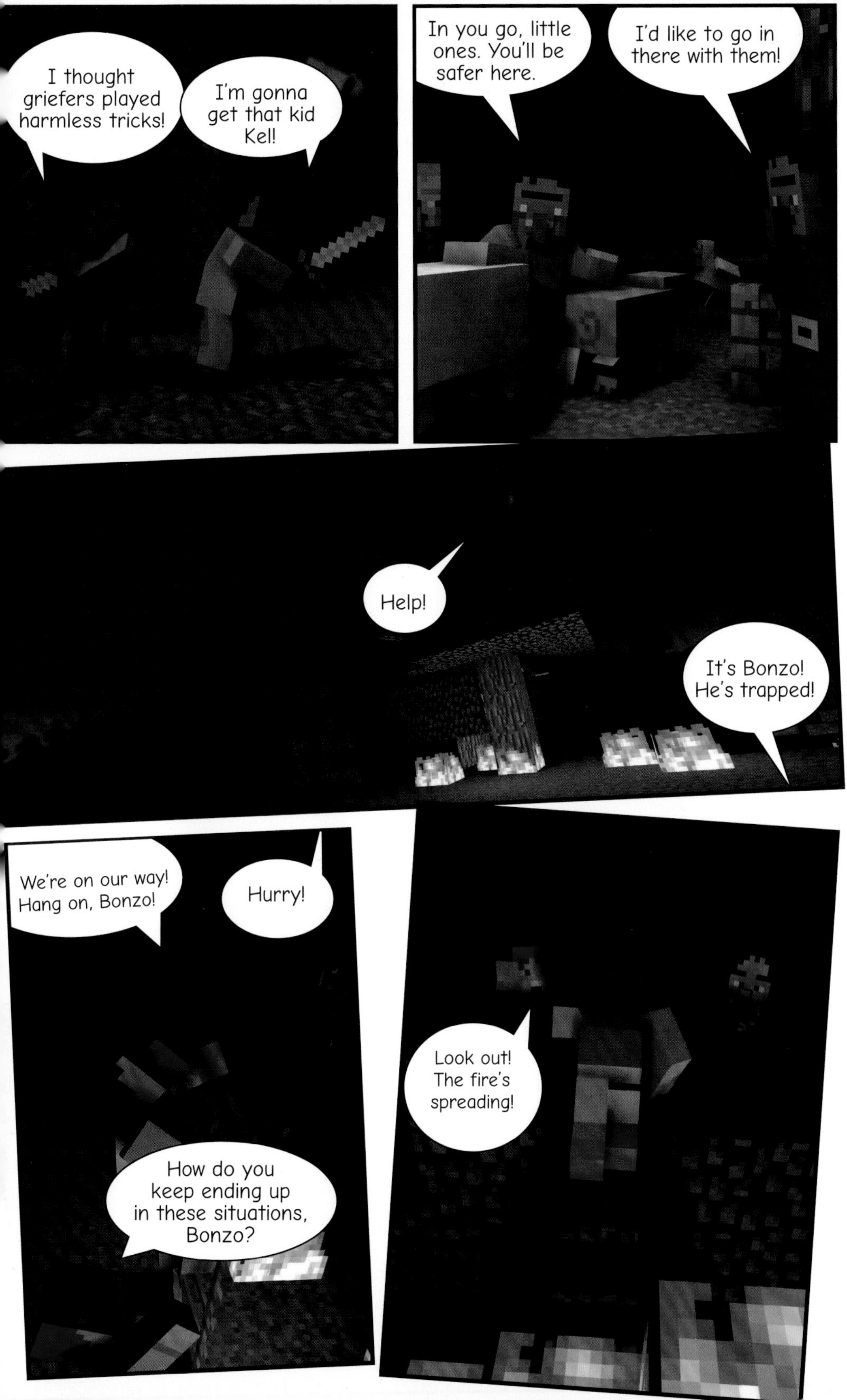
I thought griefers played harmless tricks!
I'm gonna get that kid Kel!
In you go, little ones. You'll be safer here.
I'd like to go in there with them!
Help!
It's Bonzo! He's trapped!
We're on our way! Hang on, Bonzo!
Hurry!
How do you keep ending up in these situations, Bonzo?
Look out! The fire's spreading!

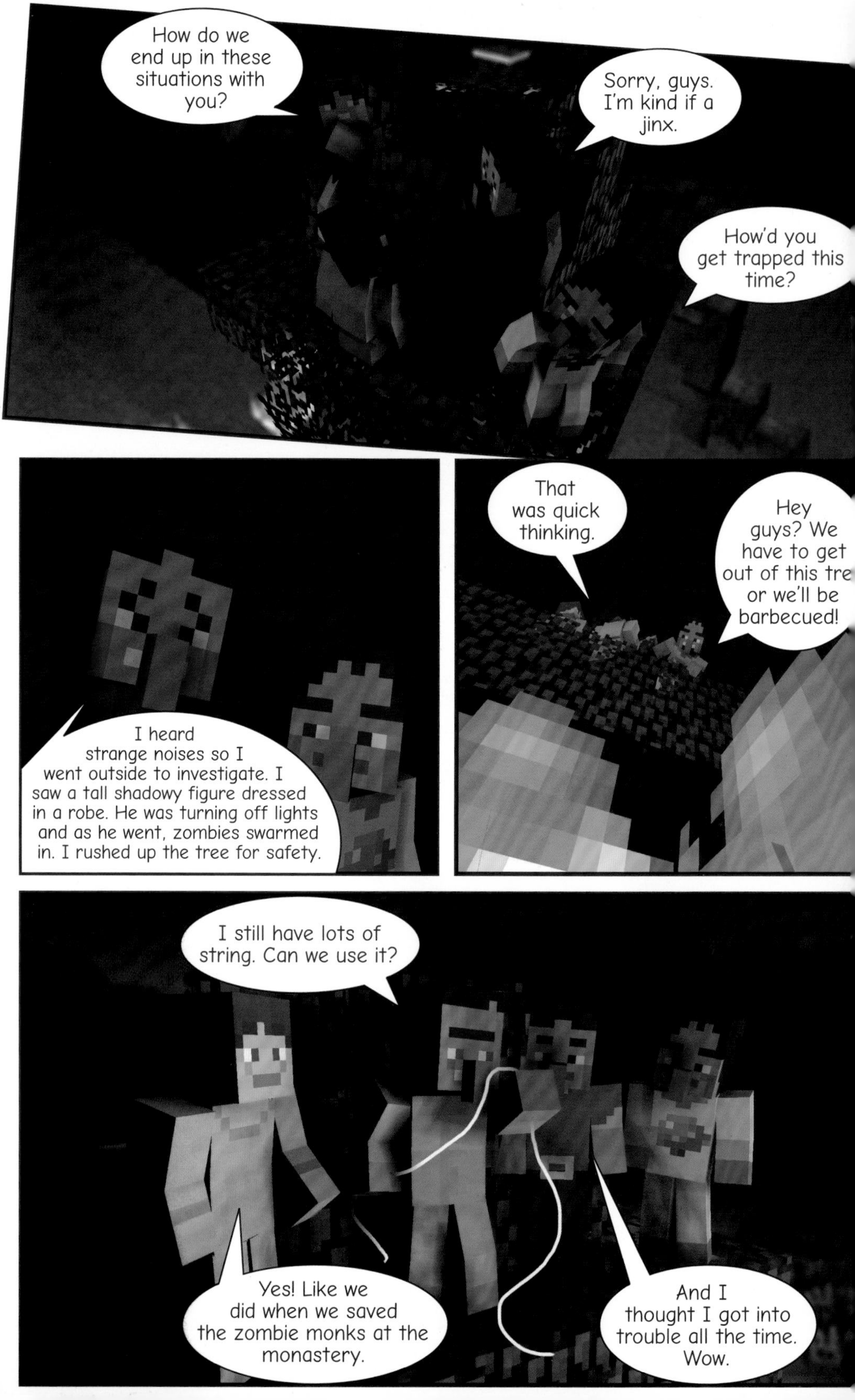
How do we end up in these situations with you?
Sorry, guys. I'm kind if a jinx.
How'd you get trapped this time?
I heard strange noises so I went outside to investigate. I saw a tall shadowy figure dressed in a robe. He was turning off lights and as he went, zombies swarmed in. I rushed up the tree for safety.
That was quick thinking.
Hey guys? We have to get out of this tre or we'll be barbecued!
I still have lots of string. Can we use it?
Yes! Like we did when we saved the zombie monks at the monastery.
And I thought I got into trouble all the time. Wow.

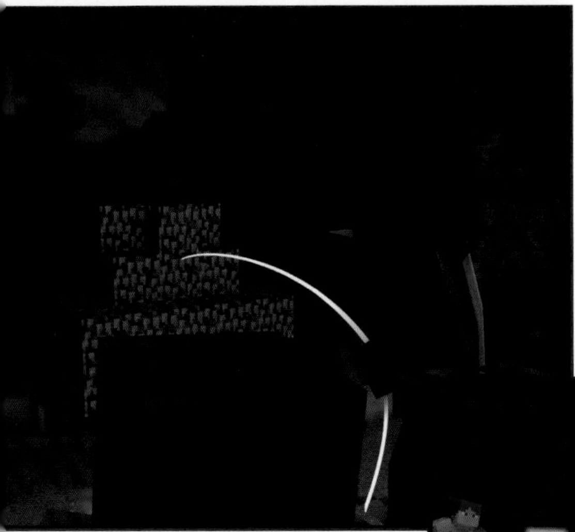
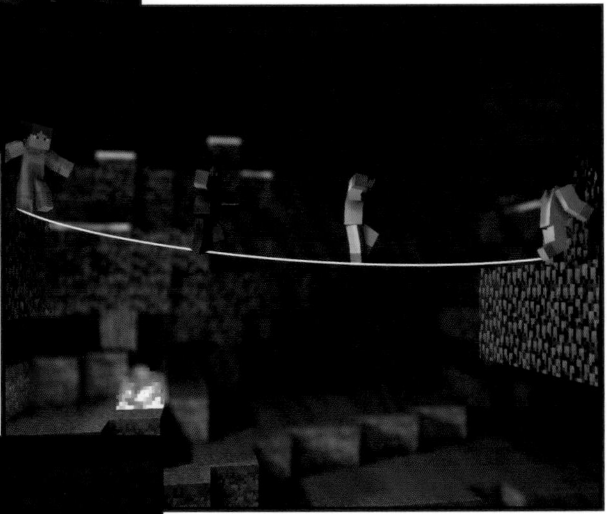
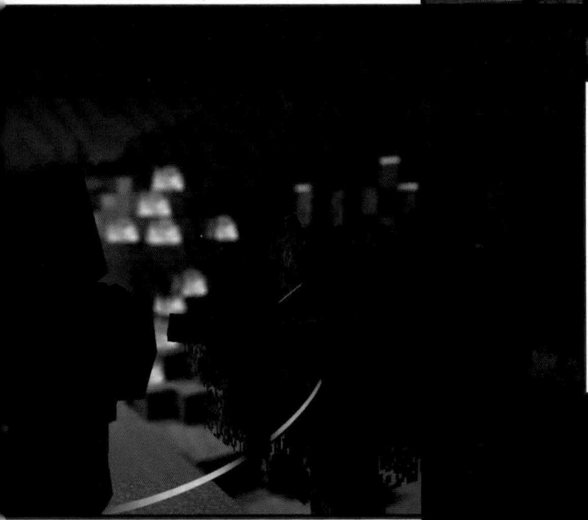
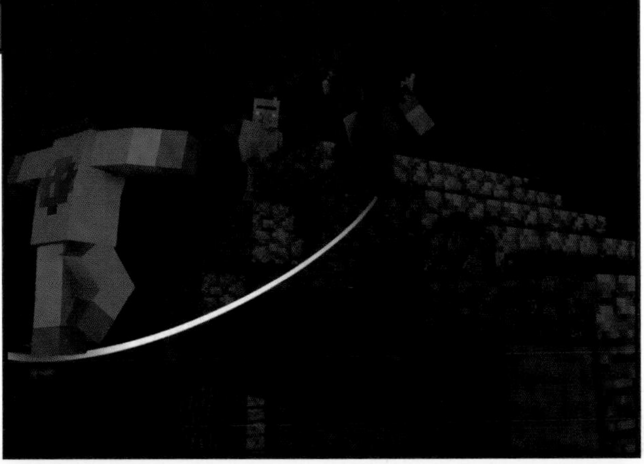

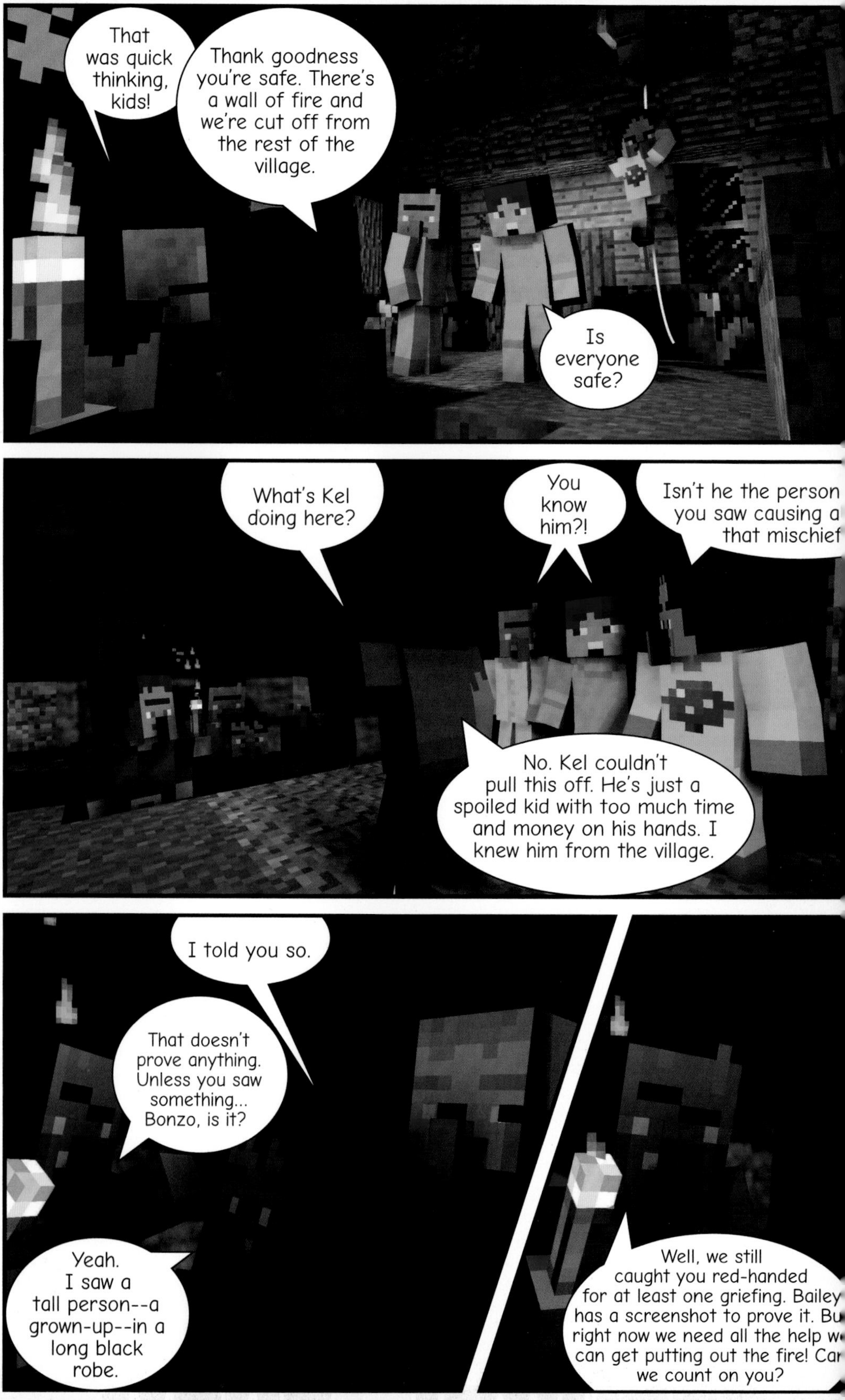

That was quick thinking, kids!
Thank goodness you're safe. There's a wall of fire and we're cut off from the rest of the village.
Is everyone safe?
What's Kel doing here?
You know him?!
Isn't he the person you saw causing a that mischief
No. Kel couldn't pull this off. He's just a spoiled kid with too much time and money on his hands. I knew him from the village.
I told you so.
That doesn't prove anything. Unless you saw something... Bonzo, is it?
Yeah. I saw a tall person--a grown-up--in a long black robe.
Well, we still caught you red-handed for at least one griefing. Bailey has a screenshot to prove it. Bu right now we need all the help w can get putting out the fire! Ca we count on you?

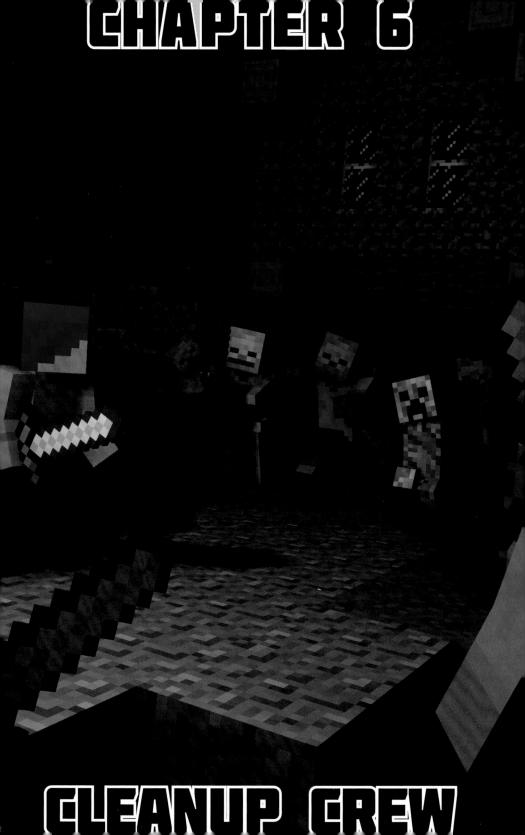

CHAPTER 6

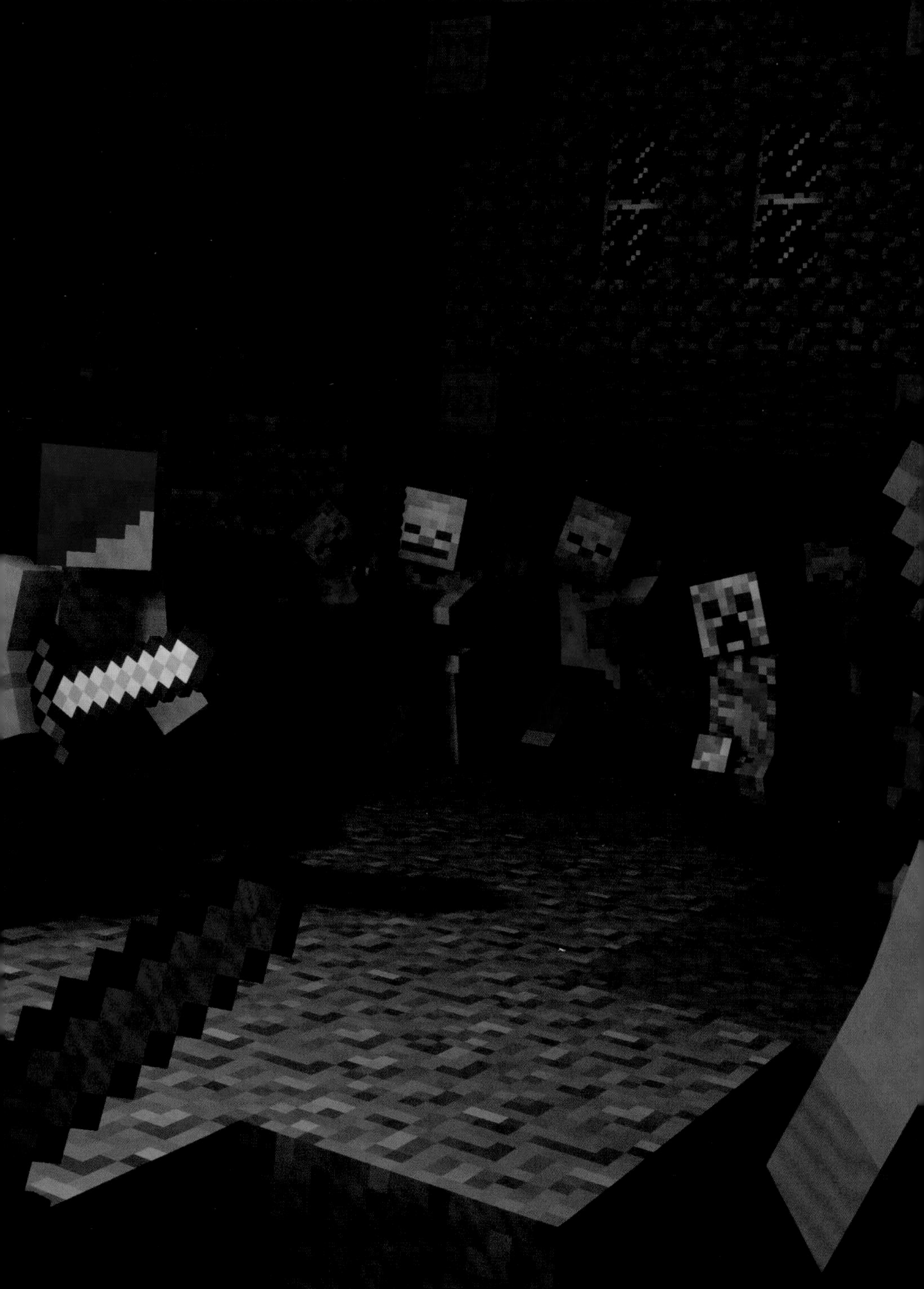

CLEANUP CREW

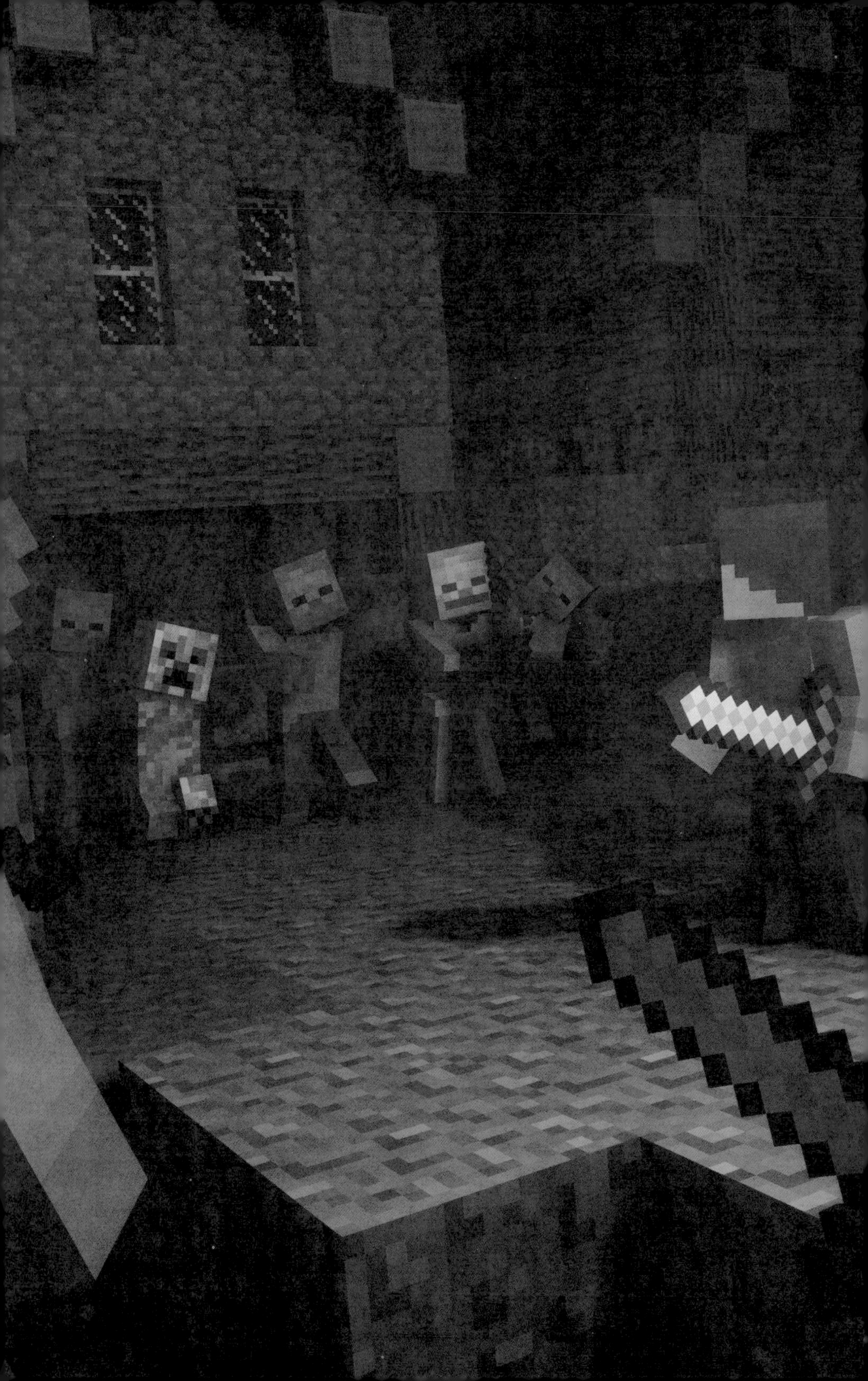

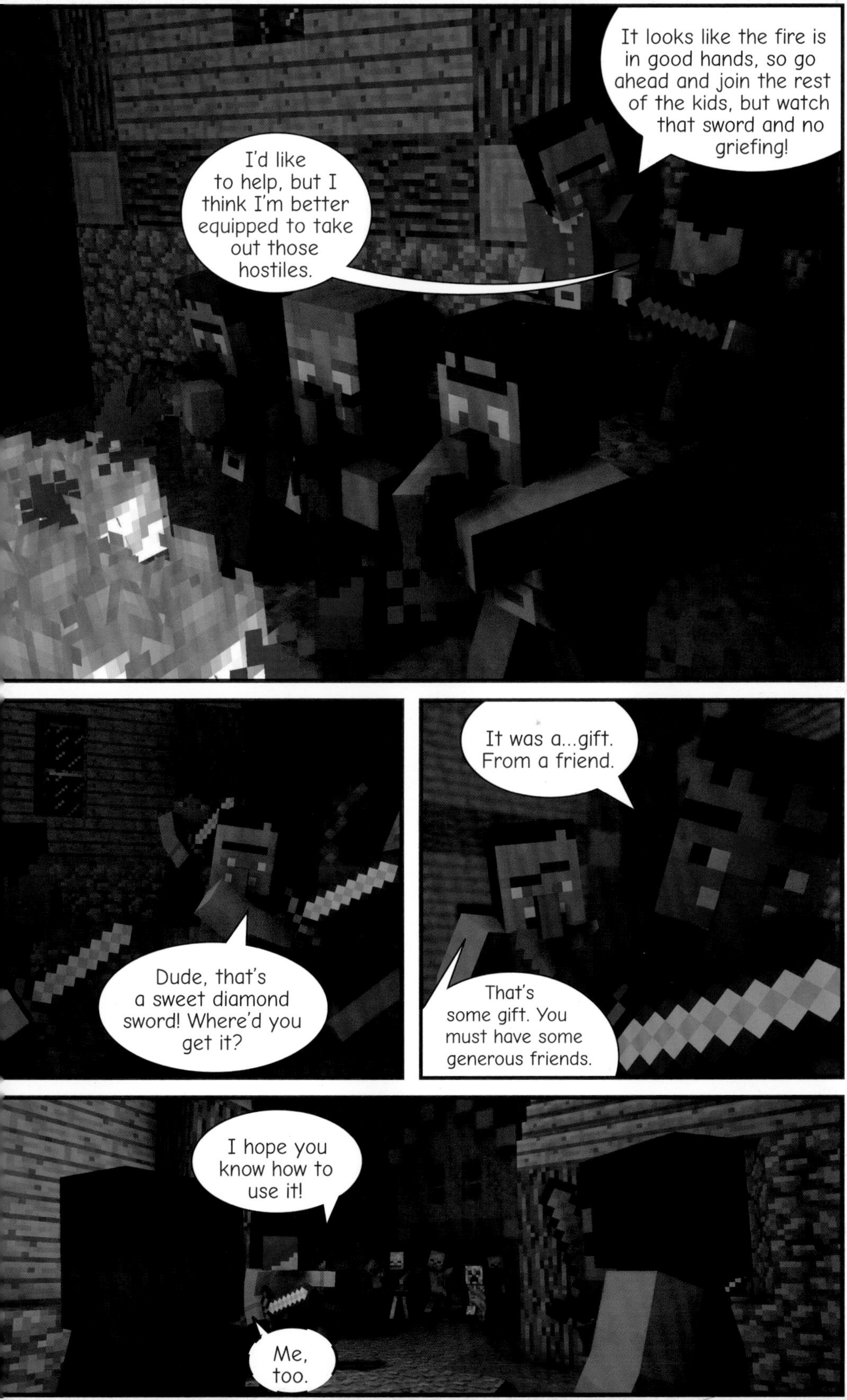
It looks like the fire is in good hands, so go ahead and join the rest of the kids, but watch that sword and no griefing!
I'd like to help, but I think I'm better equipped to take out those hostiles.
Dude, that's a sweet diamond sword! Where'd you get it?
It was a...gift. From a friend.
That's some gift. You must have some generous friends.
I hope you know how to use it!
Me, too.

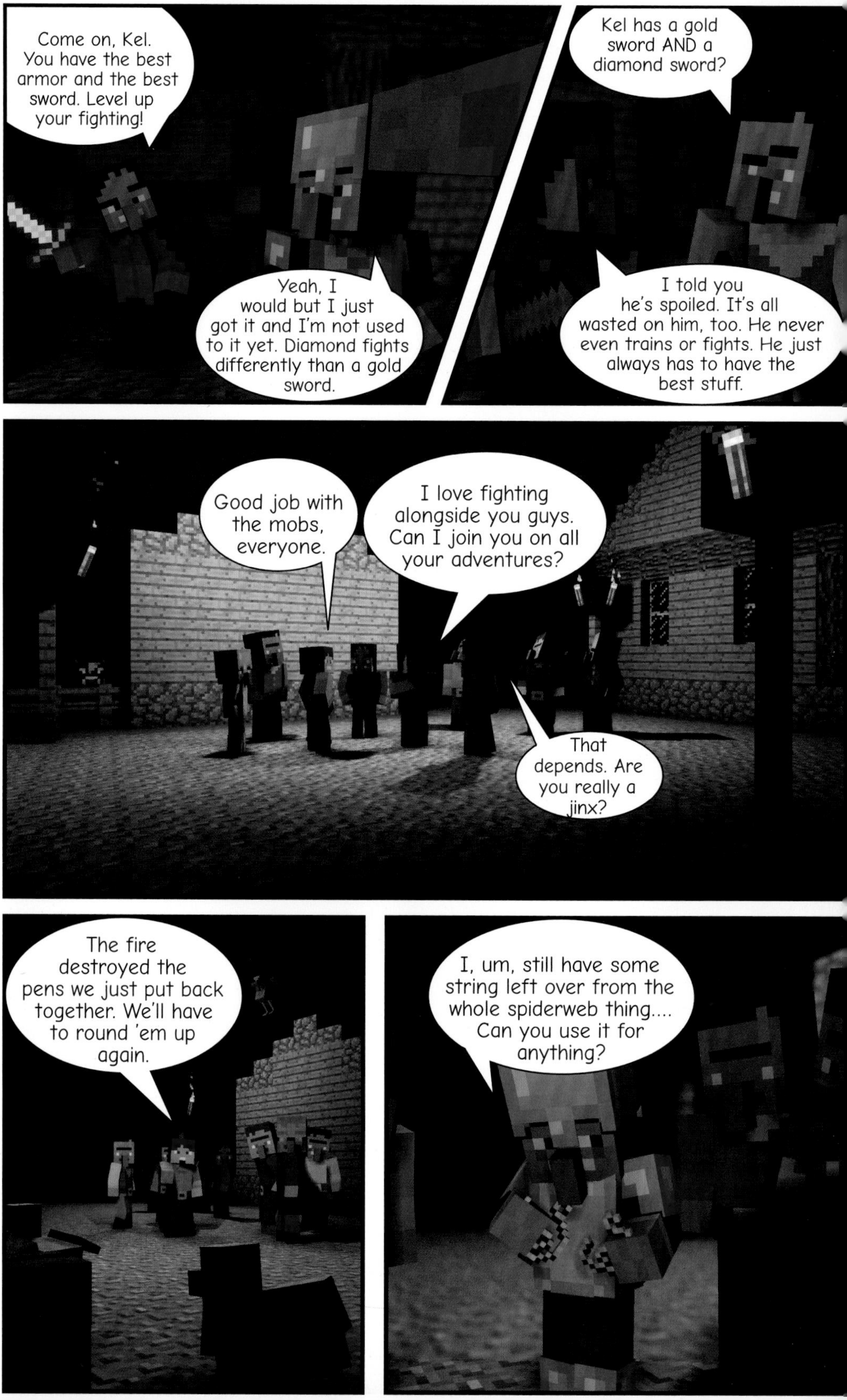
Come on, Kel. You have the best armor and the best sword. Level up your fighting!
Yeah, I would but I just got it and I'm not used to it yet. Diamond fights differently than a gold sword.
Kel has a gold sword AND a diamond sword?
I told you he's spoiled. It's all wasted on him, too. He never even trains or fights. He just always has to have the best stuff.
Good job with the mobs, everyone.
I love fighting alongside you guys. Can I join you on all your adventures?
That depends. Are you really a jinx?
The fire destroyed the pens we just put back together. We'll have to round 'em up again.
I, um, still have some string left over from the whole spiderweb thing.... Can you use it for anything?

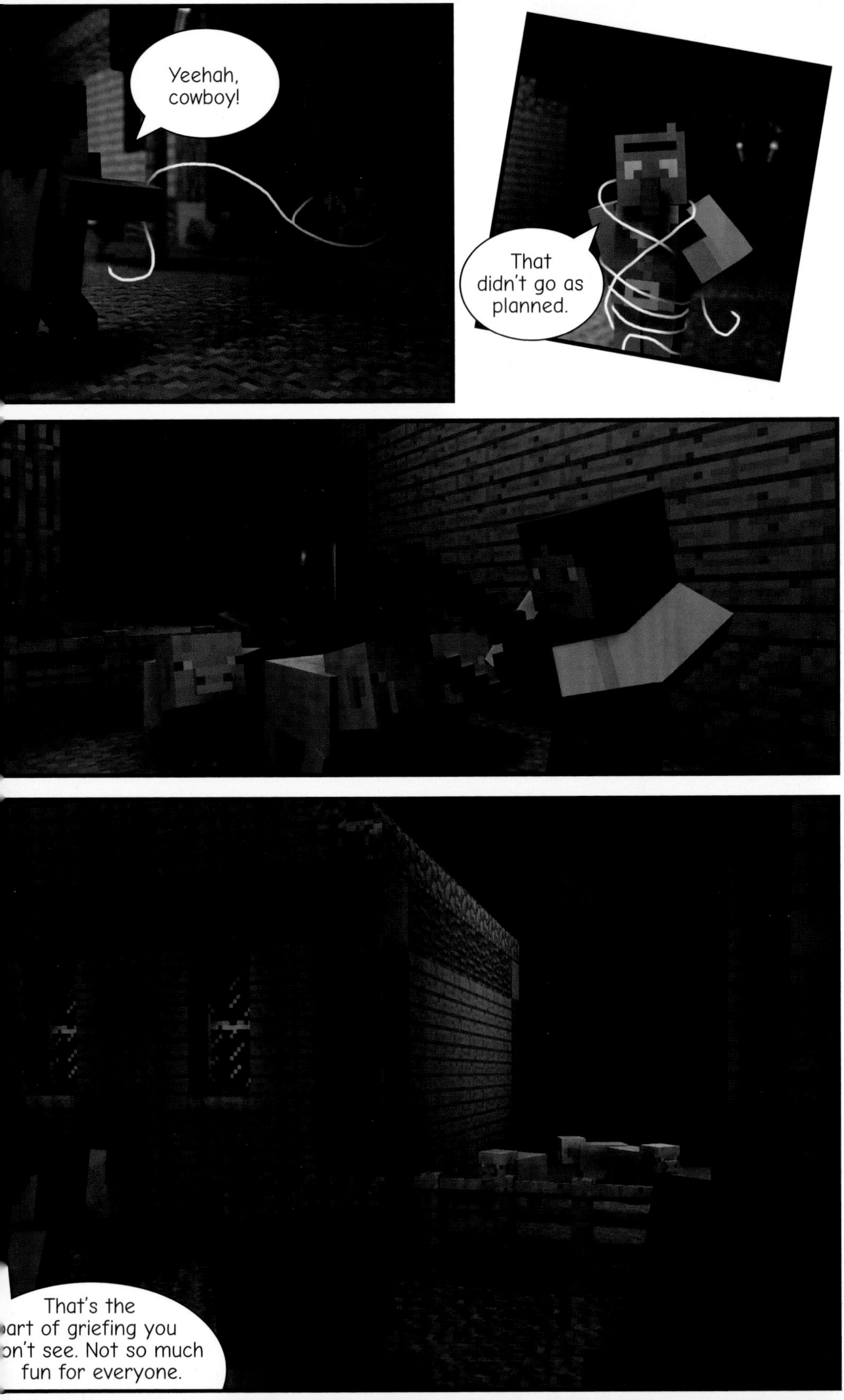
Yeehah, cowboy!
That didn't go as planned.
That's the art of griefing you on't see. Not so much fun for everyone.

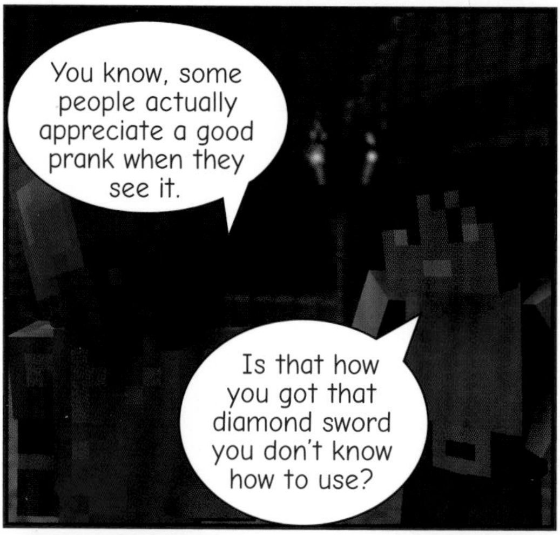
You know, some people actually appreciate a good prank when they see it.
Is that how you got that diamond sword you don't know how to use?

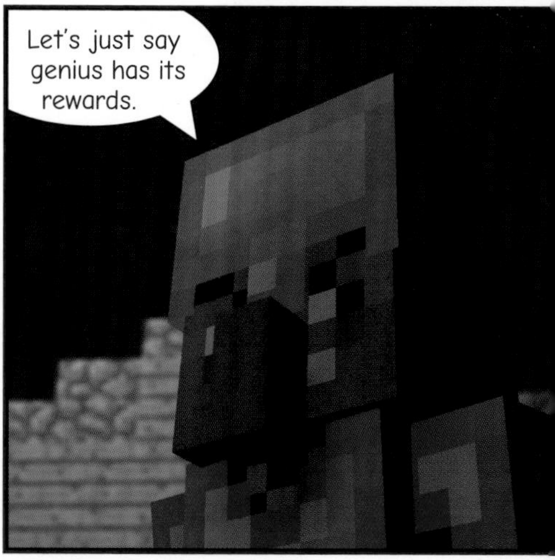
Let's just say genius has its rewards.

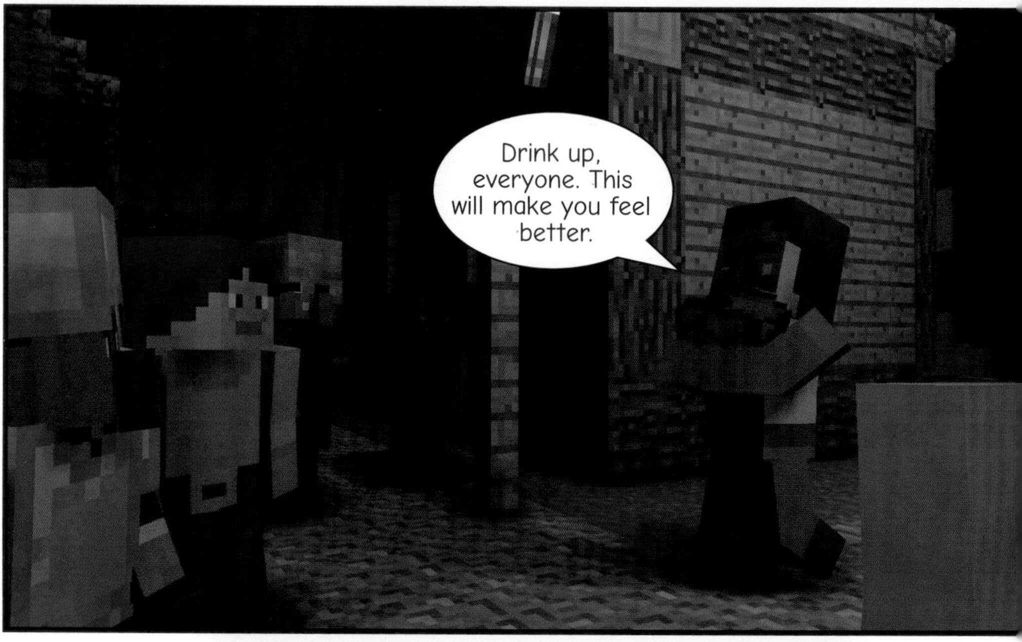
Drink up, everyone. This will make you feel better.

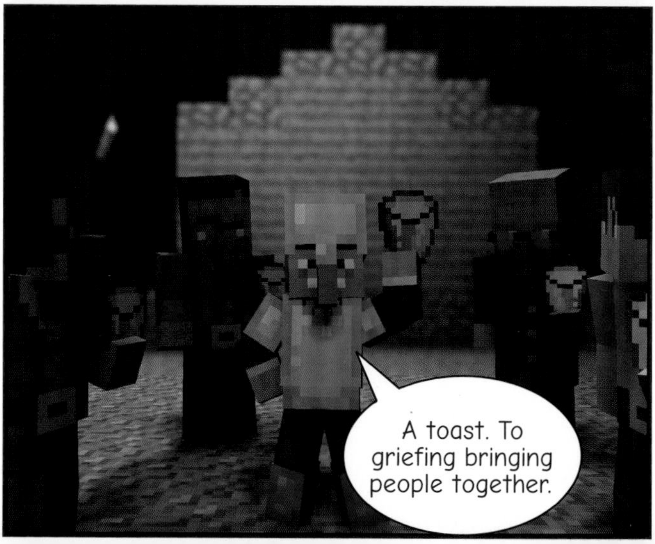
A toast. To griefing bringing people together.

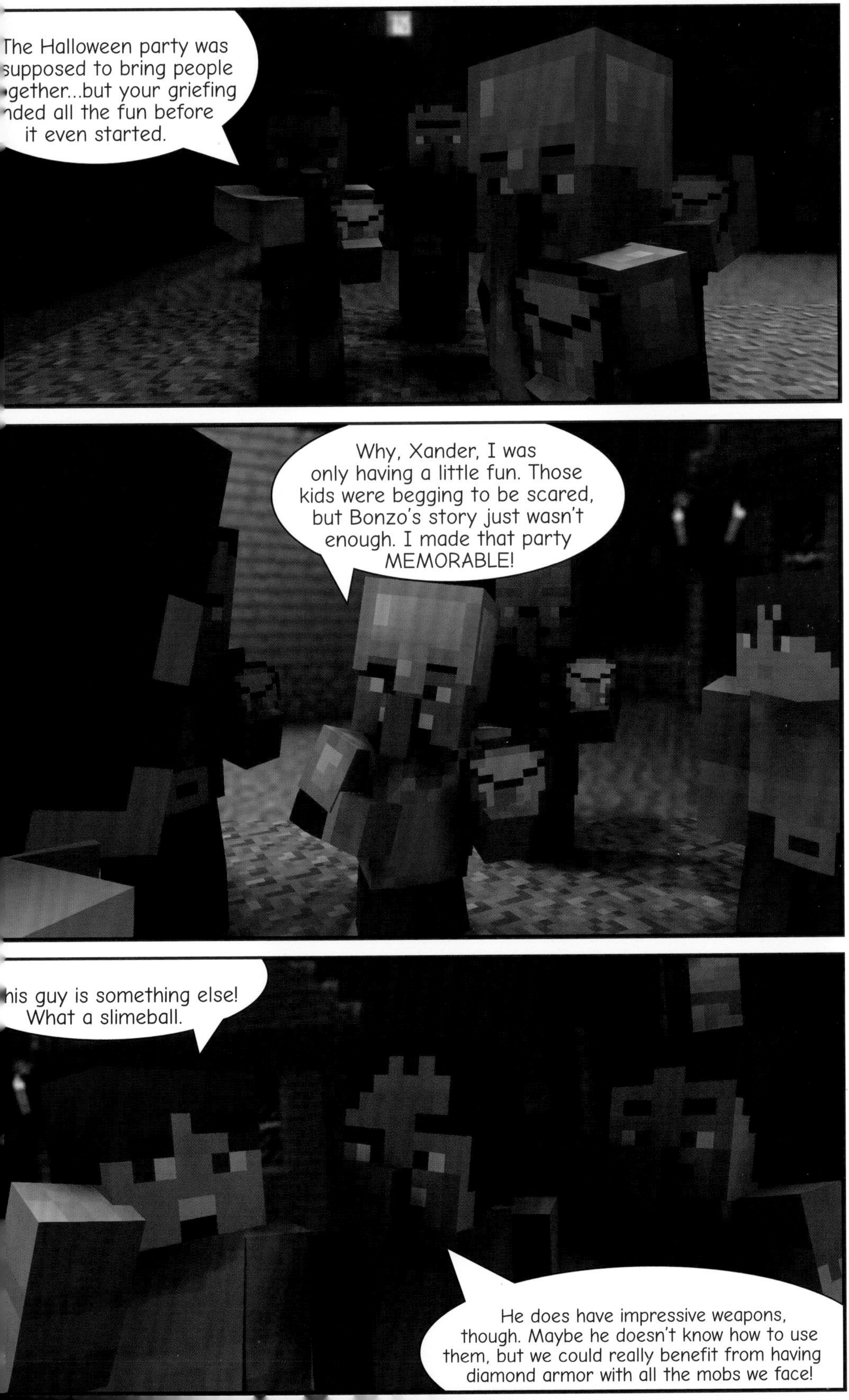
The Halloween party was supposed to bring people gether...but your griefing nded all the fun before it even started.
Why, Xander, I was only having a little fun. Those kids were begging to be scared, but Bonzo's story just wasn't enough. I made that party MEMORABLE!
his guy is something else! What a slimeball.
He does have impressive weapons, though. Maybe he doesn't know how to use them, but we could really benefit from having diamond armor with all the mobs we face!

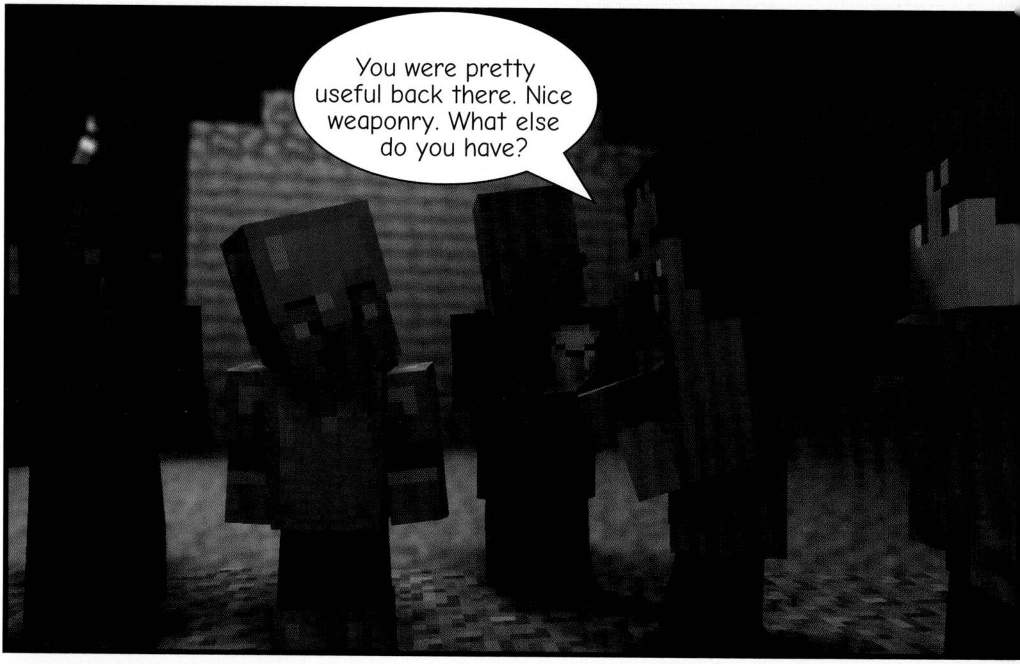
You were pretty useful back there. Nice weaponry. What else do you have?

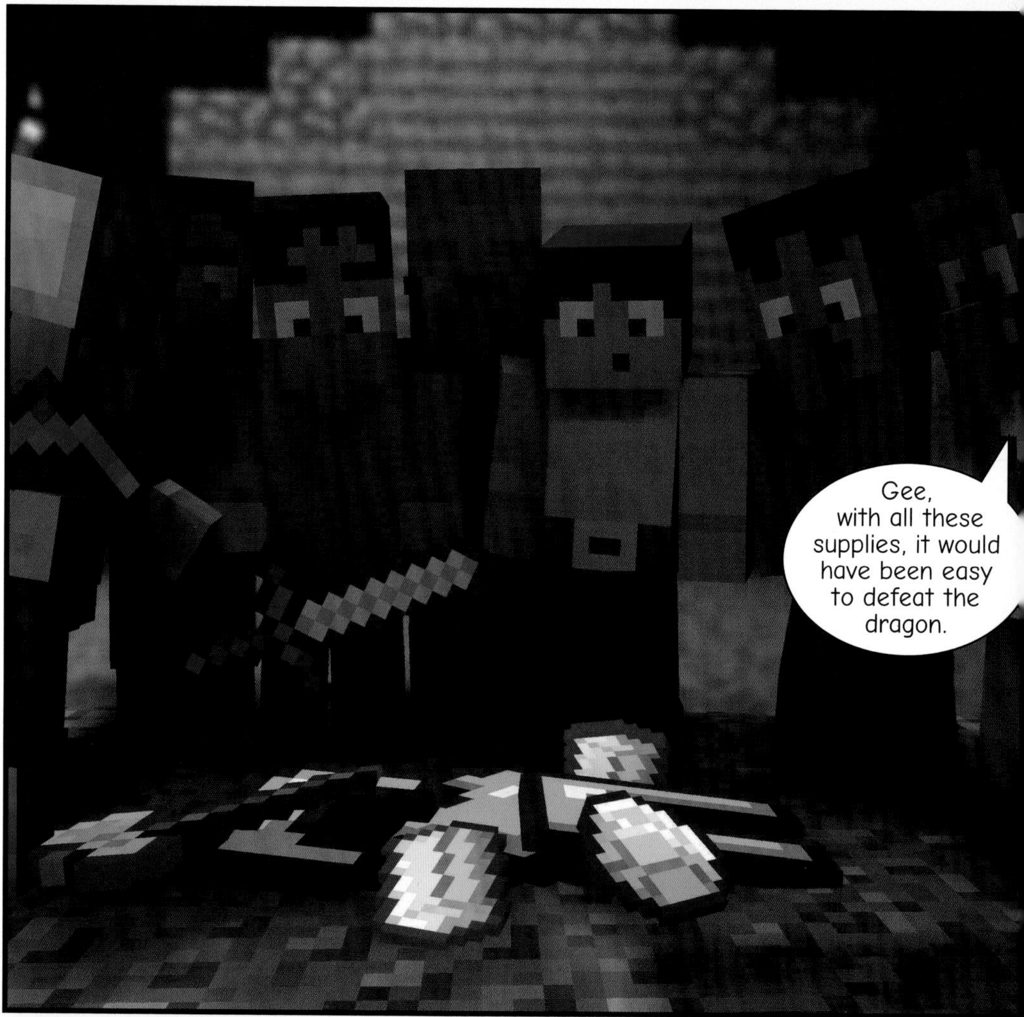
Gee, with all these supplies, it would have been easy to defeat the dragon.

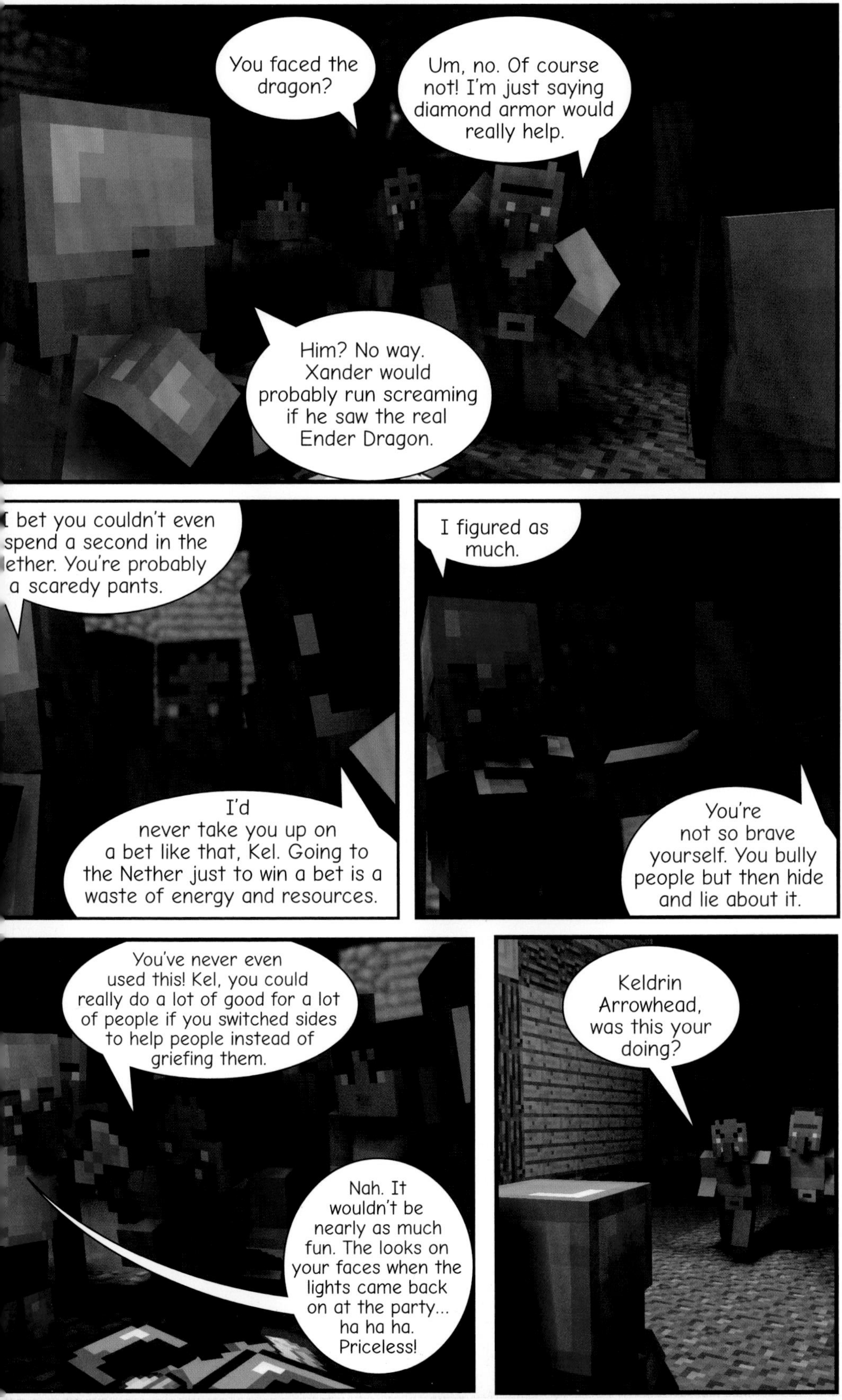
You faced the dragon?
Um, no. Of course not! I'm just saying diamond armor would really help.
Him? No way. Xander would probably run screaming if he saw the real Ender Dragon.
I bet you couldn't even spend a second in the ether. You're probably a scaredy pants.
I'd never take you up on a bet like that, Kel. Going to the Nether just to win a bet is a waste of energy and resources.
I figured as much.
You're not so brave yourself. You bully people but then hide and lie about it.
You've never even used this! Kel, you could really do a lot of good for a lot of people if you switched sides to help people instead of griefing them.
Nah. It wouldn't be nearly as much fun. The looks on your faces when the lights came back on at the party... ha ha ha. Priceless!
Keldrin Arrowhead, was this your doing?

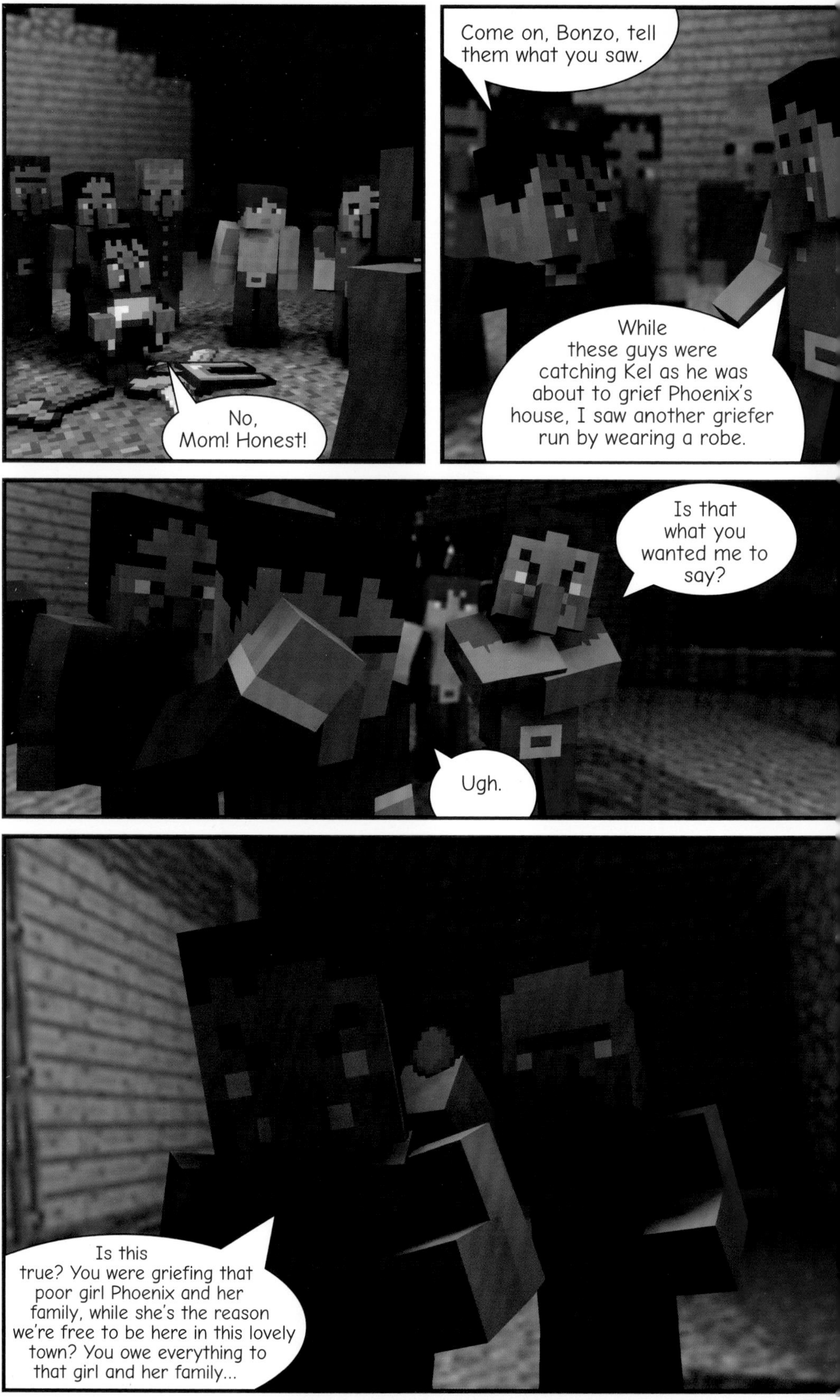
No, Mom! Honest!
Come on, Bonzo, tell them what you saw.
While these guys were catching Kel as he was about to grief Phoenix's house, I saw another griefer run by wearing a robe.
Is that what you wanted me to say?
Ugh.
Is this true? You were griefing that poor girl Phoenix and her family, while she's the reason we're free to be here in this lovely town? You owe everything to that girl and her family...

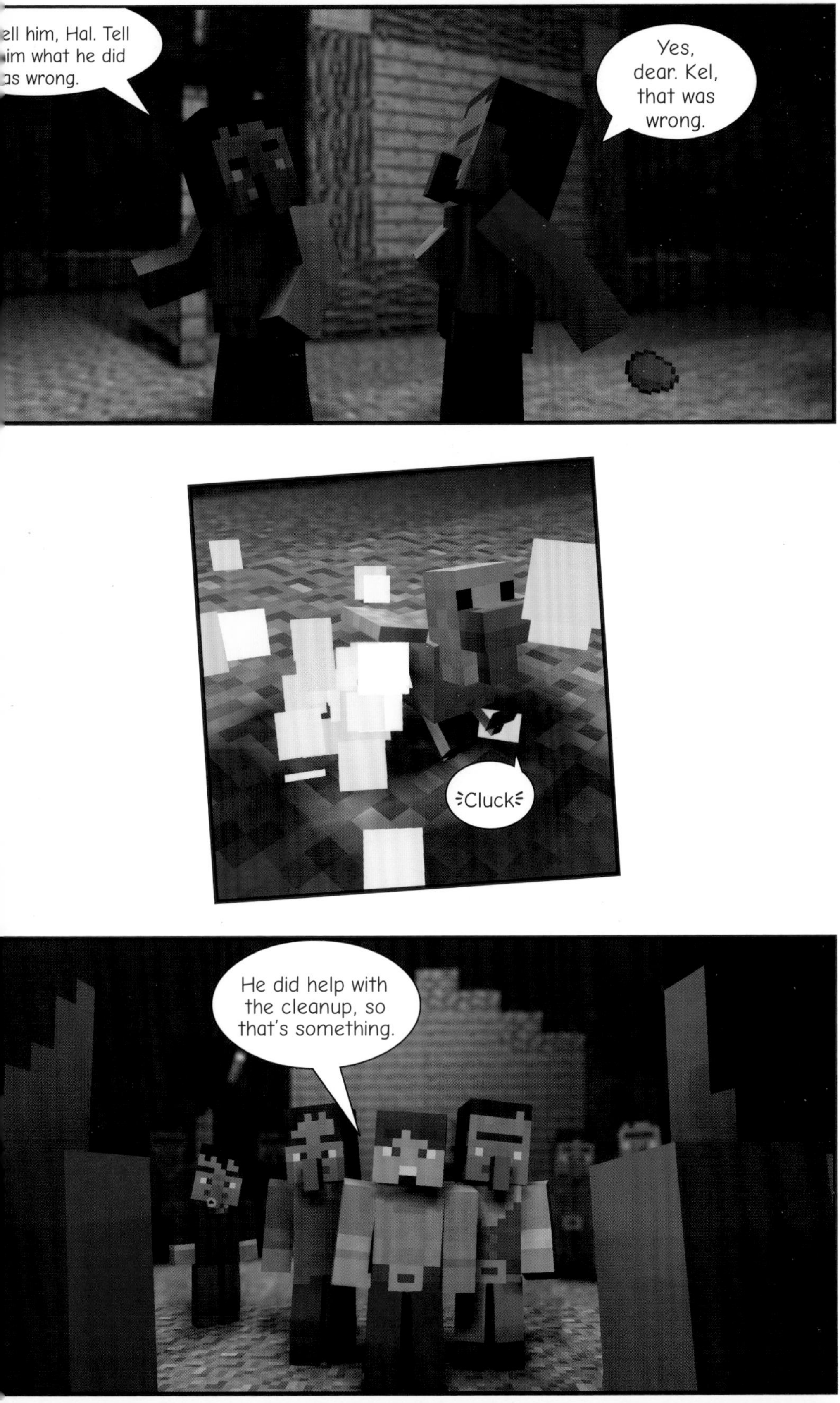
ell him, Hal. Tell im what he did as wrong.
Yes, dear. Kel, that was wrong.
Cluck
He did help with the cleanup, so that's something.

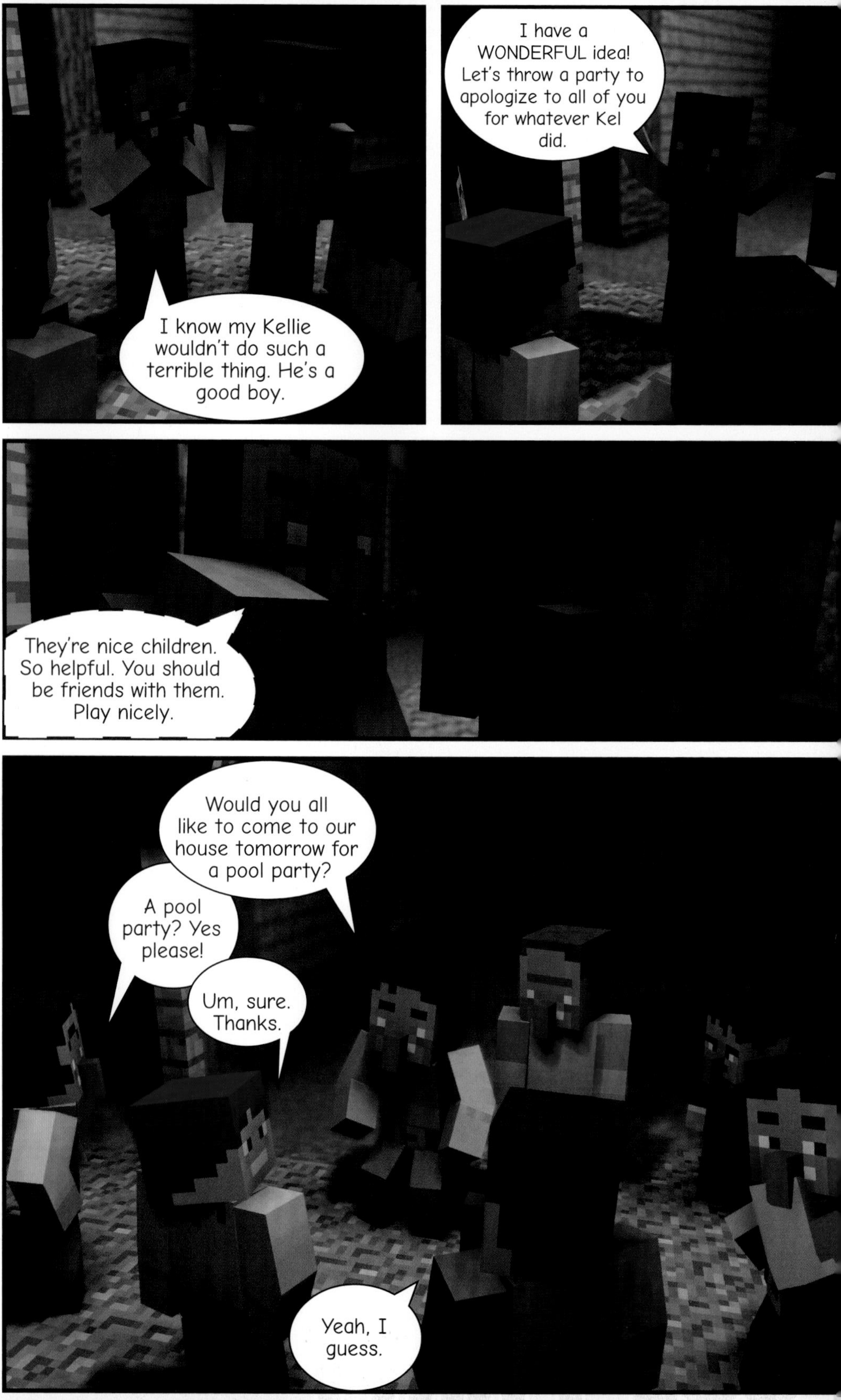
I know my Kellie wouldn't do such a terrible thing. He's a good boy.
I have a WONDERFUL idea! Let's throw a party to apologize to all of you for whatever Kel did.
They're nice children. So helpful. You should be friends with them. Play nicely.
Would you all like to come to our house tomorrow for a pool party?
A pool party? Yes please!
Um, sure. Thanks.
Yeah, I guess.

CHAPTER 7

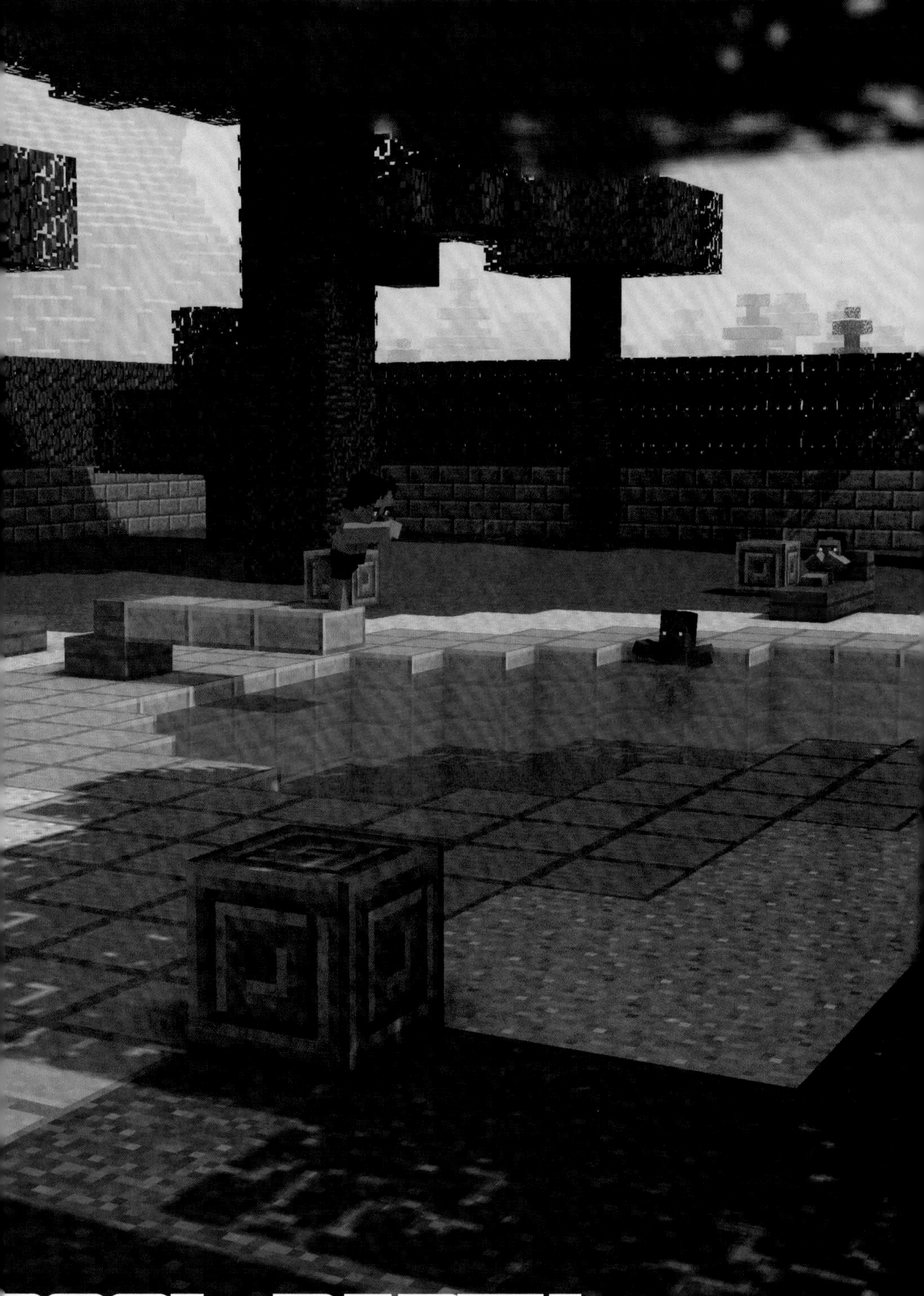

POOL PARTY

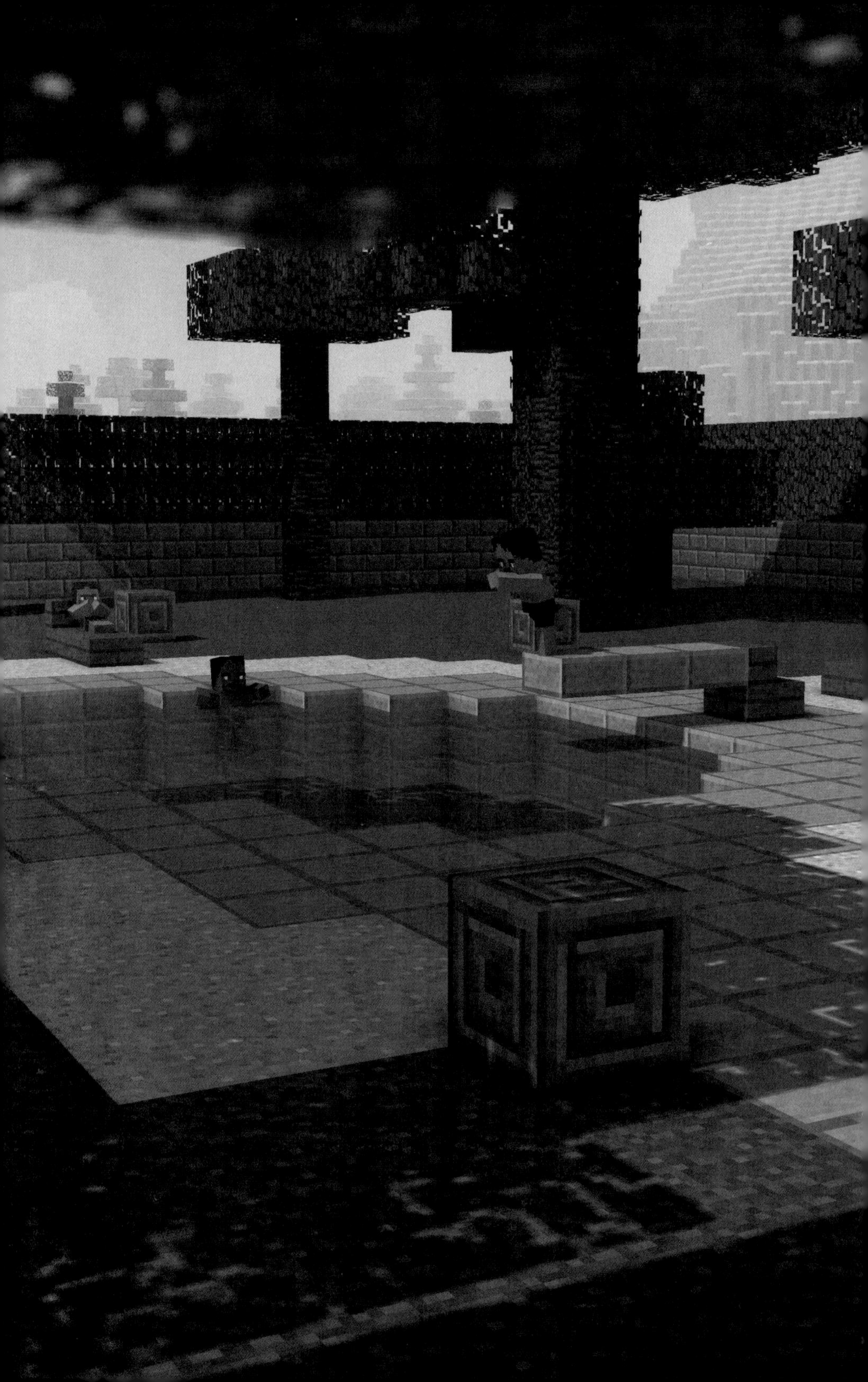

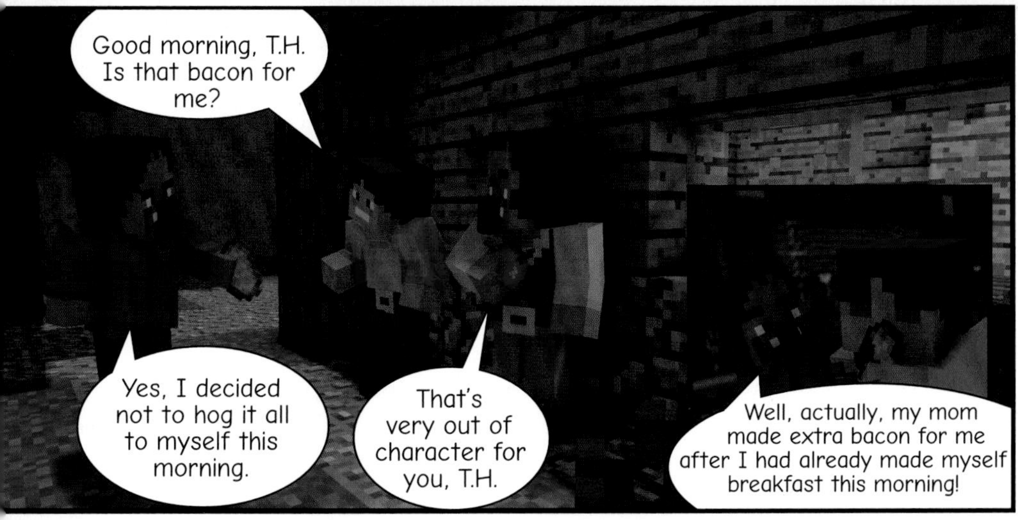
Good morning, T.H. Is that bacon for me?
Yes, I decided not to hog it all to myself this morning.
That's very out of character for you, T.H.
Well, actually, my mom made extra bacon for me after I had already made myself breakfast this morning!

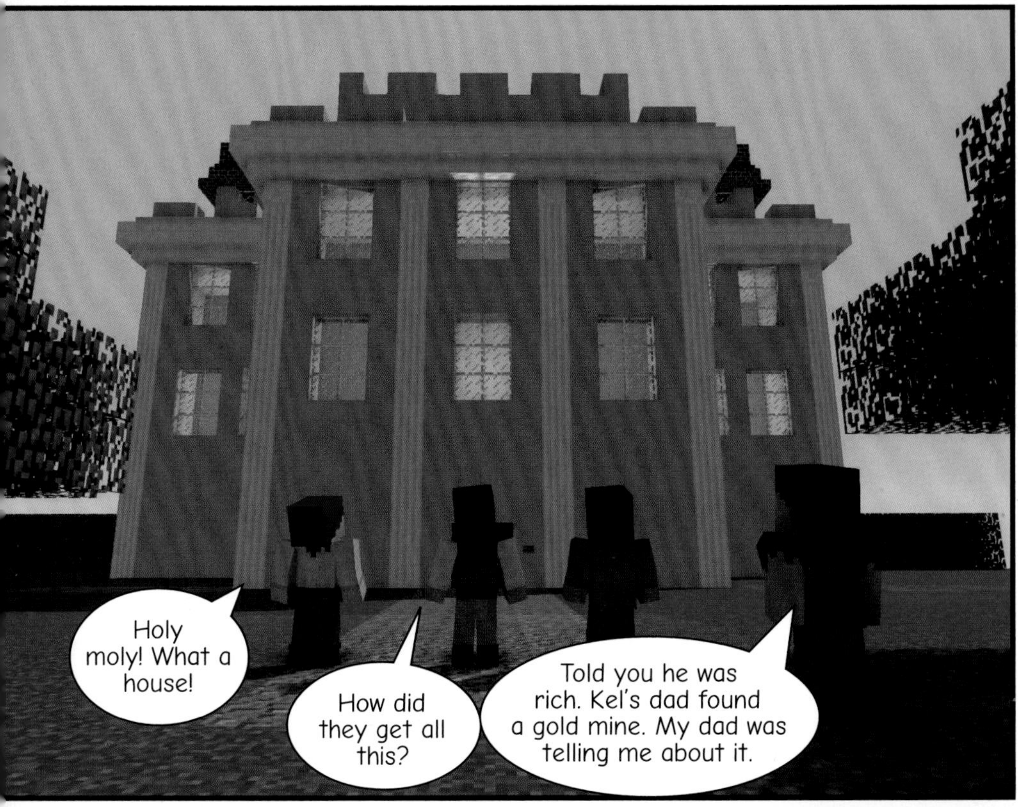
Holy moly! What a house!
How did they get all this?
Told you he was rich. Kel's dad found a gold mine. My dad was telling me about it.

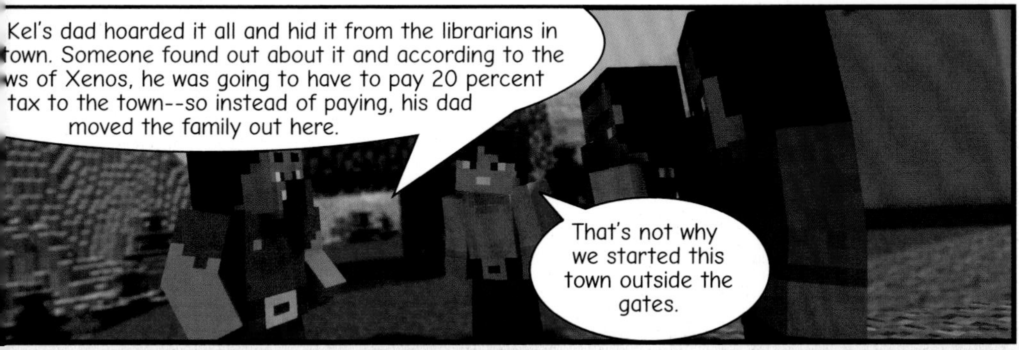
Kel's dad hoarded it all and hid it from the librarians in town. Someone found out about it and according to the ws of Xenos, he was going to have to pay 20 percent tax to the town--so instead of paying, his dad moved the family out here.
That's not why we started this town outside the gates.

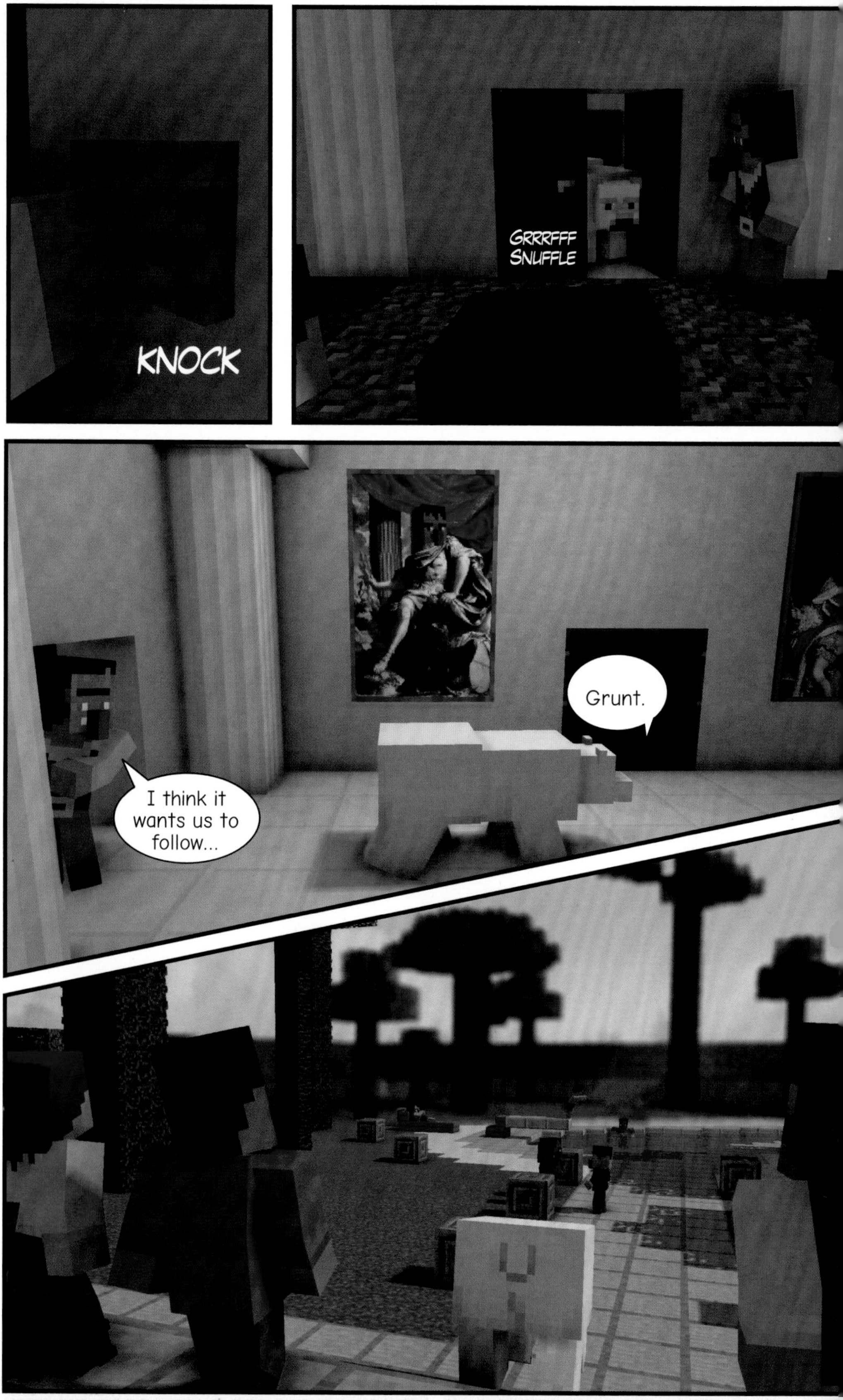
KNOCK
GRRRFFF SNUFFLE
Grunt.
I think it wants us to follow...

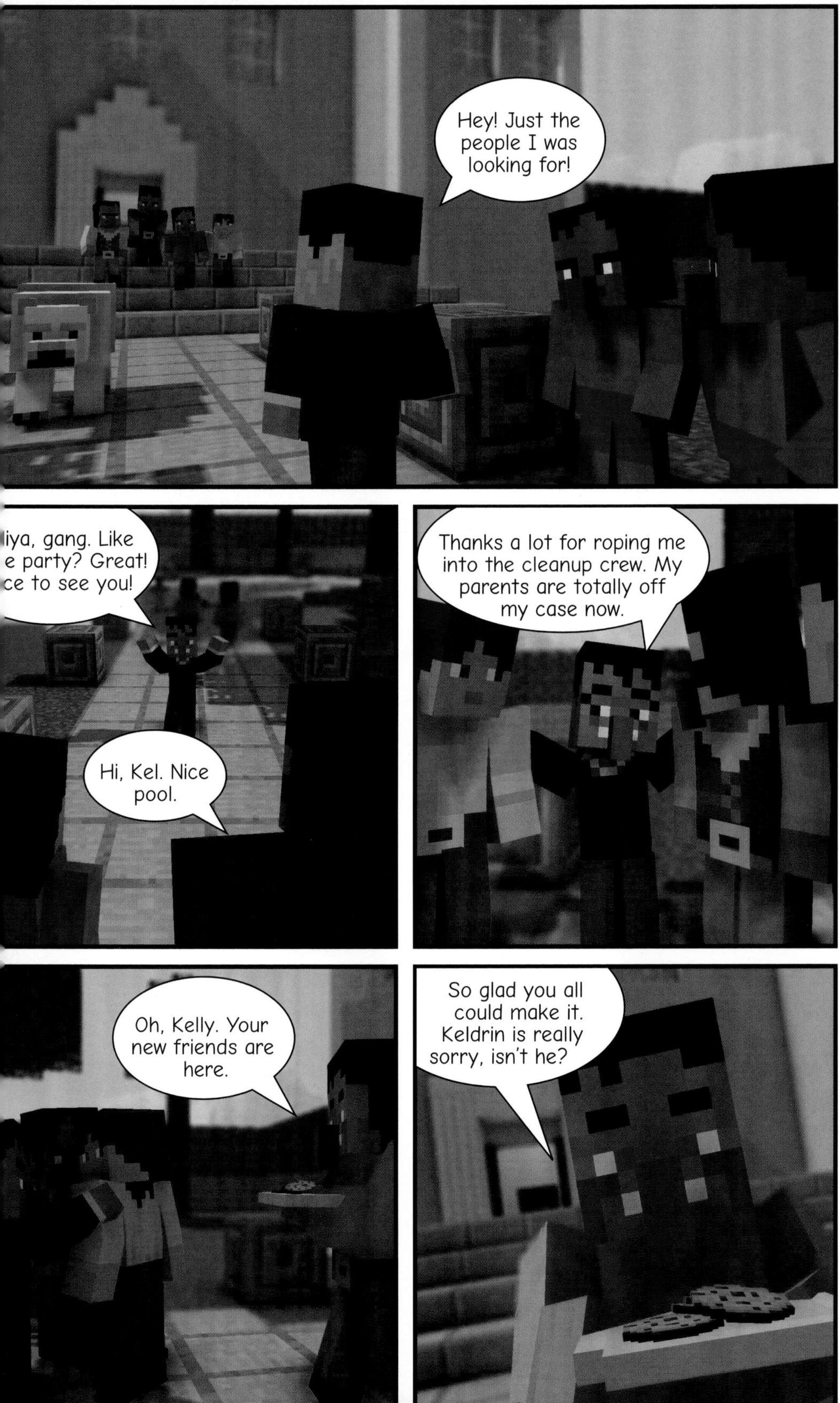
Hey! Just the people I was looking for!
iya, gang. Like e party? Great! ce to see you!
Hi, Kel. Nice pool.
Thanks a lot for roping me into the cleanup crew. My parents are totally off my case now.
Oh, Kelly. Your new friends are here.
So glad you all could make it. Keldrin is really sorry, isn't he?

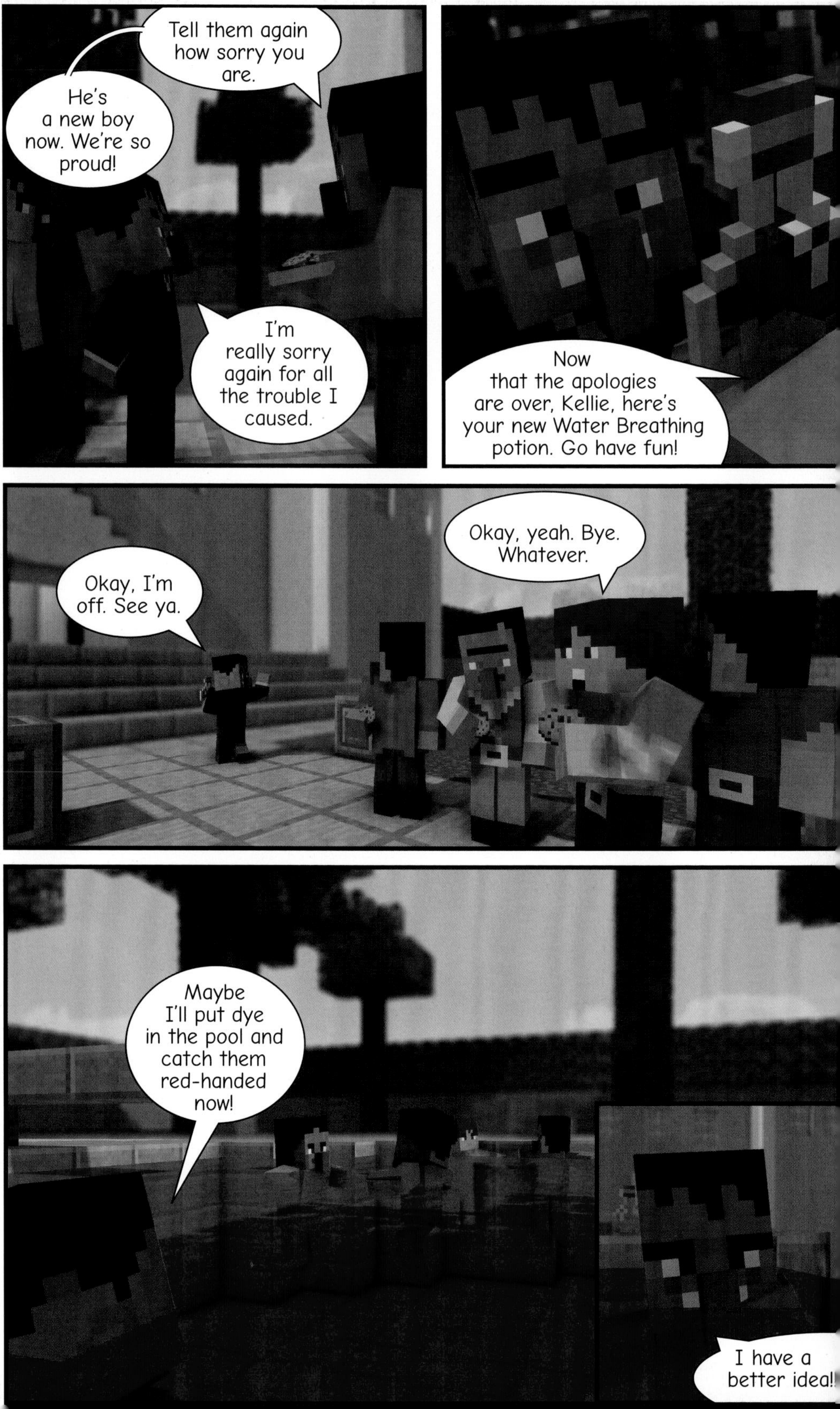
Tell them again how sorry you are.
He's a new boy now. We're so proud!
I'm really sorry again for all the trouble I caused.
Now that the apologies are over, Kellie, here's your new Water Breathing potion. Go have fun!
Okay, I'm off. See ya.
Okay, yeah. Bye. Whatever.
Maybe I'll put dye in the pool and catch them red-handed now!
I have a better idea!

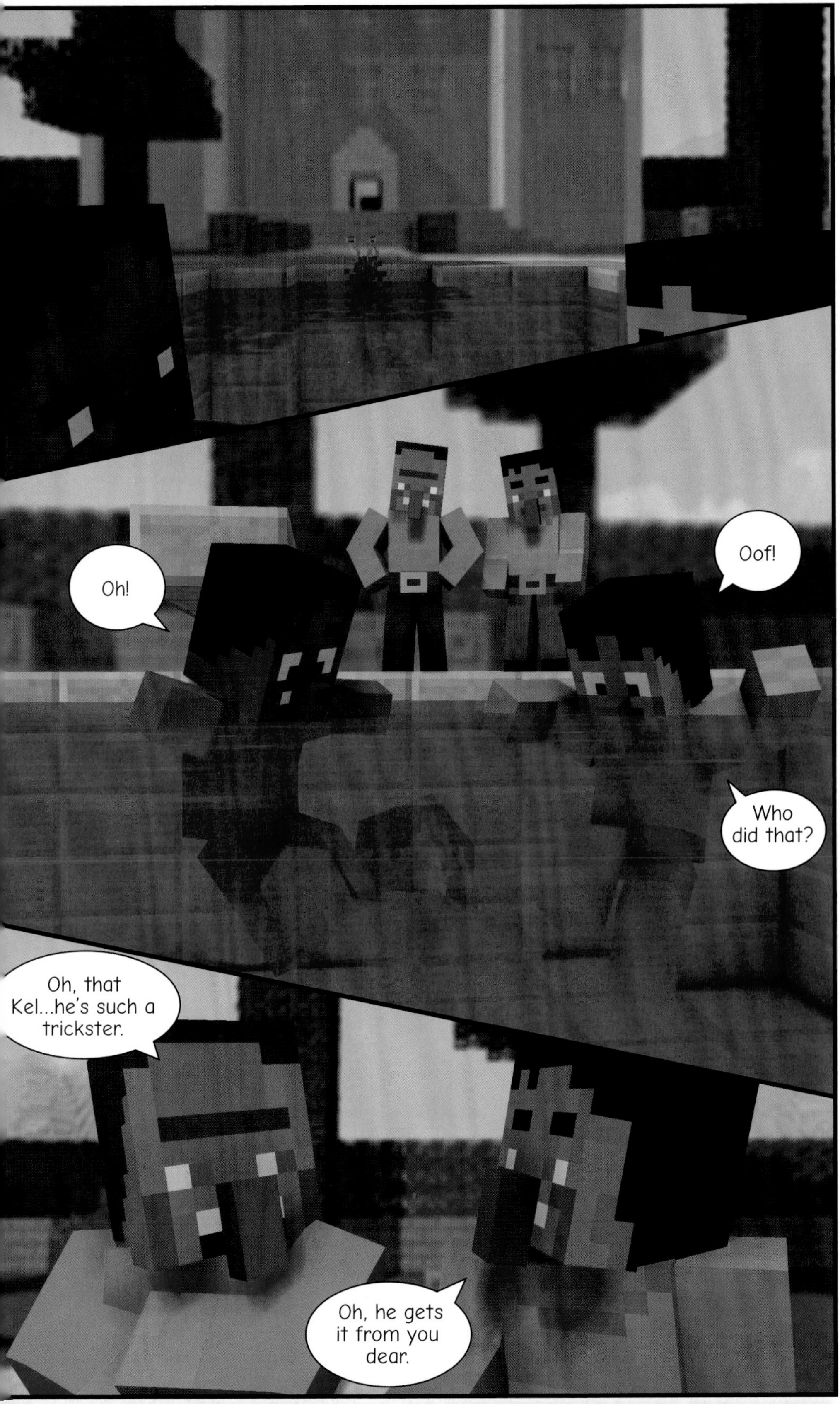
Oh!
Oof!
Who did that?
Oh, that Kel...he's such a trickster.
Oh, he gets it from you dear.

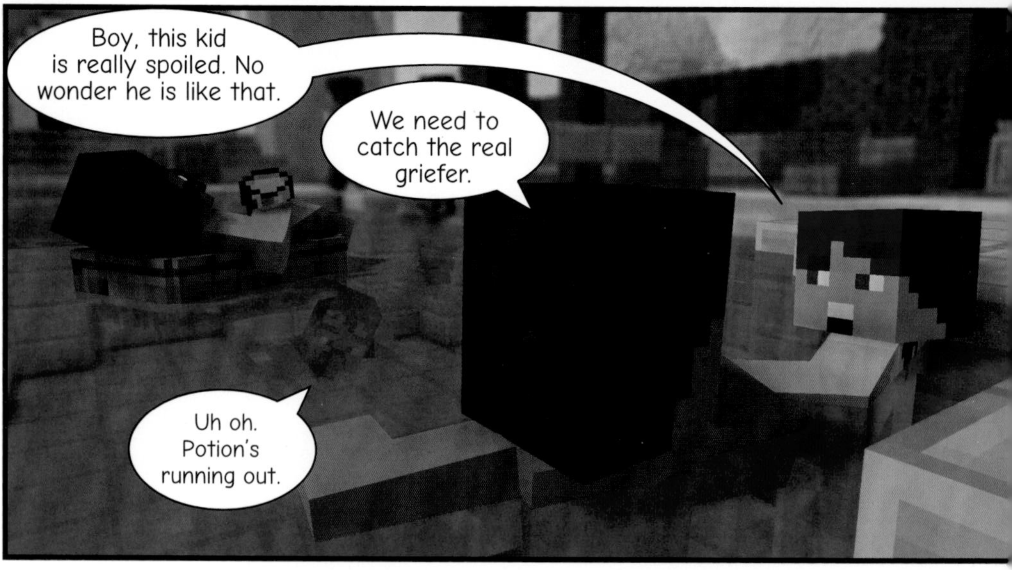
Boy, this kid is really spoiled. No wonder he is like that.
We need to catch the real griefer.
Uh oh. Potion's running out.

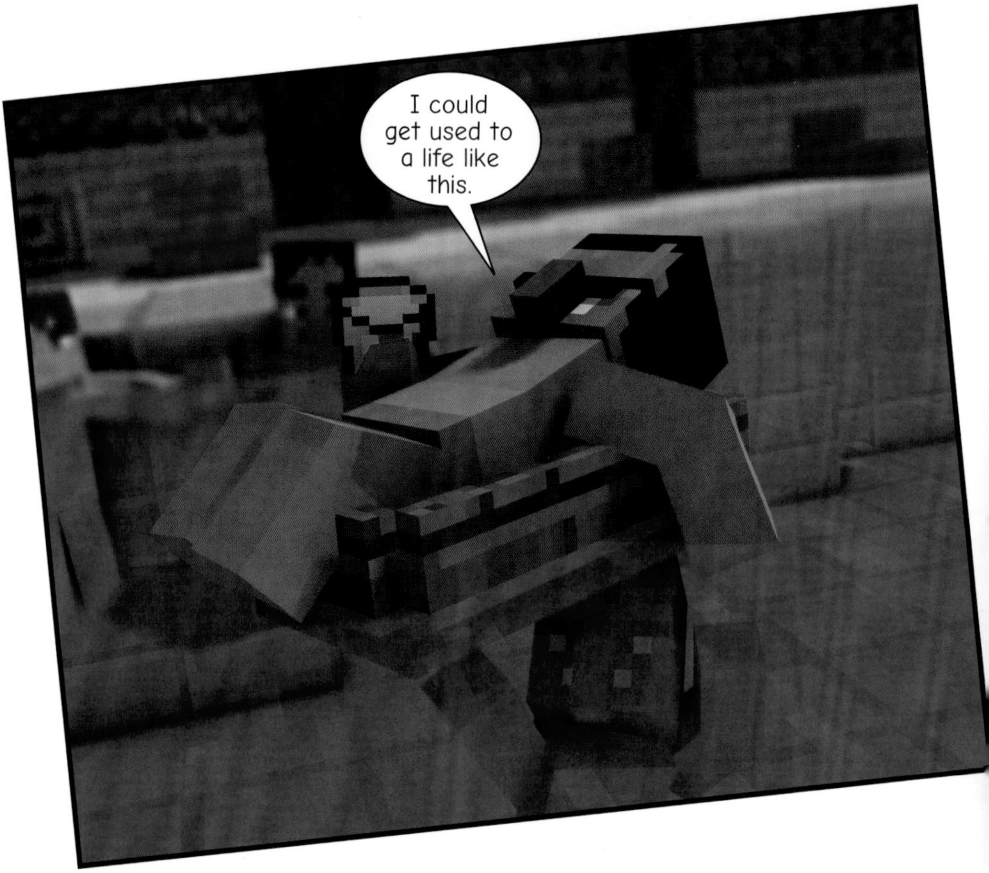
I could get used to a life like this.

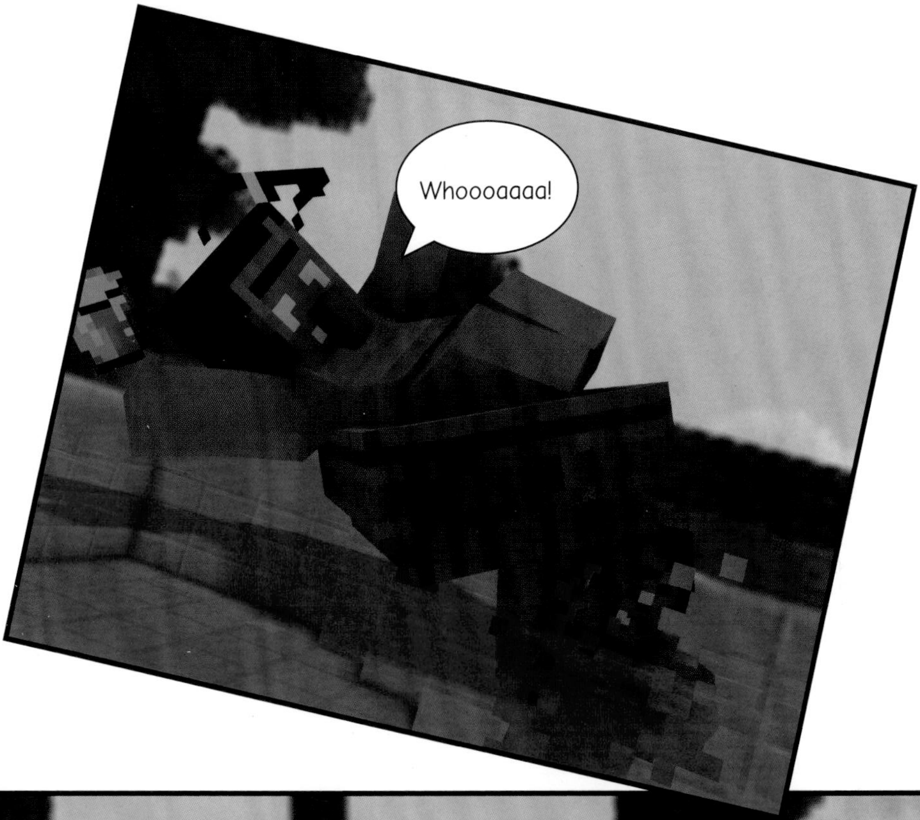
Whoooaaaa!

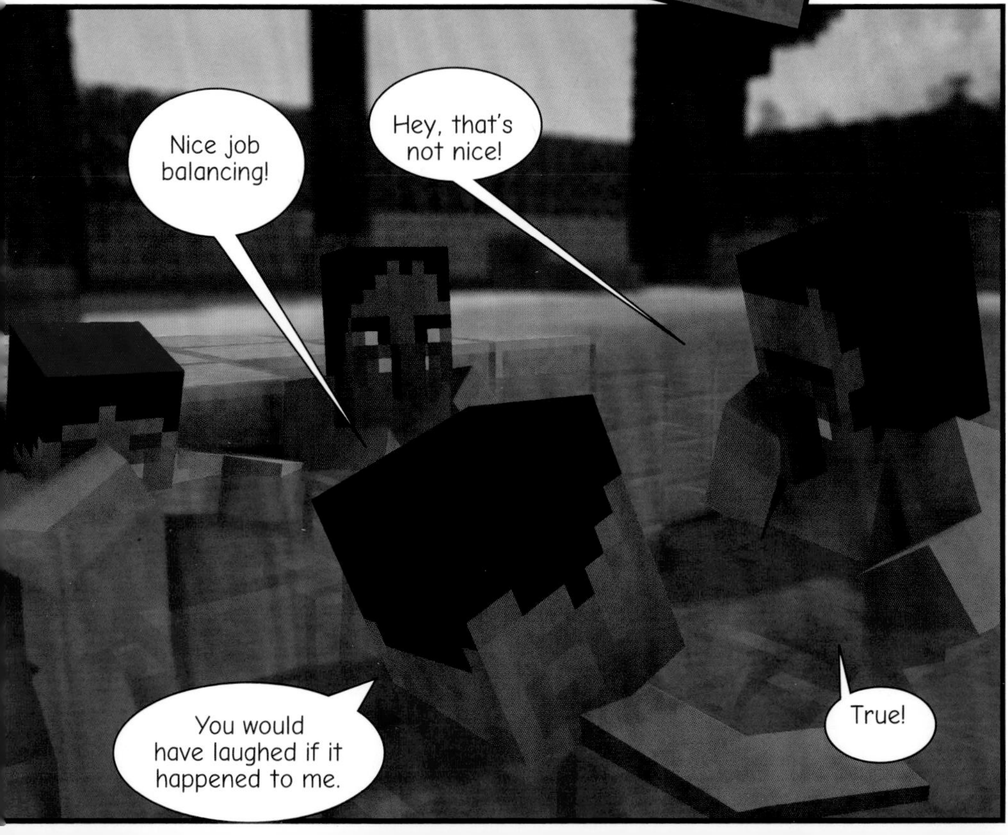
Nice job balancing!
Hey, that's not nice!
You would have laughed if it happened to me.
True!

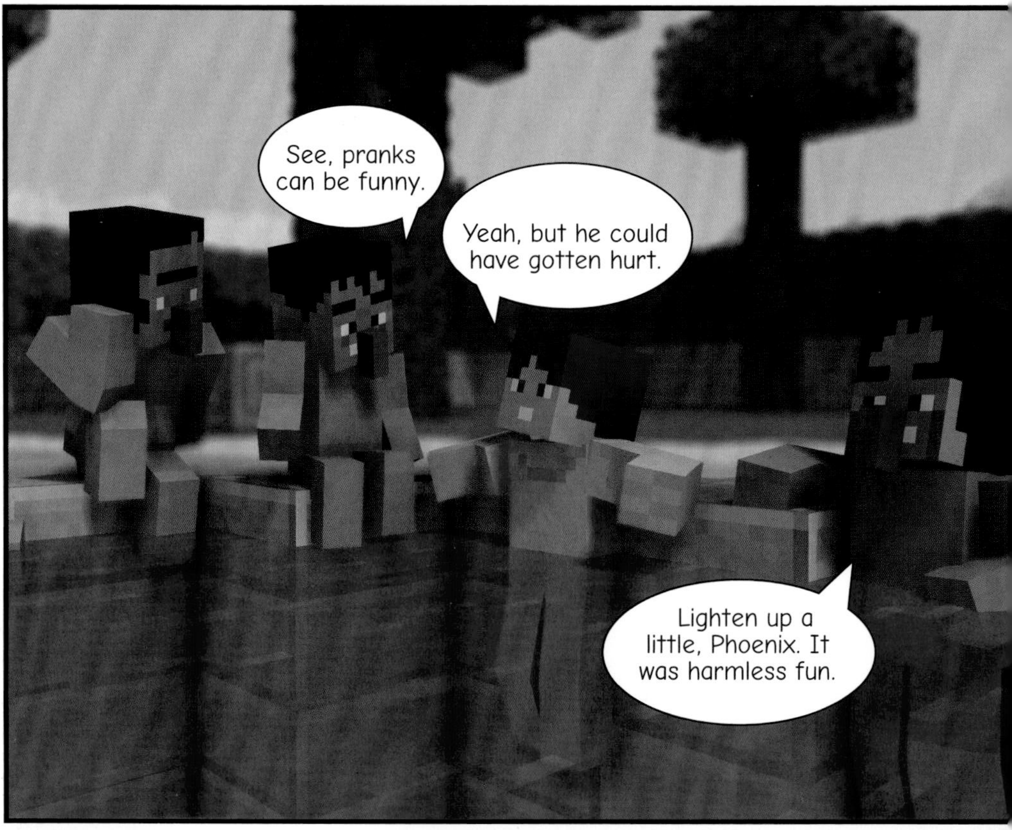
See, pranks can be funny.
Yeah, but he could have gotten hurt.
Lighten up a little, Phoenix. It was harmless fun.

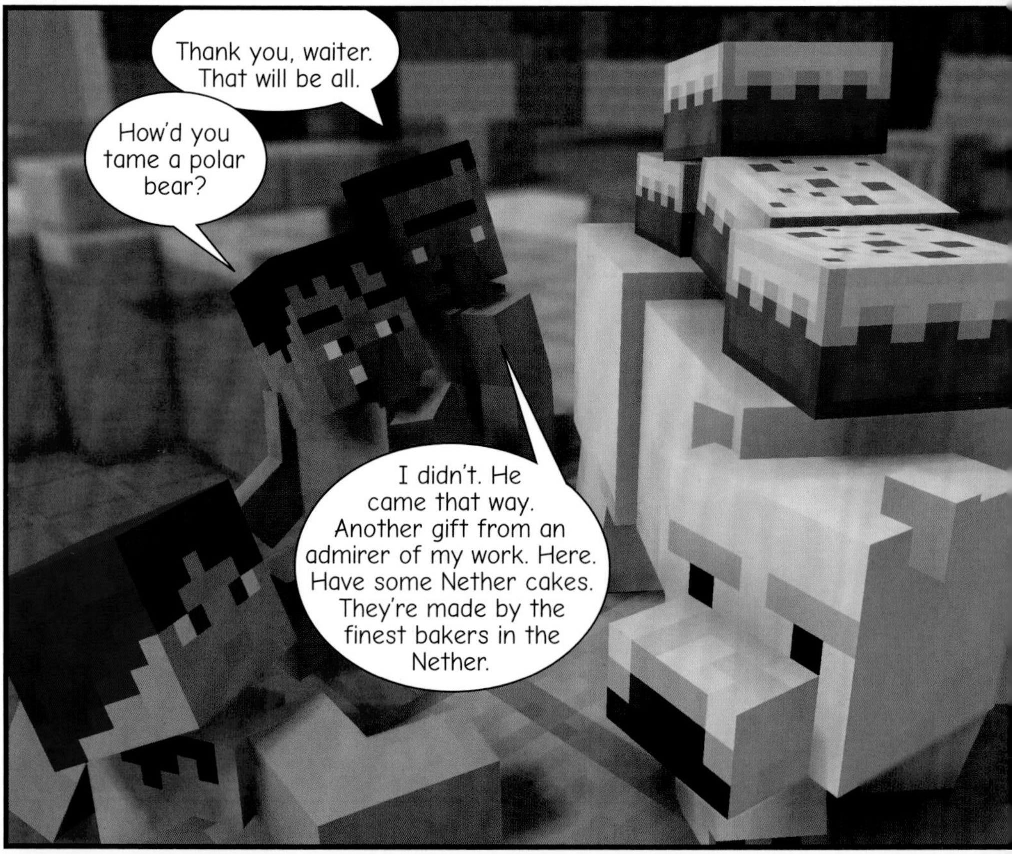
Thank you, waiter. That will be all.
How'd you tame a polar bear?
I didn't. He came that way. Another gift from an admirer of my work. Here. Have some Nether cakes. They're made by the finest bakers in the Nether.

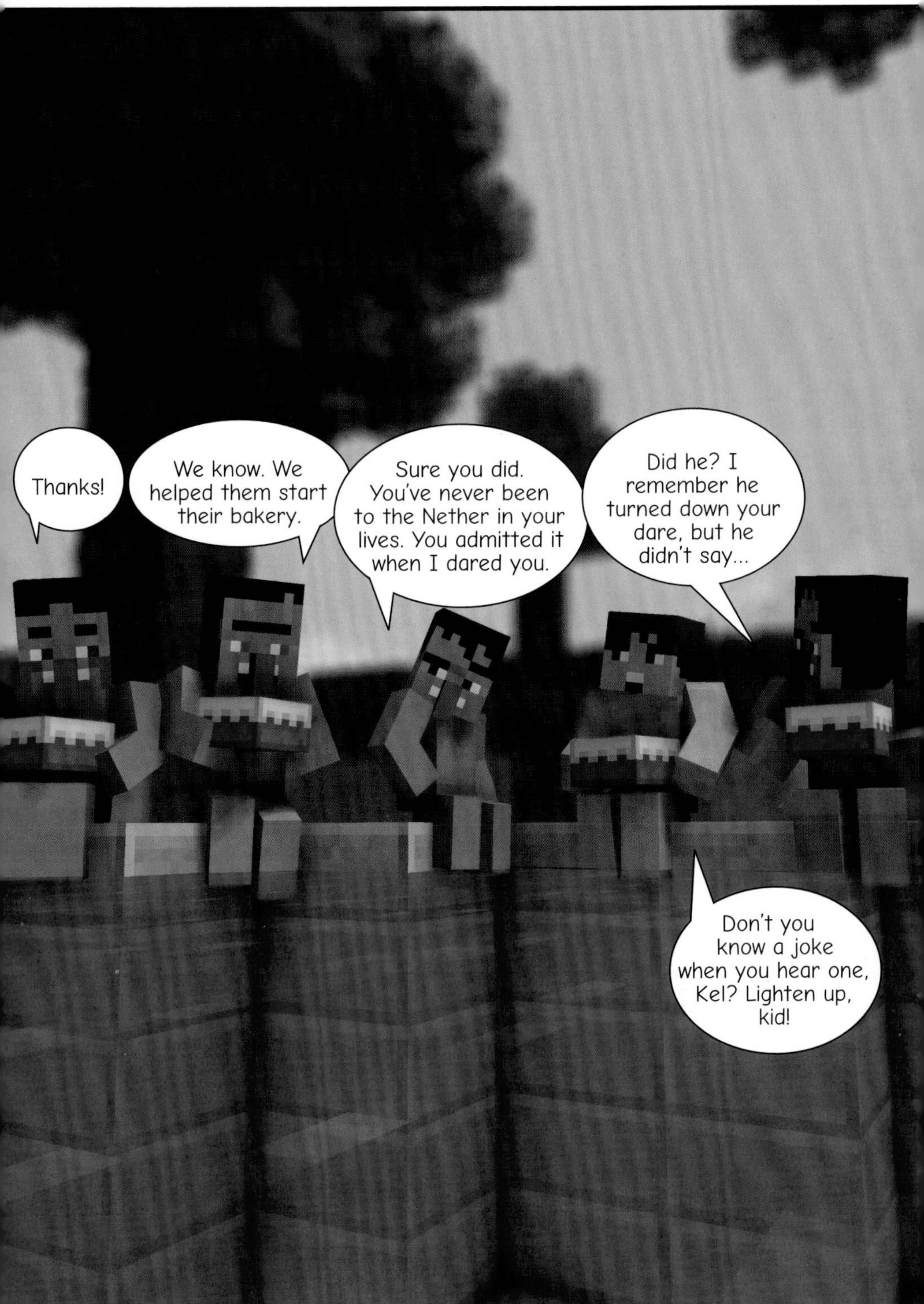
Thanks!
We know. We helped them start their bakery.
Sure you did. You've never been to the Nether in your lives. You admitted it when I dared you.
Did he? I remember he turned down your dare, but he didn't say...
Don't you know a joke when you hear one, Kel? Lighten up, kid!

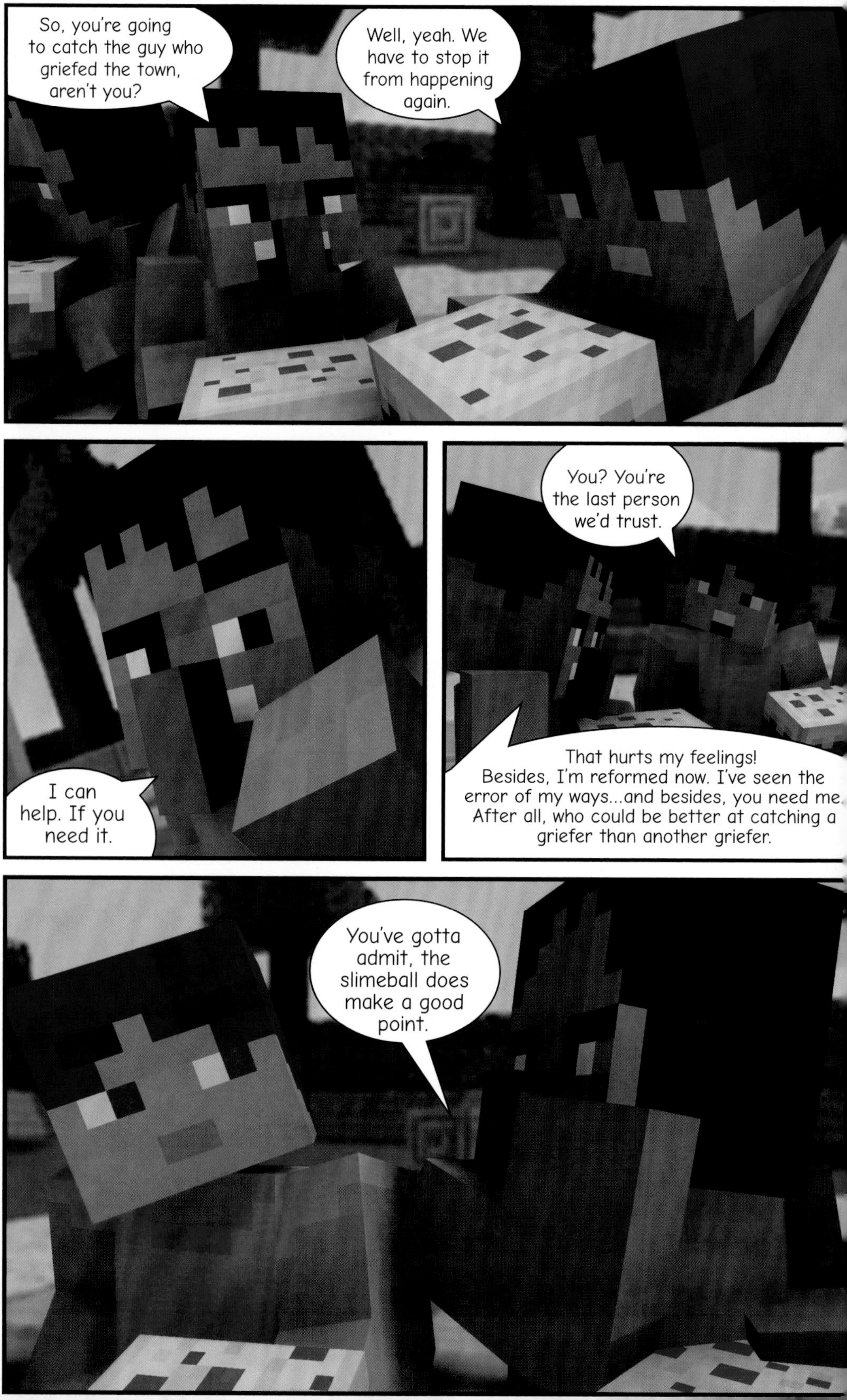
So, you're going to catch the guy who griefed the town, aren't you?
Well, yeah. We have to stop it from happening again.
I can help. If you need it.
You? You're the last person we'd trust.
That hurts my feelings! Besides, I'm reformed now. I've seen the error of my ways...and besides, you need me. After all, who could be better at catching a griefer than another griefer.
You've gotta admit, the slimeball does make a good point.

CHAPTER 8

THE PLOT THICKENS

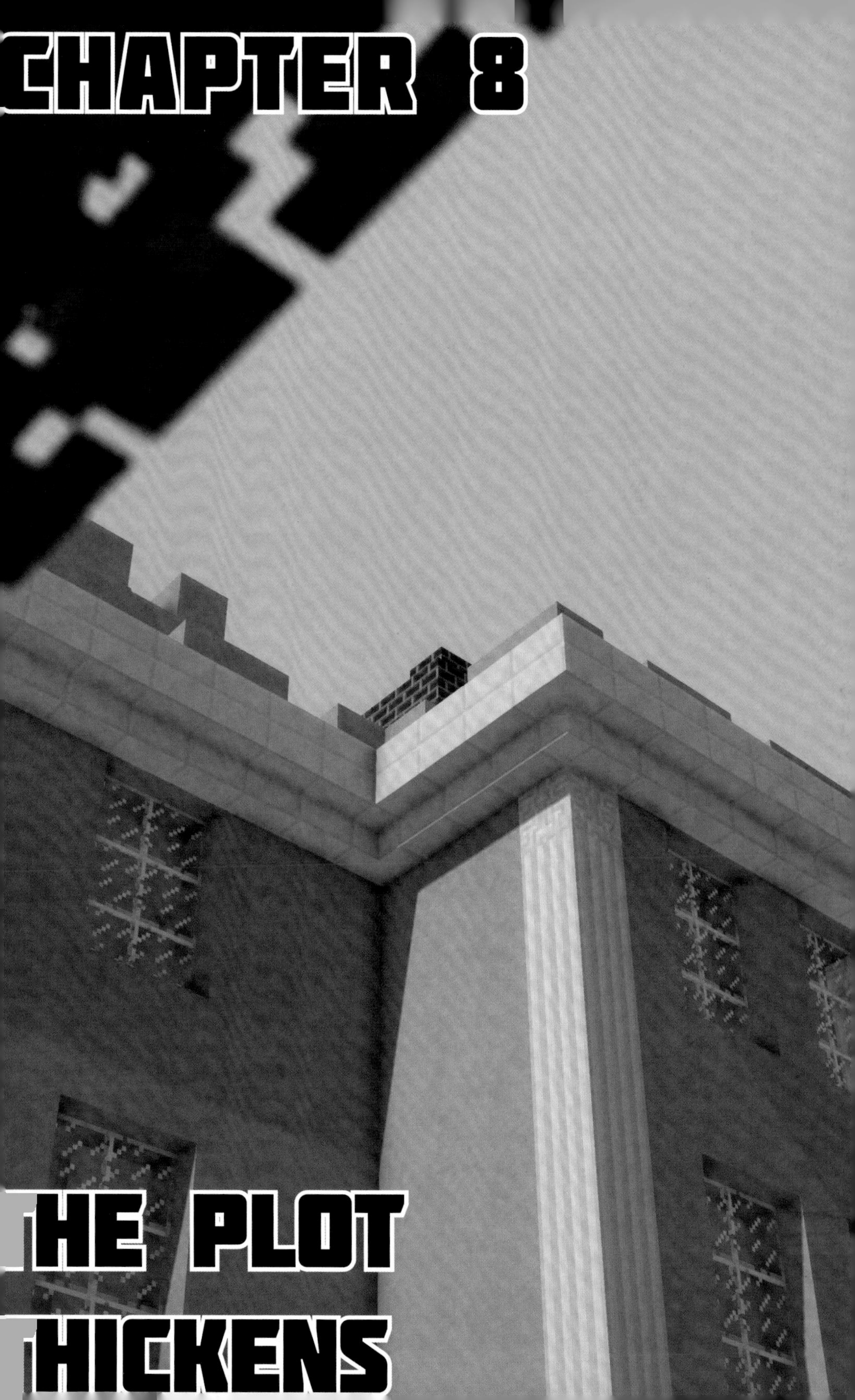

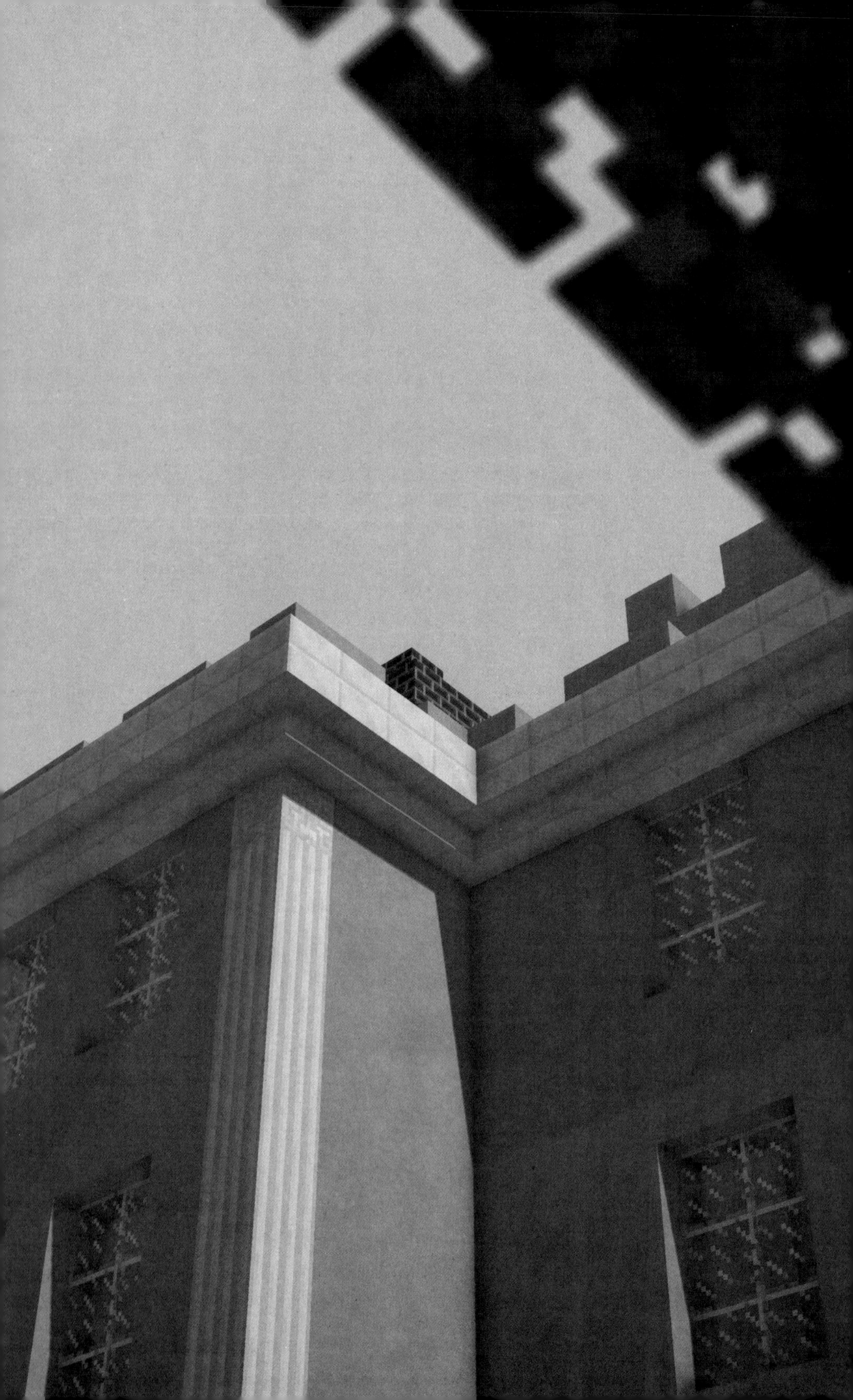

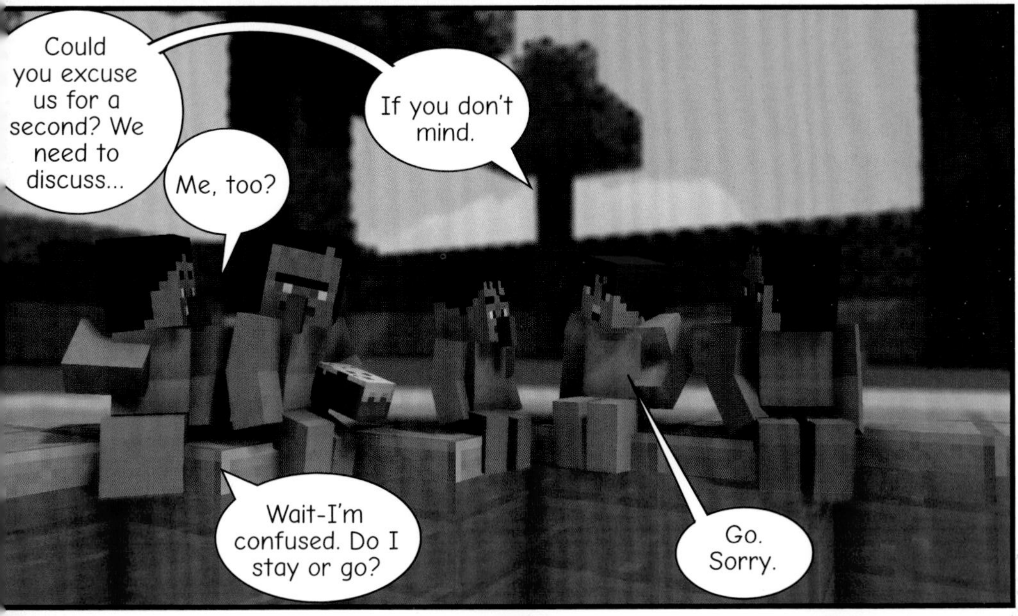
Could you excuse us for a second? We need to discuss...
If you don't mind.
Me, too?
Wait-I'm confused. Do I stay or go?
Go. Sorry.

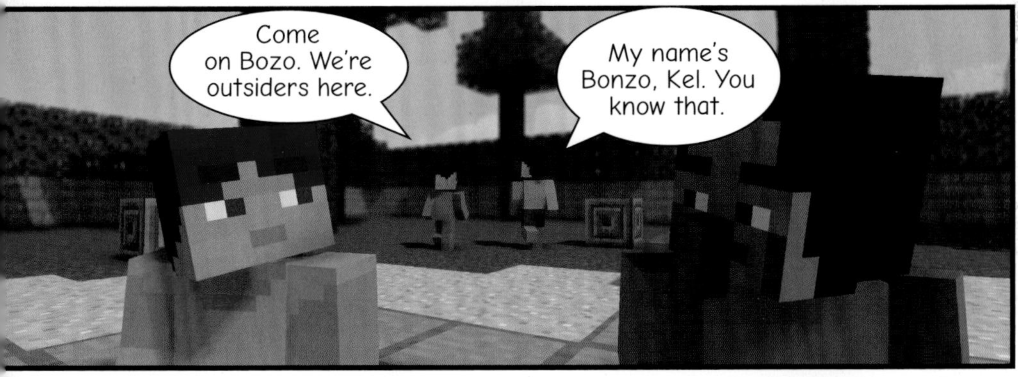
Come on Bozo. We're outsiders here.
My name's Bonzo, Kel. You know that.

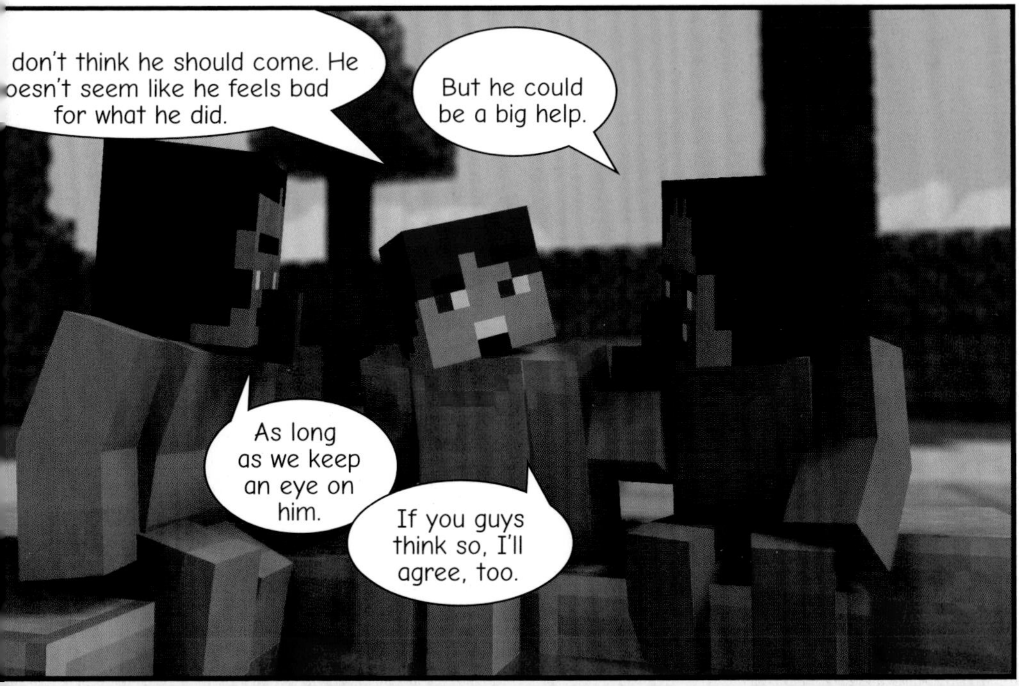
don't think he should come. He oesn't seem like he feels bad for what he did.
But he could be a big help.
As long as we keep an eye on him.
If you guys think so, I'll agree, too.

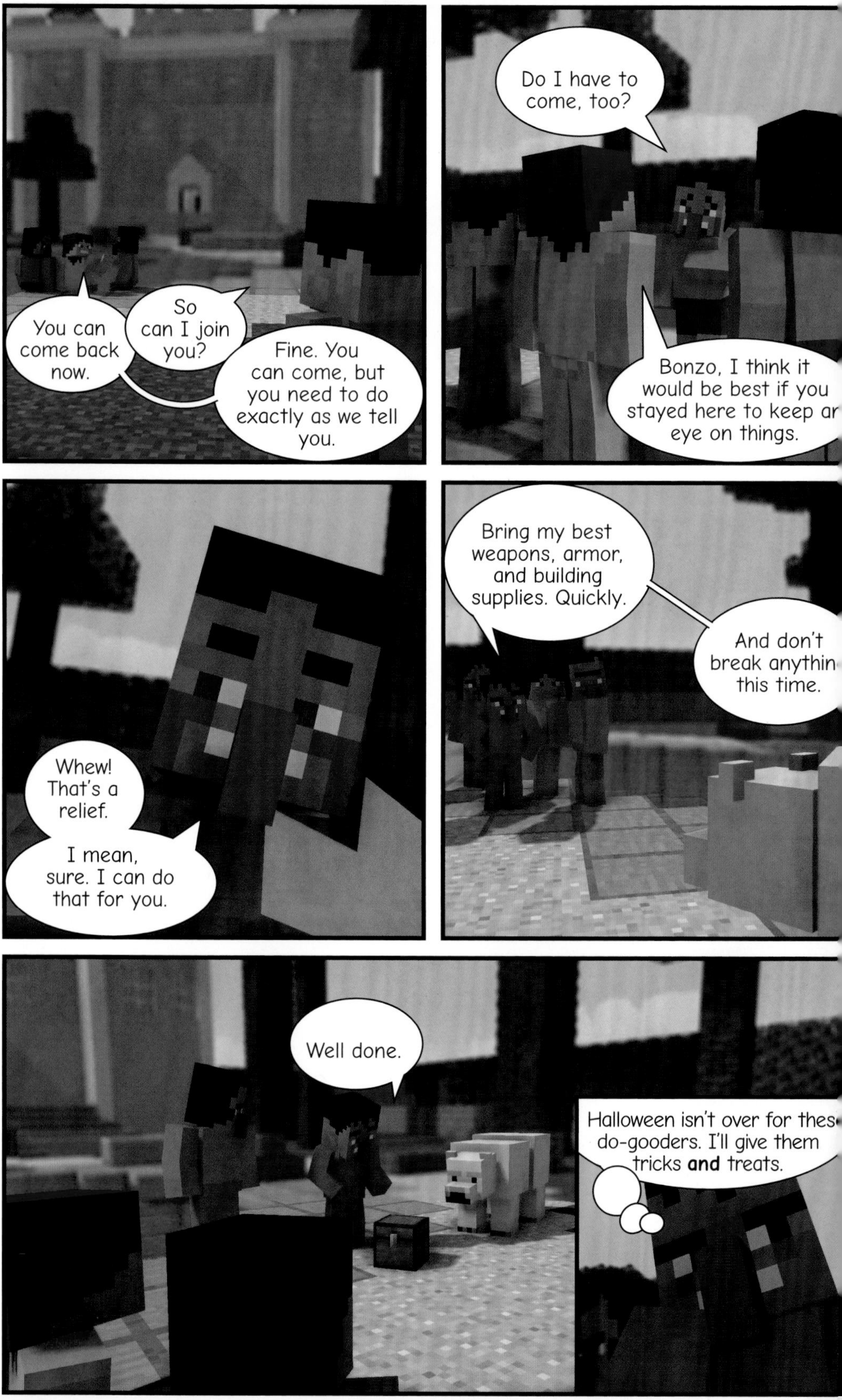
You can come back now.
So can I join you?
Fine. You can come, but you need to do exactly as we tell you.
Do I have to come, too?
Bonzo, I think it would be best if you stayed here to keep ar eye on things.
Whew! That's a relief.
I mean, sure. I can do that for you.
Bring my best weapons, armor, and building supplies. Quickly.
And don't break anythin this time.
Well done.
Halloween isn't over for thes do-gooders. I'll give them tricks **and** treats.

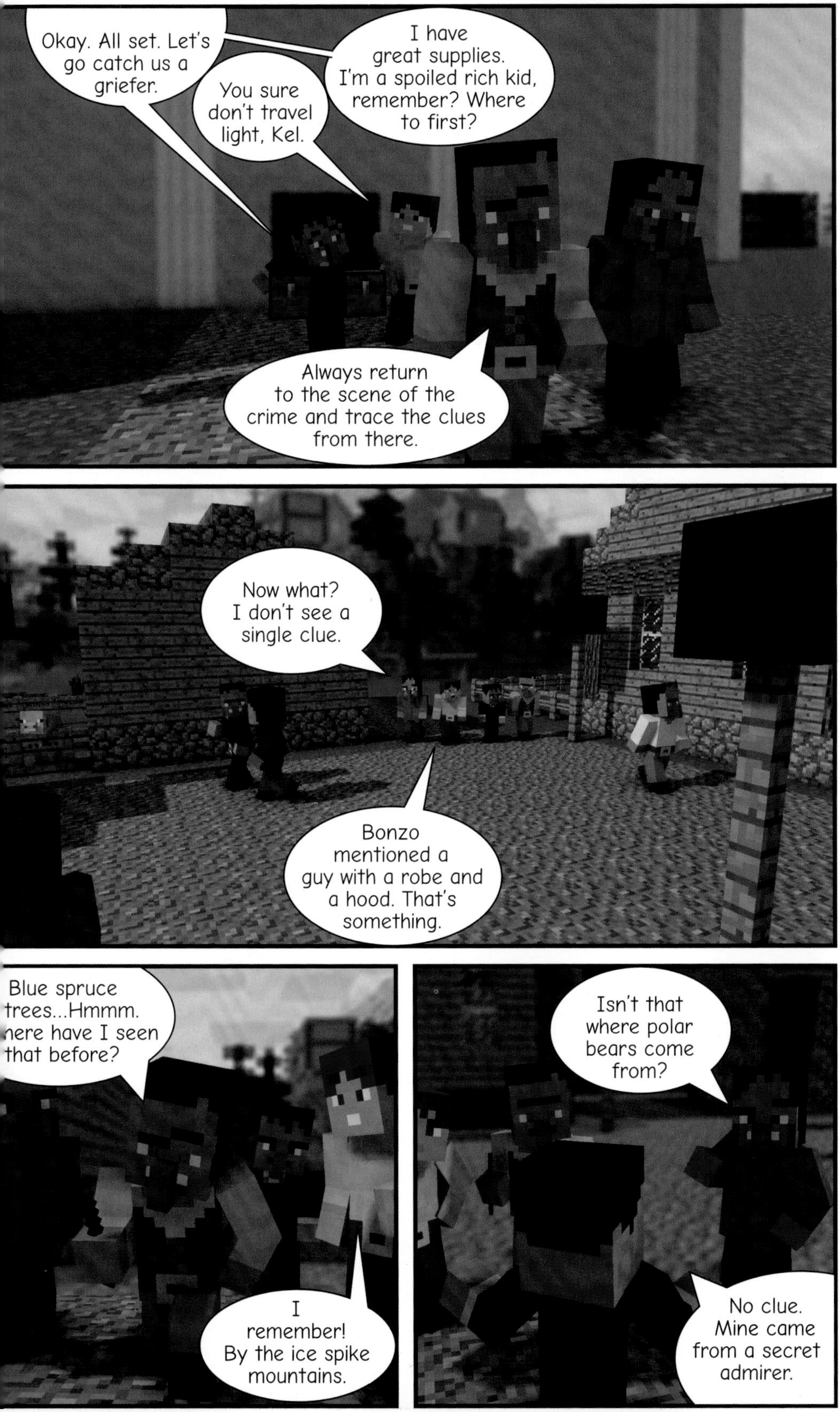

Okay. All set. Let's go catch us a griefer.
I have great supplies. I'm a spoiled rich kid, remember? Where to first?
You sure don't travel light, Kel.
Always return to the scene of the crime and trace the clues from there.
Now what? I don't see a single clue.
Bonzo mentioned a guy with a robe and a hood. That's something.
Blue spruce trees...Hmmm. here have I seen that before?
I remember! By the ice spike mountains.
Isn't that where polar bears come from?
No clue. Mine came from a secret admirer.

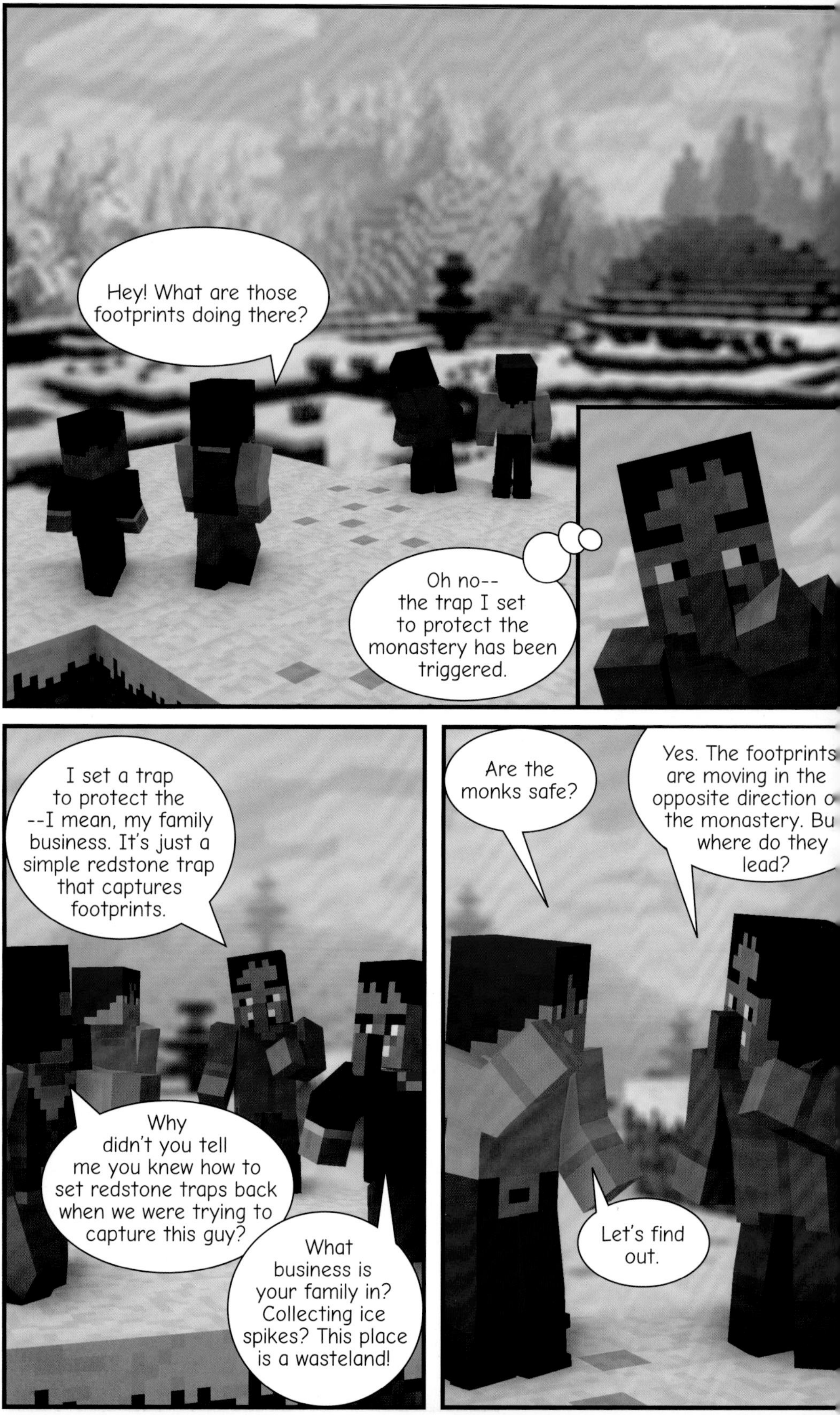
Hey! What are those footprints doing there?
Oh no-- the trap I set to protect the monastery has been triggered.
I set a trap to protect the --I mean, my family business. It's just a simple redstone trap that captures footprints.
Why didn't you tell me you knew how to set redstone traps back when we were trying to capture this guy?
What business is your family in? Collecting ice spikes? This place is a wasteland!
Are the monks safe?
Yes. The footprints are moving in the opposite direction o the monastery. Bu where do they lead?
Let's find out.

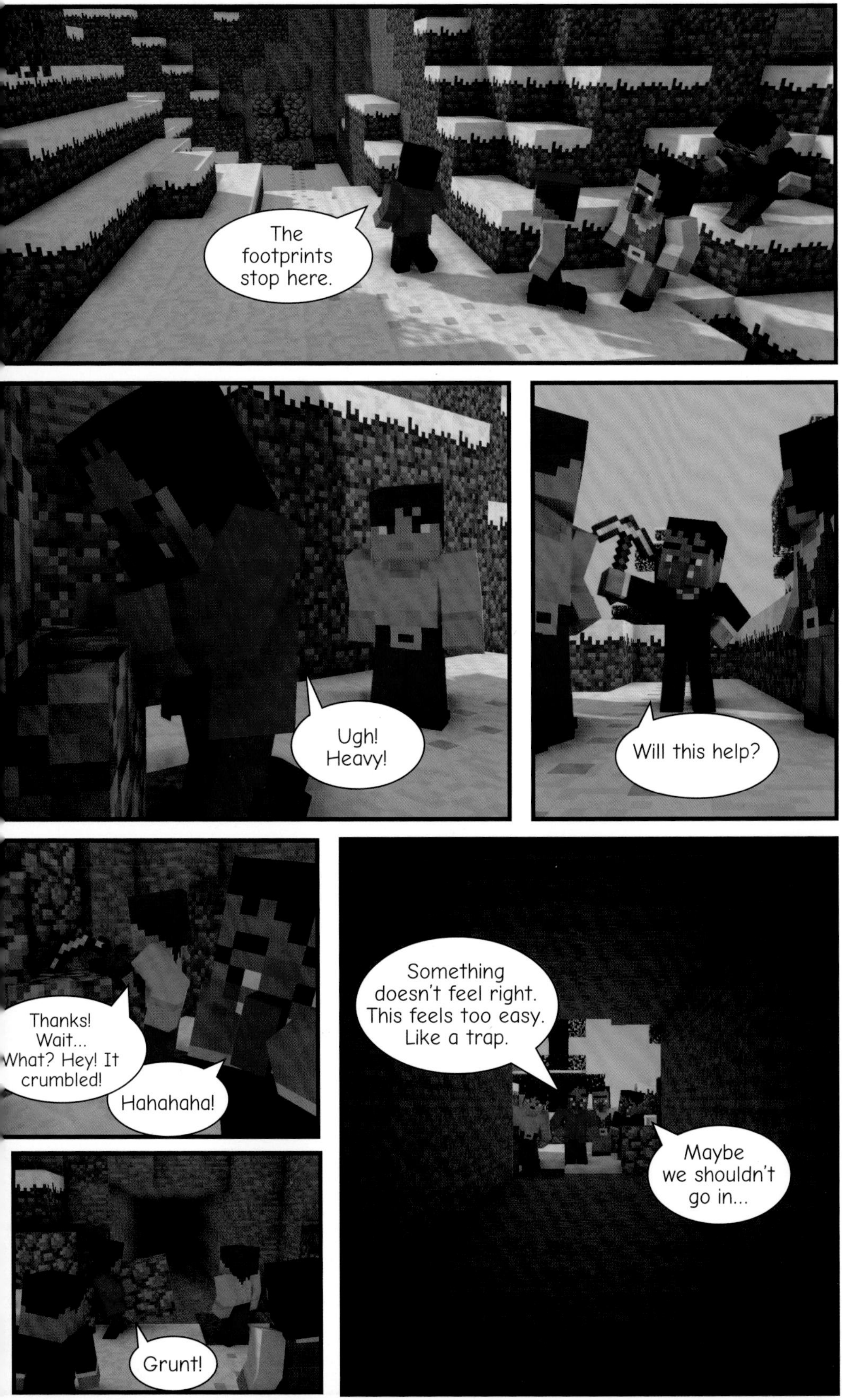
The footprints stop here.
Ugh! Heavy!
Will this help?
Thanks! Wait... What? Hey! It crumbled!
Hahahaha!
Grunt!
Something doesn't feel right. This feels too easy. Like a trap.
Maybe we shouldn't go in...

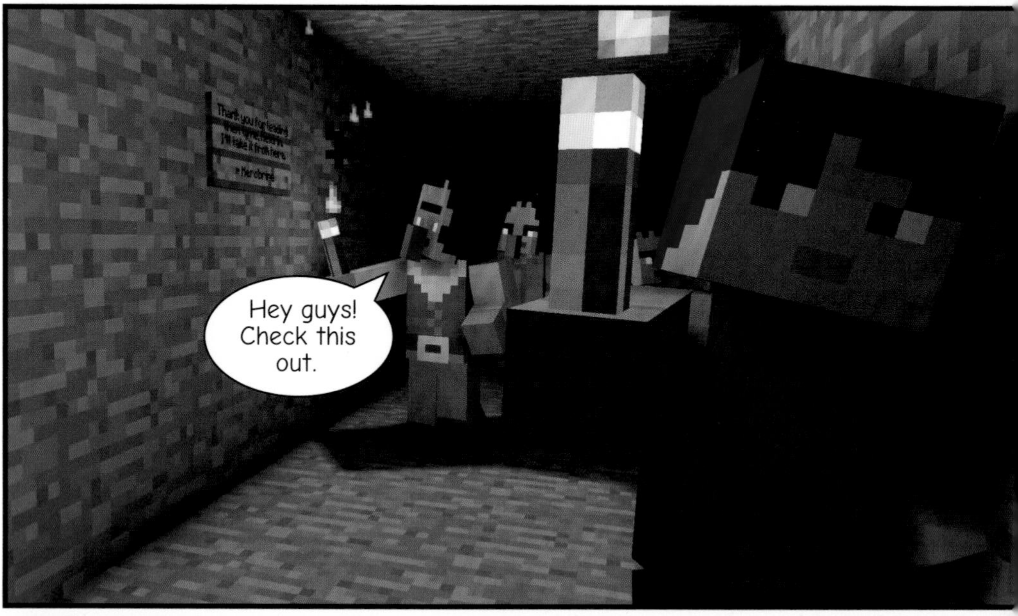
Hey guys! Check this out.

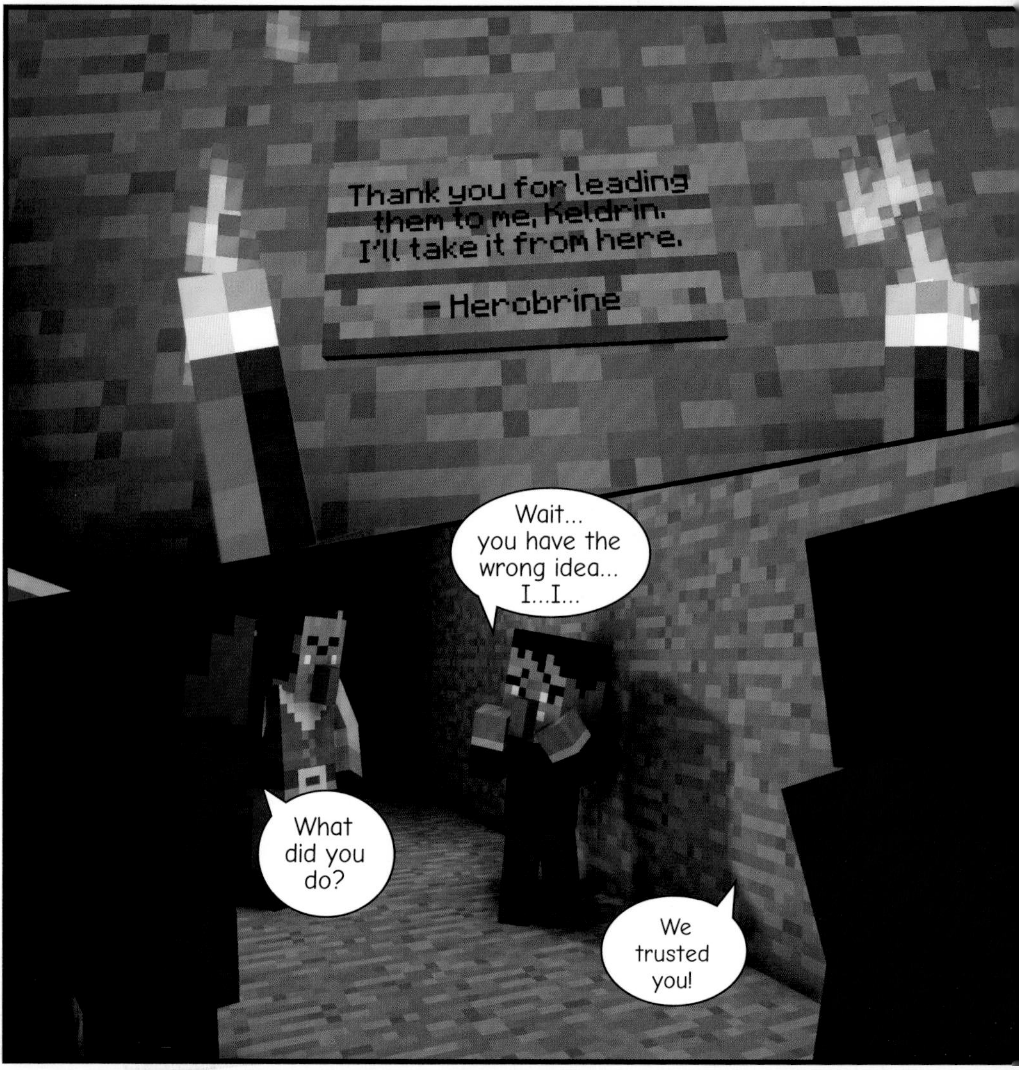
Thank you for leading them to me, Keldrin. I'll take it from here.
- Herobrine
Wait... you have the wrong idea... I...I...
What did you do?
We trusted you!

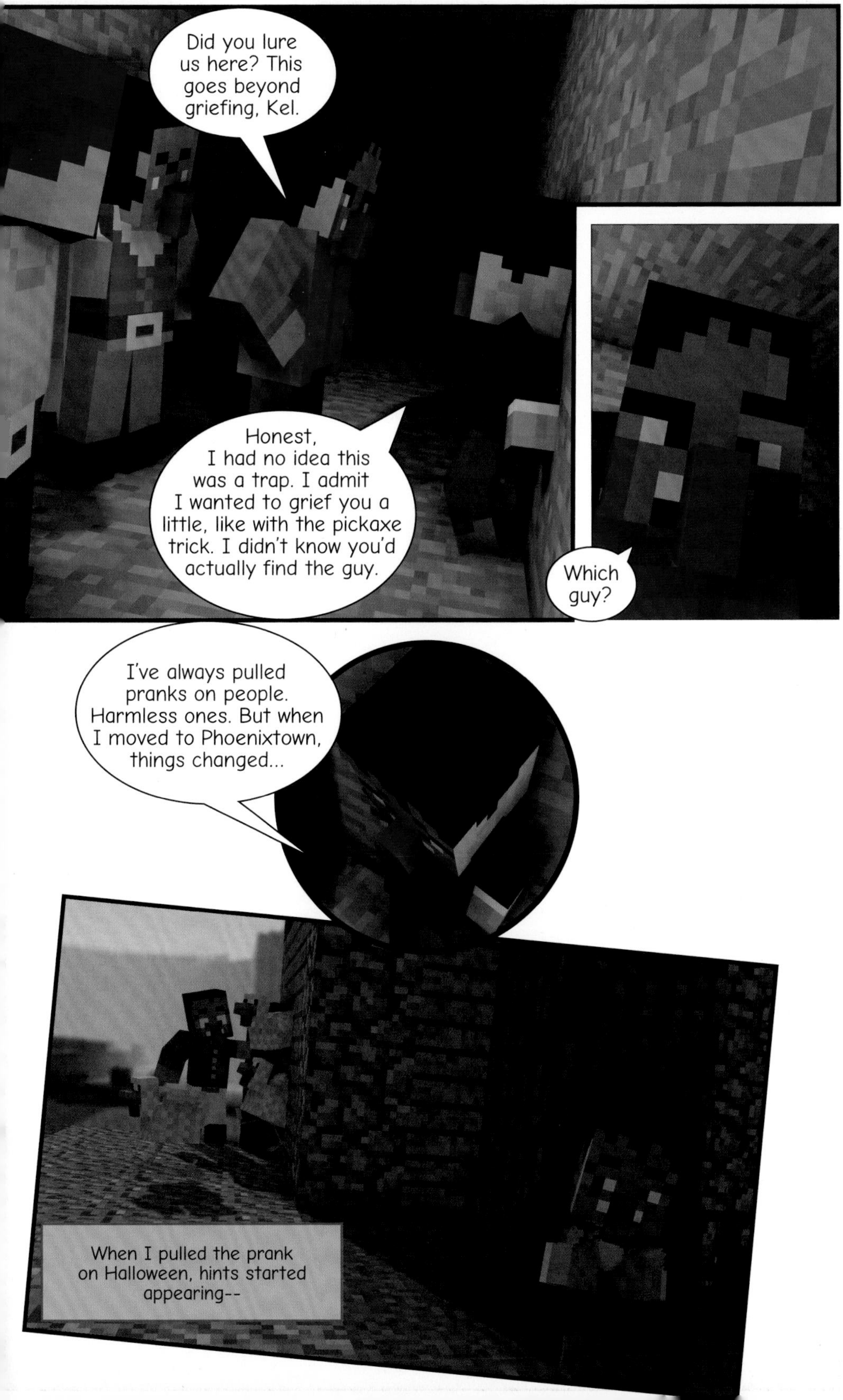
Did you lure us here? This goes beyond griefing, Kel.
Honest, I had no idea this was a trap. I admit I wanted to grief you a little, like with the pickaxe trick. I didn't know you'd actually find the guy.
Which guy?
I've always pulled pranks on people. Harmless ones. But when I moved to Phoenixtown, things changed...
When I pulled the prank on Halloween, hints started appearing--

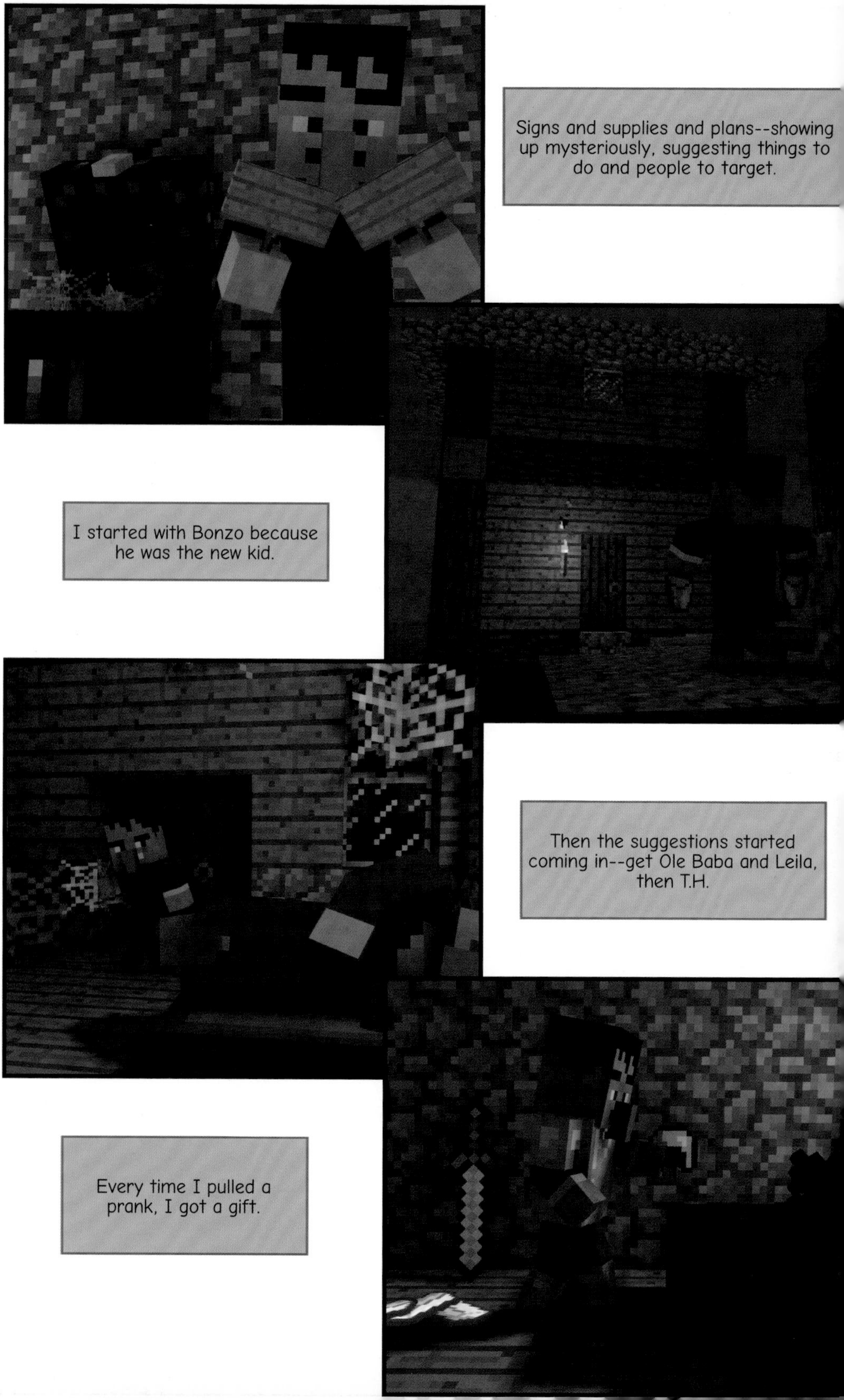
Signs and supplies and plans--showing up mysteriously, suggesting things to do and people to target.
I started with Bonzo because he was the new kid.
Then the suggestions started coming in--get Ole Baba and Leila, then T.H.
Every time I pulled a prank, I got a gift.

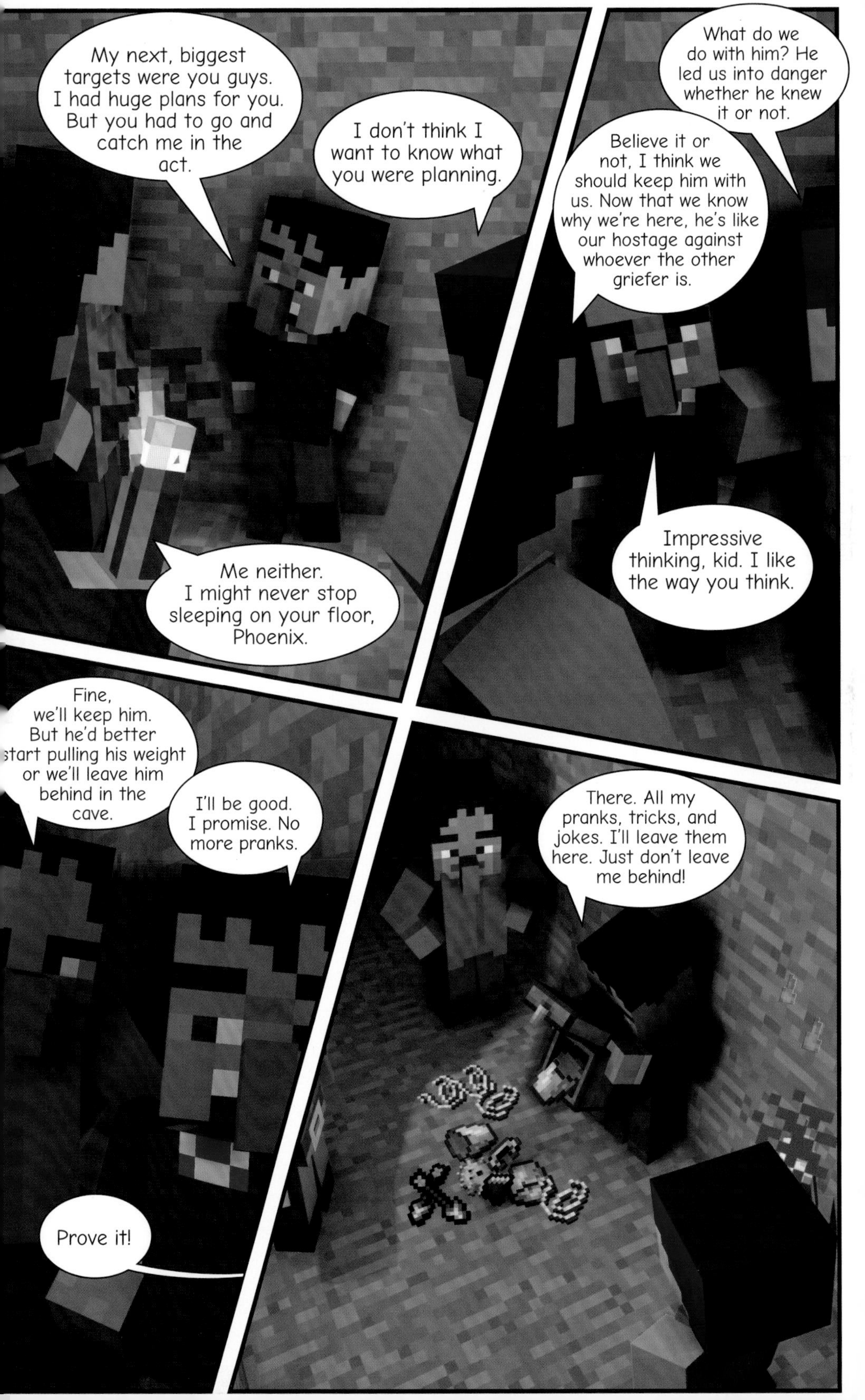
My next, biggest targets were you guys. I had huge plans for you. But you had to go and catch me in the act.
I don't think I want to know what you were planning.
Me neither. I might never stop sleeping on your floor, Phoenix.
What do we do with him? He led us into danger whether he knew it or not.
Believe it or not, I think we should keep him with us. Now that we know why we're here, he's like our hostage against whoever the other griefer is.
Impressive thinking, kid. I like the way you think.
Fine, we'll keep him. But he'd better start pulling his weight or we'll leave him behind in the cave.
I'll be good. I promise. No more pranks.
Prove it!
There. All my pranks, tricks, and jokes. I'll leave them here. Just don't leave me behind!

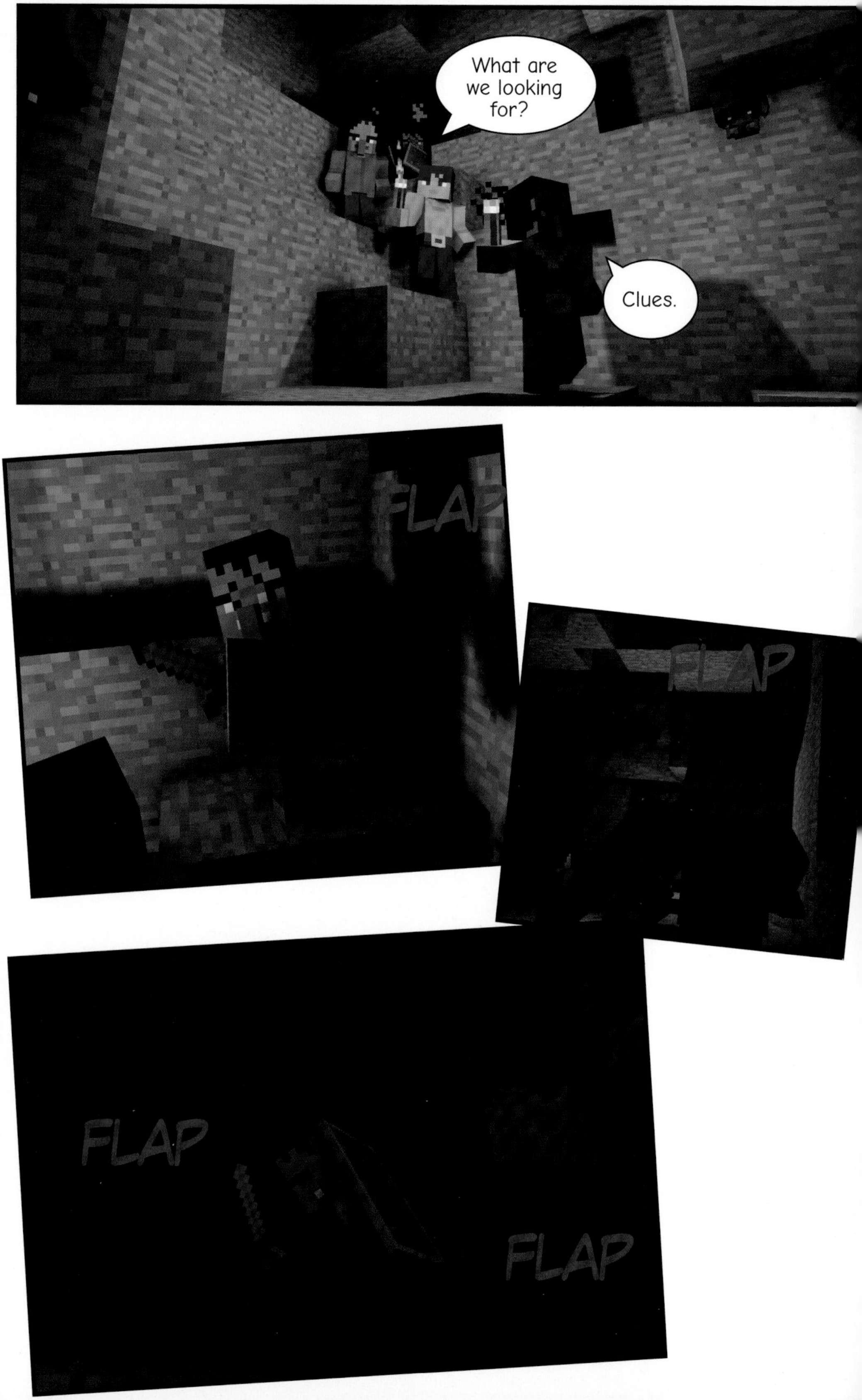
What are we looking for?
Clues.
FLAP
FLAP
FLAP
FLAP

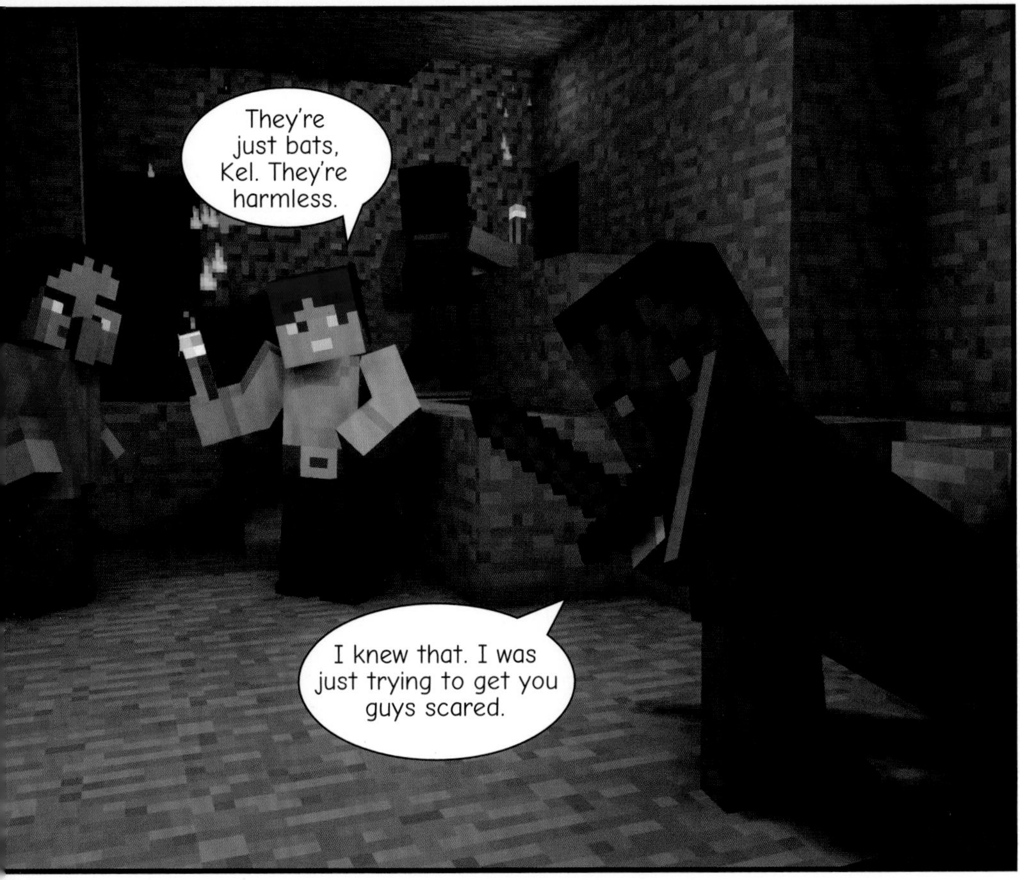
They're just bats, Kel. They're harmless.
I knew that. I was just trying to get you guys scared.

HUMMM

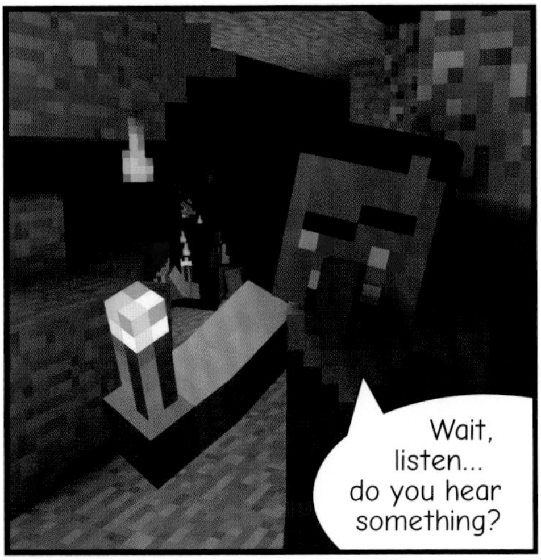
Wait, listen... do you hear something?

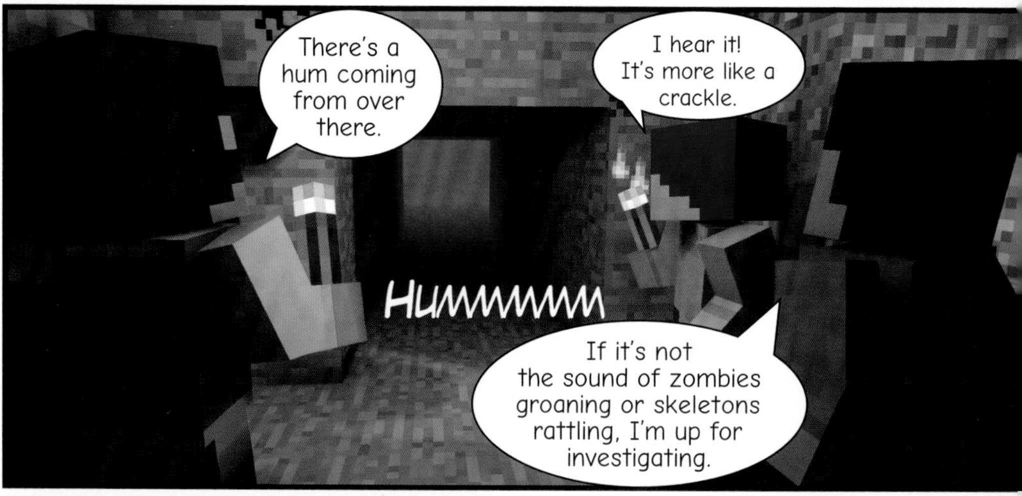
There's a hum coming from over there.
I hear it! It's more like a crackle.
HUMMMMMM
If it's not the sound of zombies groaning or skeletons rattling, I'm up for investigating.

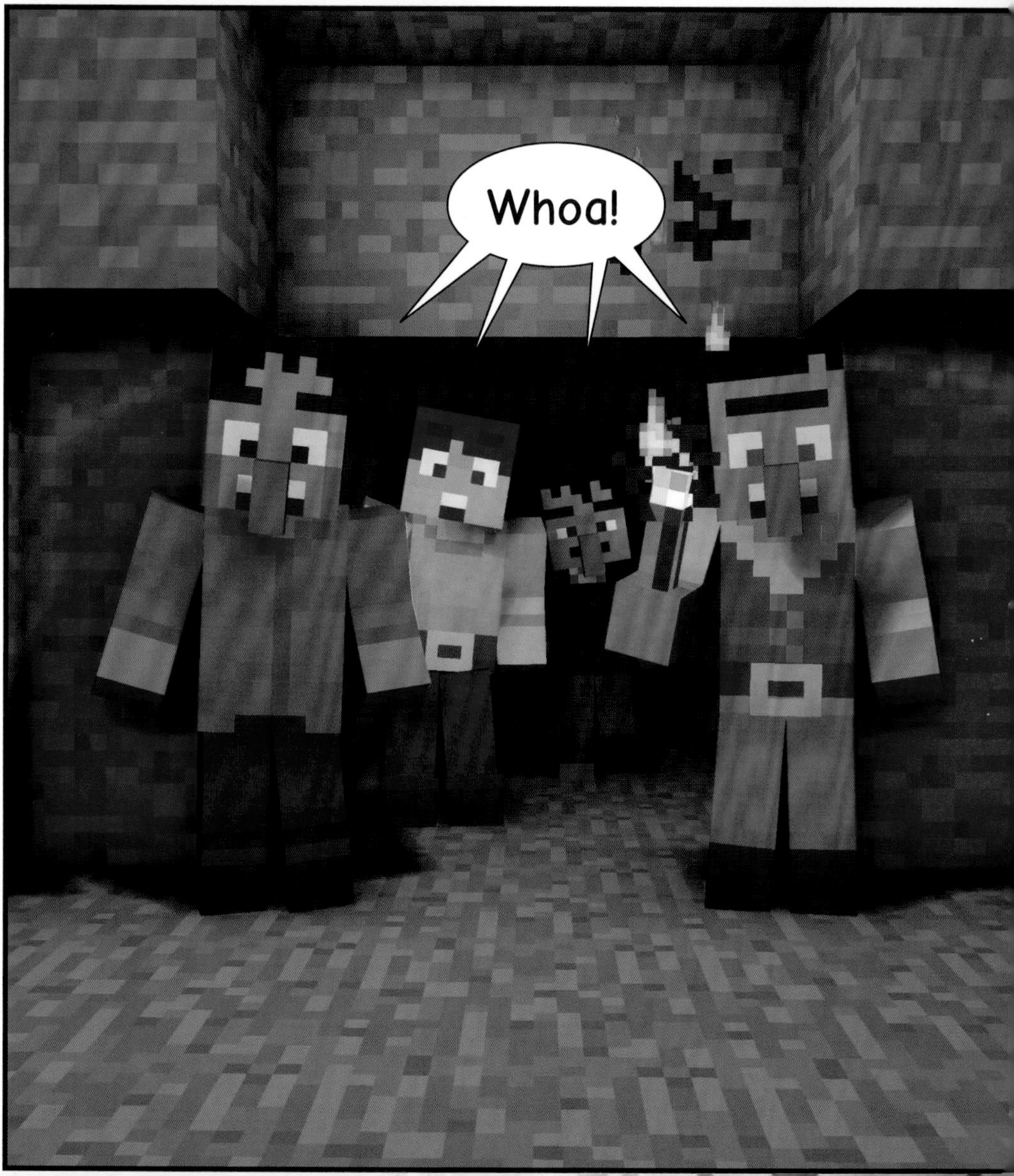
Whoa!

CHAPTER 9

DOWN TO THE NETHER

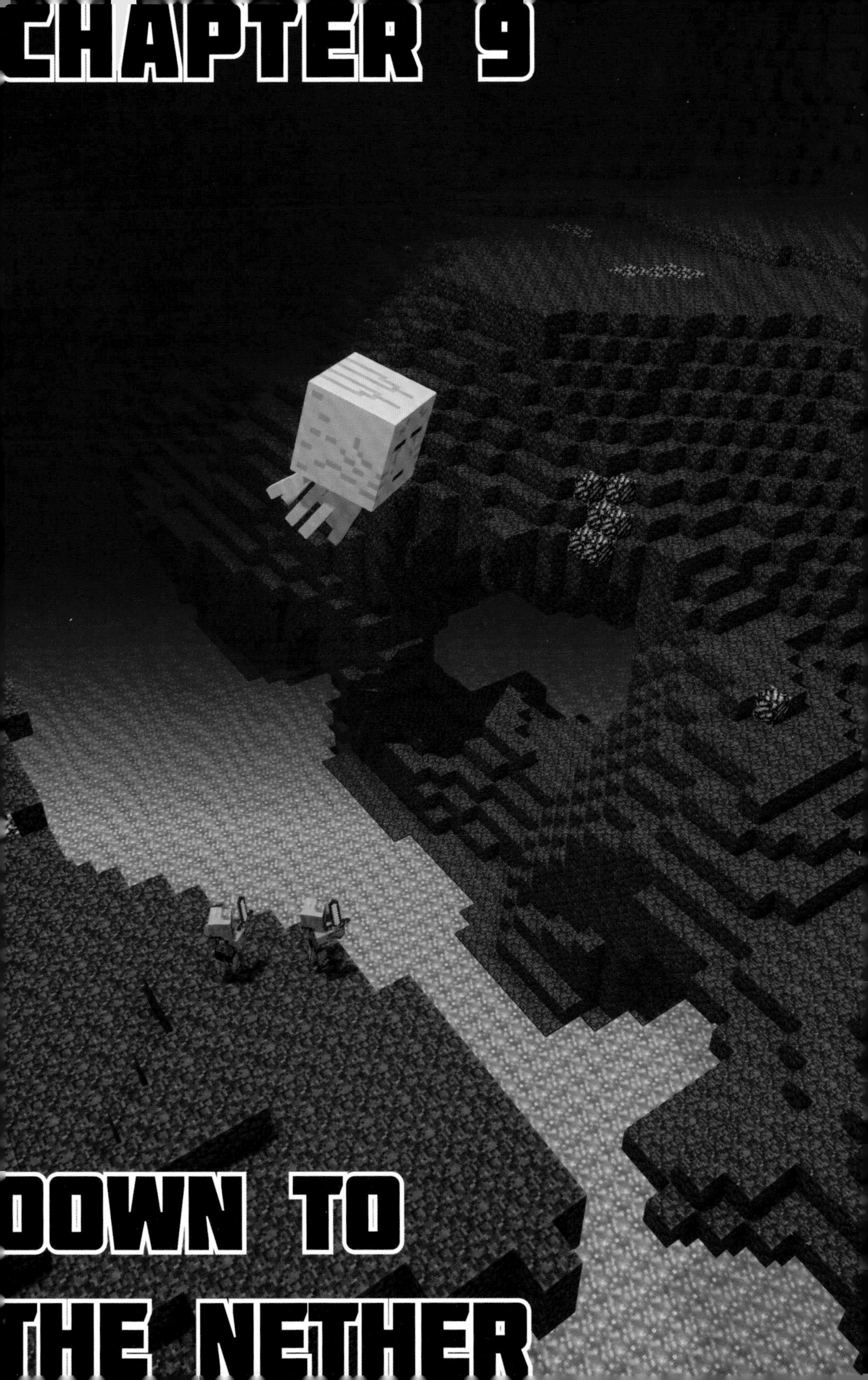

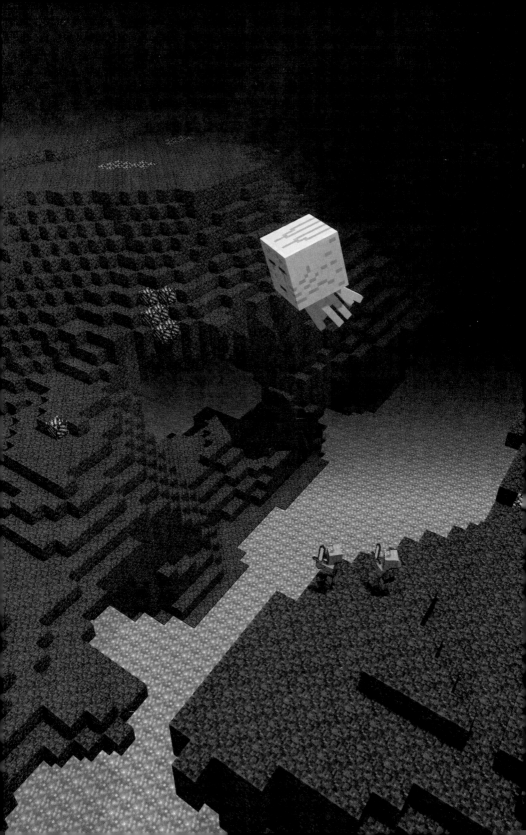

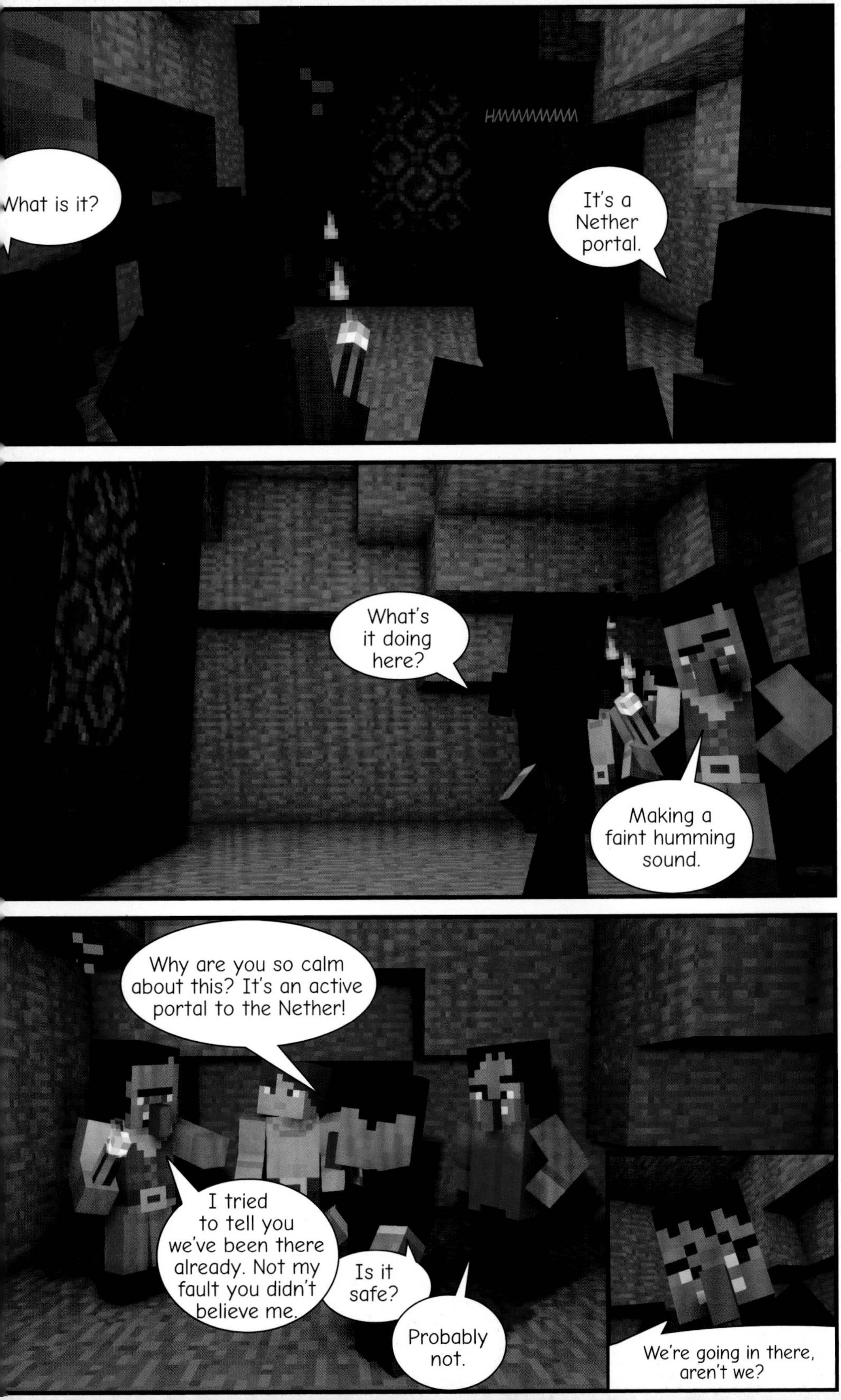
HMMMMMMMM
What is it?
It's a Nether portal.
What's it doing here?
Making a faint humming sound.
Why are you so calm about this? It's an active portal to the Nether!
I tried to tell you we've been there already. Not my fault you didn't believe me.
Is it safe?
Probably not.
We're going in there, aren't we?

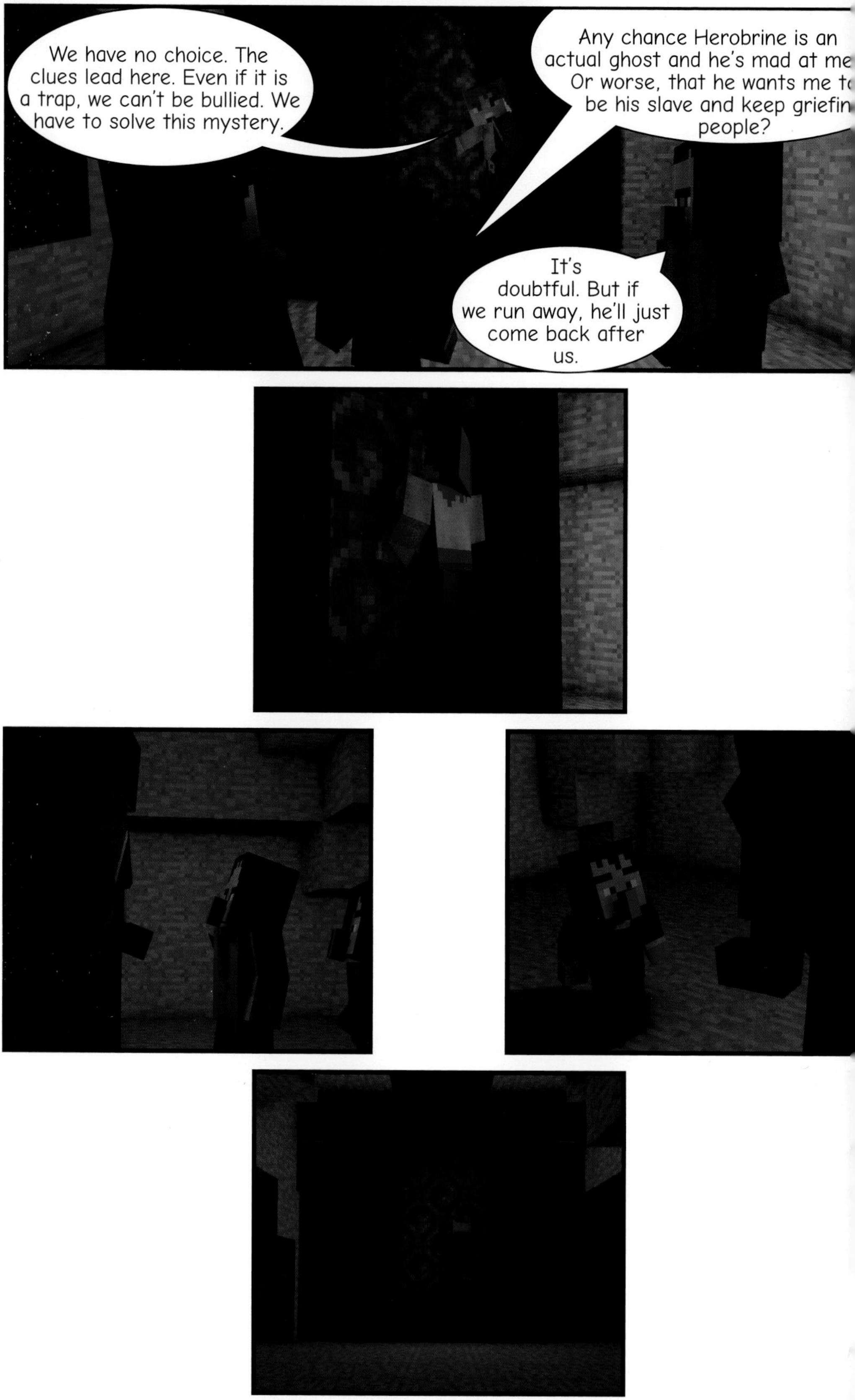
We have no choice. The clues lead here. Even if it is a trap, we can't be bullied. We have to solve this mystery.
Any chance Herobrine is an actual ghost and he's mad at me Or worse, that he wants me t be his slave and keep griefin people?
It's doubtful. But if we run away, he'll just come back after us.

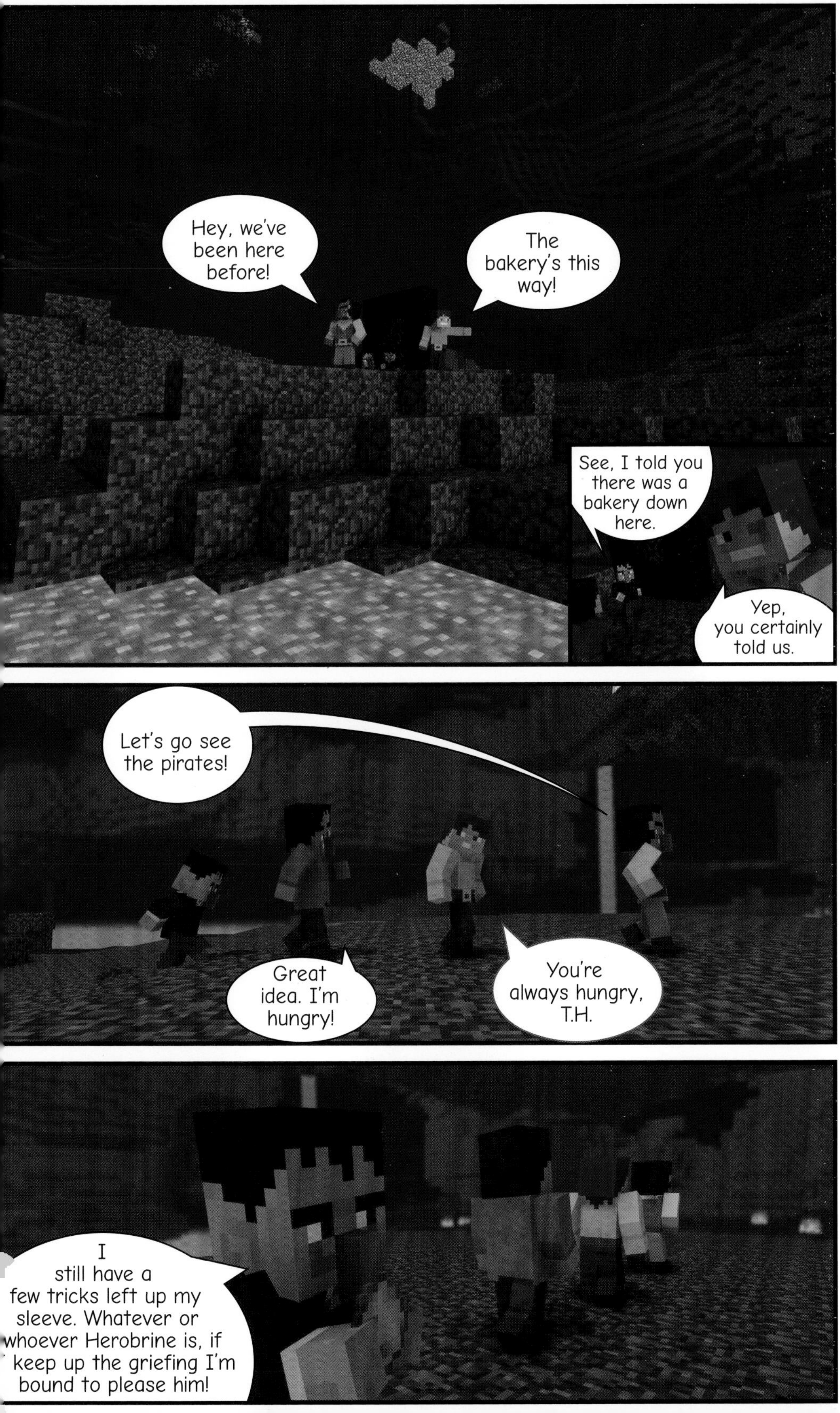
Hey, we've been here before!
The bakery's this way!
See, I told you there was a bakery down here.
Yep, you certainly told us.
Let's go see the pirates!
Great idea. I'm hungry!
You're always hungry, T.H.
I still have a few tricks left up my sleeve. Whatever or whoever Herobrine is, if keep up the griefing I'm bound to please him!

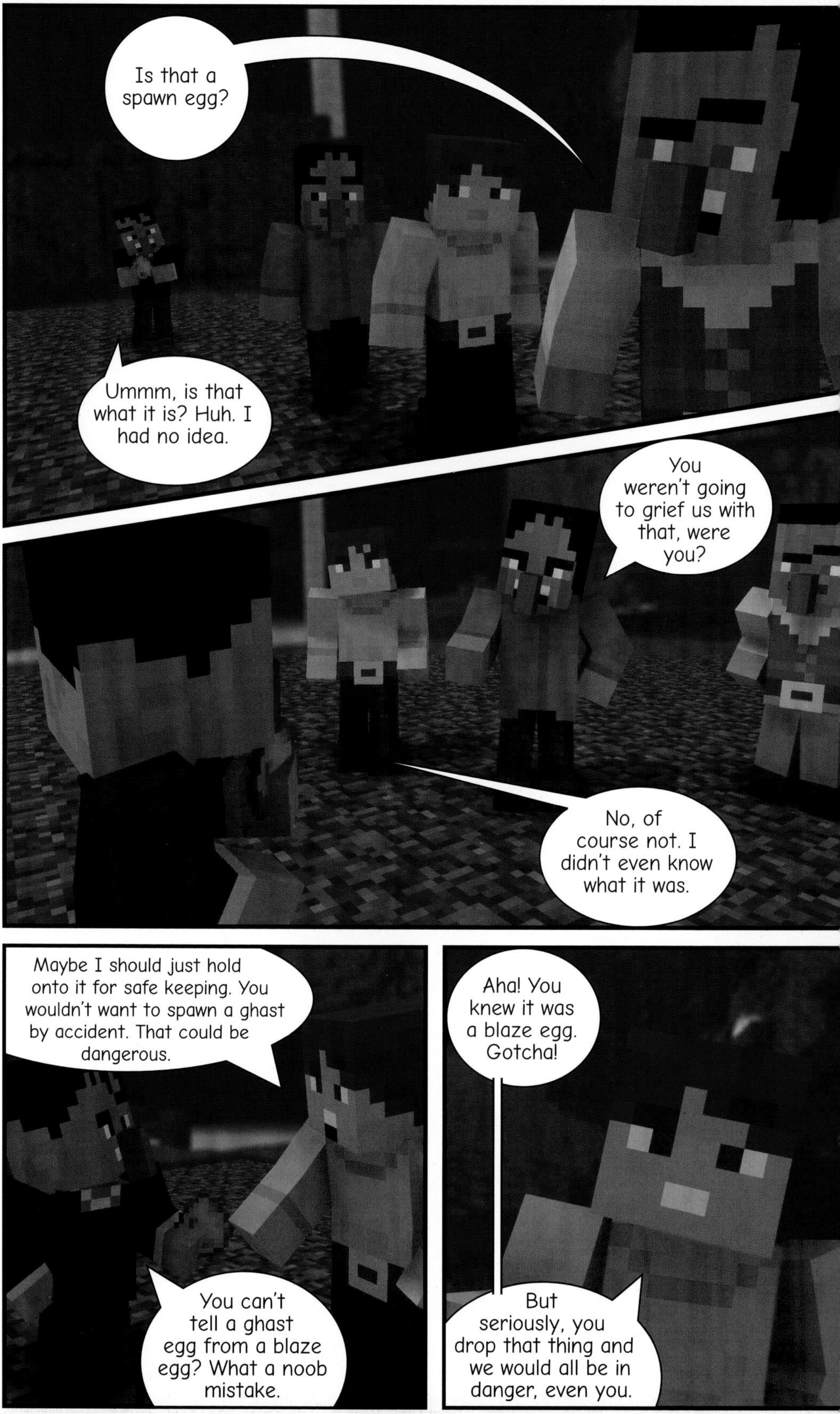
Is that a spawn egg?
Ummm, is that what it is? Huh. I had no idea.
You weren't going to grief us with that, were you?
No, of course not. I didn't even know what it was.
Maybe I should just hold onto it for safe keeping. You wouldn't want to spawn a ghast by accident. That could be dangerous.
You can't tell a ghast egg from a blaze egg? What a noob mistake.
Aha! You knew it was a blaze egg. Gotcha!
But seriously, you drop that thing and we would all be in danger, even you.

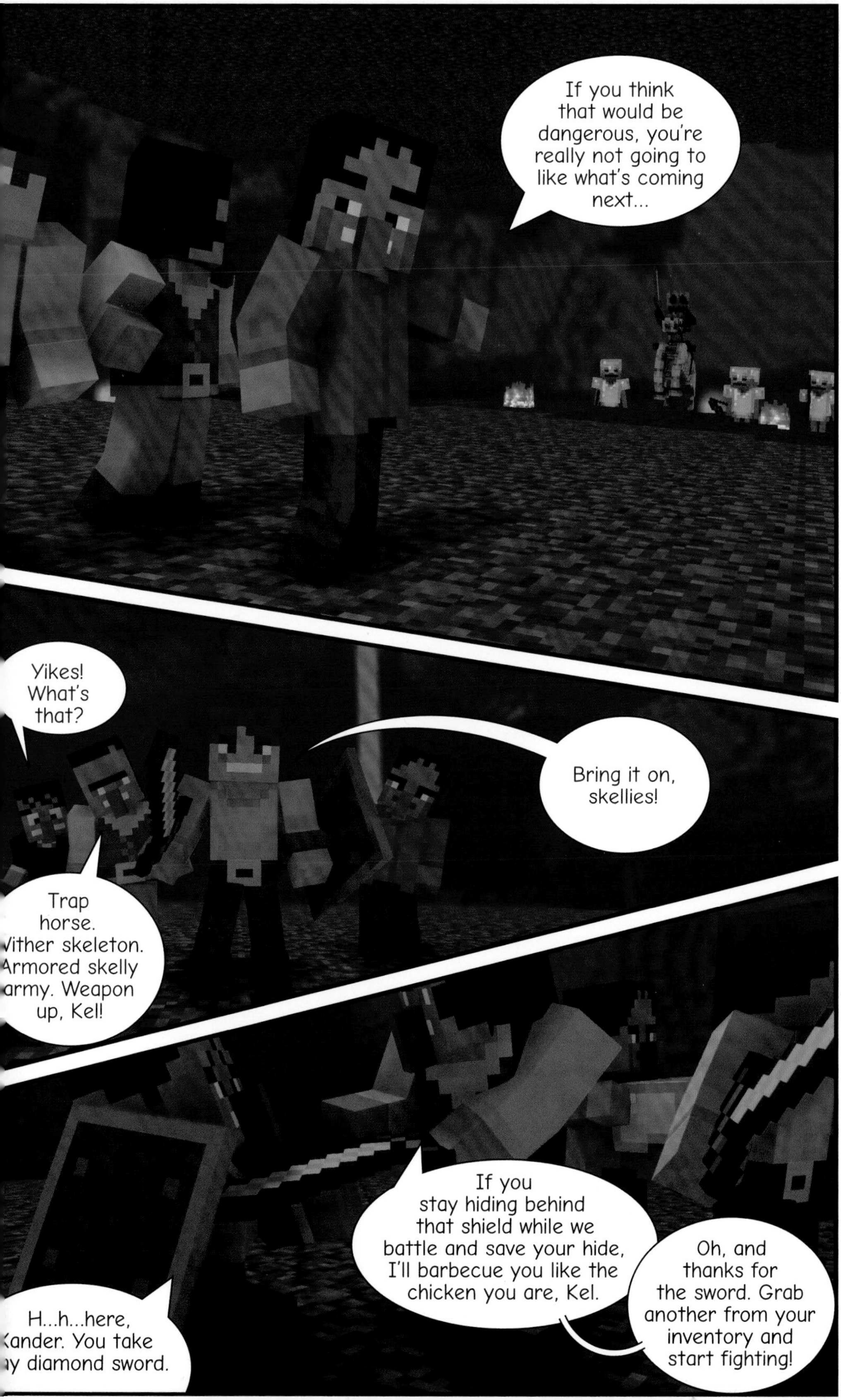

If you think that would be dangerous, you're really not going to like what's coming next...
Yikes! What's that?
Bring it on, skellies!
Trap horse. Vither skeleton. Armored skelly army. Weapon up, Kel!
H...h...here, (ander. You take y diamond sword.
If you stay hiding behind that shield while we battle and save your hide, I'll barbecue you like the chicken you are, Kel.
Oh, and thanks for the sword. Grab another from your inventory and start fighting!

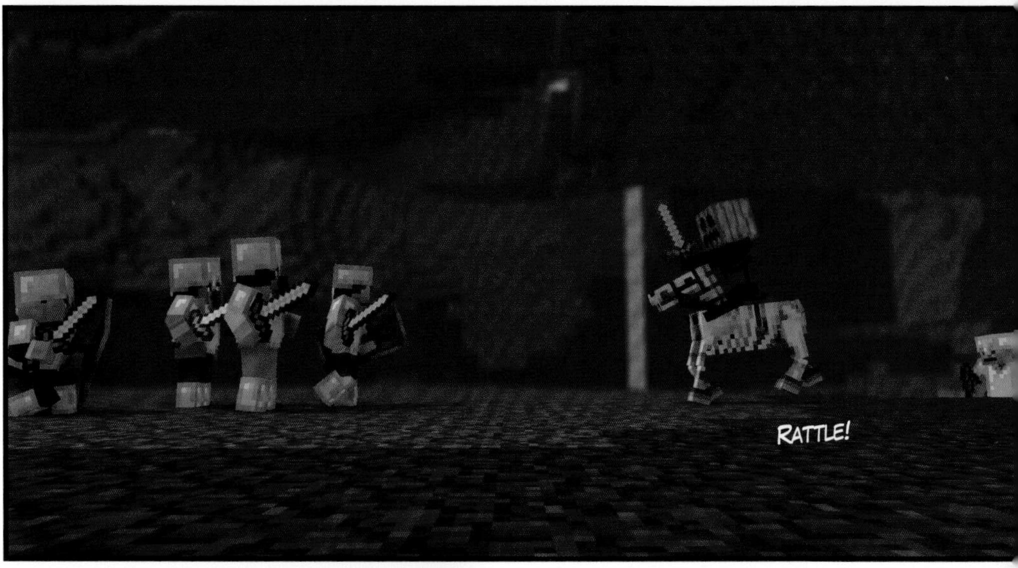
RATTLE!
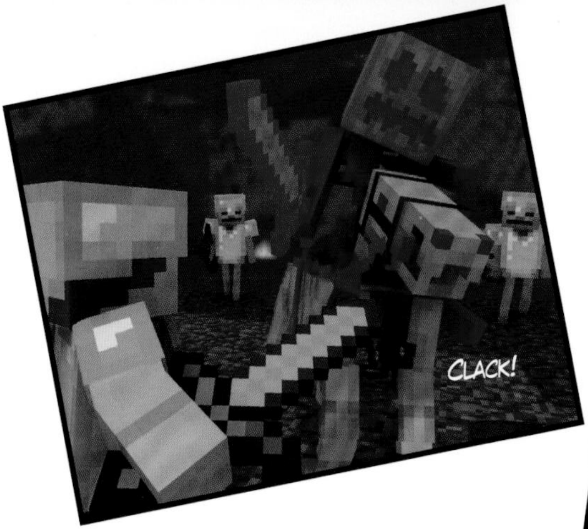
CLACK!
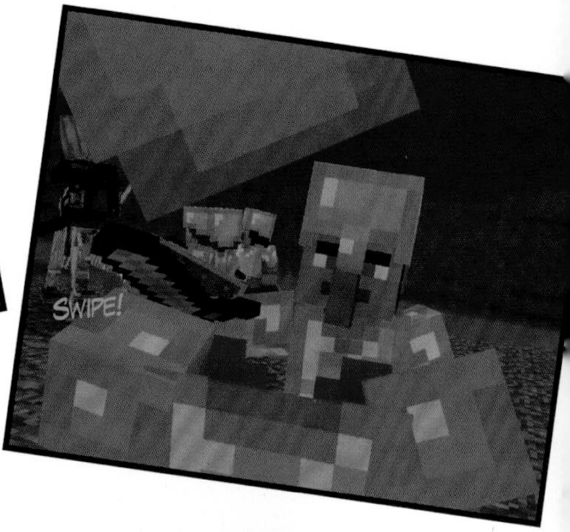
SWIPE!
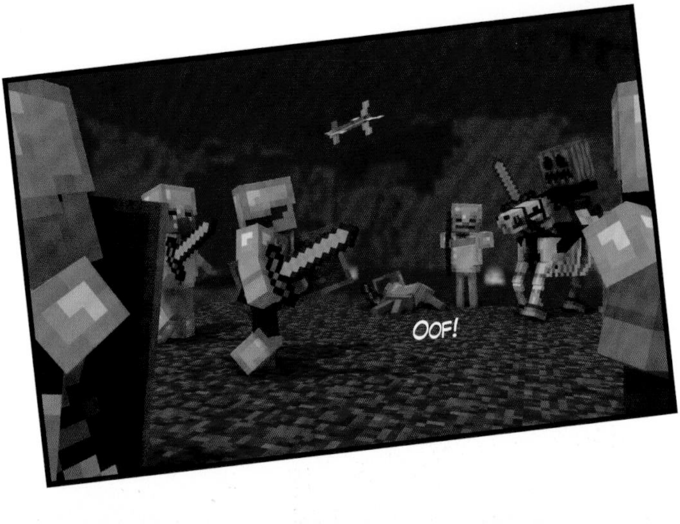
OOF!

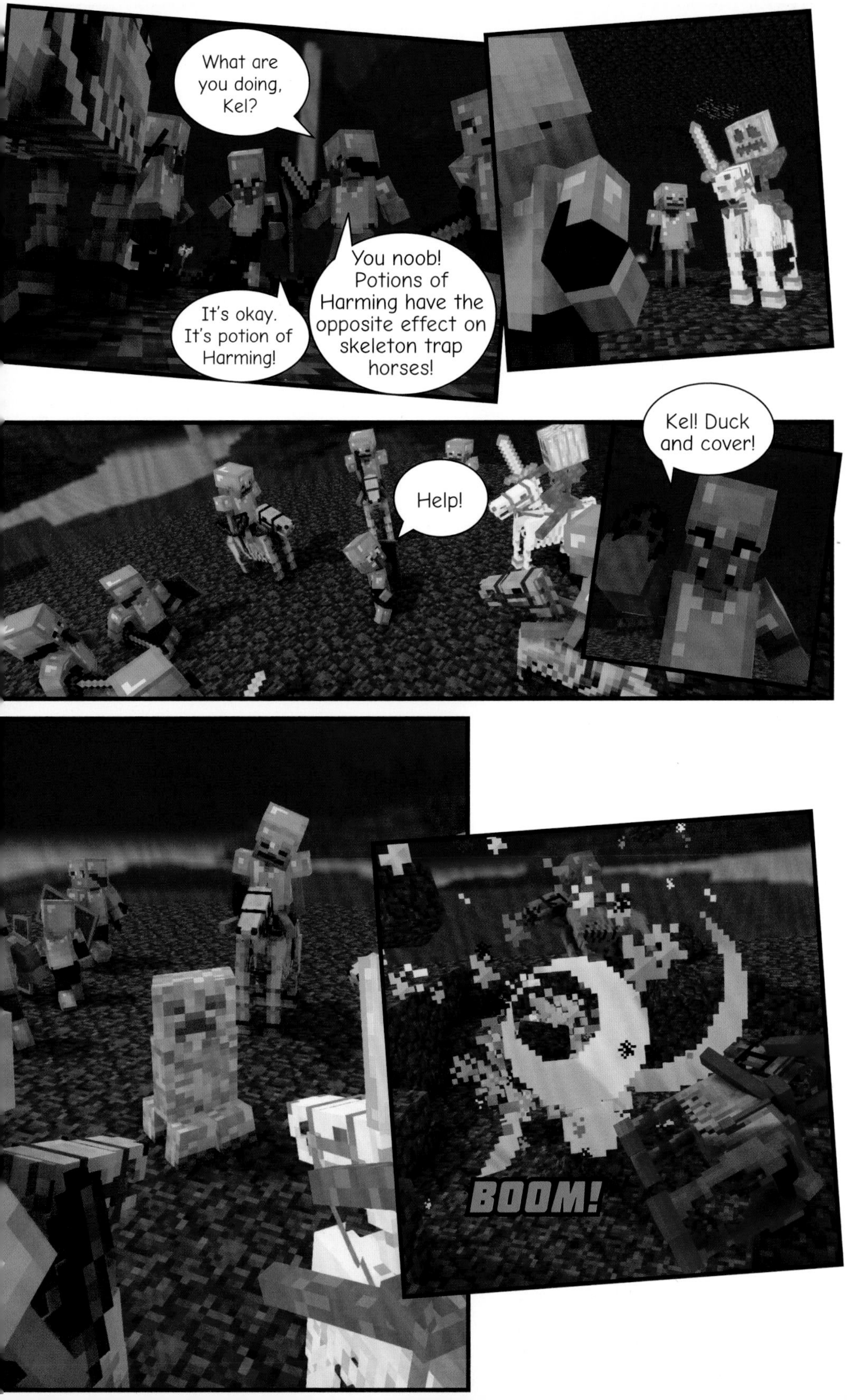
What are you doing, Kel?
It's okay. It's potion of Harming!
You noob! Potions of Harming have the opposite effect on skeleton trap horses!
Help!
Kel! Duck and cover!
BOOM!

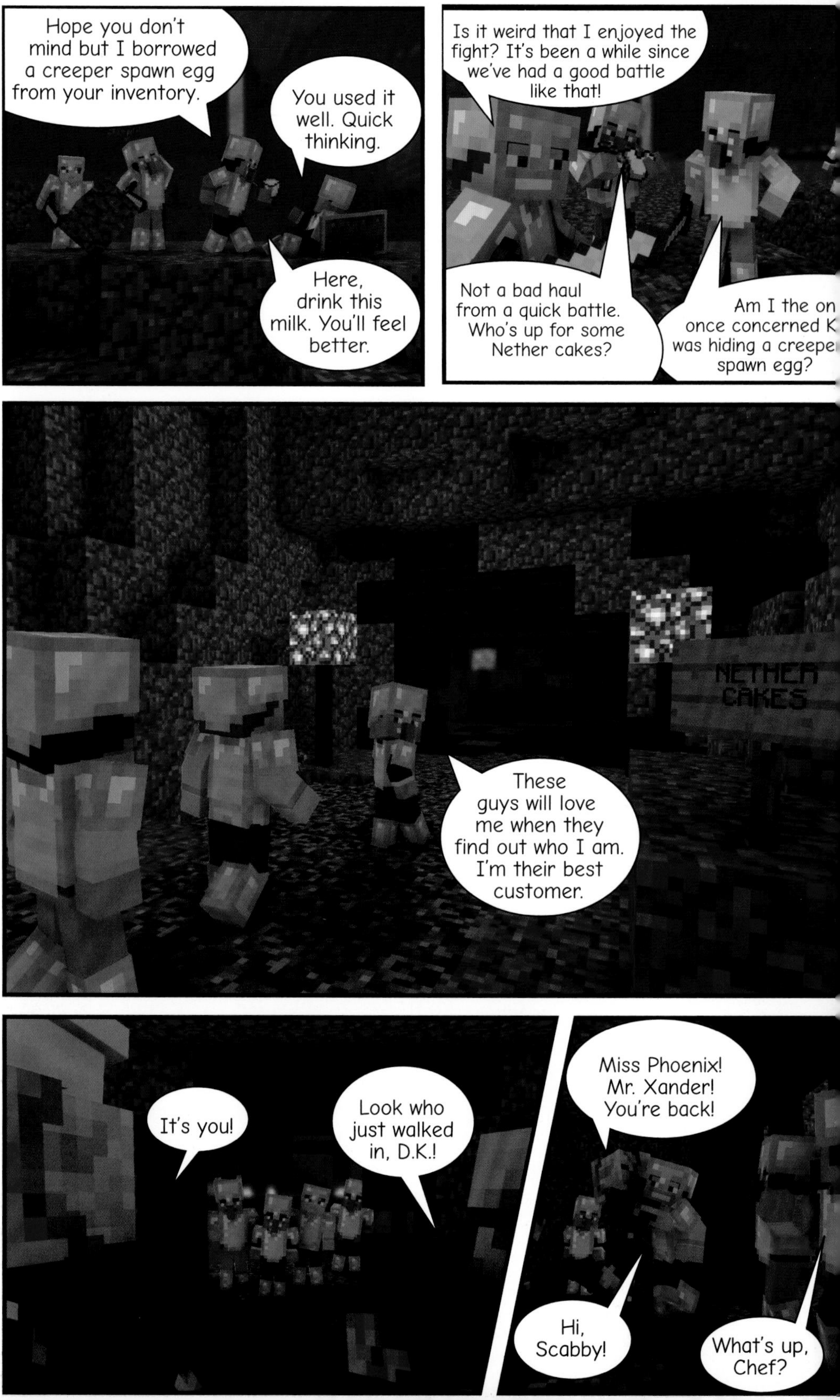
Hope you don't mind but I borrowed a creeper spawn egg from your inventory.
You used it well. Quick thinking.
Here, drink this milk. You'll feel better.
Is it weird that I enjoyed the fight? It's been a while since we've had a good battle like that!
Not a bad haul from a quick battle. Who's up for some Nether cakes?
Am I the on once concerned K was hiding a creepe spawn egg?
NETHER CAKES
These guys will love me when they find out who I am. I'm their best customer.
It's you!
Look who just walked in, D.K.!
Miss Phoenix! Mr. Xander! You're back!
Hi, Scabby!
What's up, Chef?

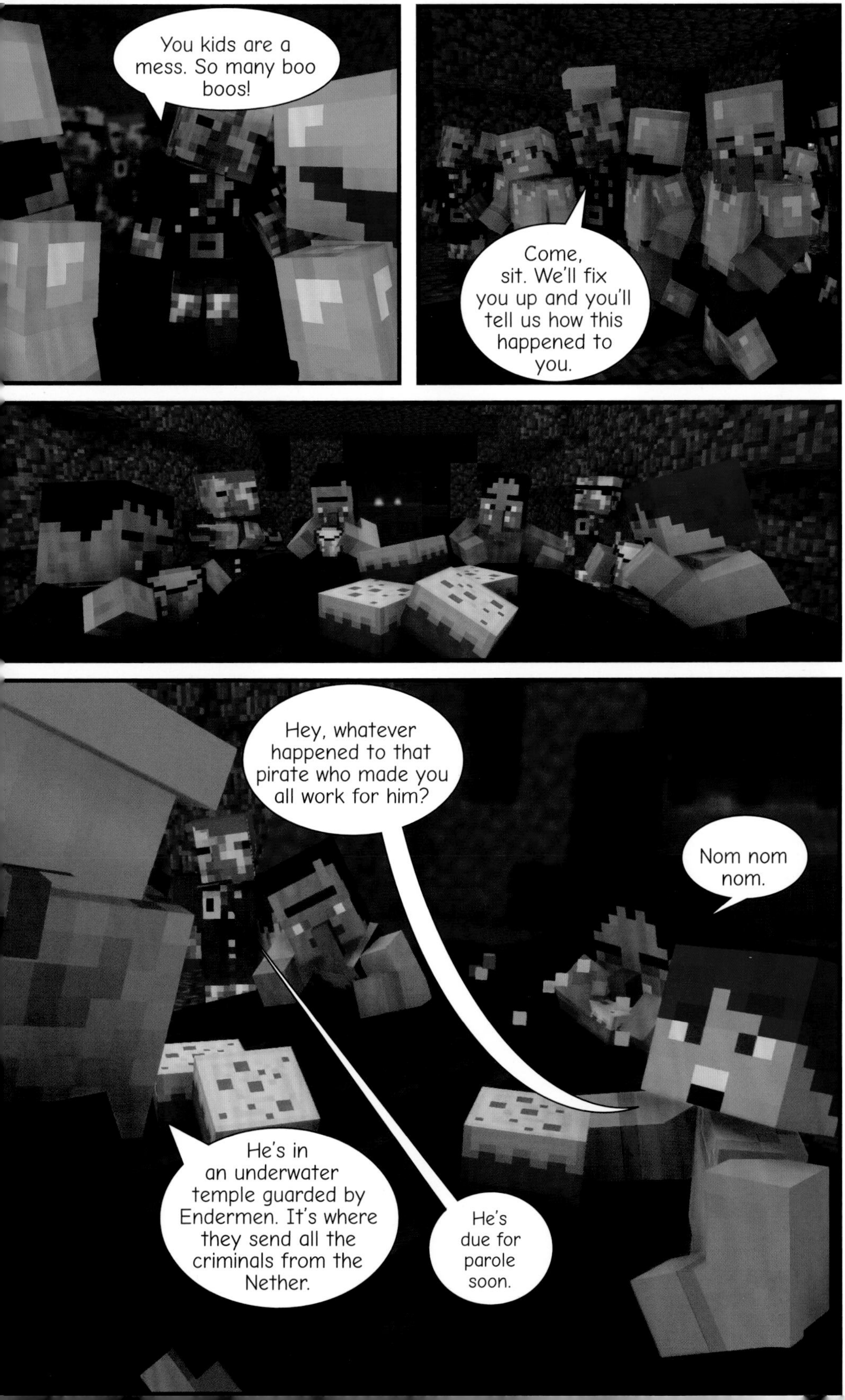
You kids are a mess. So many boo boos!
Come, sit. We'll fix you up and you'll tell us how this happened to you.
Hey, whatever happened to that pirate who made you all work for him?
Nom nom nom.
He's in an underwater temple guarded by Endermen. It's where they send all the criminals from the Nether.
He's due for parole soon.

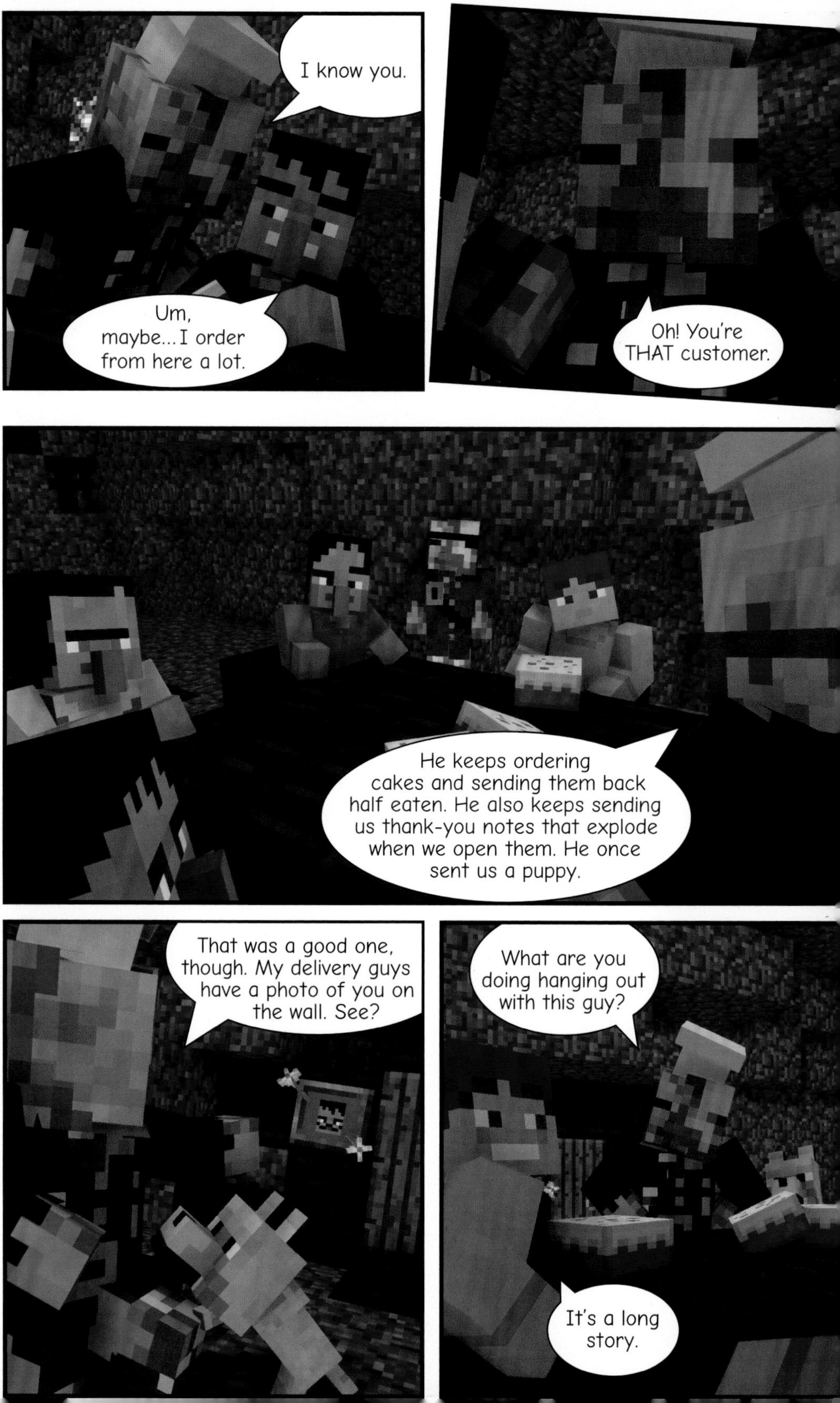
I know you.
Um, maybe... I order from here a lot.
Oh! You're THAT customer.
He keeps ordering cakes and sending them back half eaten. He also keeps sending us thank-you notes that explode when we open them. He once sent us a puppy.
That was a good one, though. My delivery guys have a photo of you on the wall. See?
What are you doing hanging out with this guy?
It's a long story.

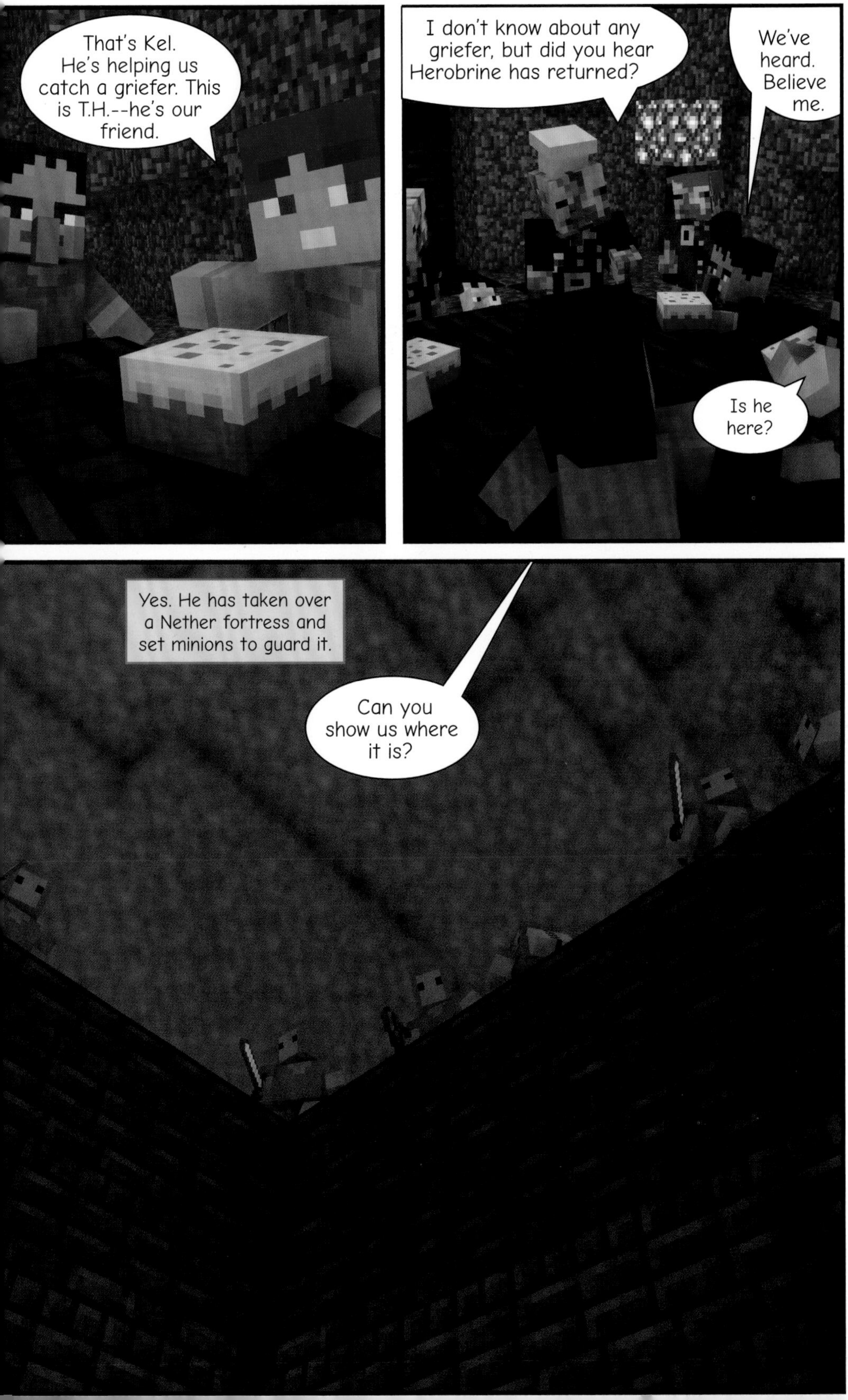
That's Kel. He's helping us catch a griefer. This is T.H.--he's our friend.
I don't know about any griefer, but did you hear Herobrine has returned?
We've heard. Believe me.
Is he here?
Yes. He has taken over a Nether fortress and set minions to guard it.
Can you show us where it is?

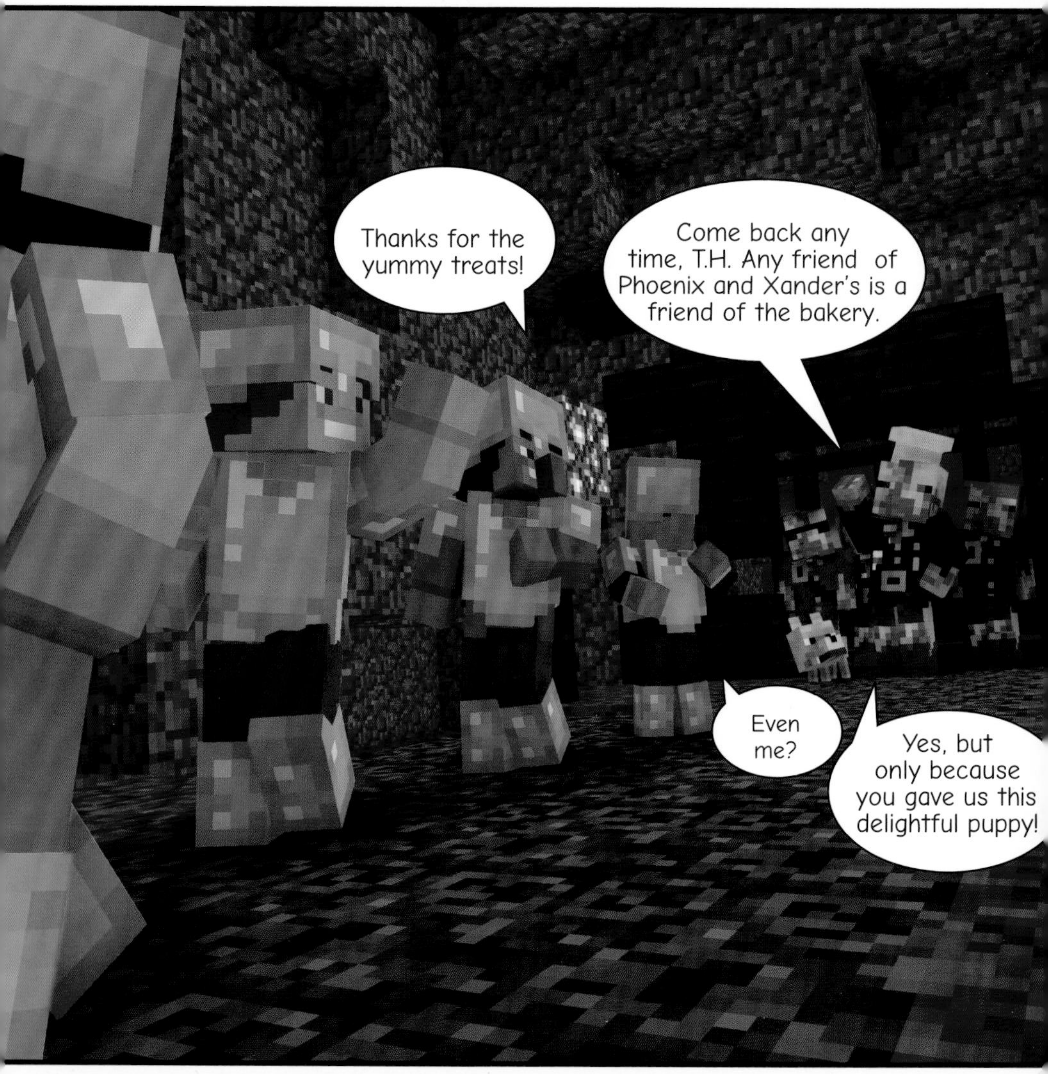
Thanks for the yummy treats!
Come back any time, T.H. Any friend of Phoenix and Xander's is a friend of the bakery.
Even me?
Yes, but only because you gave us this delightful puppy!

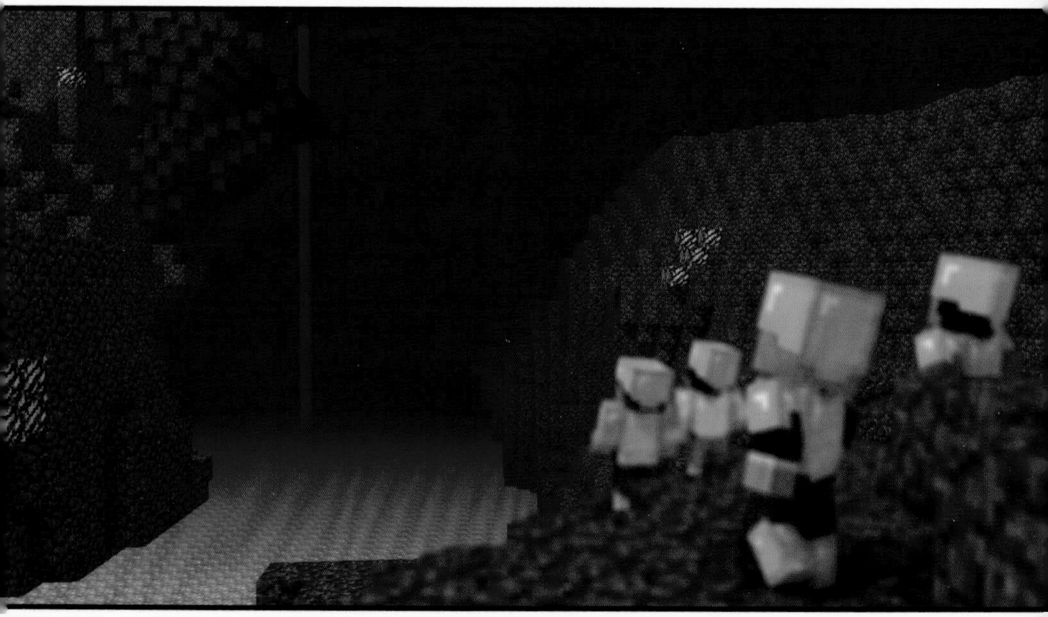

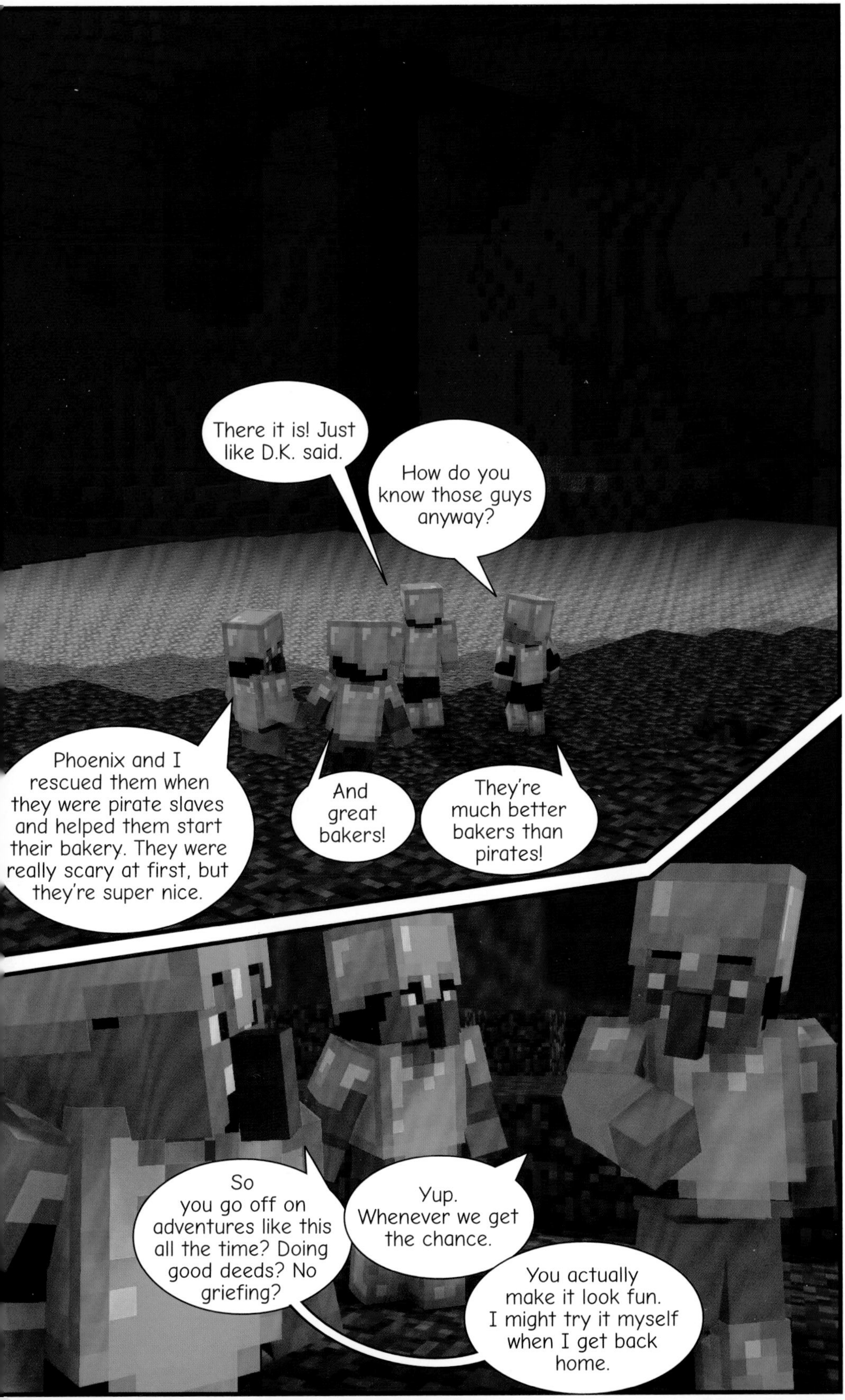
There it is! Just like D.K. said.
How do you know those guys anyway?
Phoenix and I rescued them when they were pirate slaves and helped them start their bakery. They were really scary at first, but they're super nice.
And great bakers!
They're much better bakers than pirates!
So you go off on adventures like this all the time? Doing good deeds? No griefing?
Yup. Whenever we get the chance.
You actually make it look fun. I might try it myself when I get back home.

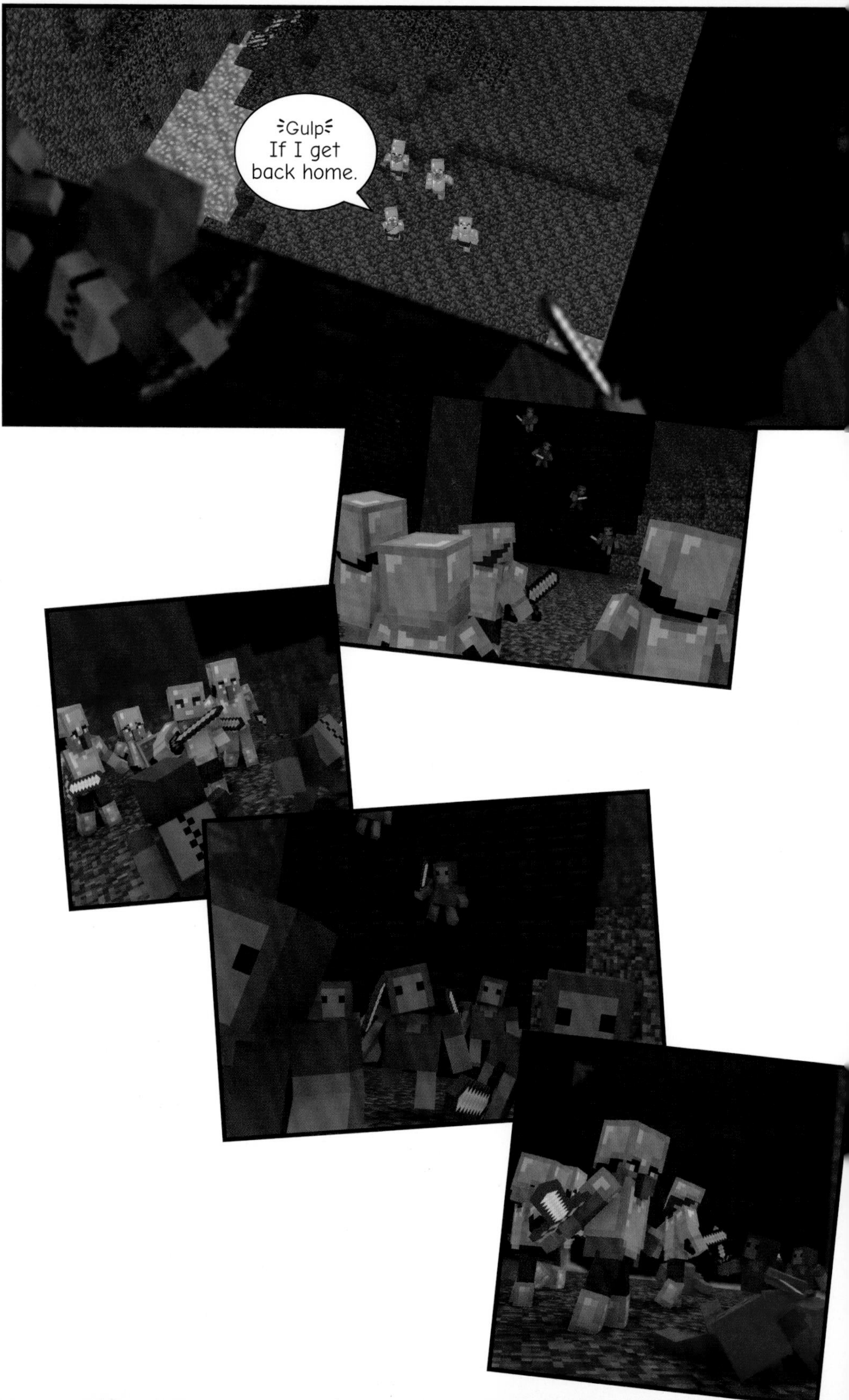
Gulp
If I get back home.

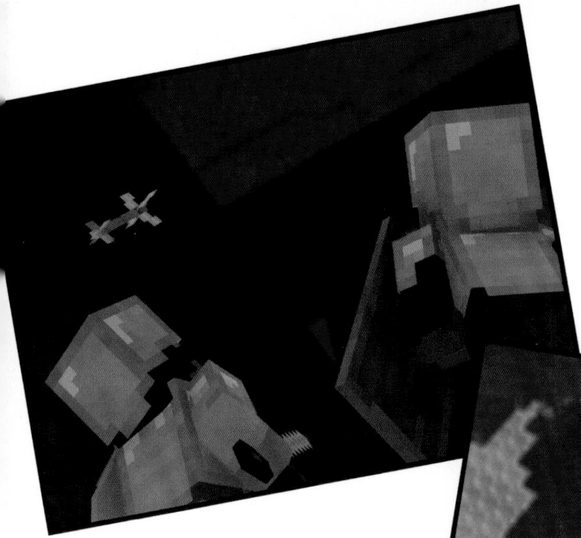
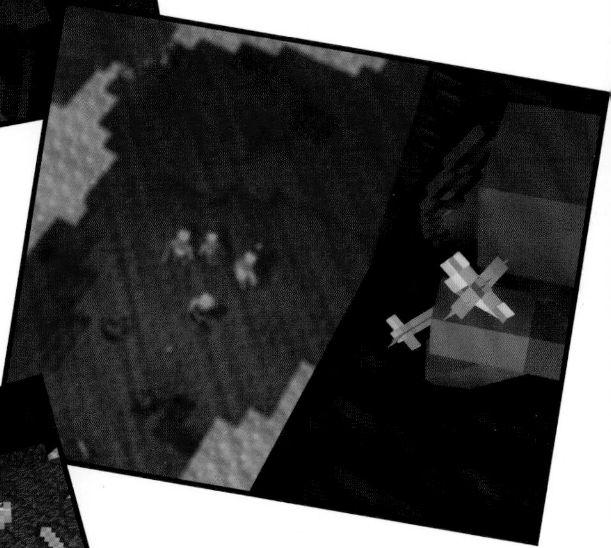
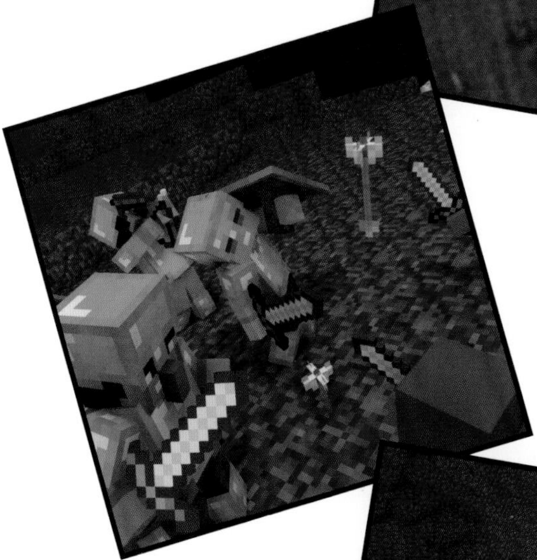
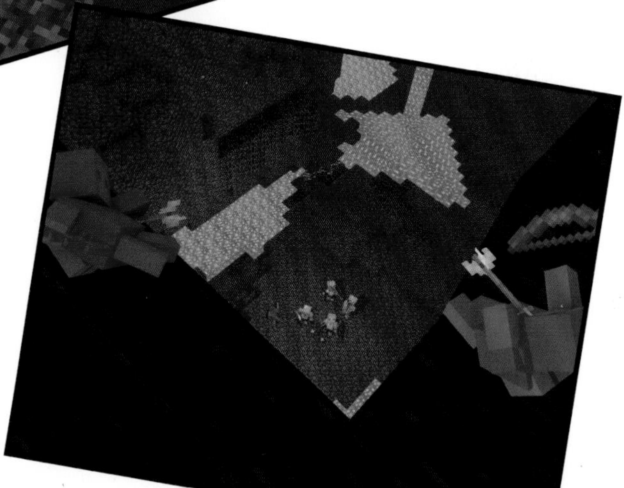

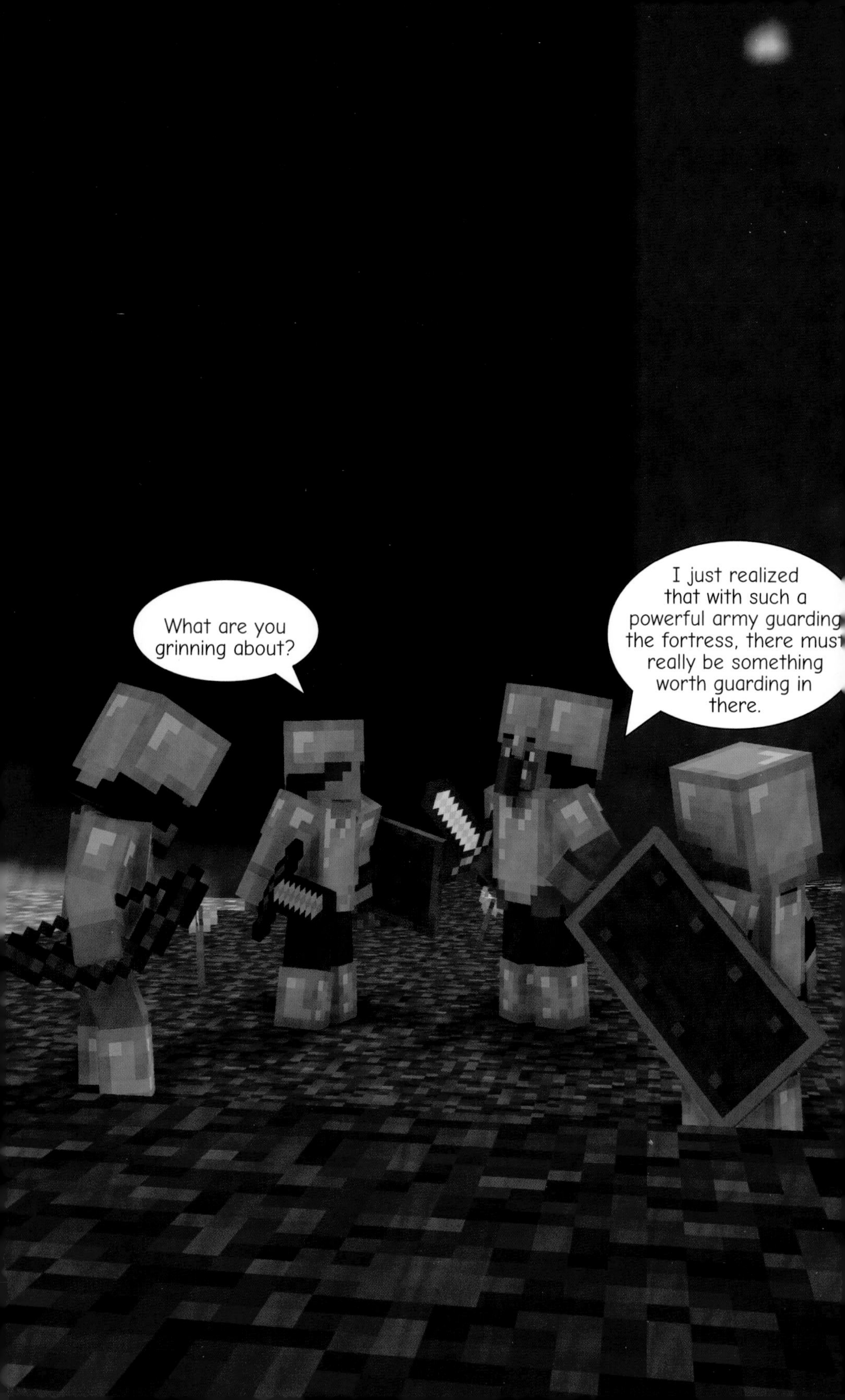
What are you grinning about?
I just realized that with such a powerful army guarding the fortress, there must really be something worth guarding in there.

CHAPTER 10

THE FORTRESS SHADOW

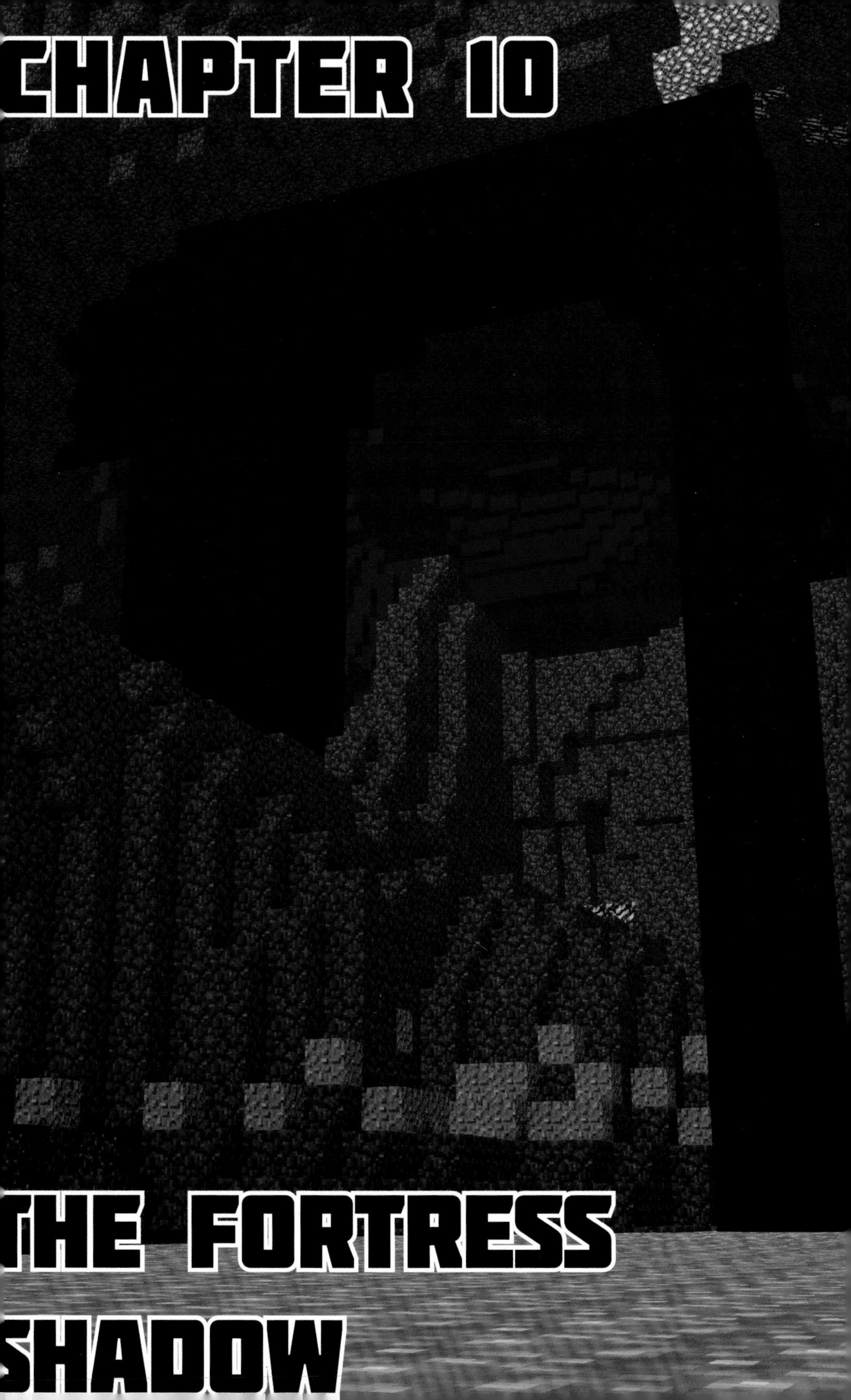

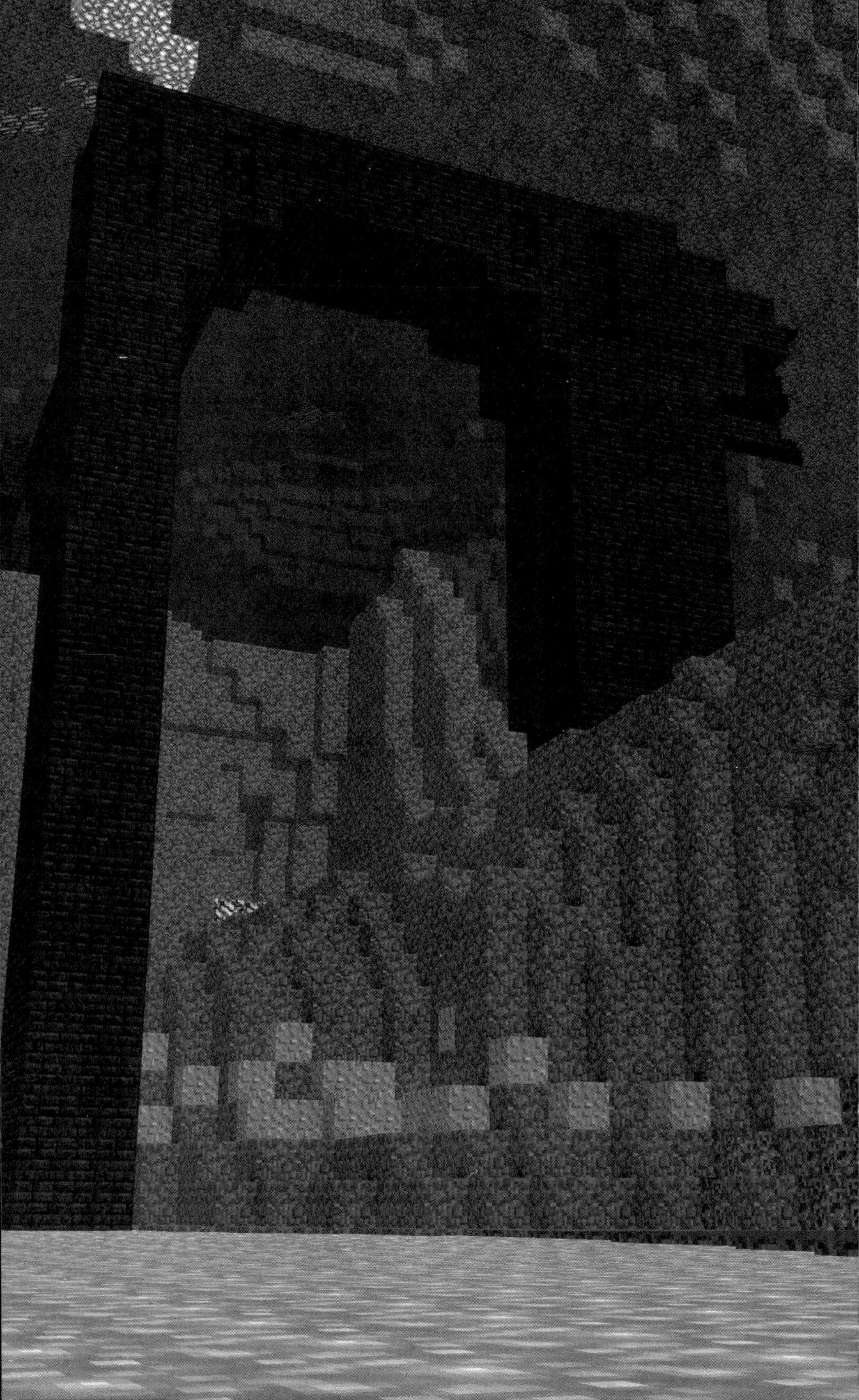

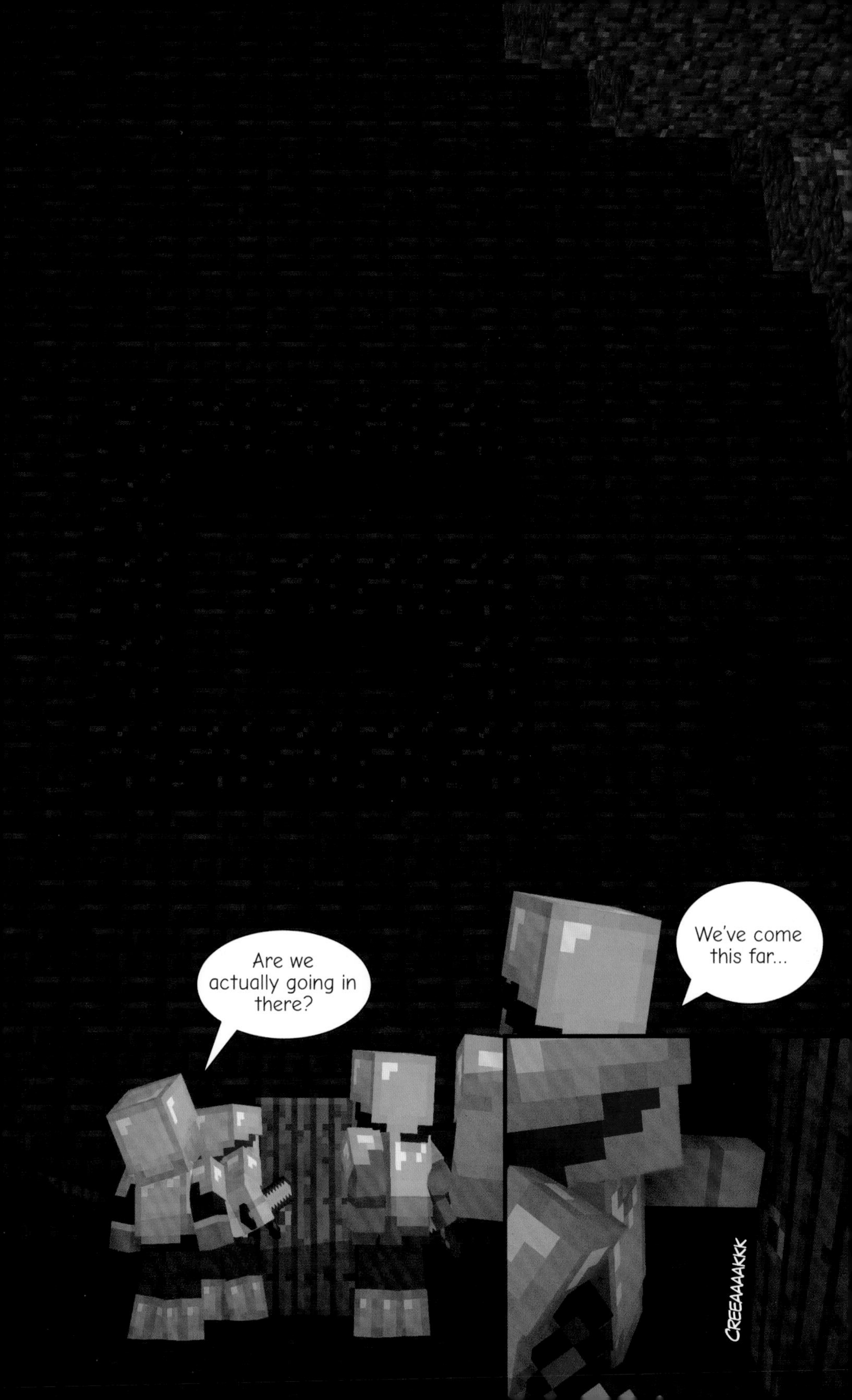
Are we actually going in there?
We've come this far...
CREEAAAKKK

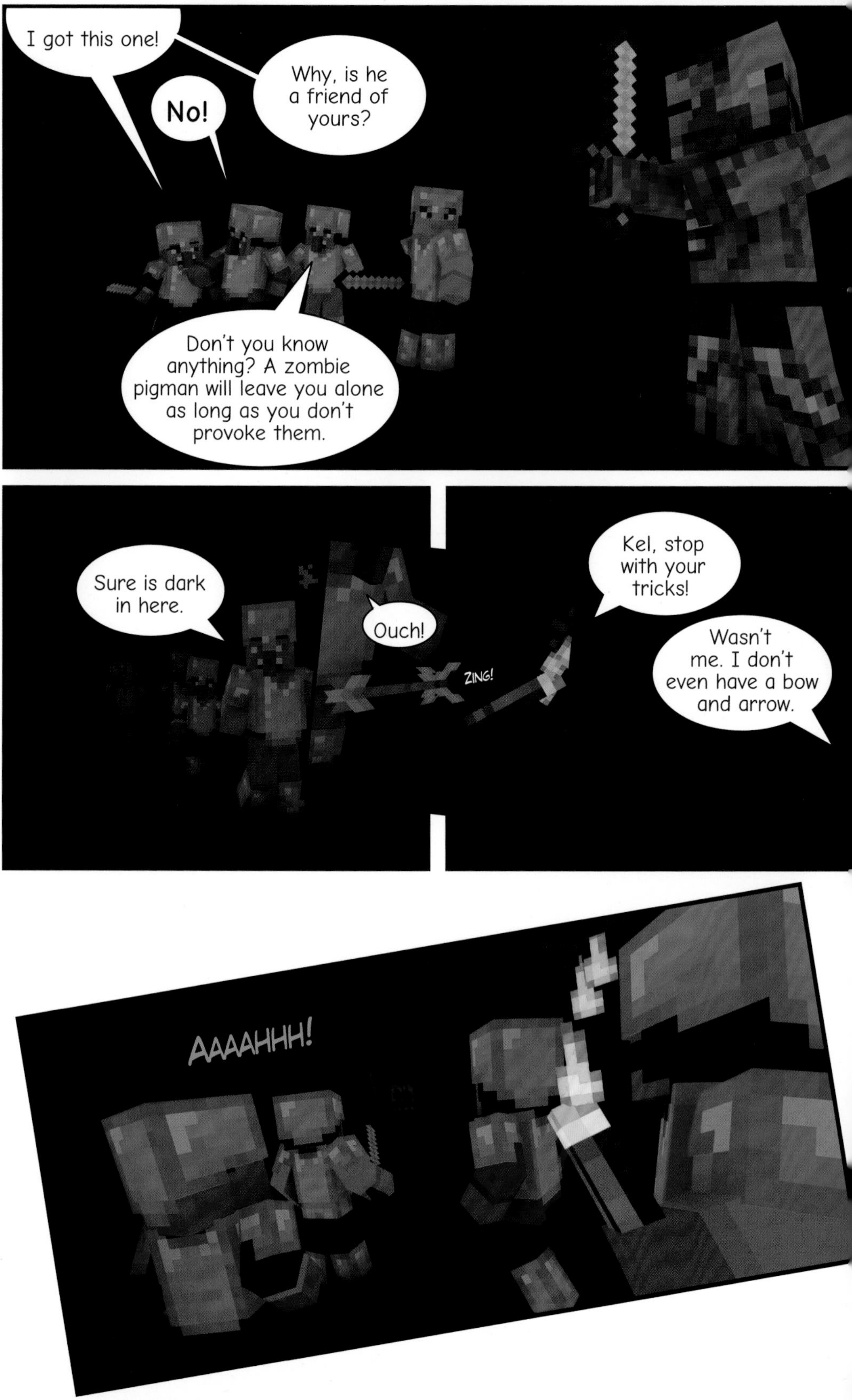
I got this one!
Why, is he a friend of yours?
No!
Don't you know anything? A zombie pigman will leave you alone as long as you don't provoke them.
Sure is dark in here.
Ouch!
ZING!
Kel, stop with your tricks!
Wasn't me. I don't even have a bow and arrow.
AAAAHHH!

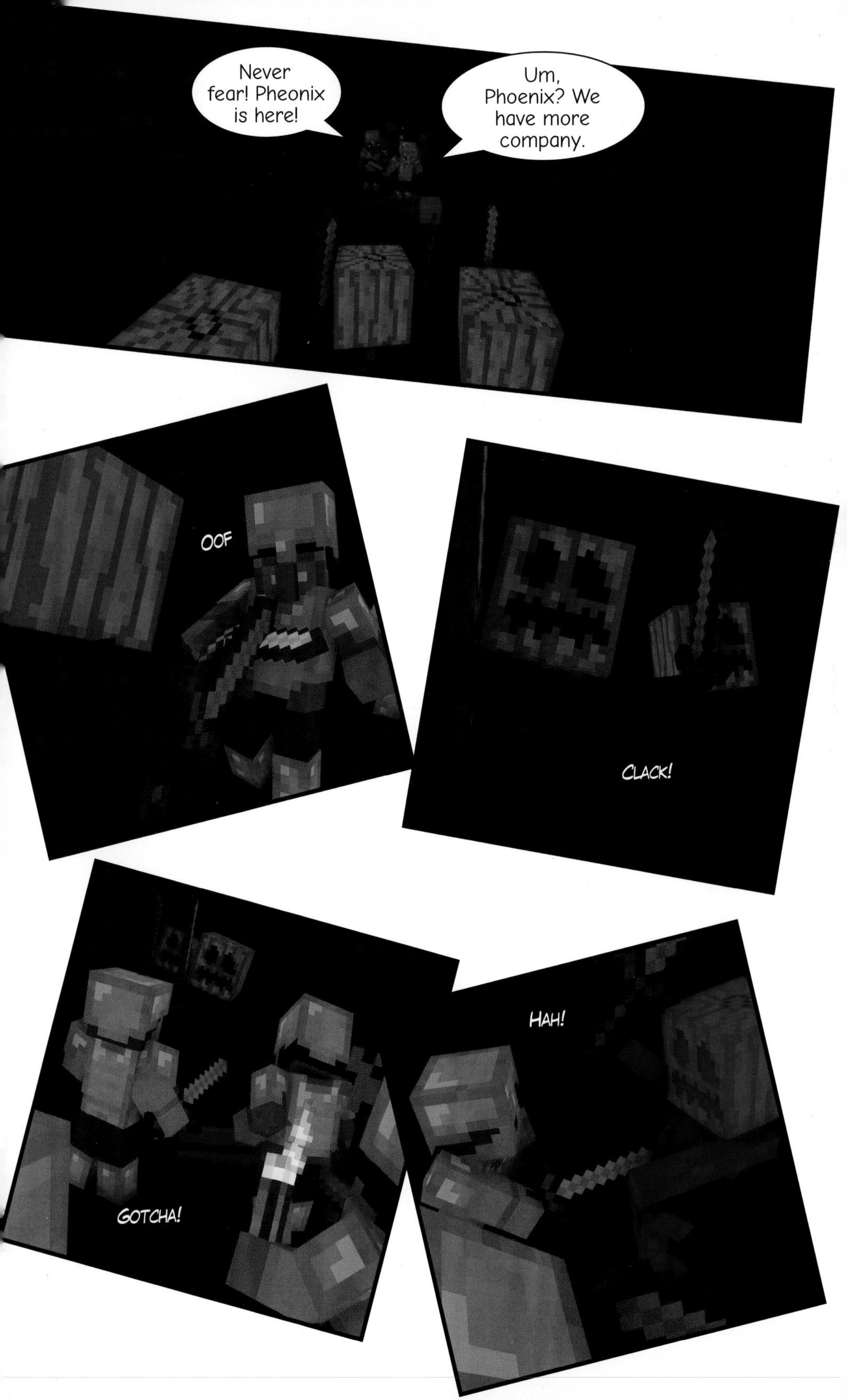
Never fear! Pheonix is here!
Um, Phoenix? We have more company.
OOF
CLACK!
GOTCHA!
HAH!

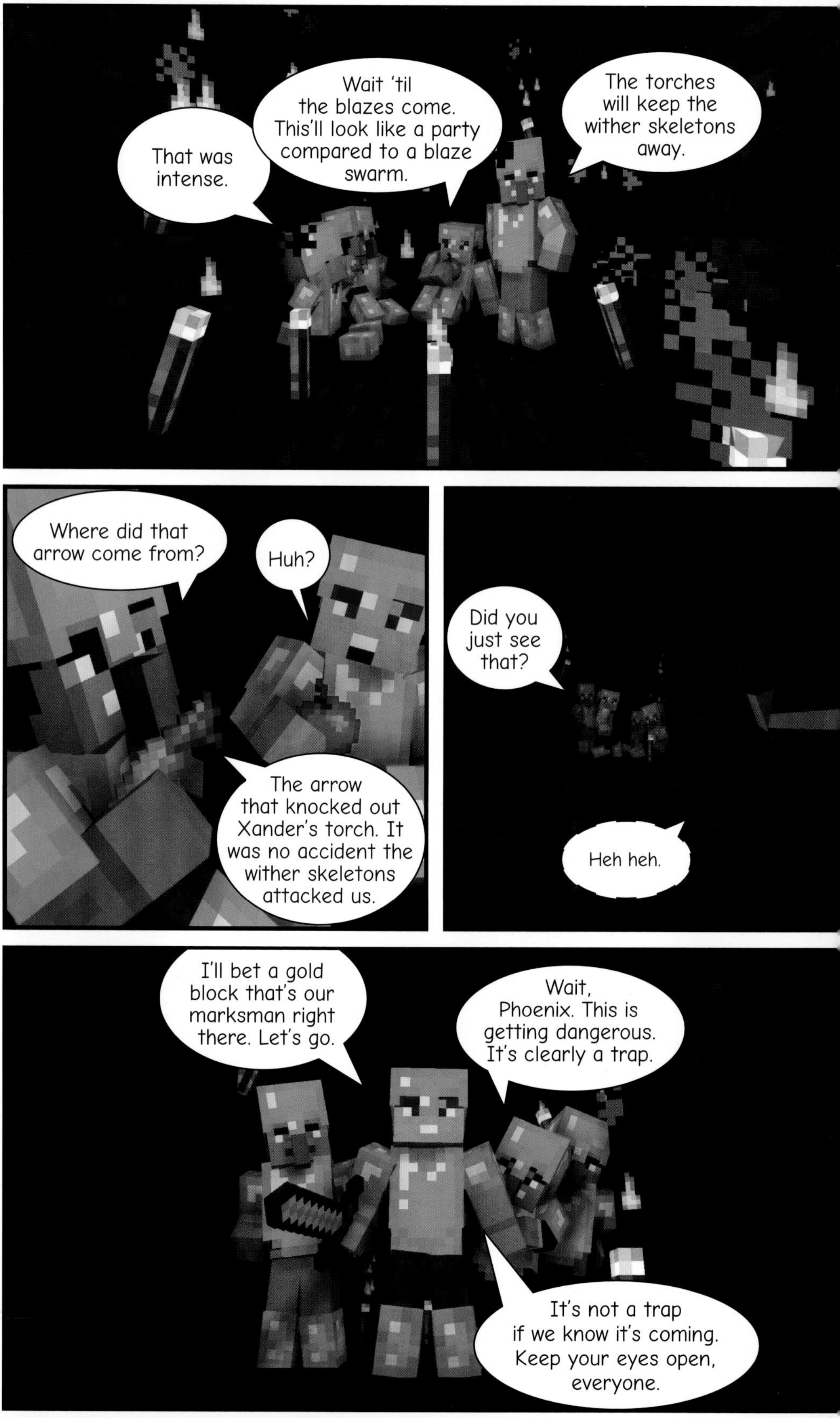
That was intense.
Wait 'til the blazes come. This'll look like a party compared to a blaze swarm.
The torches will keep the wither skeletons away.
Where did that arrow come from?
Huh?
The arrow that knocked out Xander's torch. It was no accident the wither skeletons attacked us.
Did you just see that?
Heh heh.
I'll bet a gold block that's our marksman right there. Let's go.
Wait, Phoenix. This is getting dangerous. It's clearly a trap.
It's not a trap if we know it's coming. Keep your eyes open, everyone.

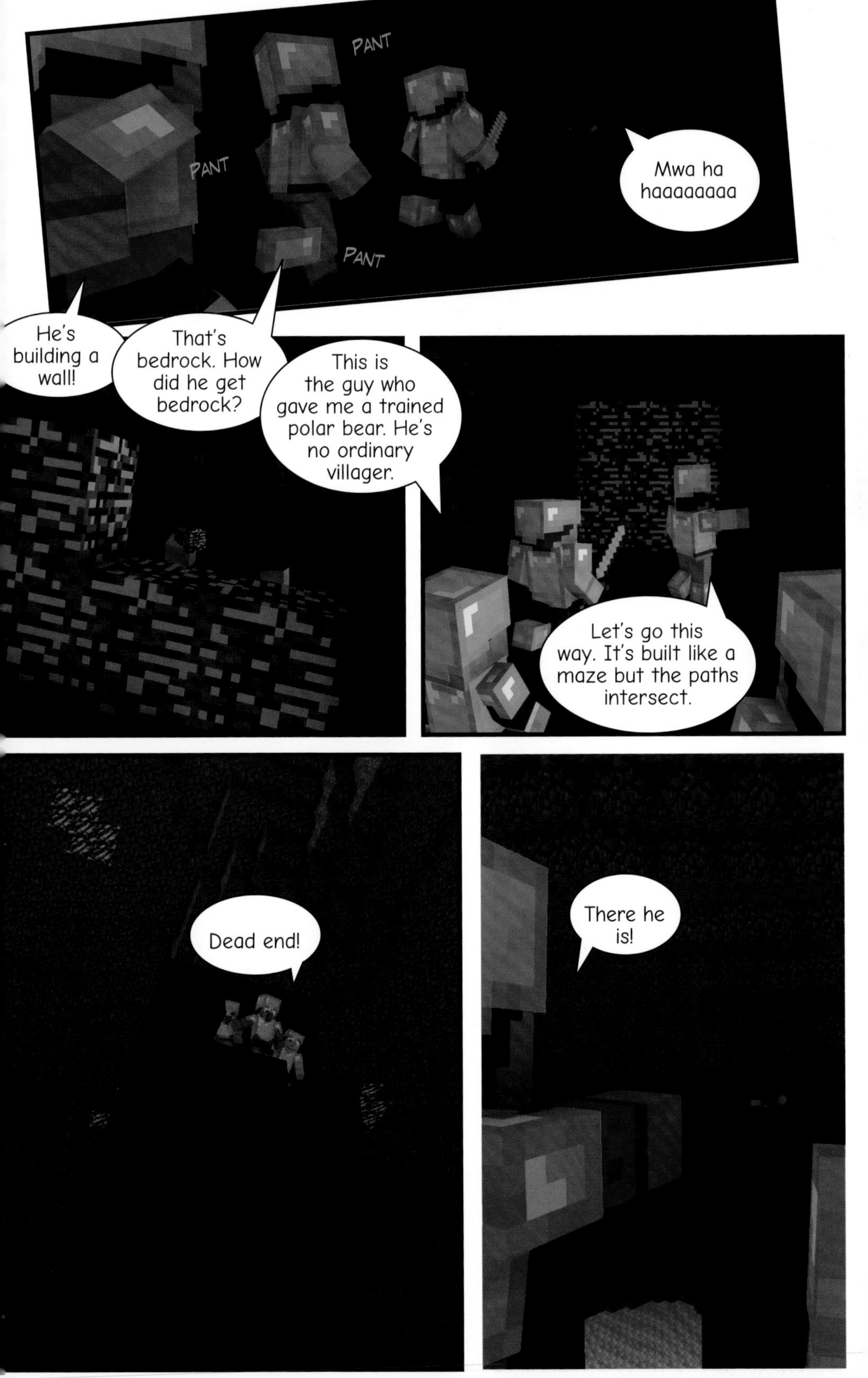
PANT
PANT
PANT
Mwa ha haaaaaaaa
He's building a wall!
That's bedrock. How did he get bedrock?
This is the guy who gave me a trained polar bear. He's no ordinary villager.
Let's go this way. It's built like a maze but the paths intersect.
Dead end!
There he is!

SIZZLE. CRACKLE.
Look out--there's blaze nearby!
Good idea, Kel. You draw his fire. I'll catch him while he recharges.
I did not do that on purpose! And I'm not doing it again, so make your shot count.
Don't blazes know the dangers of secondhand fires? Or smoking? How rude.
This way!

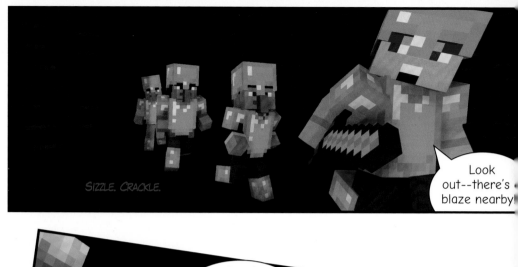

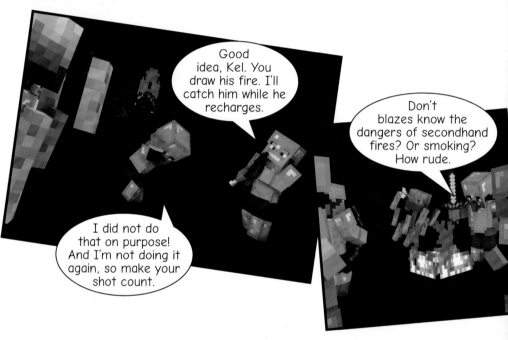

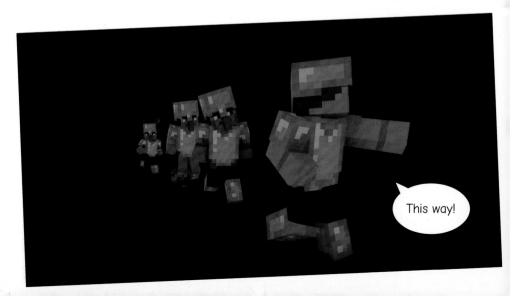

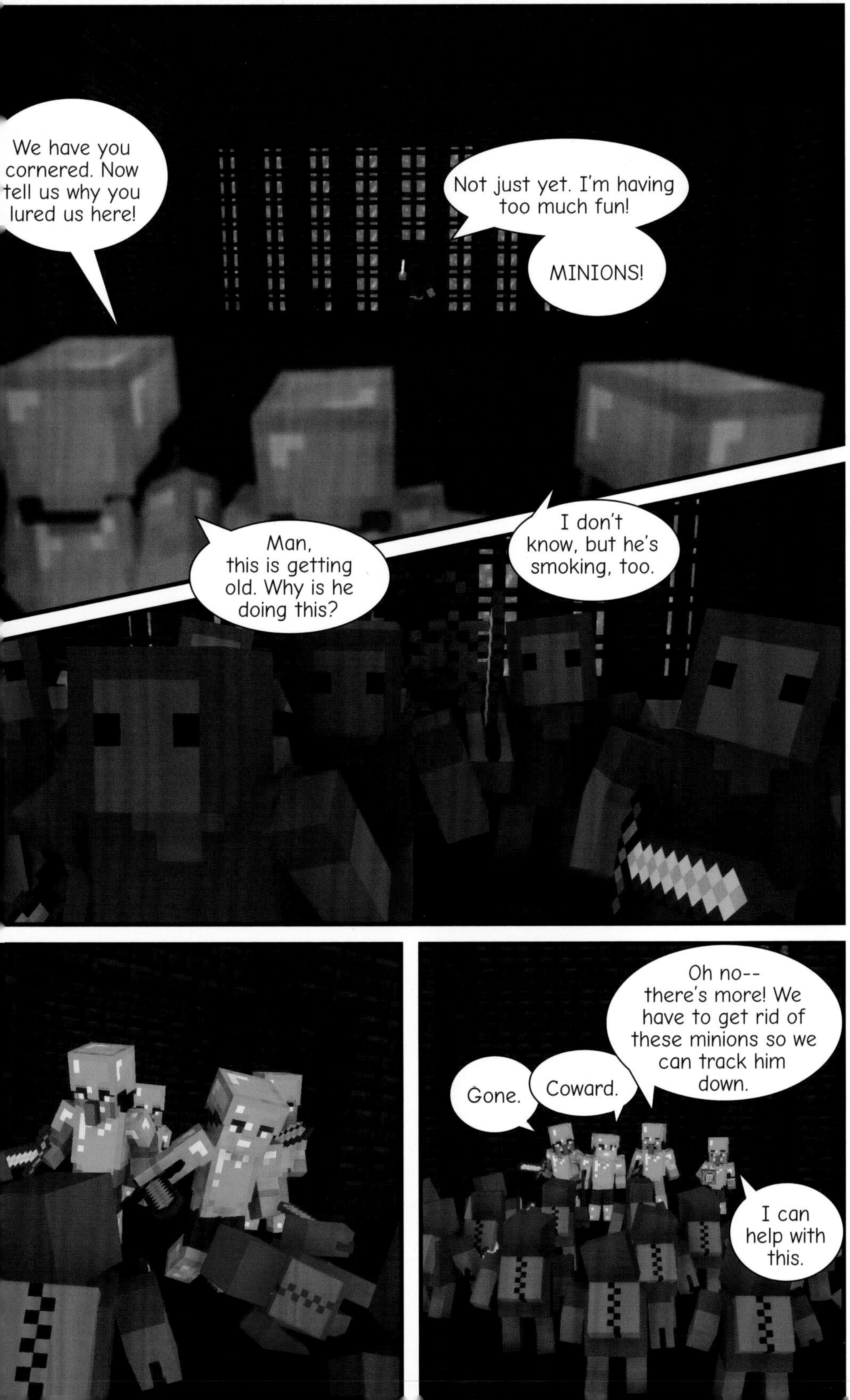
We have you cornered. Now tell us why you lured us here!
Not just yet. I'm having too much fun!
MINIONS!
Man, this is getting old. Why is he doing this?
I don't know, but he's smoking, too.
Gone.
Coward.
Oh no-- there's more! We have to get rid of these minions so we can track him down.
I can help with this.

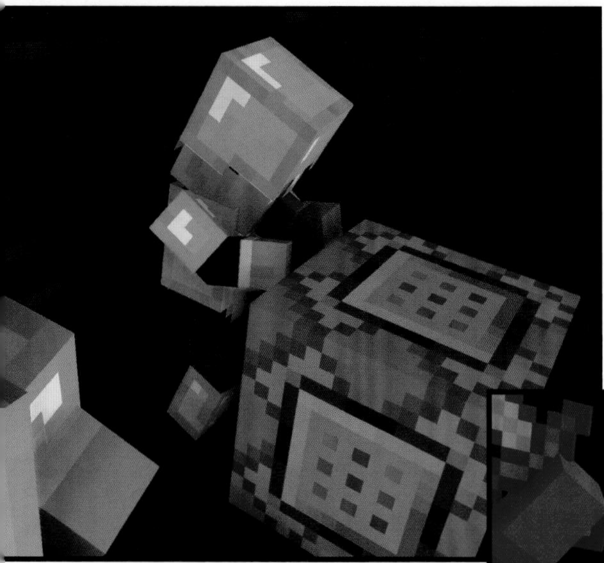
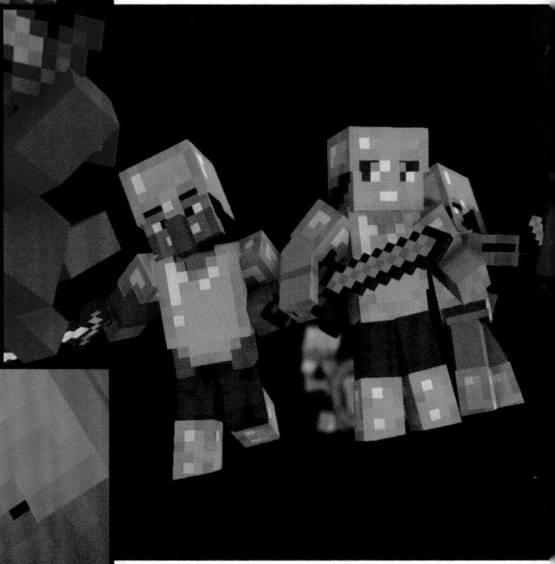
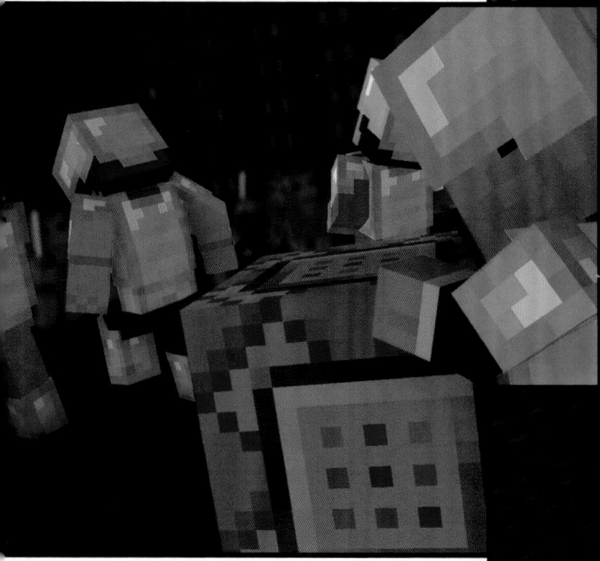
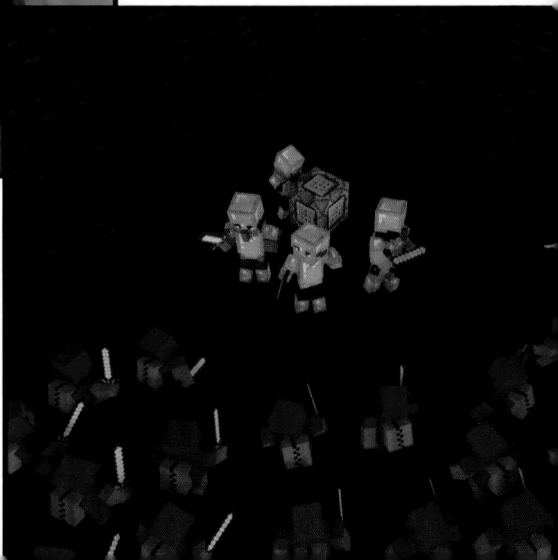

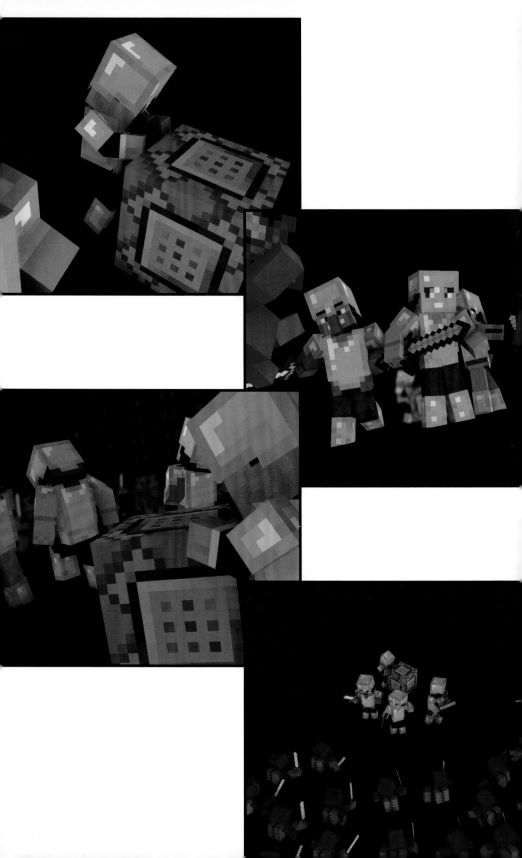

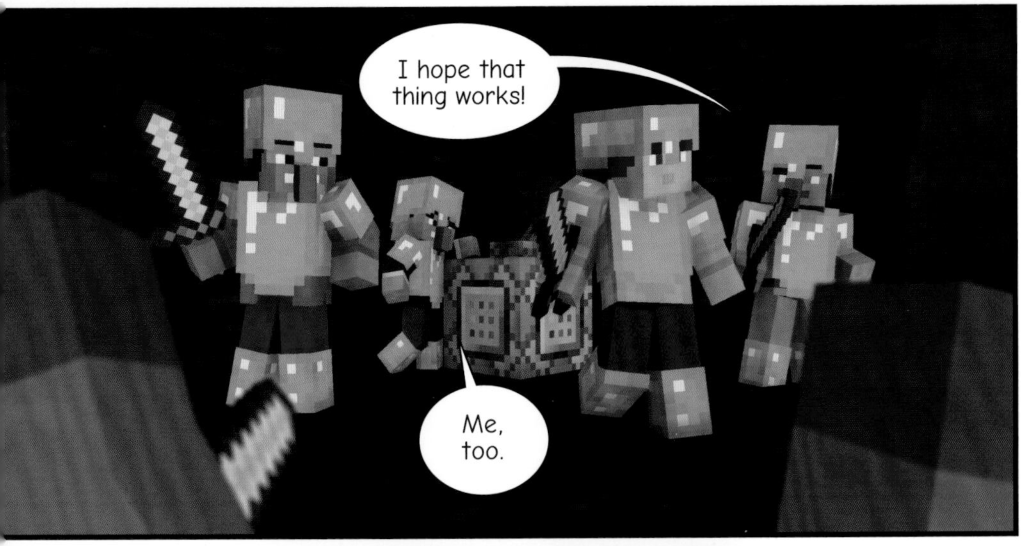
I hope that thing works!
Me, too.

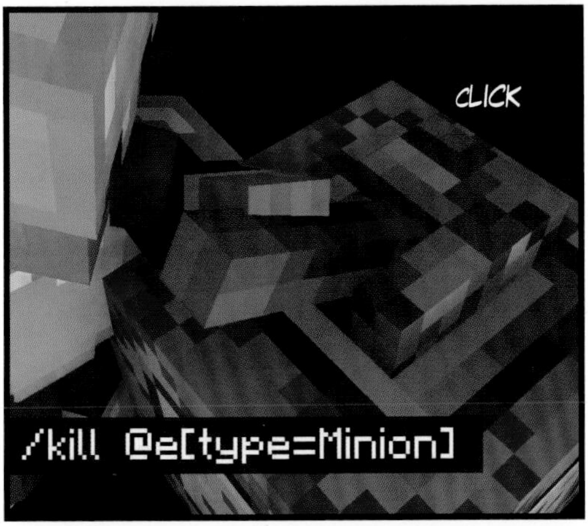
CLICK
/kill @e[type=Minion]

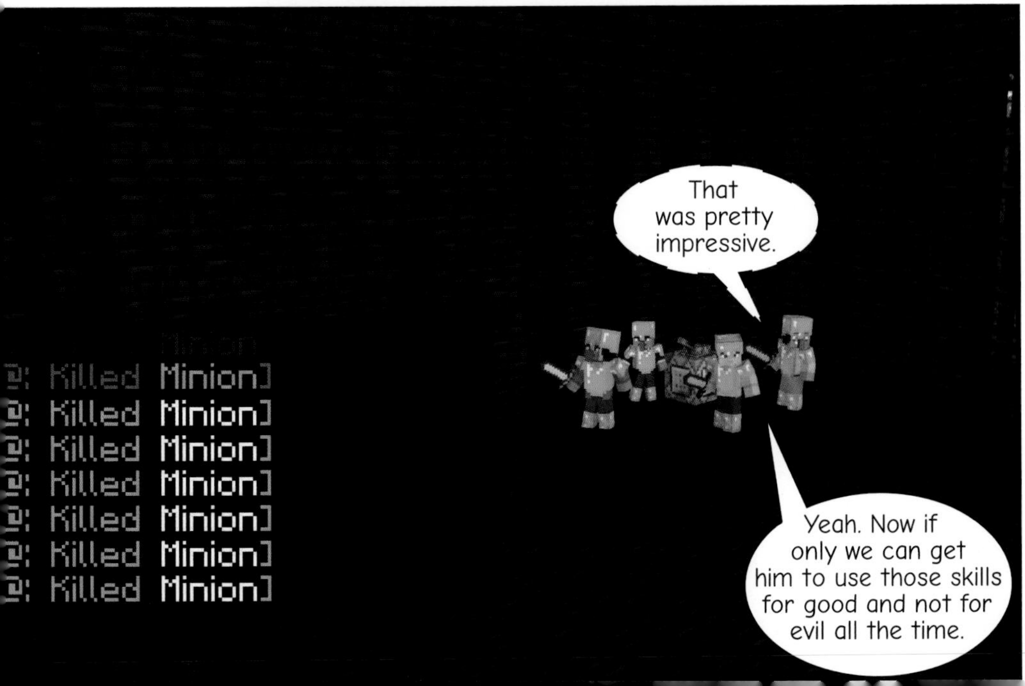
@: Killed Minion]
@: Killed Minion]
@: Killed Minion]
@: Killed Minion]
@: Killed Minion]
@: Killed Minion]
@: Killed Minion]
That was pretty impressive.
Yeah. Now if only we can get him to use those skills for good and not for evil all the time.

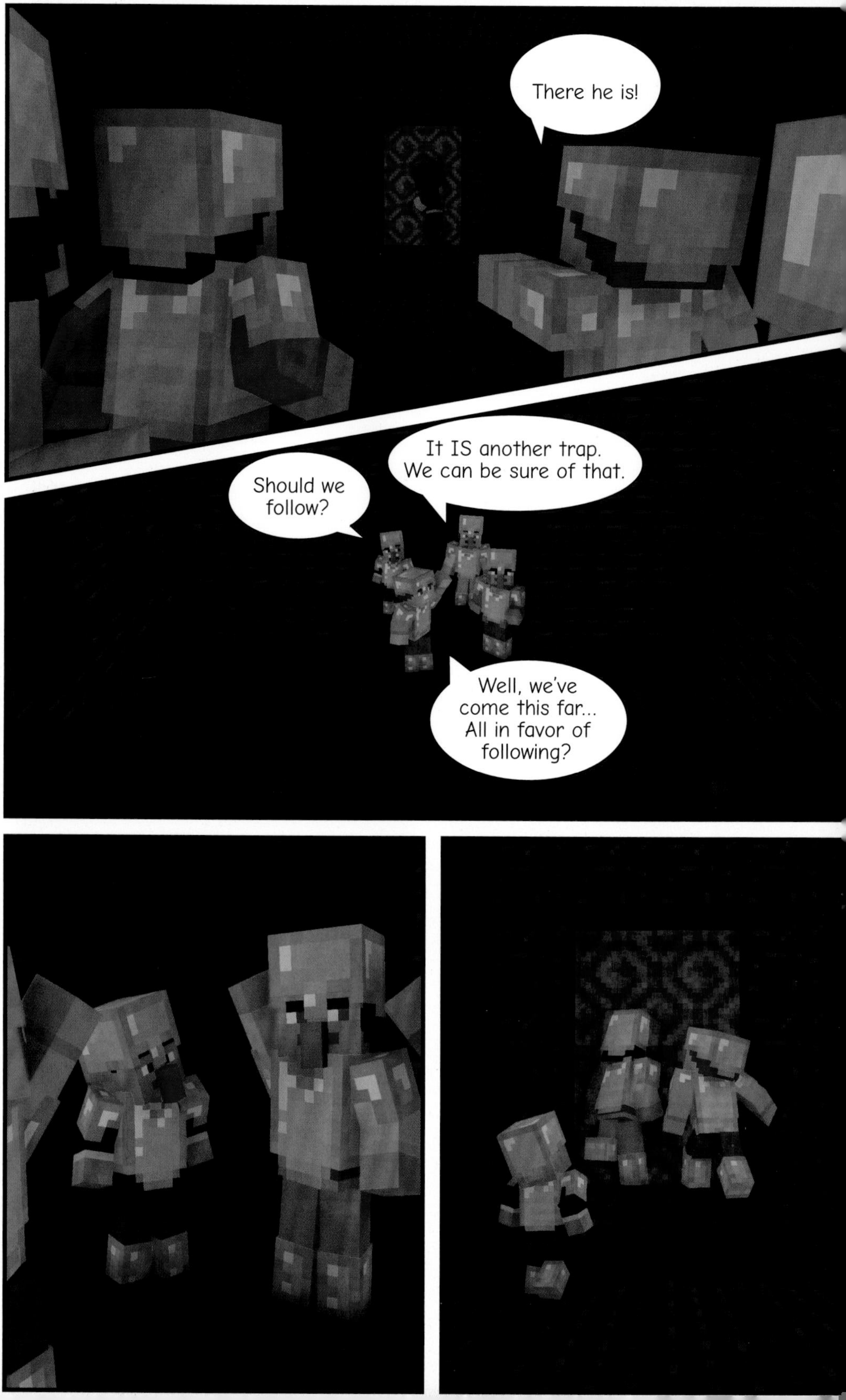
There he is!
Should we follow?
It IS another trap. We can be sure of that.
Well, we've come this far... All in favor of following?

CHAPTER II

CORNERED

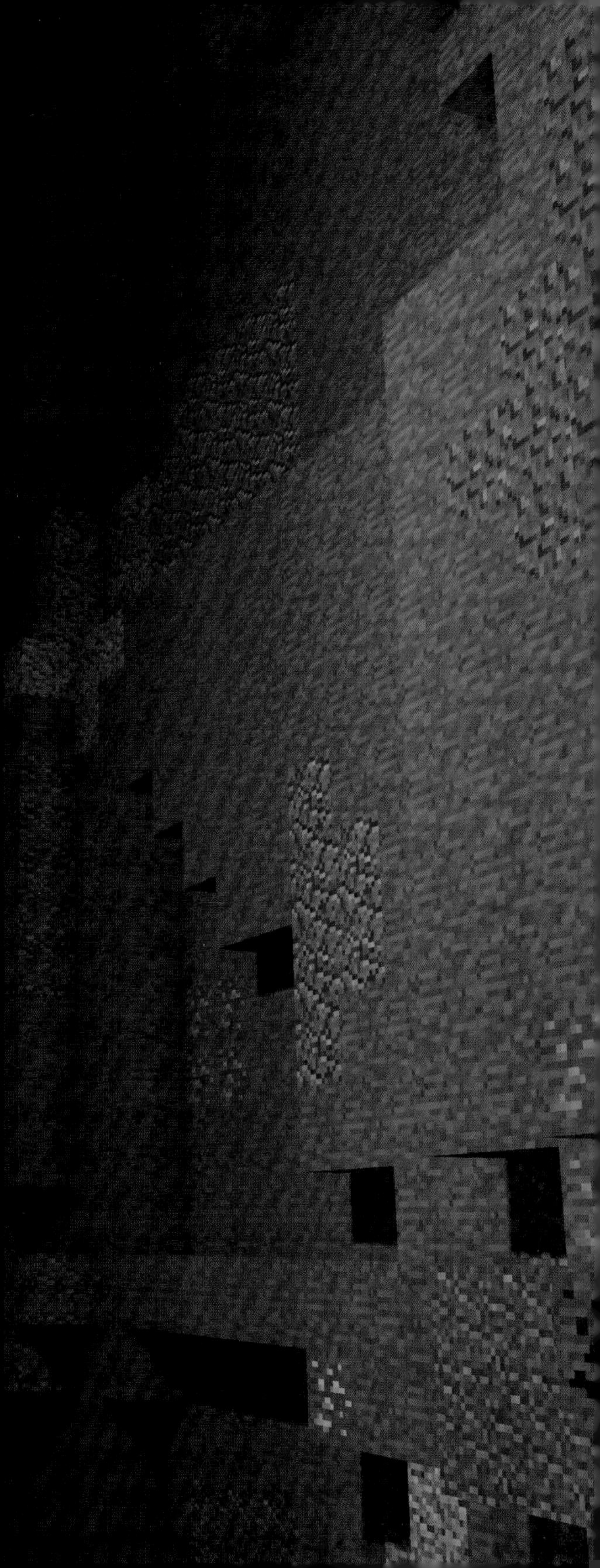

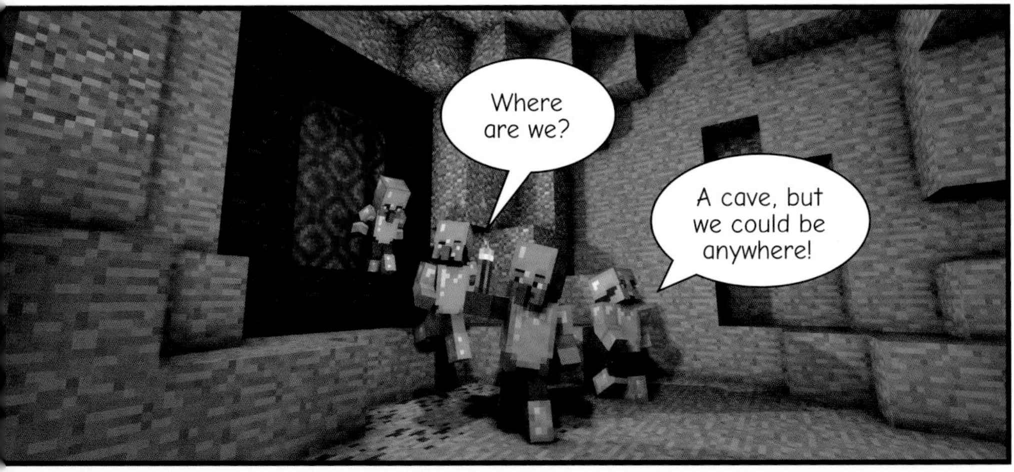
Where are we?
A cave, but we could be anywhere!

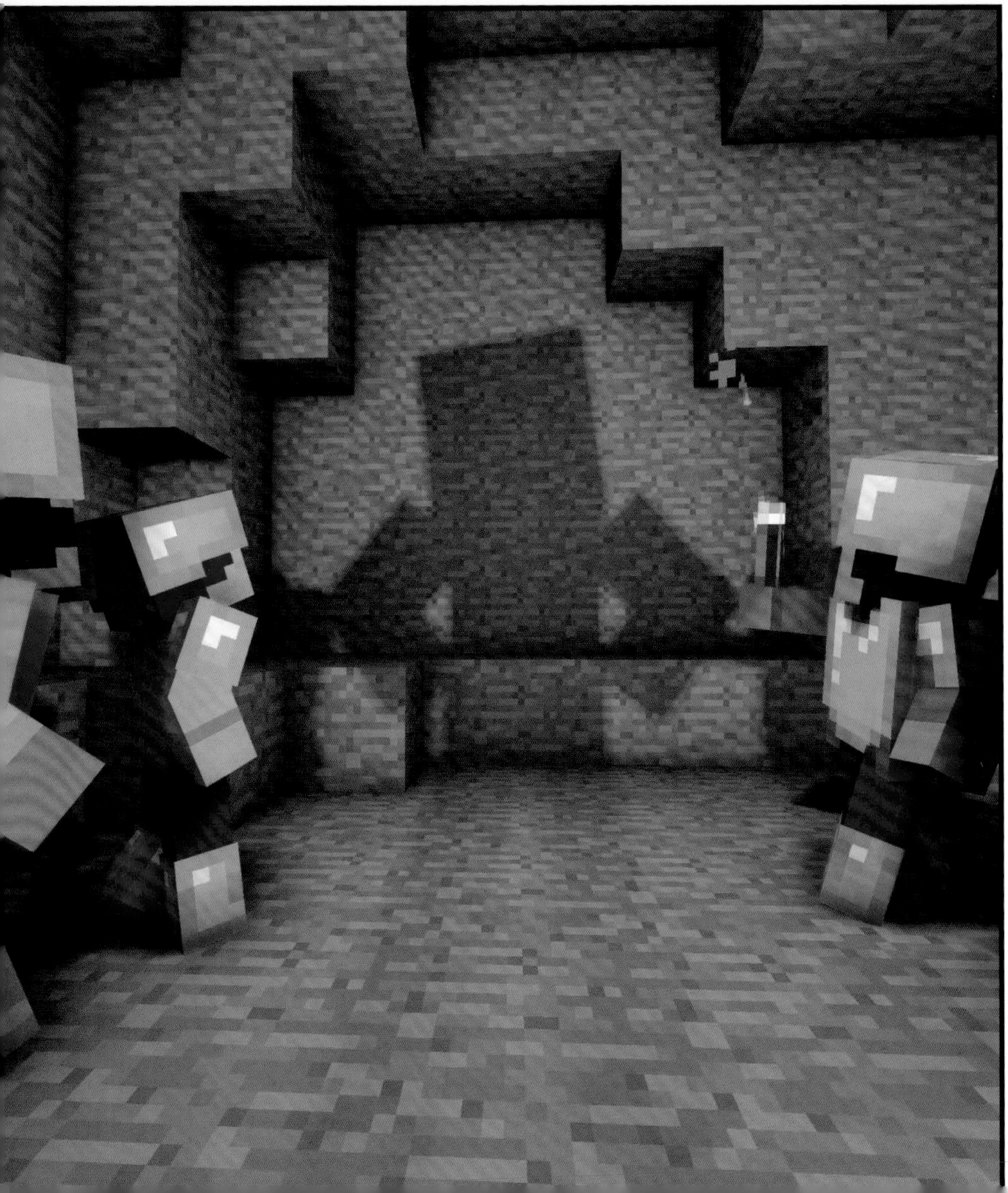

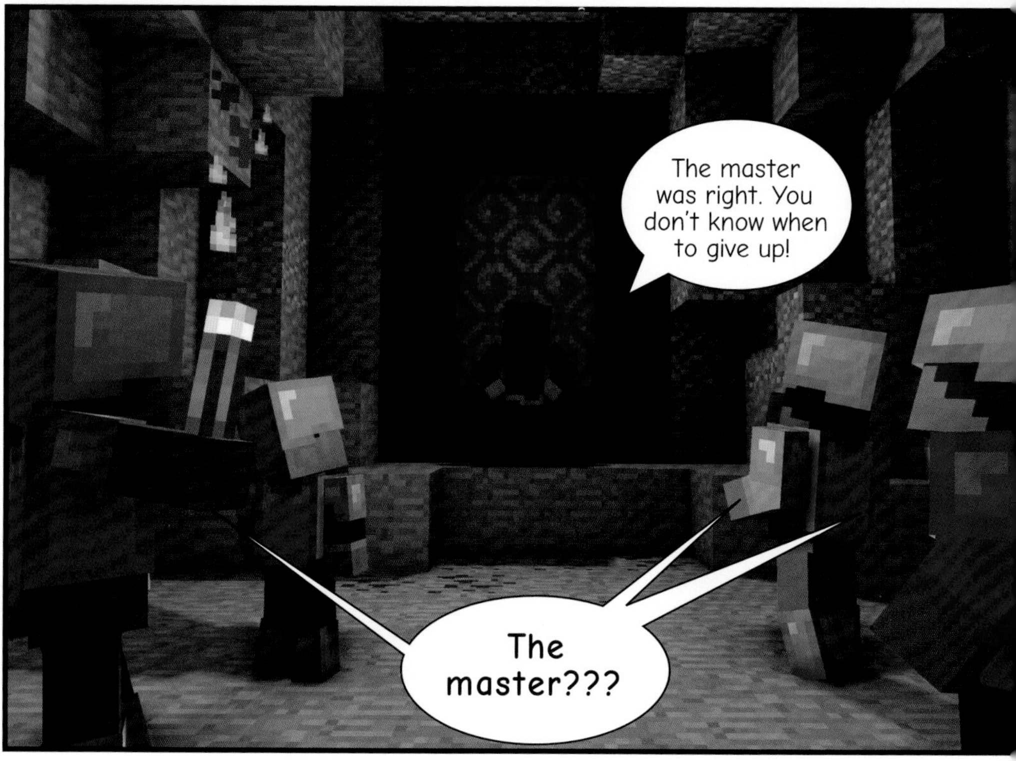
The master was right. You don't know when to give up!
The master???

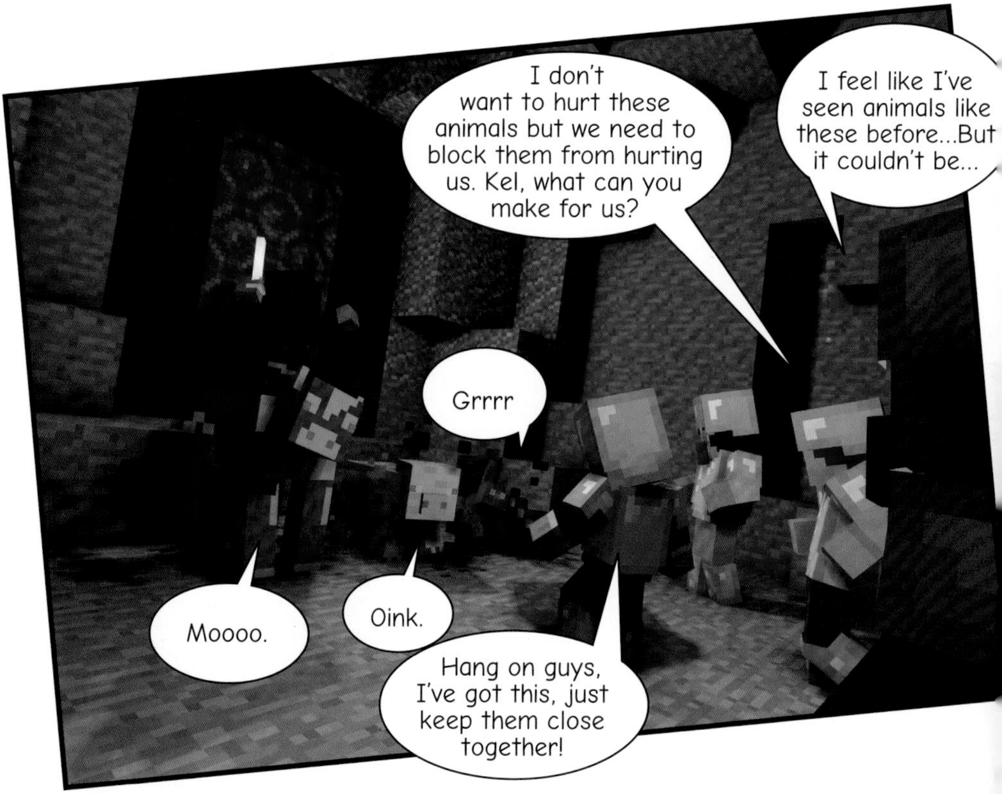
I don't want to hurt these animals but we need to block them from hurting us. Kel, what can you make for us?
I feel like I've seen animals like these before...But it couldn't be...
Grrrr
Moooo.
Oink.
Hang on guys, I've got this, just keep them close together!

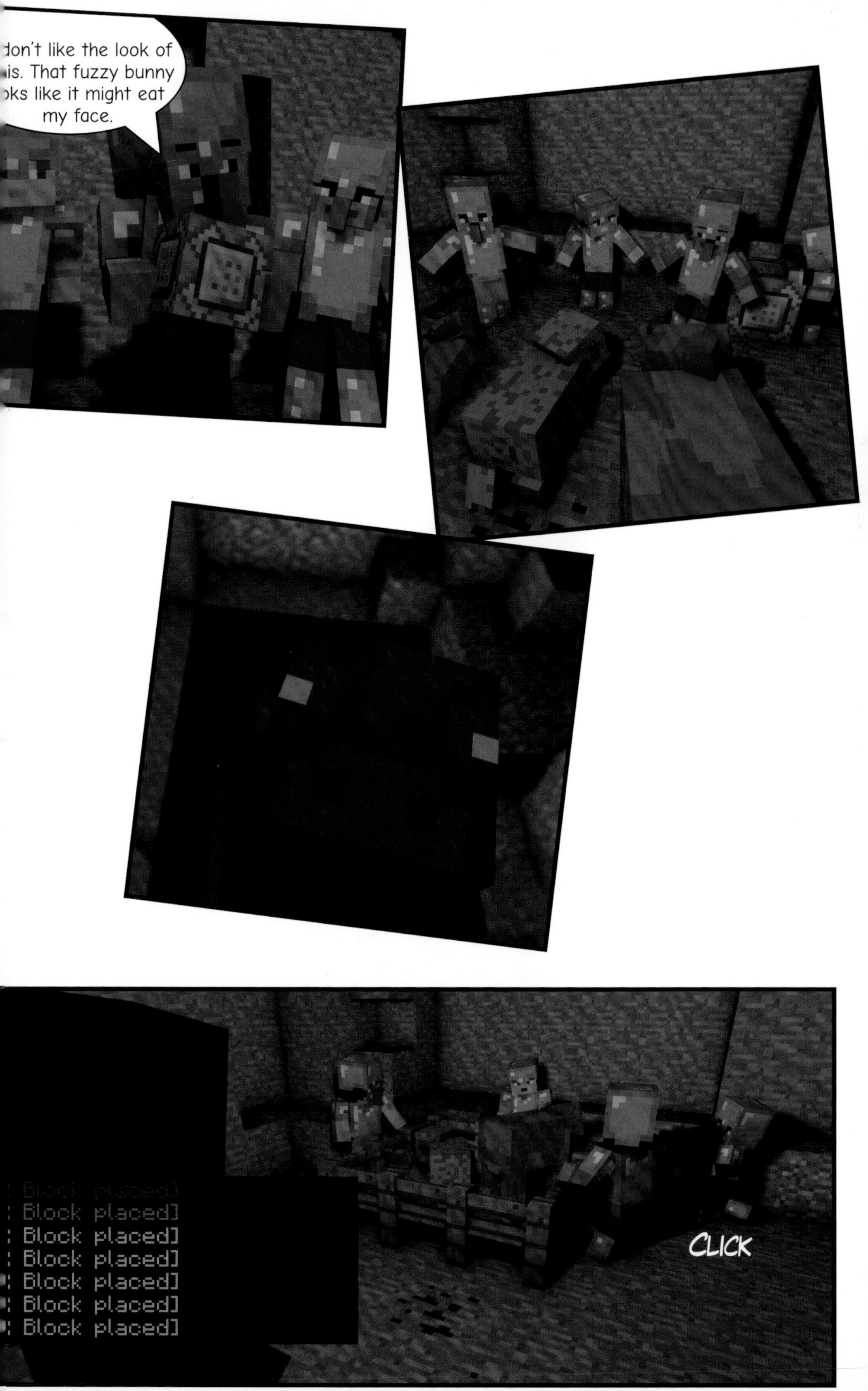

don't like the look of
is. That fuzzy bunny
oks like it might eat
my face.
: Block placed]
: Block placed]
: Block placed]
: Block placed]
: Block placed]
: Block placed]
: Block placed]
CLICK

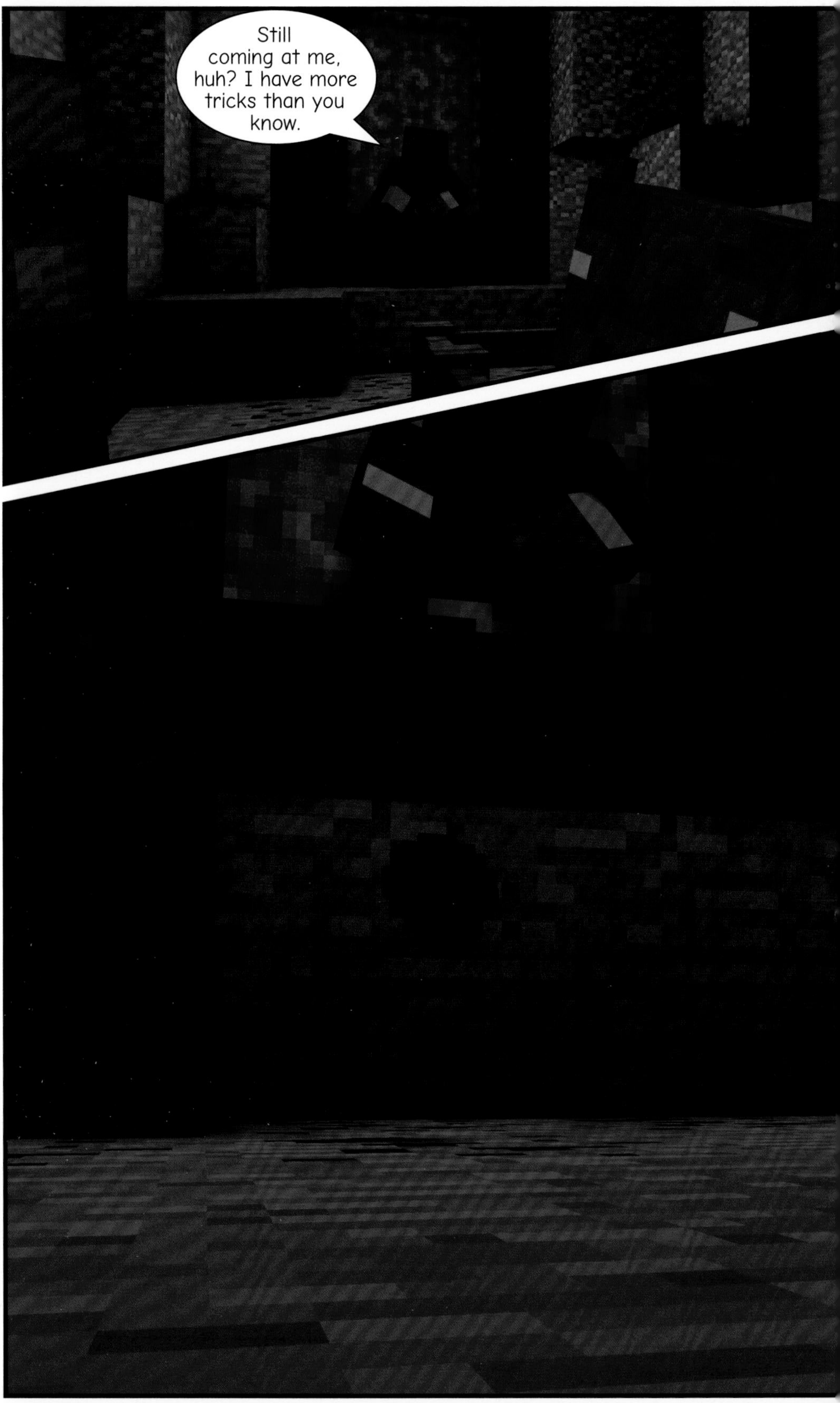
Still coming at me, huh? I have more tricks than you know.

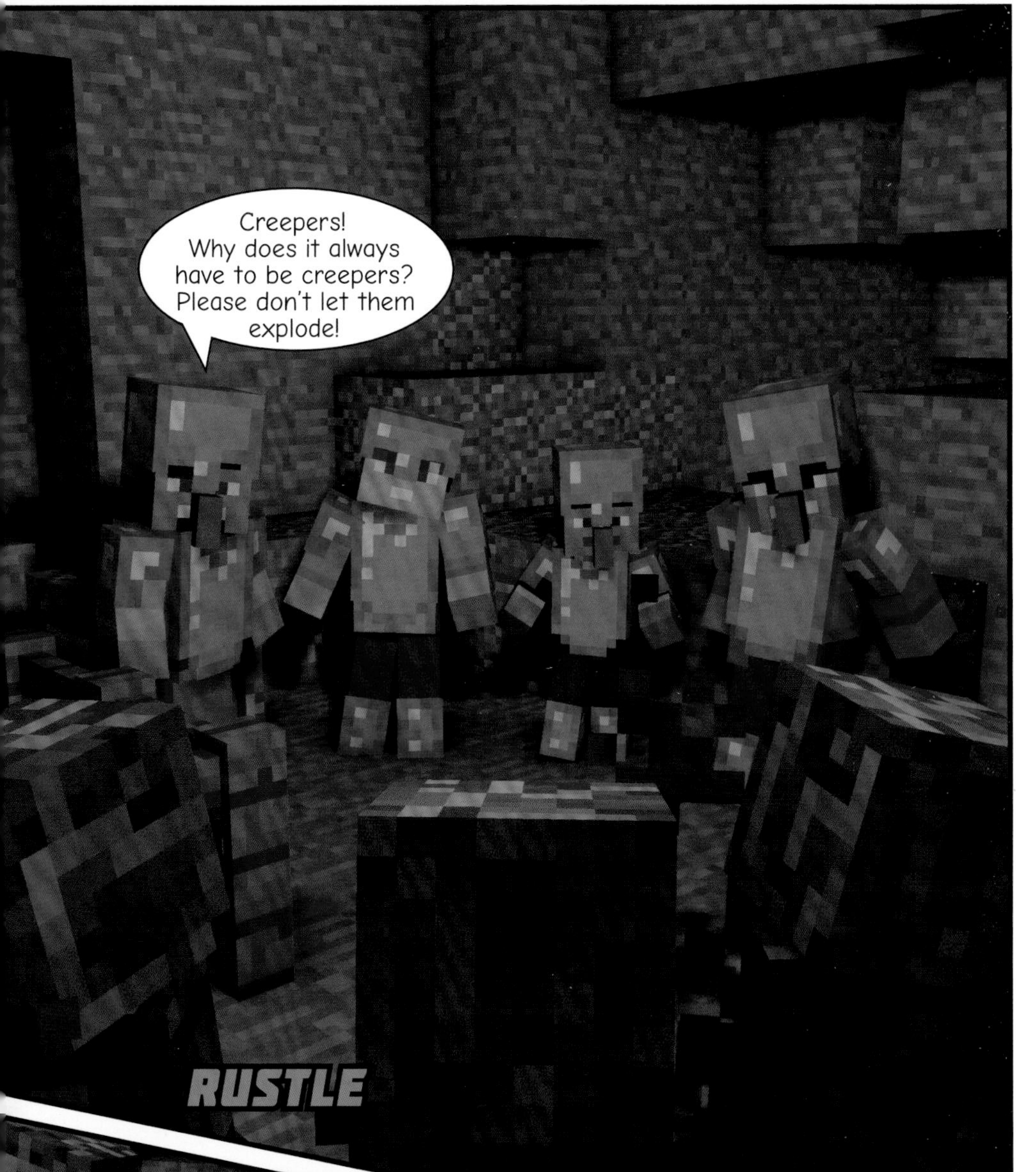
Creepers! Why does it always have to be creepers? Please don't let them explode!
RUSTLE

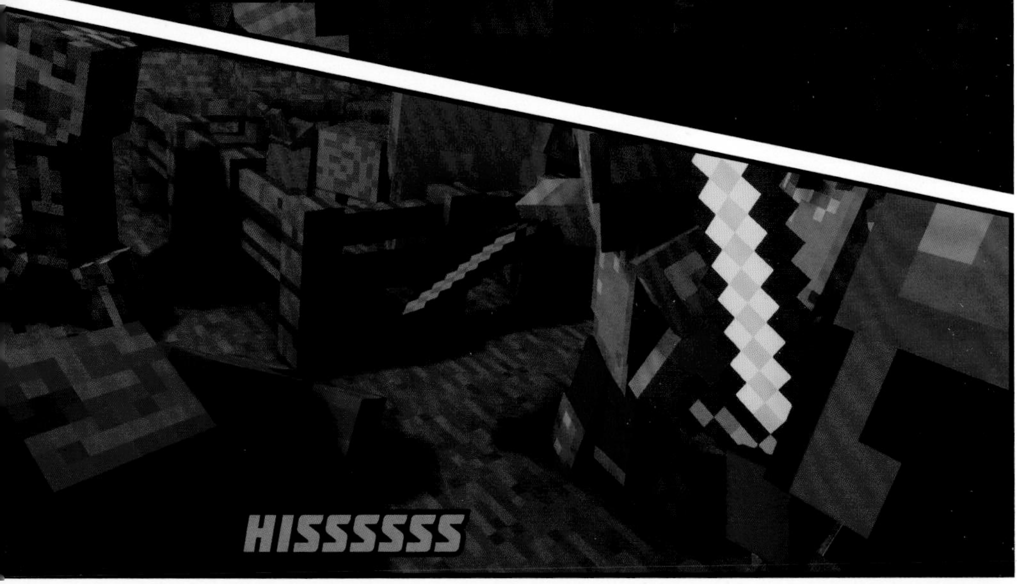
HISSSSSS

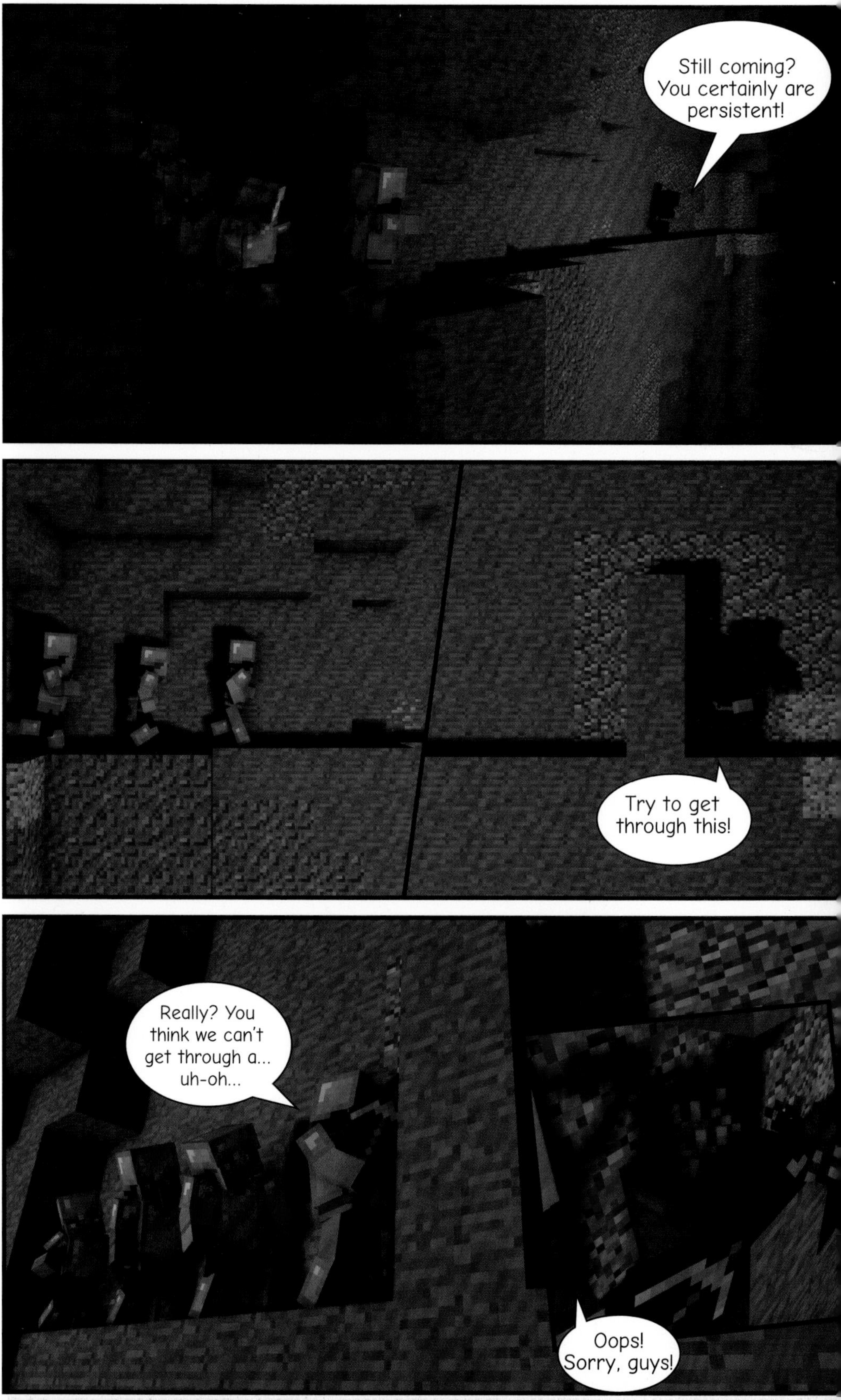
Still coming? You certainly are persistent!
Try to get through this!
Really? You think we can't get through a... uh-oh...
Oops! Sorry, guys!

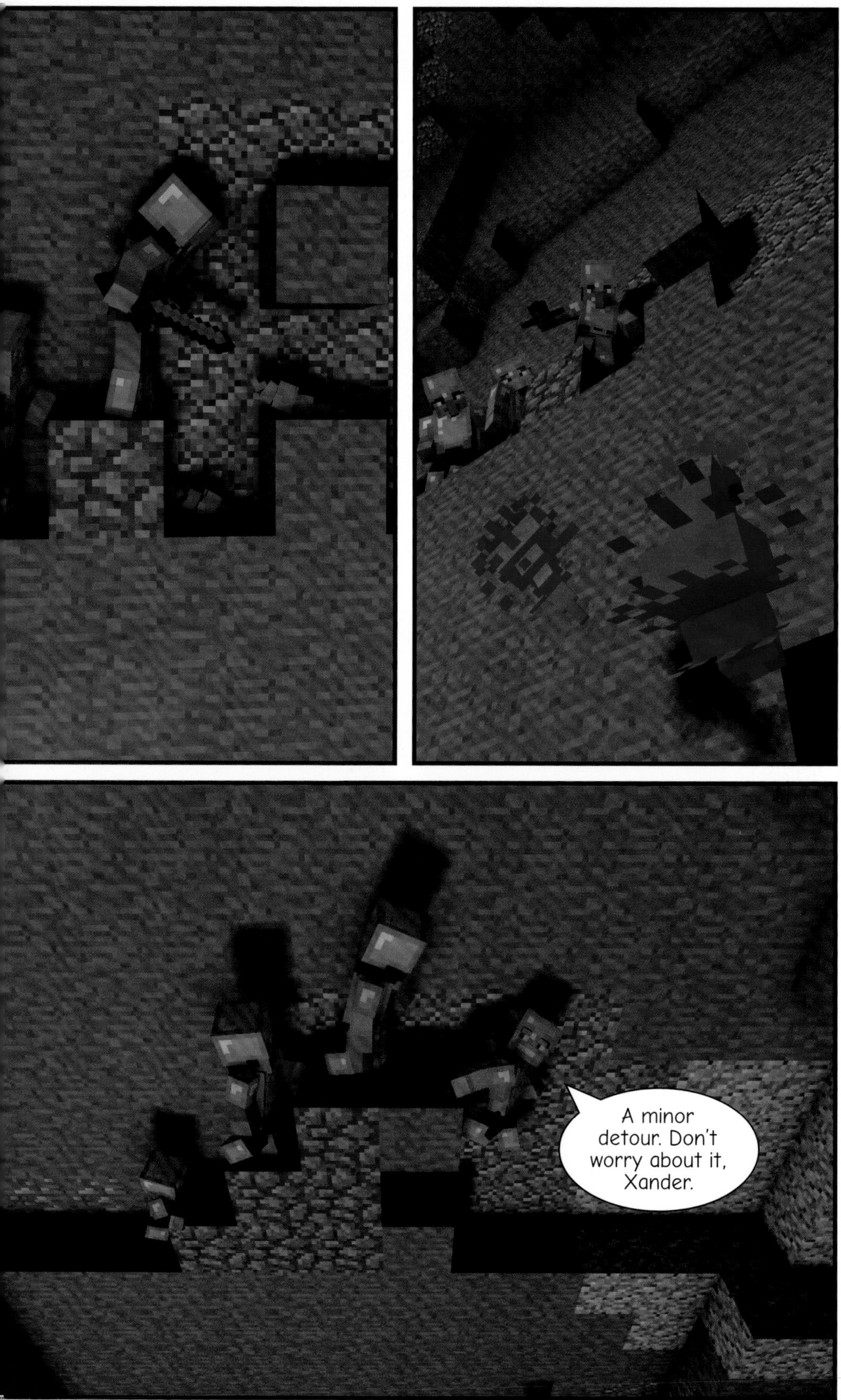
A minor detour. Don't worry about it, Xander.

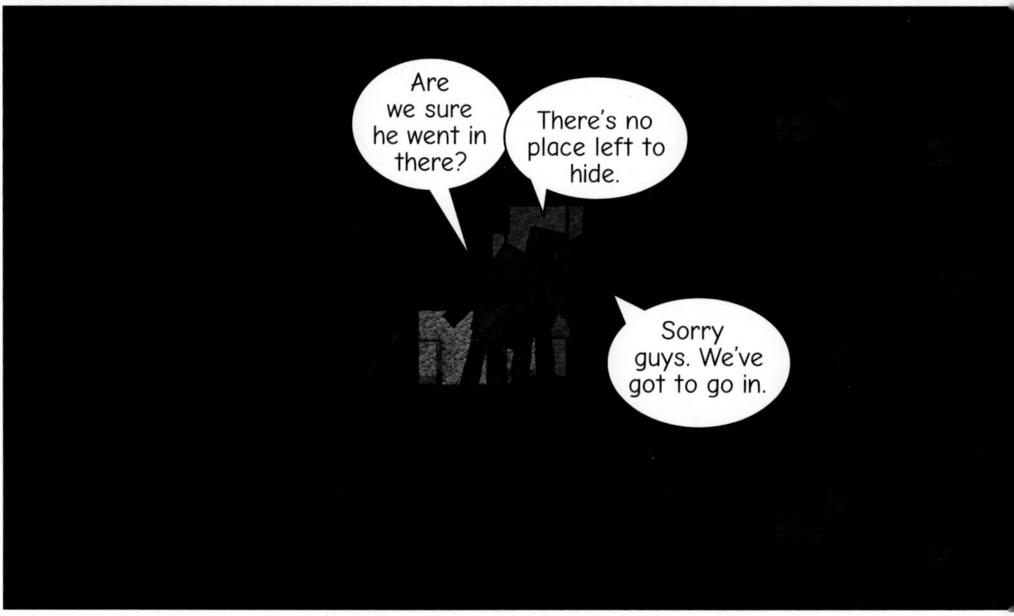
Are we sure he went in there?
There's no place left to hide.
Sorry guys. We've got to go in.

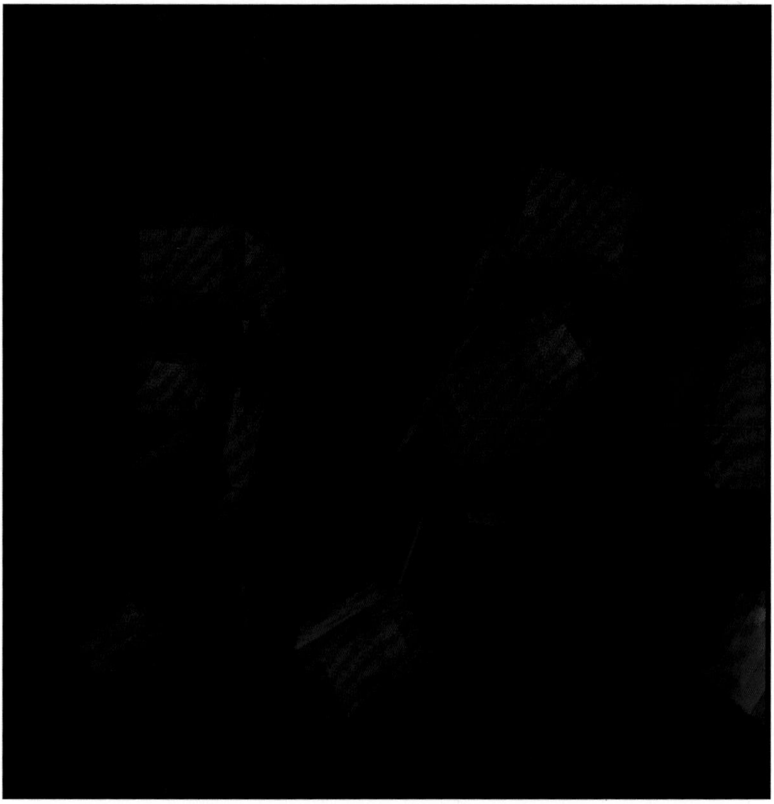

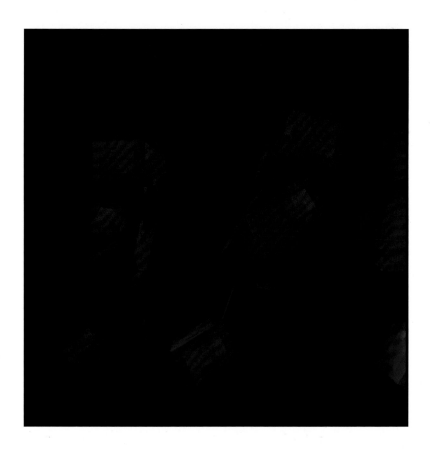

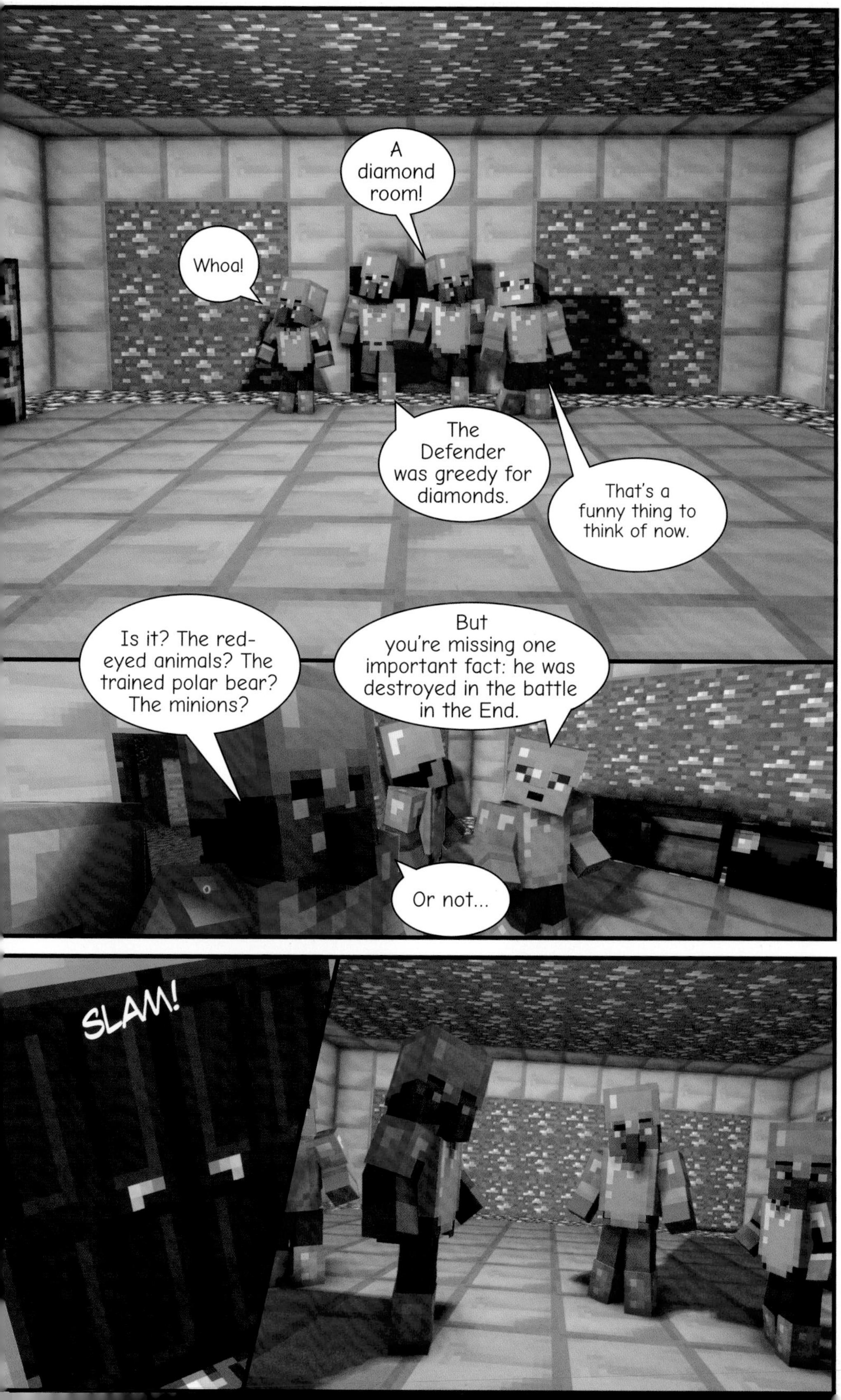
Whoa!
A diamond room!
The Defender was greedy for diamonds.
That's a funny thing to think of now.
Is it? The red-eyed animals? The trained polar bear? The minions?
But you're missing one important fact: he was destroyed in the battle in the End.
Or not...
SLAM!

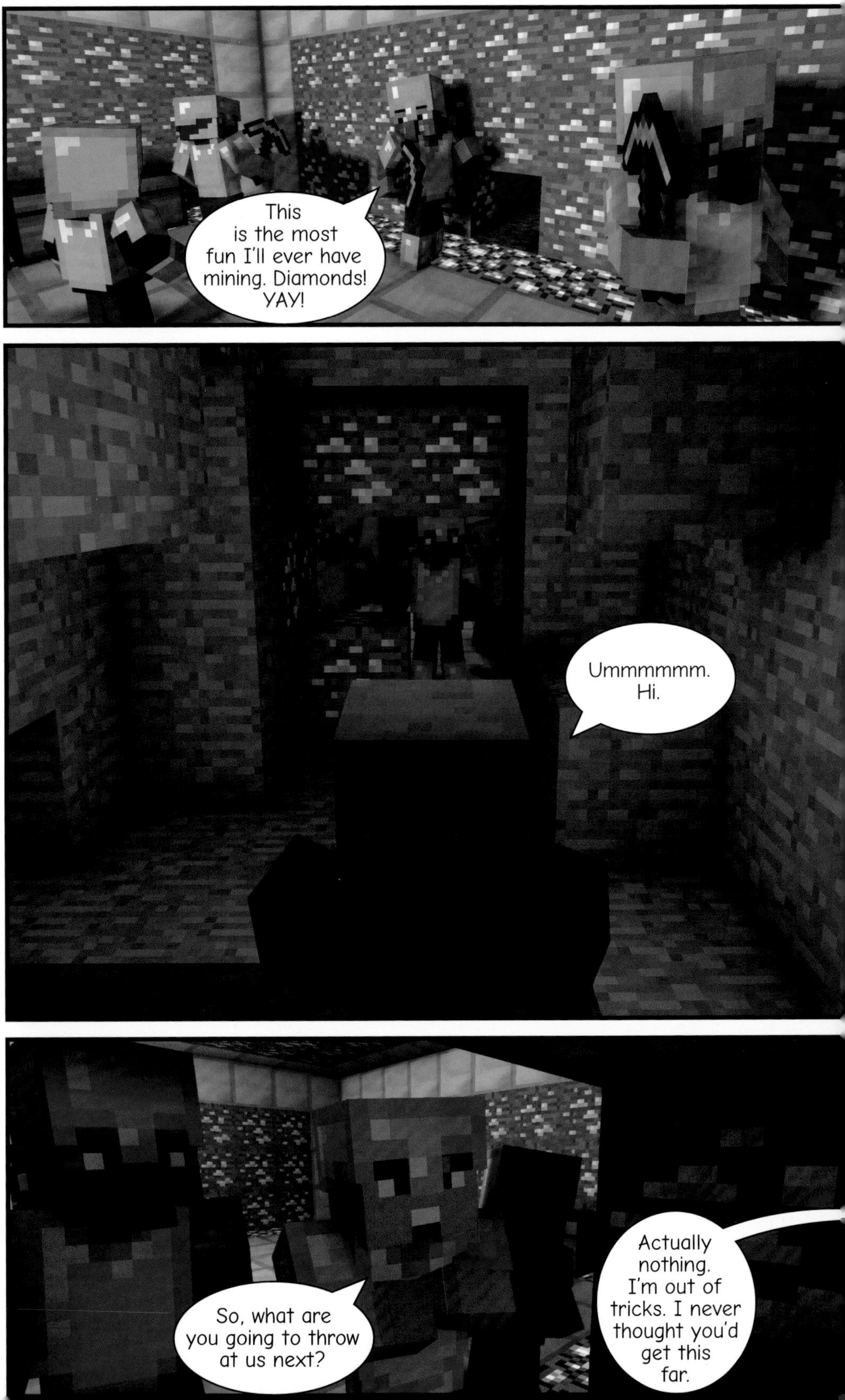
This is the most fun I'll ever have mining. Diamonds! YAY!
Ummmmmm. Hi.
So, what are you going to throw at us next?
Actually nothing. I'm out of tricks. I never thought you'd get this far.

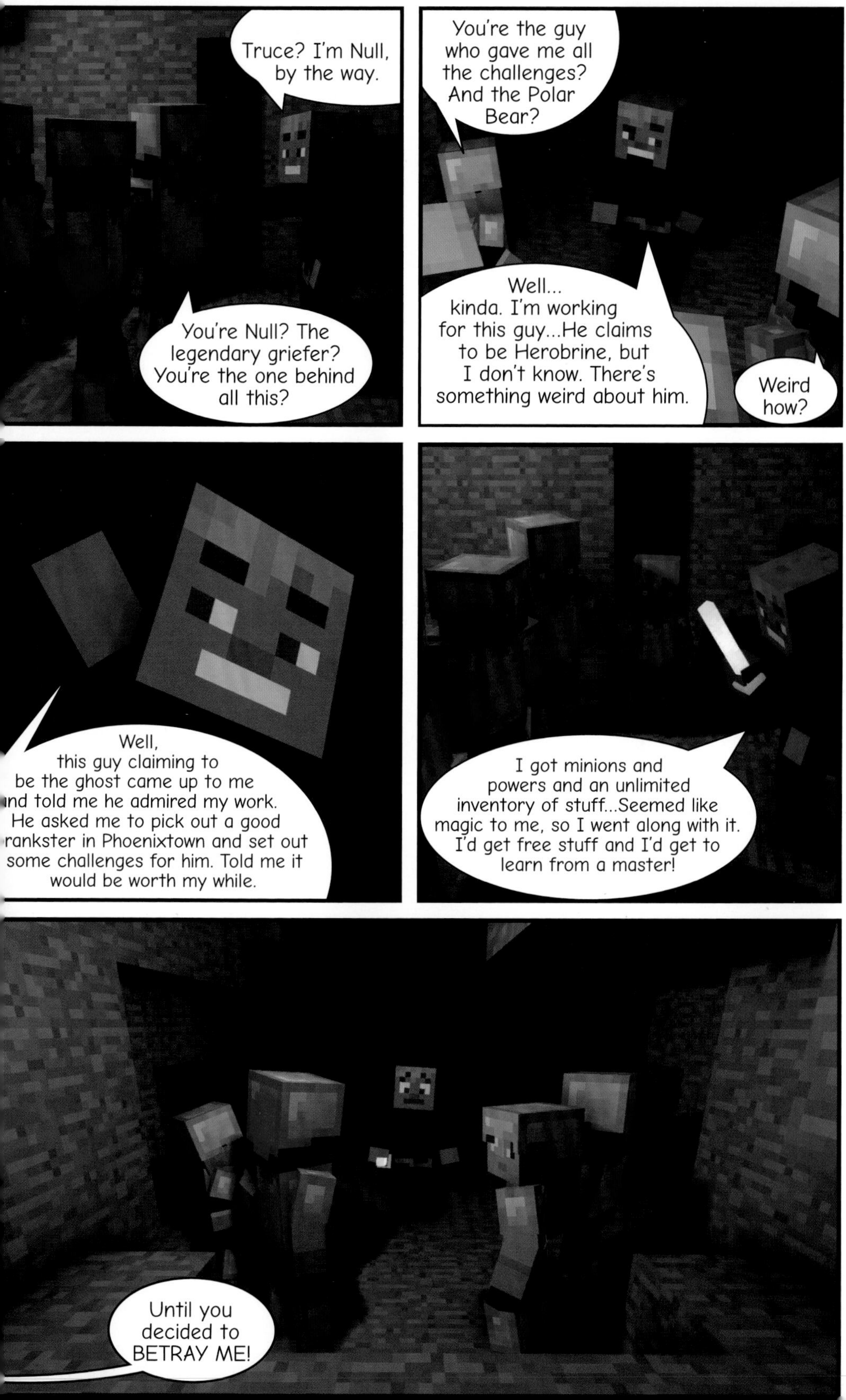

Truce? I'm Null, by the way.
You're Null? The legendary griefer? You're the one behind all this?
You're the guy who gave me all the challenges? And the Polar Bear?
Well... kinda. I'm working for this guy...He claims to be Herobrine, but I don't know. There's something weird about him.
Weird how?
Well, this guy claiming to be the ghost came up to me ınd told me he admired my work. He asked me to pick out a good rankster in Phoenixtown and set out some challenges for him. Told me it would be worth my while.
I got minions and powers and an unlimited inventory of stuff...Seemed like magic to me, so I went along with it. I'd get free stuff and I'd get to learn from a master!
Until you decided to BETRAY ME!

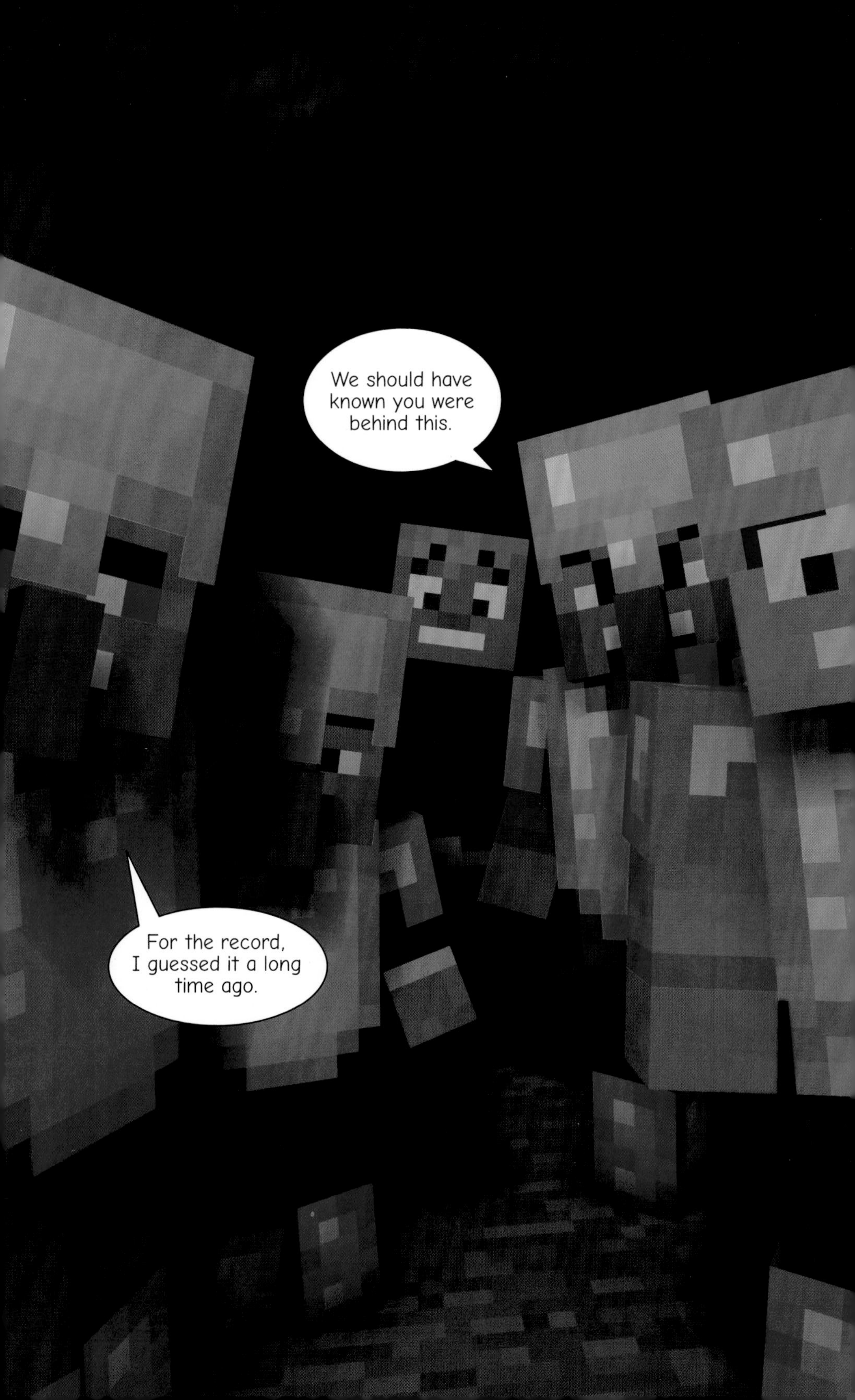
We should have known you were behind this.
For the record, I guessed it a long time ago.

CHAPTER 12

BACK FROM THE DEAD

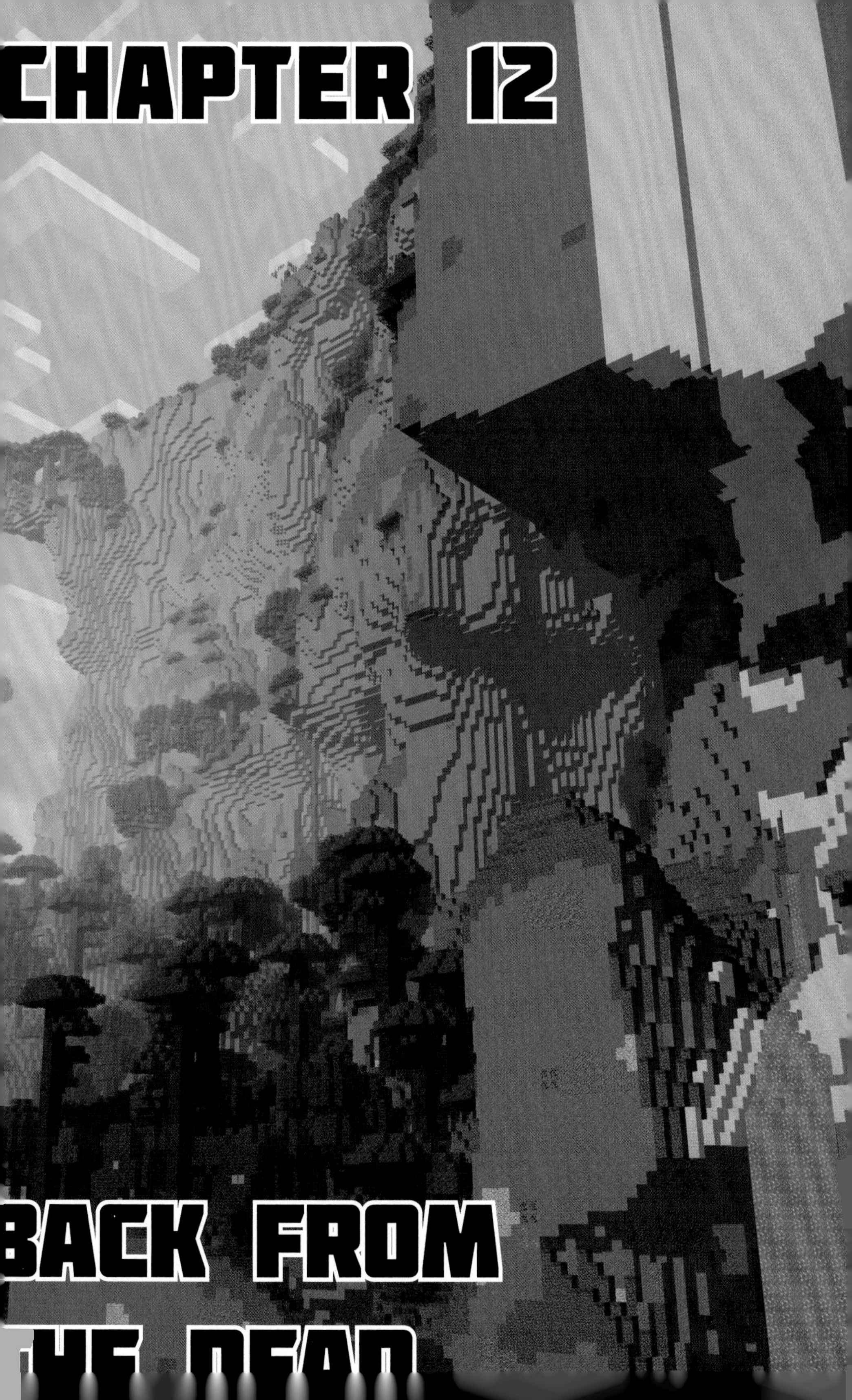

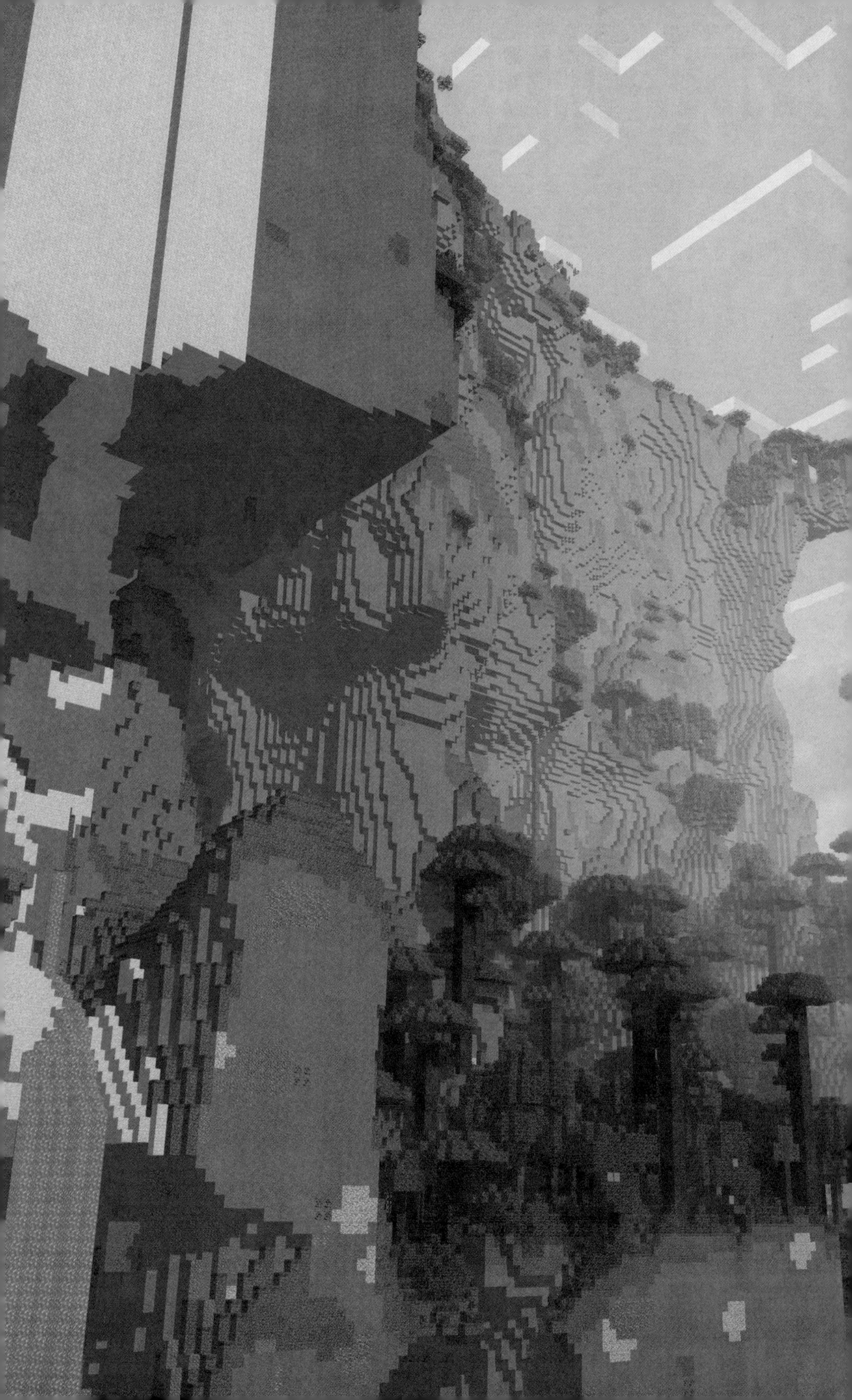

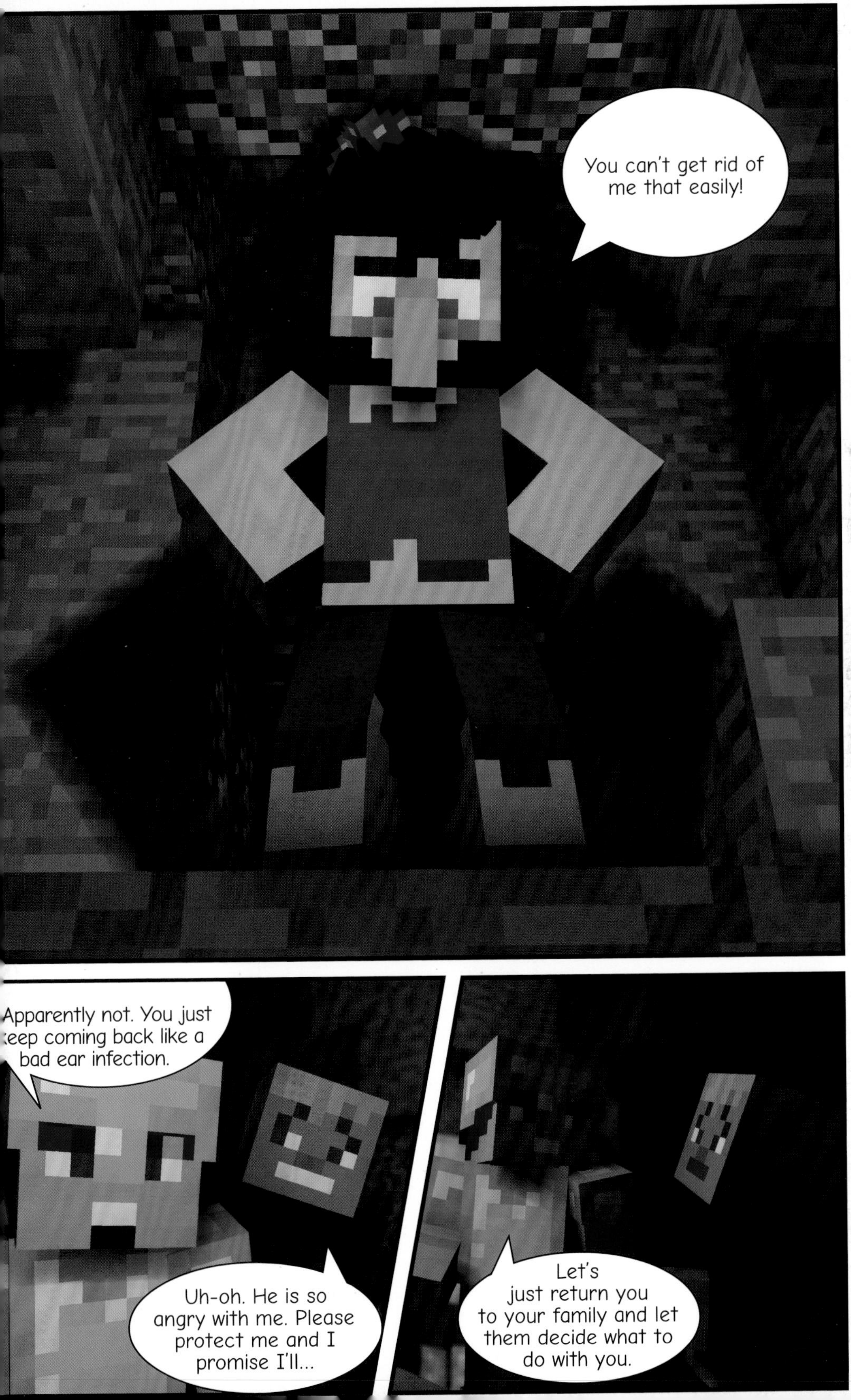
You can't get rid of me that easily!
Apparently not. You just eep coming back like a bad ear infection.
Uh-oh. He is so angry with me. Please protect me and I promise I'll...
Let's just return you to your family and let them decide what to do with you.

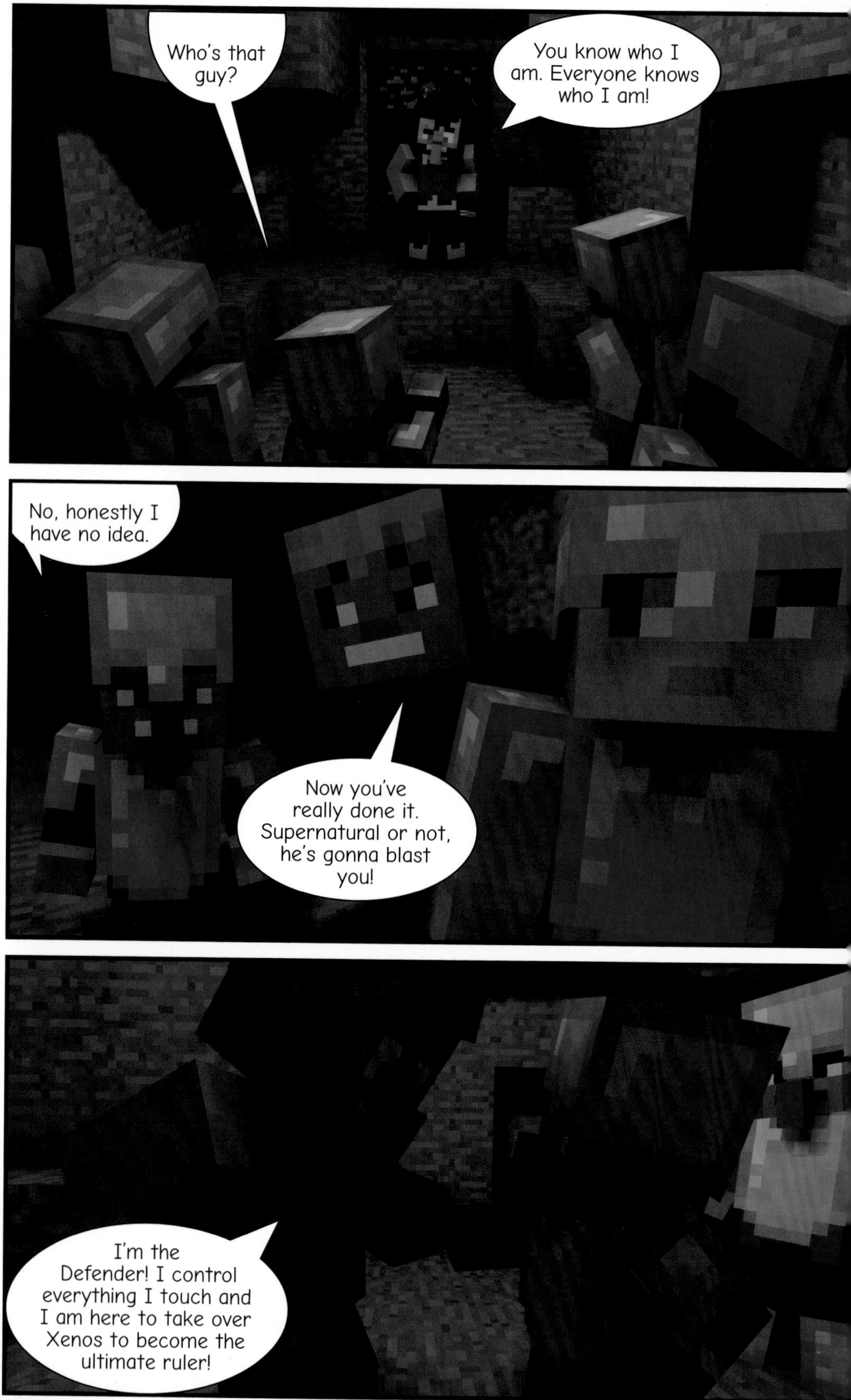
Who's that guy?
You know who I am. Everyone knows who I am!
No, honestly I have no idea.
Now you've really done it. Supernatural or not, he's gonna blast you!
I'm the Defender! I control everything I touch and I am here to take over Xenos to become the ultimate ruler!

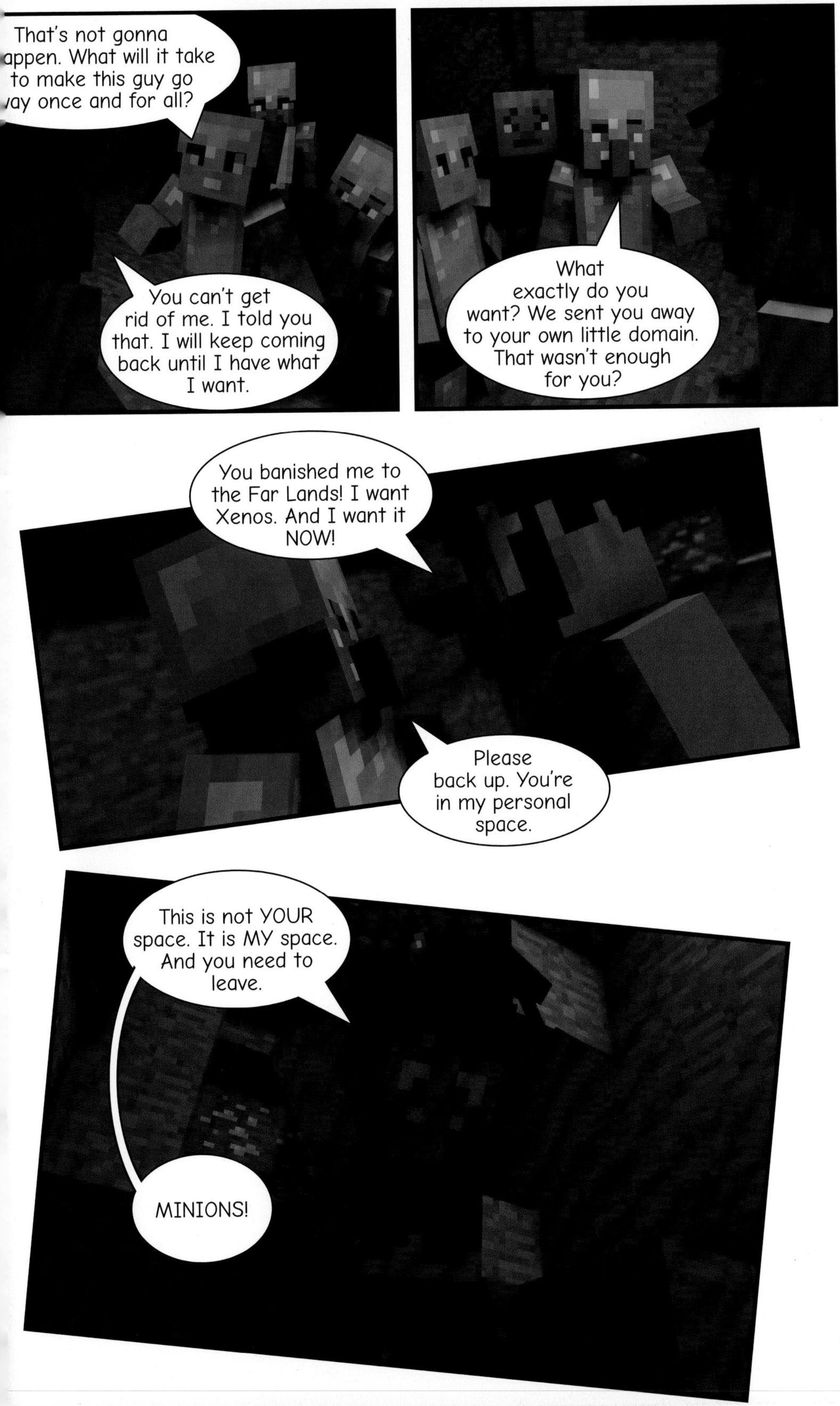
That's not gonna appen. What will it take to make this guy go ay once and for all?
You can't get rid of me. I told you that. I will keep coming back until I have what I want.
What exactly do you want? We sent you away to your own little domain. That wasn't enough for you?
You banished me to the Far Lands! I want Xenos. And I want it NOW!
Please back up. You're in my personal space.
This is not YOUR space. It is MY space. And you need to leave.
MINIONS!

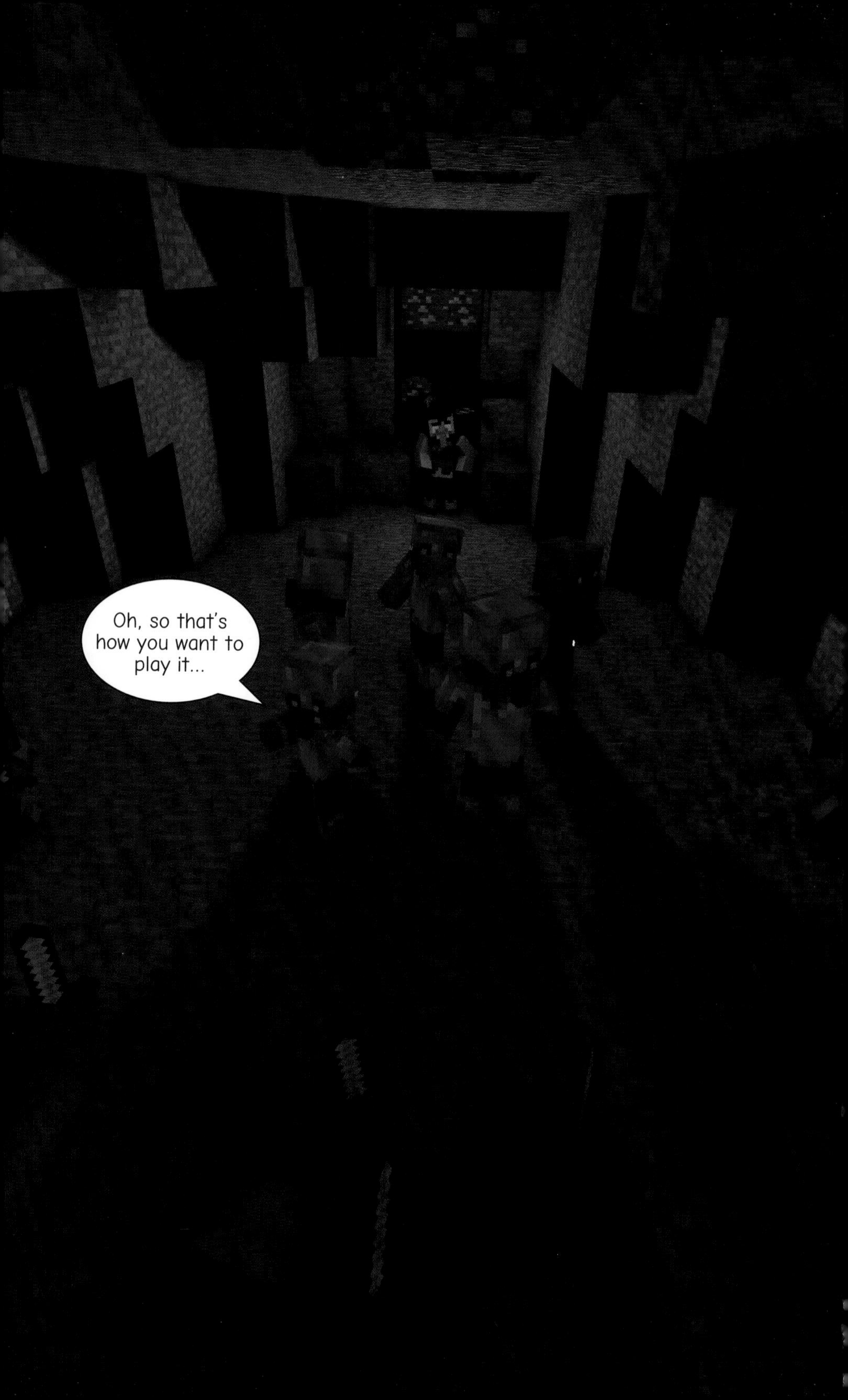
Oh, so that's how you want to play it...

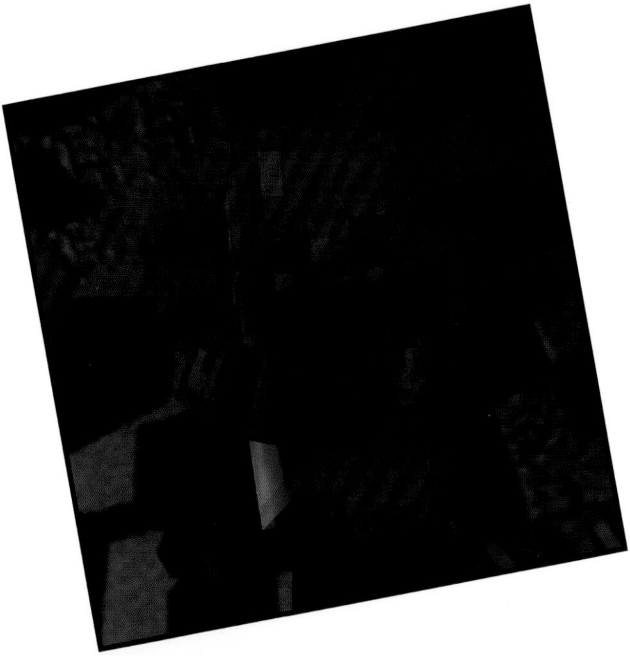

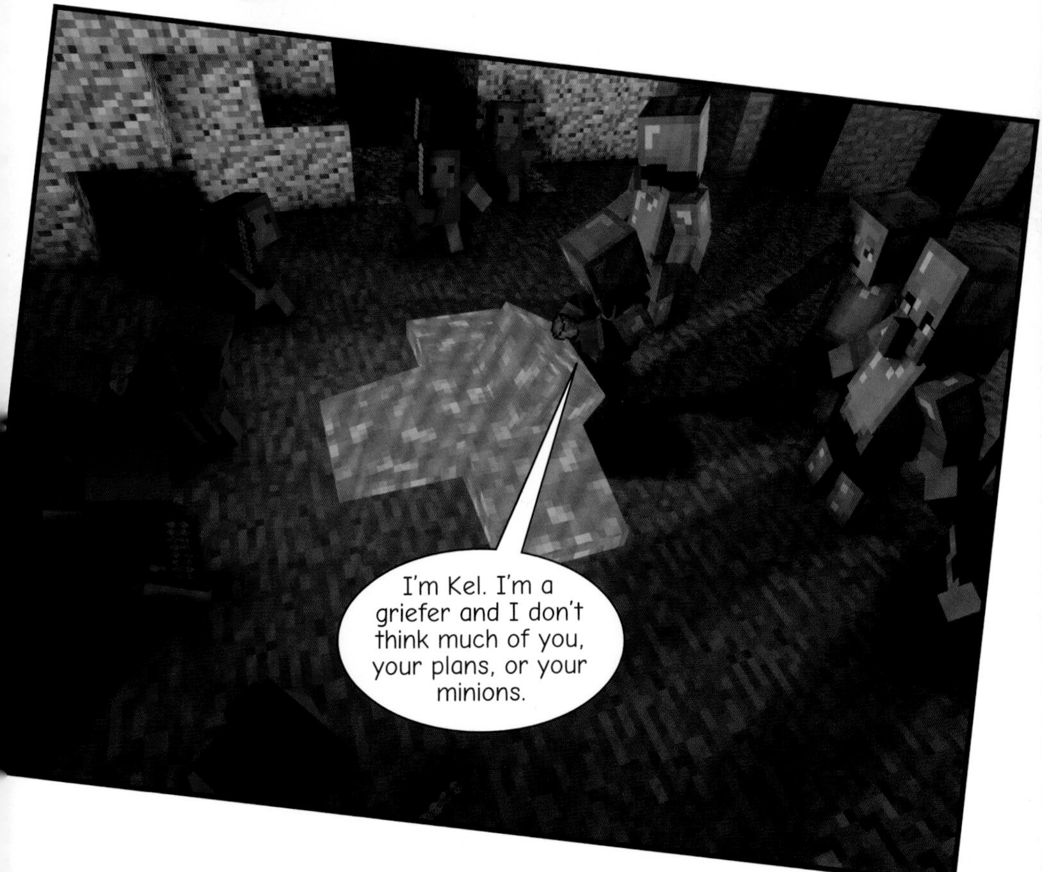
I'm Kel. I'm a griefer and I don't think much of you, your plans, or your minions.

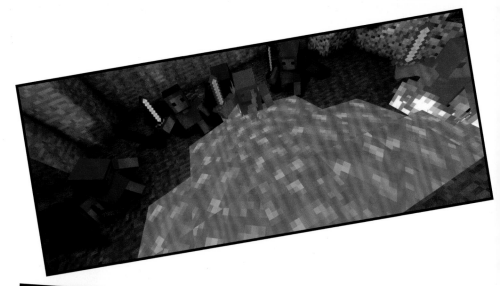

Come back here and do my bidding!

You kids are always ruining my plans!

And you're just useless.

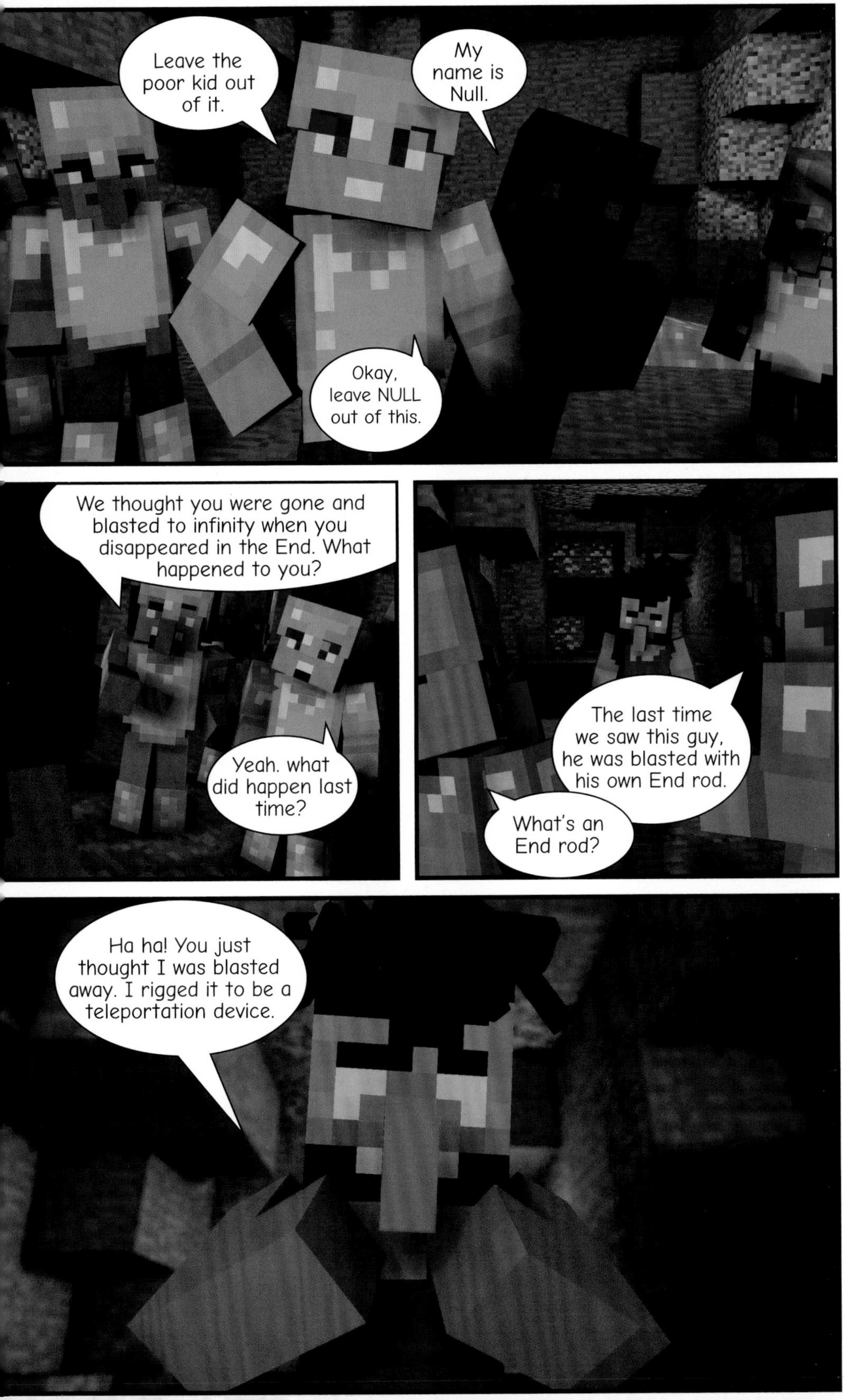
Leave the poor kid out of it.
My name is Null.
Okay, leave NULL out of this.
We thought you were gone and blasted to infinity when you disappeared in the End. What happened to you?
Yeah. what did happen last time?
The last time we saw this guy, he was blasted with his own End rod.
What's an End rod?
Ha ha! You just thought I was blasted away. I rigged it to be a teleportation device.

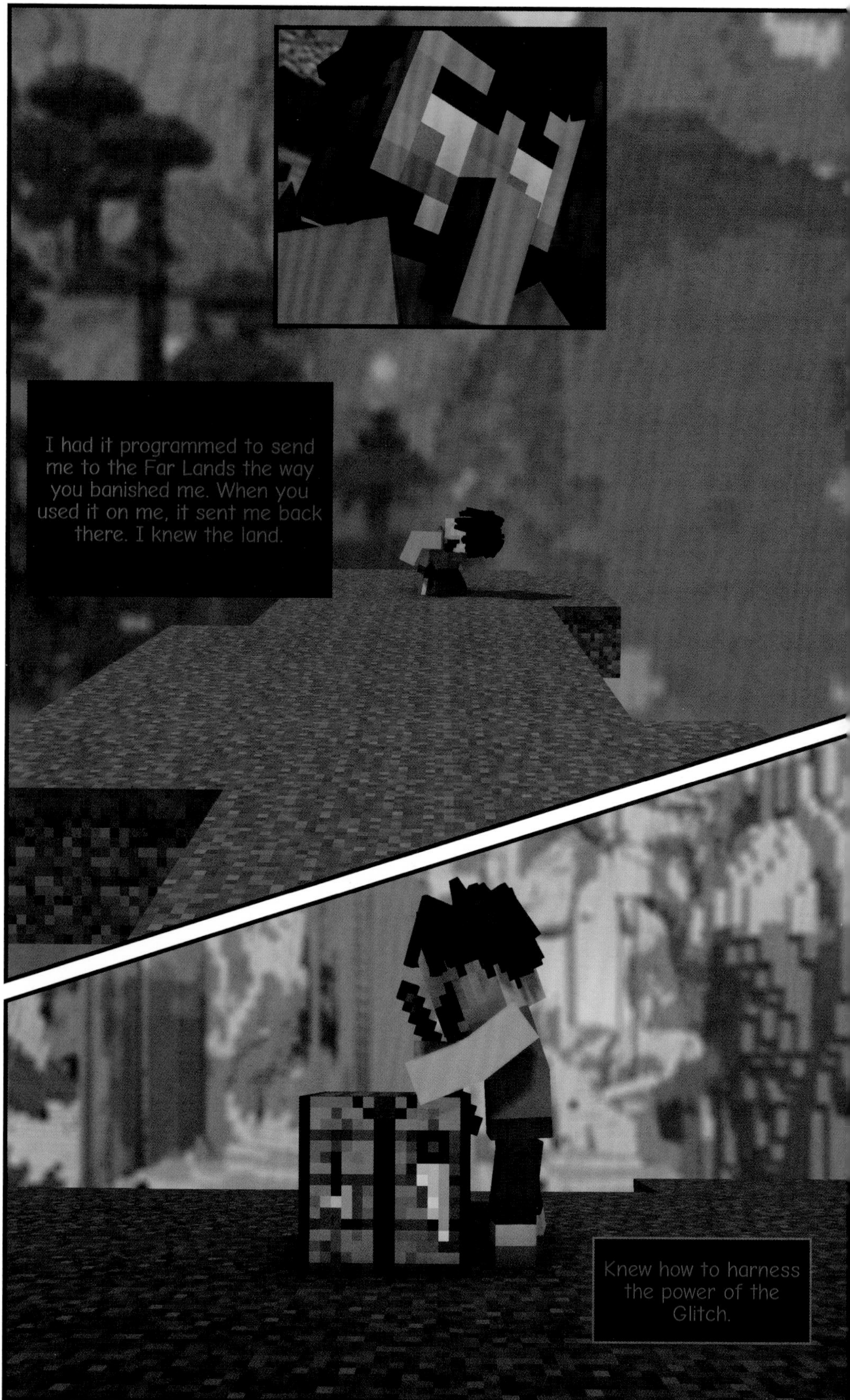
I had it programmed to send me to the Far Lands the way you banished me. When you used it on me, it sent me back there. I knew the land.
Knew how to harness the power of the Glitch.

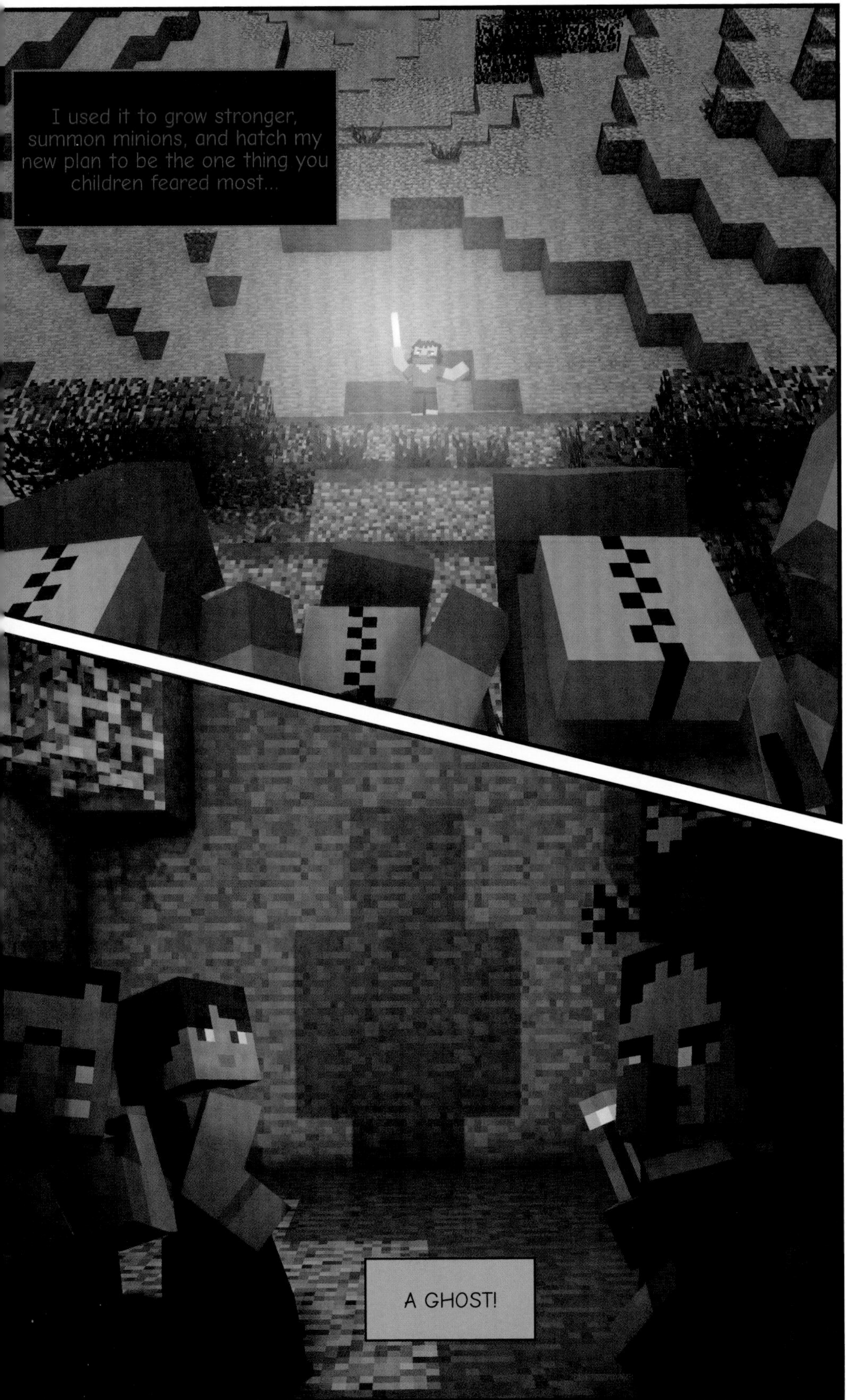
I used it to grow stronger, summon minions, and hatch my new plan to be the one thing you children feared most...
A GHOST!

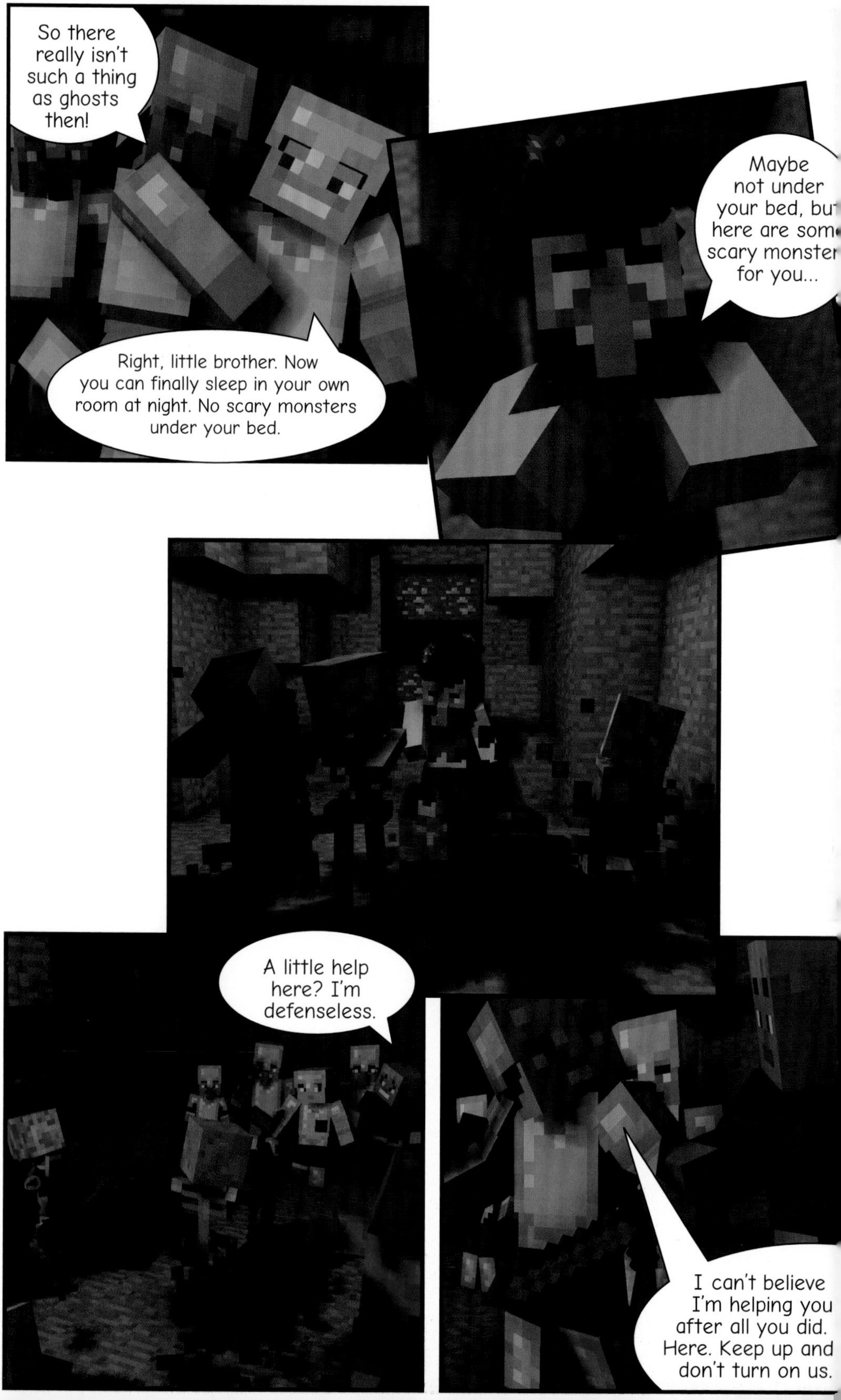
So there really isn't such a thing as ghosts then!
Right, little brother. Now you can finally sleep in your own room at night. No scary monsters under your bed.
Maybe not under your bed, bu here are som scary monster for you...
A little help here? I'm defenseless.
I can't believe I'm helping you after all you did. Here. Keep up and don't turn on us.

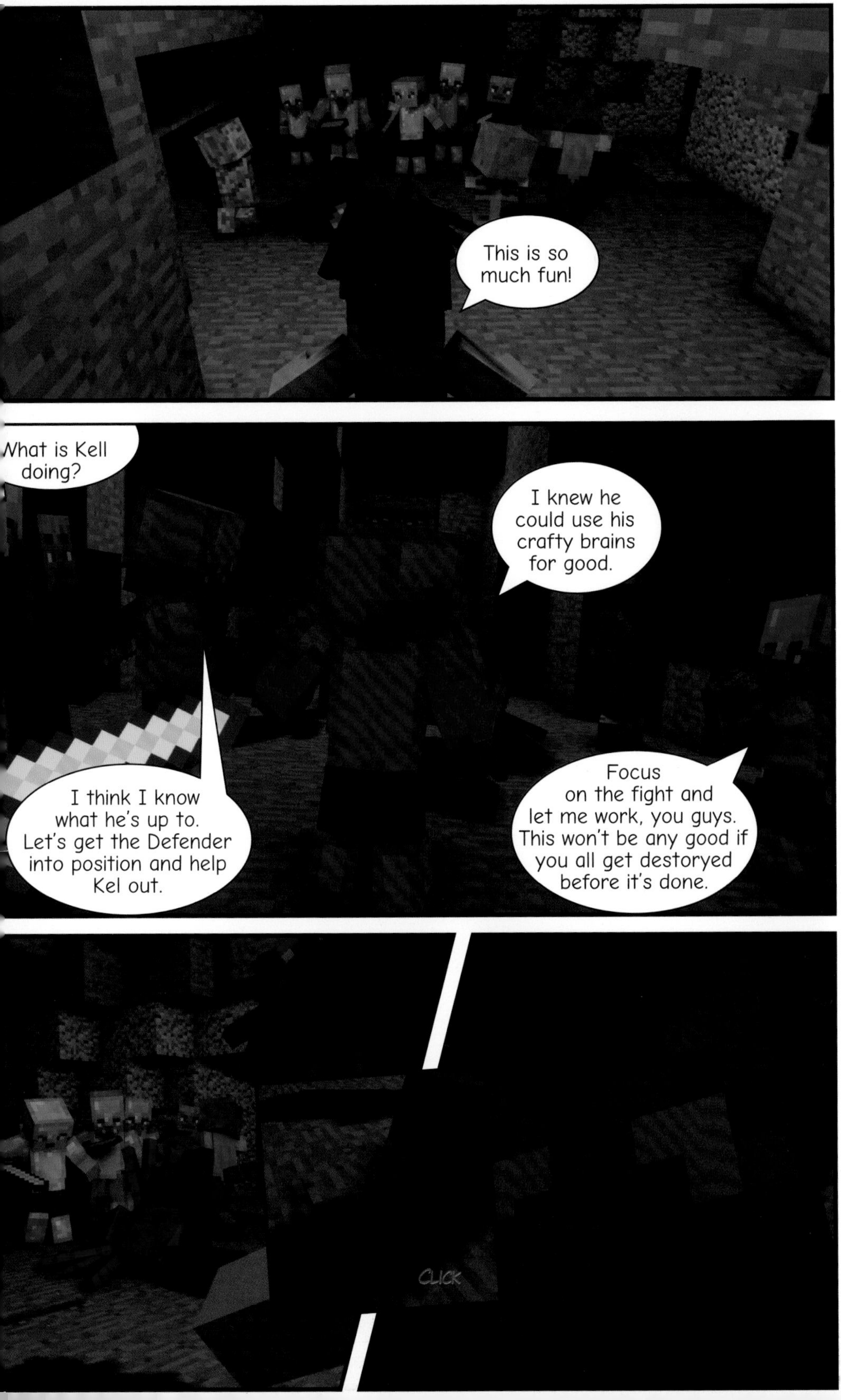
This is so much fun!
What is Kell doing?
I knew he could use his crafty brains for good.
I think I know what he's up to. Let's get the Defender into position and help Kel out.
Focus on the fight and let me work, you guys. This won't be any good if you all get destoryed before it's done.
CLICK

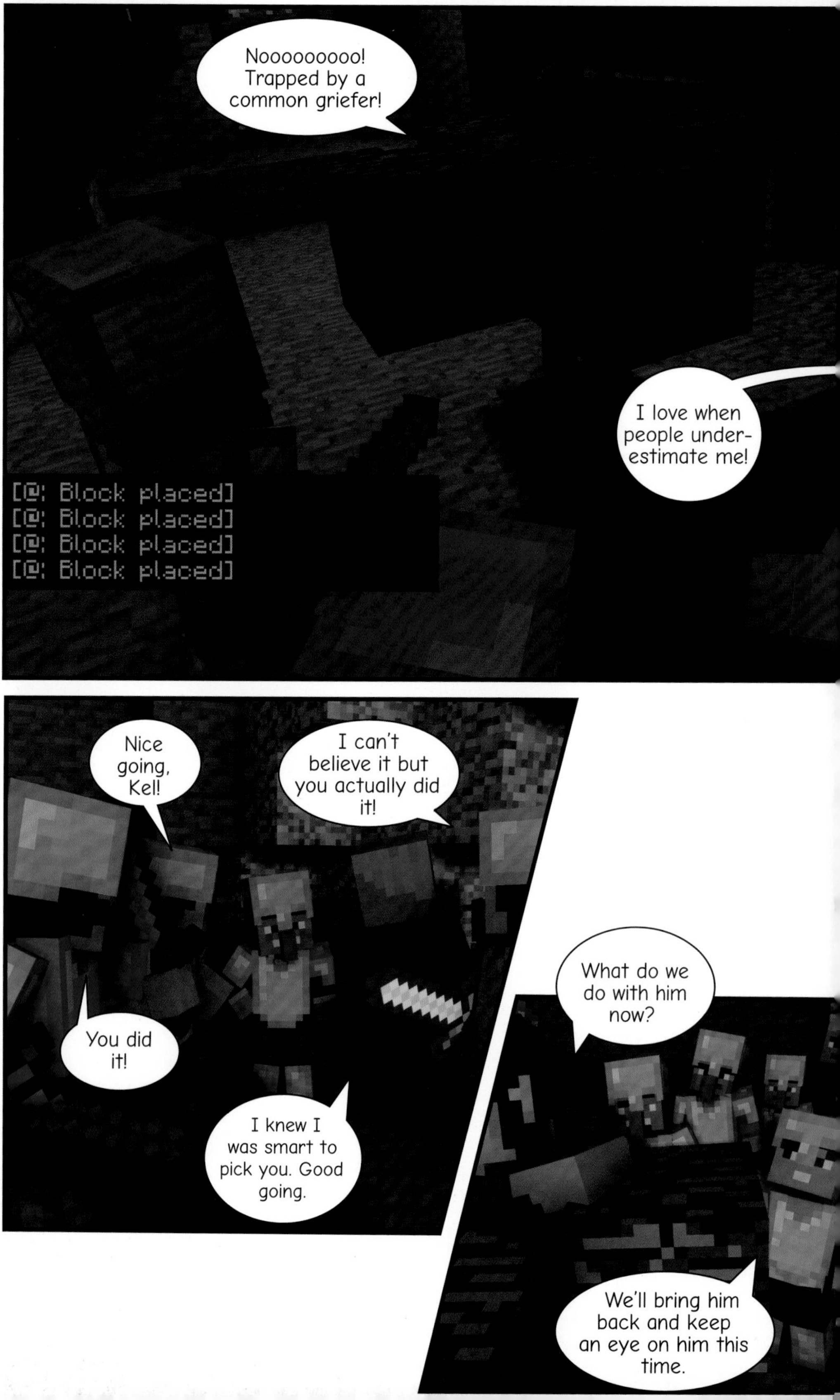
Noooooooooo! Trapped by a common griefer!
I love when people under-estimate me!
[@: Block placed]
[@: Block placed]
[@: Block placed]
[@: Block placed]
Nice going, Kel!
I can't believe it but you actually did it!
You did it!
I knew I was smart to pick you. Good going.
What do we do with him now?
We'll bring him back and keep an eye on him this time.

CHAPTER 13

PARTY ON

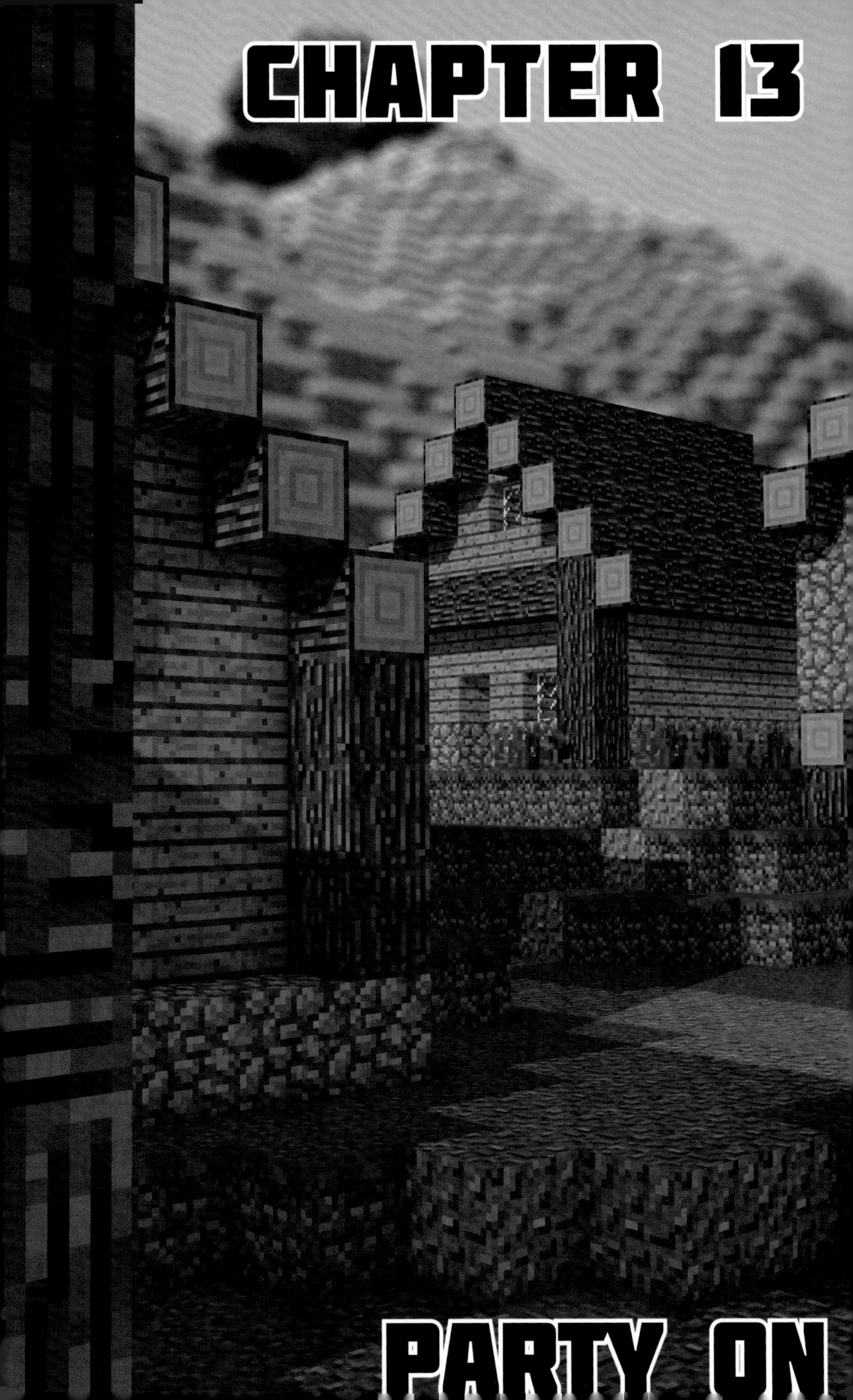

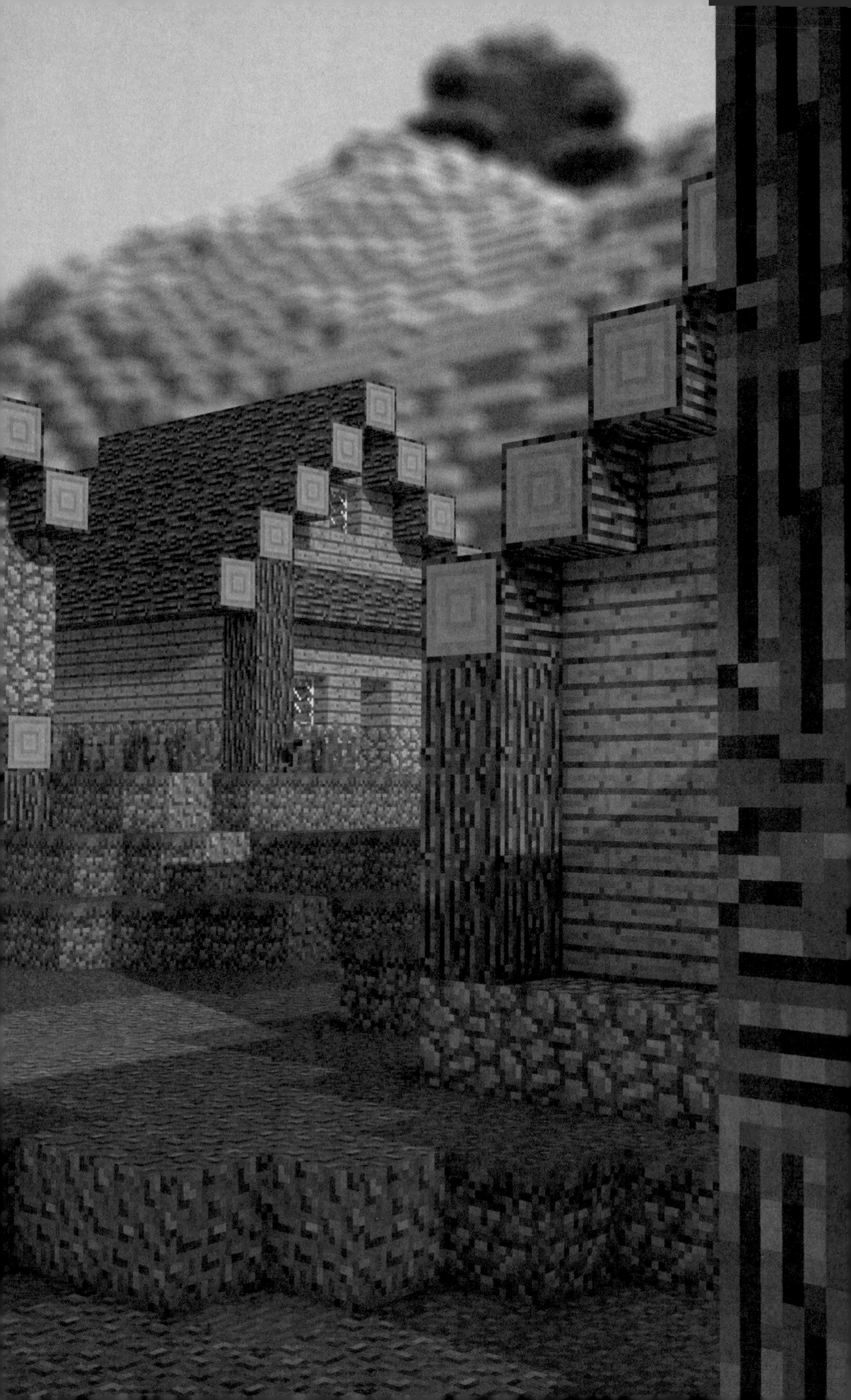

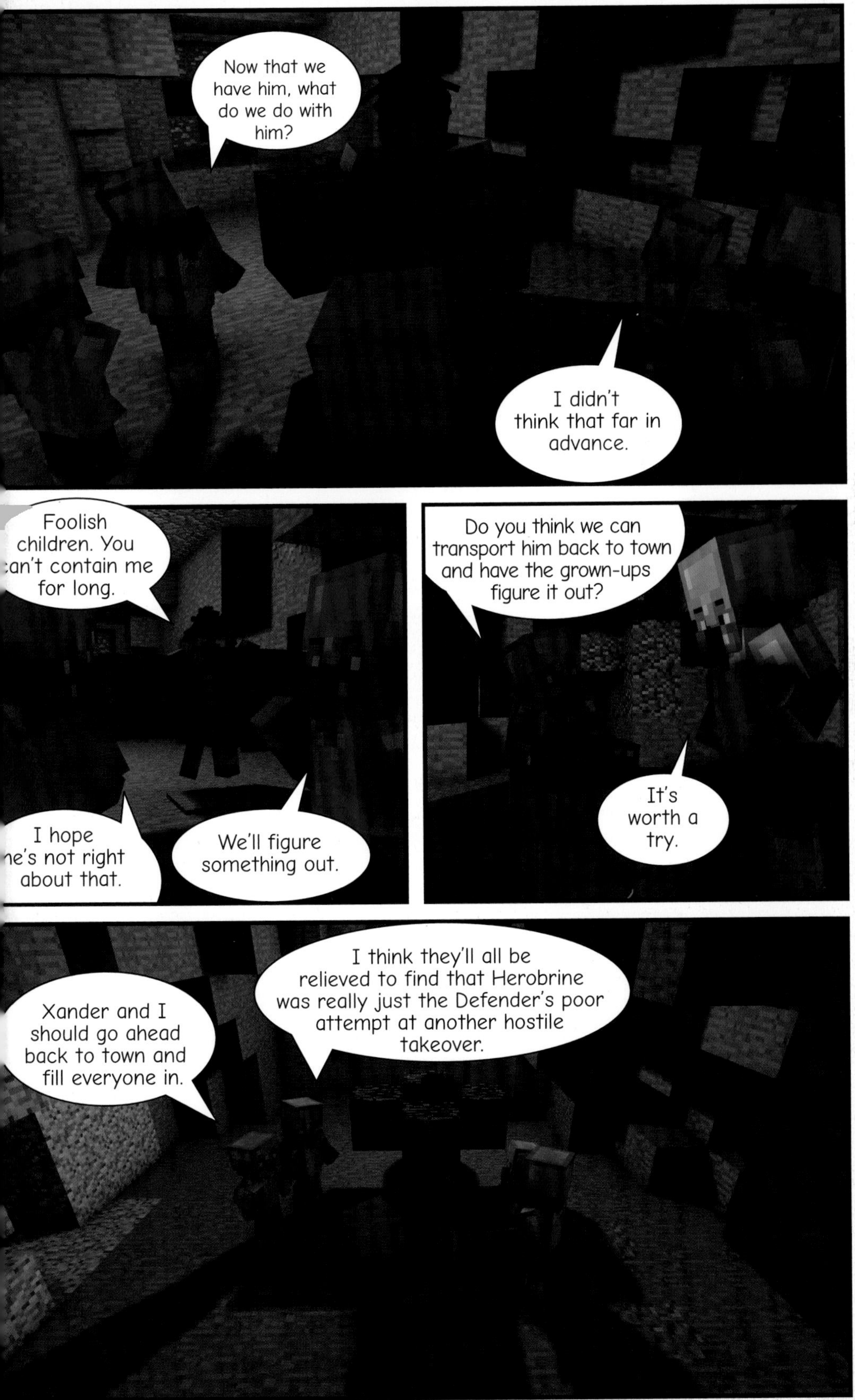
Now that we have him, what do we do with him?
I didn't think that far in advance.
Foolish children. You an't contain me for long.
I hope e's not right about that.
We'll figure something out.
Do you think we can transport him back to town and have the grown-ups figure it out?
It's worth a try.
Xander and I should go ahead back to town and fill everyone in.
I think they'll all be relieved to find that Herobrine was really just the Defender's poor attempt at another hostile takeover.

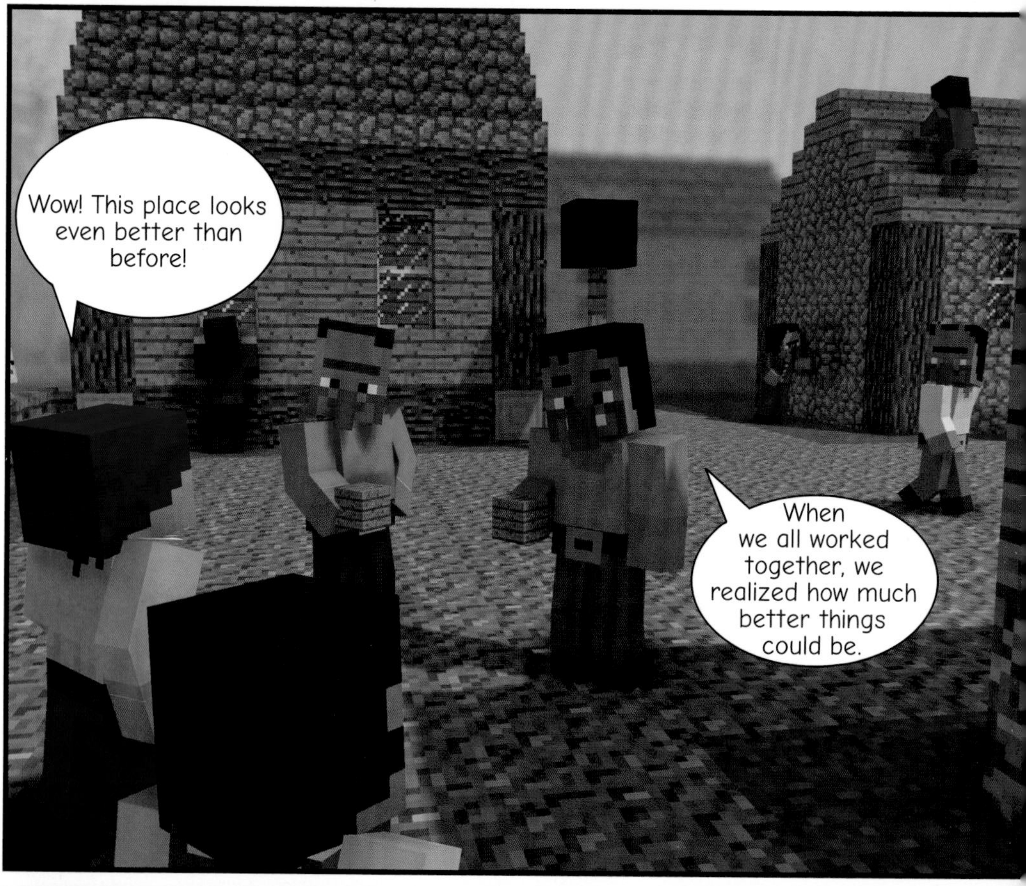
Wow! This place looks even better than before!
When we all worked together, we realized how much better things could be.

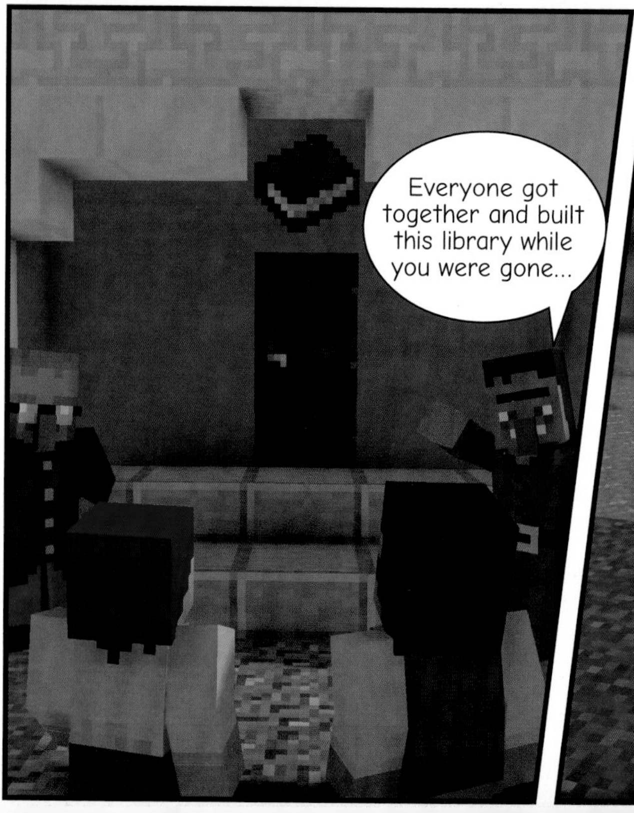
Everyone got together and built this library while you were gone...

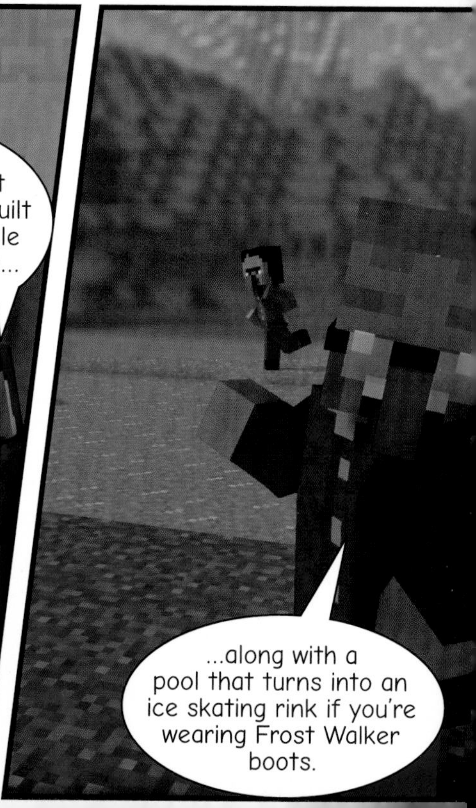
...along with a pool that turns into an ice skating rink if you're wearing Frost Walker boots.

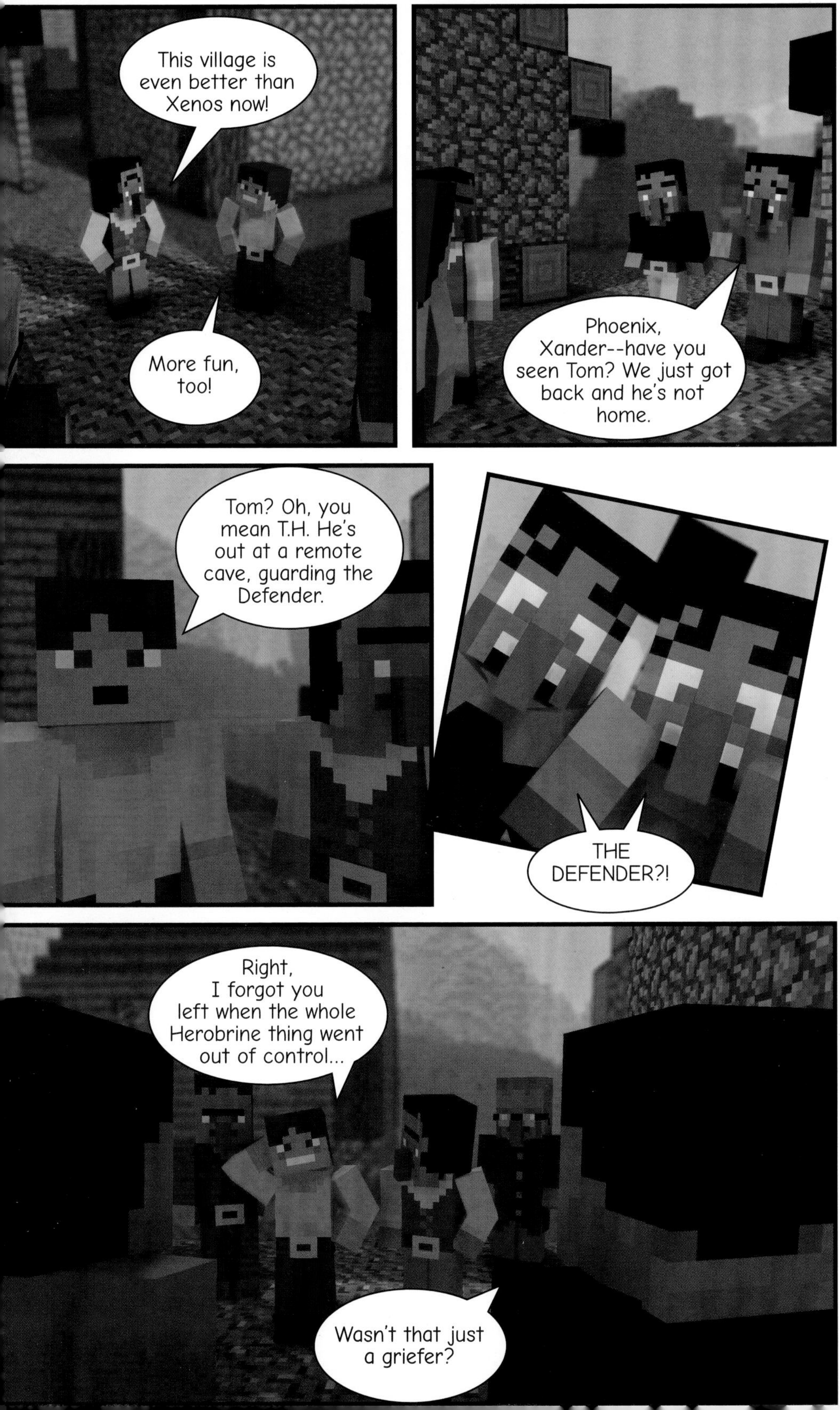
This village is even better than Xenos now!
More fun, too!
Phoenix, Xander--have you seen Tom? We just got back and he's not home.
Tom? Oh, you mean T.H. He's out at a remote cave, guarding the Defender.
THE DEFENDER?!
Right, I forgot you left when the whole Herobrine thing went out of control...
Wasn't that just a griefer?

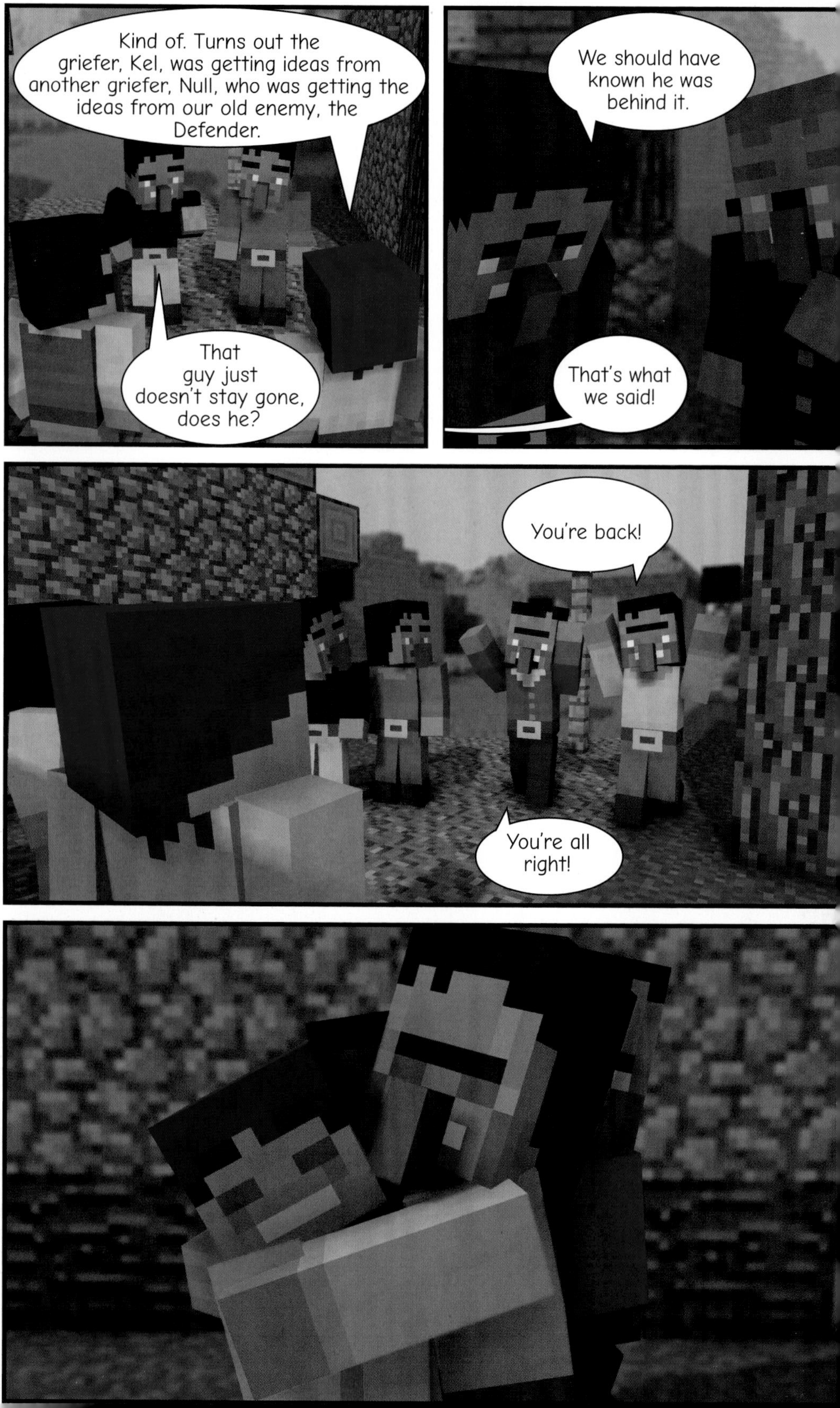
Kind of. Turns out the griefer, Kel, was getting ideas from another griefer, Null, who was getting the ideas from our old enemy, the Defender.
That guy just doesn't stay gone, does he?
We should have known he was behind it.
That's what we said!
You're back!
You're all right!

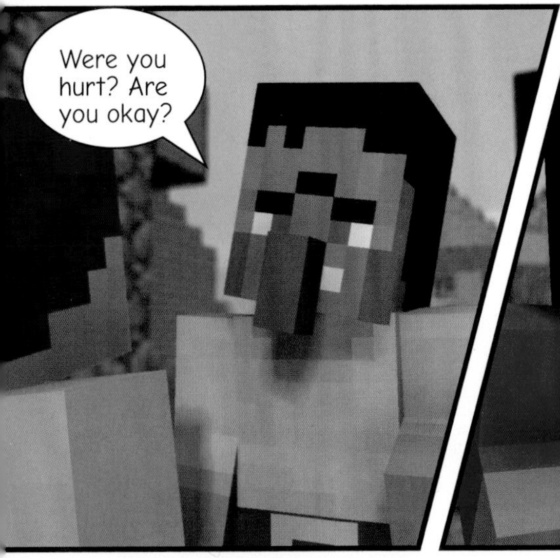
Were you hurt? Are you okay?

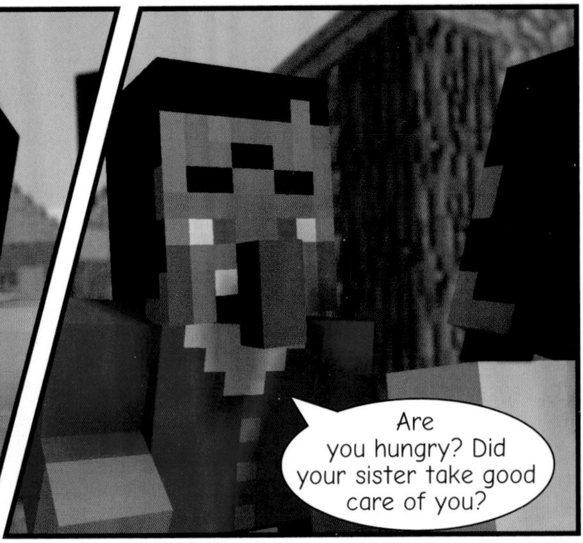
Are you hungry? Did your sister take good care of you?

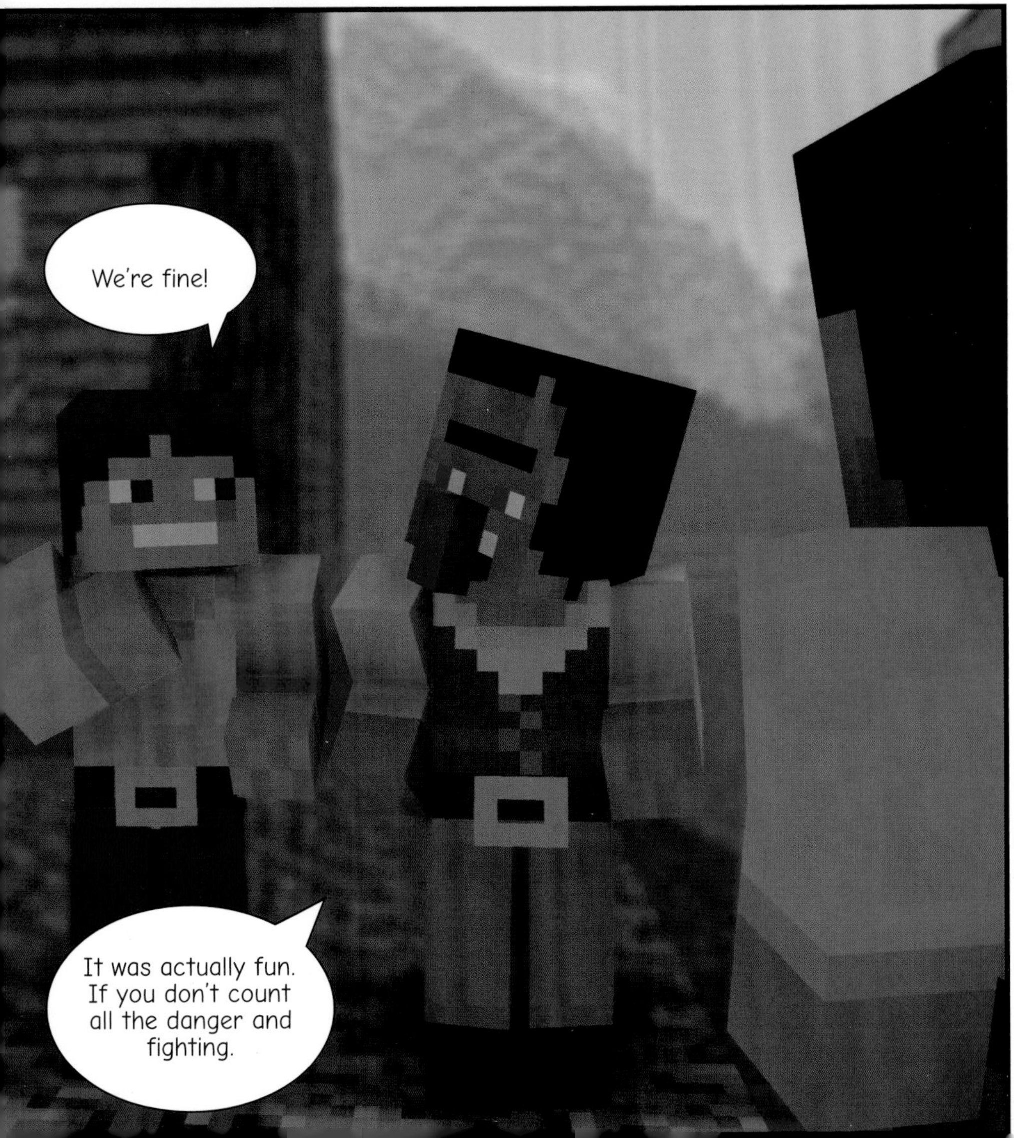
We're fine!
It was actually fun. If you don't count all the danger and fighting.

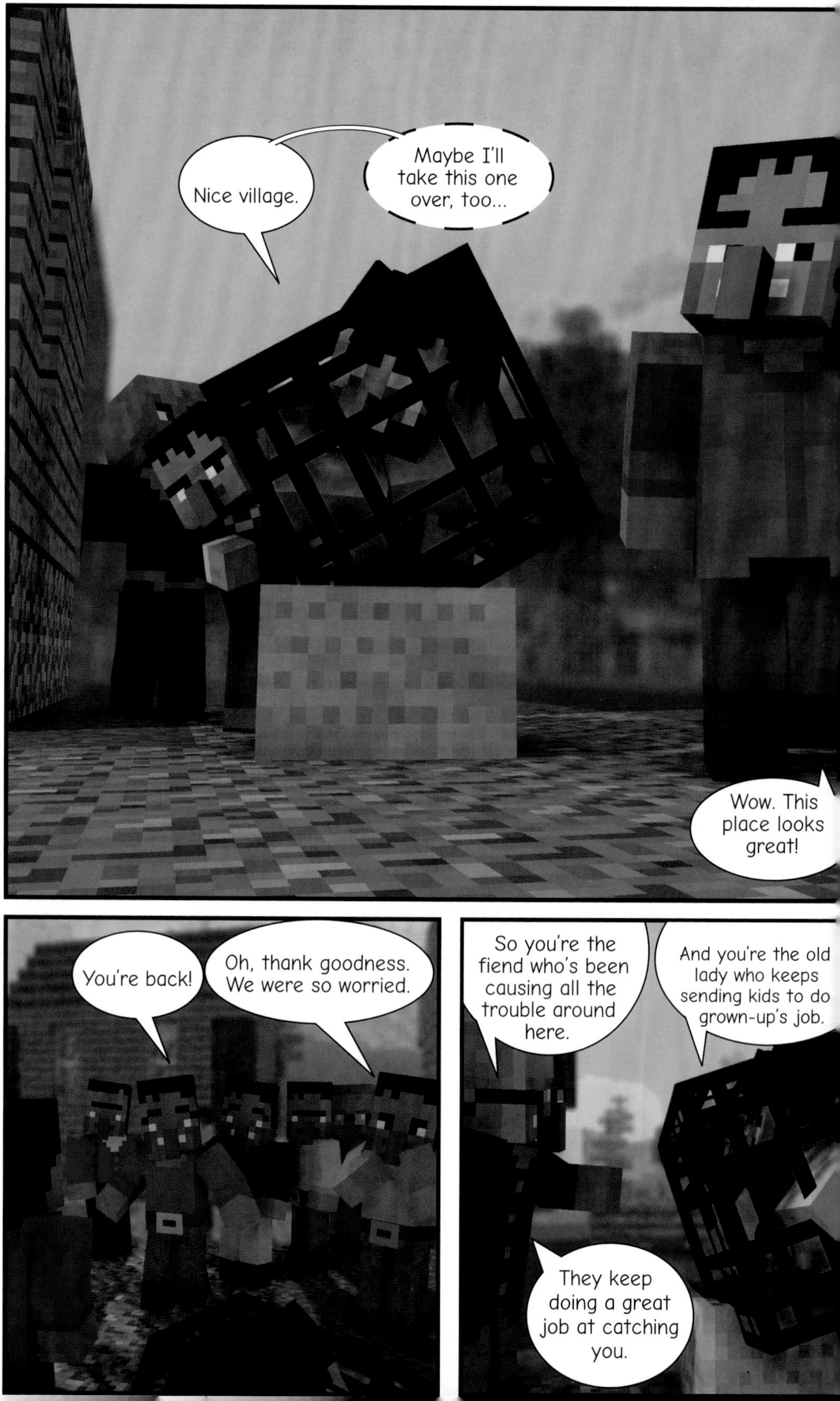
Nice village.
Maybe I'll take this one over, too...
Wow. This place looks great!
You're back!
Oh, thank goodness. We were so worried.
So you're the fiend who's been causing all the trouble around here.
And you're the old lady who keeps sending kids to do grown-up's job.
They keep doing a great job at catching you.

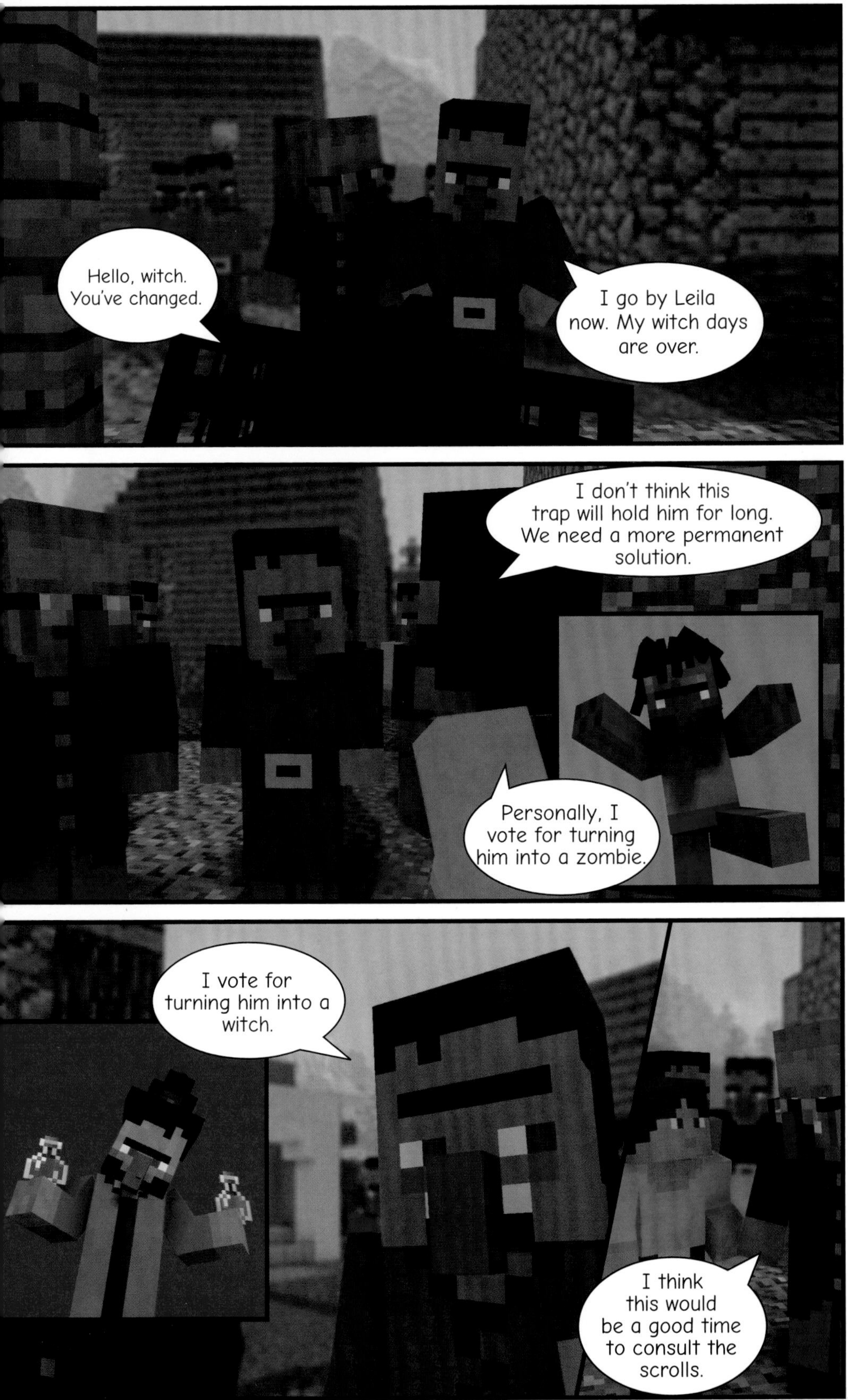
Hello, witch. You've changed.
I go by Leila now. My witch days are over.
I don't think this trap will hold him for long. We need a more permanent solution.
Personally, I vote for turning him into a zombie.
I vote for turning him into a witch.
I think this would be a good time to consult the scrolls.

Can you guys keep your eyes on him for a bit? Ole Baba--I mean, Bailey and I are going to figure out what to do with the Defender once and for all.

That's a great idea.

So we found the Defender, back from the dead.

I know, and you want to know what to do with him now?

Yep, so what do you recommend?

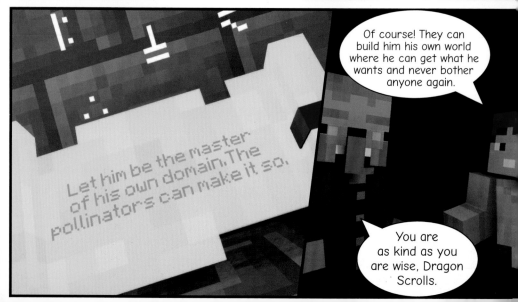

Let him be the master of his own domain. The pollinators can make it so.

Of course! They can build him his own world where he can get what he wants and never bother anyone again.

You are as kind as you are wise, Dragon Scrolls.

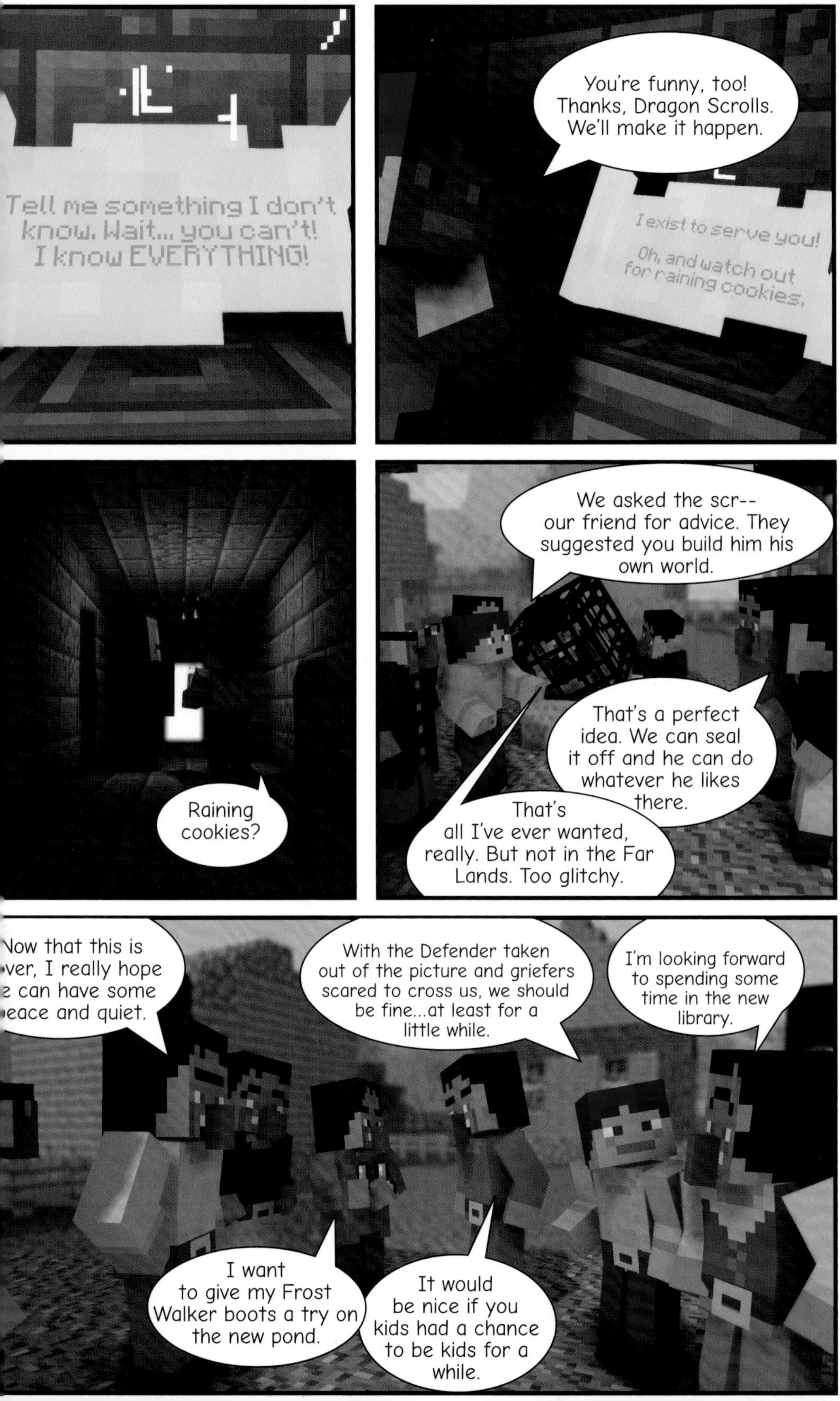

Tell me something I don't know. Wait... you can't! I know EVERYTHING!
You're funny, too! Thanks, Dragon Scrolls. We'll make it happen.
I exist to serve you! Oh, and watch out for raining cookies.
Raining cookies?
We asked the scr-- our friend for advice. They suggested you build him his own world.
That's a perfect idea. We can seal it off and he can do whatever he likes there.
That's all I've ever wanted, really. But not in the Far Lands. Too glitchy.
Now that this is ver, I really hope e can have some eace and quiet.
With the Defender taken out of the picture and griefers scared to cross us, we should be fine...at least for a little while.
I'm looking forward to spending some time in the new library.
I want to give my Frost Walker boots a try on the new pond.
It would be nice if you kids had a chance to be kids for a while.

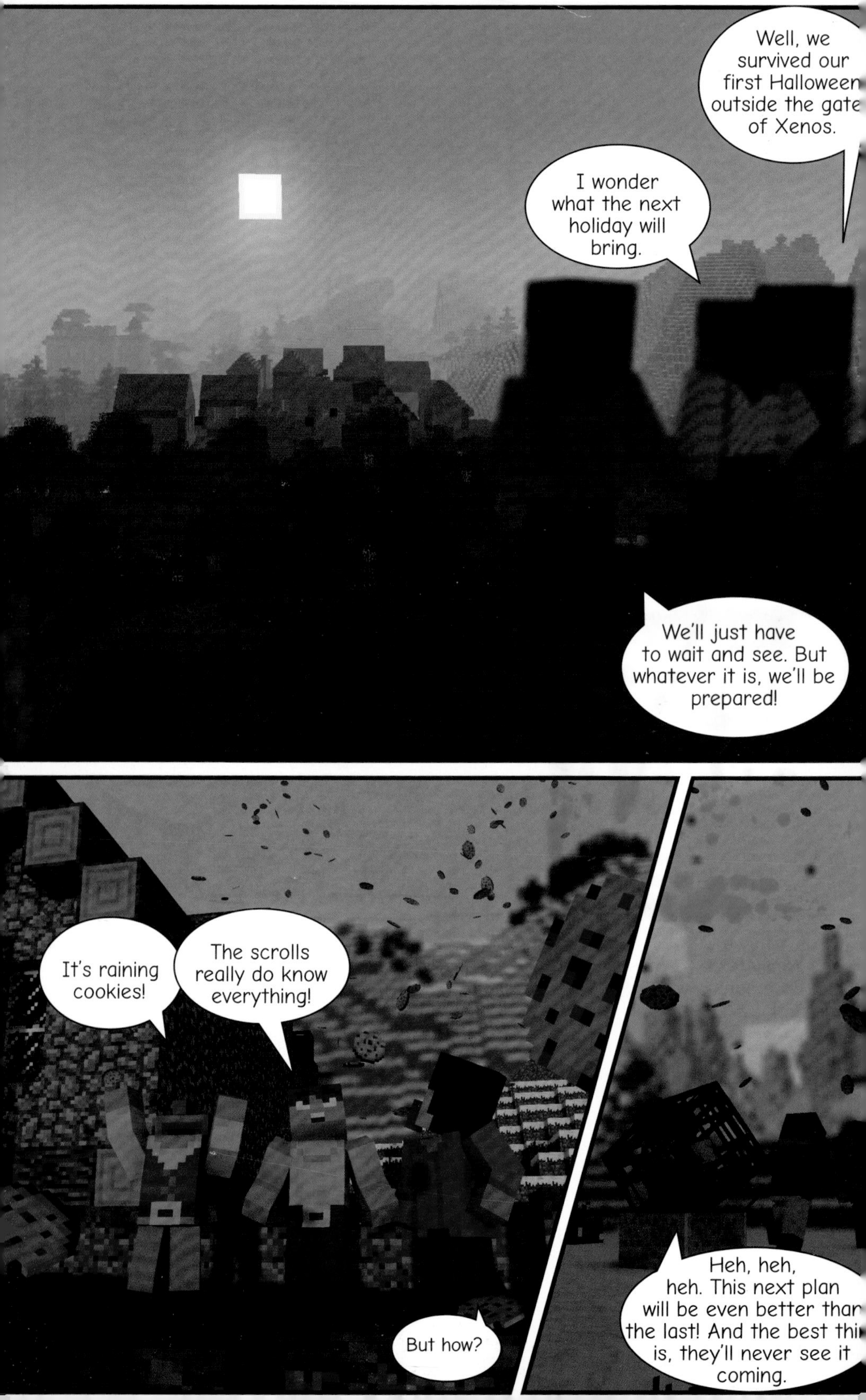
Well, we survived our first Halloween outside the gate of Xenos.
I wonder what the next holiday will bring.
We'll just have to wait and see. But whatever it is, we'll be prepared!
It's raining cookies!
The scrolls really do know everything!
But how?
Heh, heh, heh. This next plan will be even better than the last! And the best thi is, they'll never see it coming.